About th

When Kate Dreyer was seven years old, she wrote a children's book optimistically titled *Animal Story 1*, in which a young girl rescues a fox. She bound it herself, using a cereal box as a hardback cover. Although she never completed the much-anticipated sequel, she subsequently devoured all the animal stories on which she could get her hands.

More recently, her love for animals has manifested itself in other creative ways, namely painting, getting tattoos and looking out of office windows longingly. Writing has always been there in the background, but one day it tapped her on the shoulder and asked why she wasn't doing more of it. She said she didn't know, so she started doing more of it.

The Fox of Richmond Park is her first 'proper' novel, sparked by eight years of living in London and working in dull office jobs. Kate's ultimate dream is to write, paint and look after animals for a living. Or to be a magpie.

THE FOX OF RICHMOND PARK

THE FOX OF RICHMOND PARK

KATE DREYER

This edition first published in 2017

Unbound
6th Floor Mutual House, 70 Conduit Street,
London W1S 2GF

www.unbound.com

ISBN (eBook): 978-1911586333
ISBN (Paperback): 978-1911586340

Design by Mecob

Cover images:

© Shutterstock.com/Jef Thompson
© Textures.com
Fox image by www.animalsclipart.com

Dedicated to Nate, whose answer to my most frequently asked question: 'Is this ridiculous?' is always: 'Yes. I love it.'

Dear Reader,

The book you are holding came about in a rather different way from most others. It was funded directly by readers through a new website: Unbound.

Unbound is the creation of three writers. We started the company because we believed there had to be a better deal for both writers and readers. On the Unbound website, authors share the ideas for the books they want to write directly with readers. If enough of you support the book by pledging for it in advance, we produce a beautifully bound special subscribers' edition and distribute a regular edition and e-book wherever books are sold, in shops and online.

This new way of publishing is actually a very old idea (Samuel Johnson funded his dictionary this way). We're just using the internet to build each writer a network of patrons. Here, at the back of this book, you'll find the names of all the people who made it happen.

Publishing in this way means readers are no longer just passive consumers of the books they buy, and authors are free to write the books they really want. They get a much fairer return too – half the profits their books generate, rather than a tiny percentage of the cover price.

If you're not yet a subscriber, we hope that you'll want to join our publishing revolution and have your name listed in one of our books in the future. To get you started, here is a £5 discount on your first pledge. Just visit unbound.com, make your pledge and type VINCE17 in the promo code box when you check out.

Thank you for your support,

Dan, Justin and John
Founders, Unbound

Super Patrons

Kirsten Beacock
Laura Brown
Stephanie Cave
Sarah Conway
Madge & Ron Dreyer
Jessica Groenendijk
Andrew Hoyle
Allison Hoyle
Josh Jordan
Dan Kieran
Robert Kinns
Nate Lanxon
David Martin
Lexi Mills
John Mitchinson
Michael Parsons
Justin Pollard
Brad Rice
David Riley
Sally Russo
Daphne Shinn
Jennie Smith
Colin Smith
Charlotte Steggz
Lisa Taylor
Susie Thompson
Richard Trenholm
David Whitney
Louisa Wilson

1

'Why I should leave,' Vince snarled as he prowled back and forth in the semi-circle of bare earth that marked the entrance to his den, black ears flat to his head, 'just because some over-entitled deer want to be near the lake?'

'It's not like that. And you can dig a new, bigger den in a day or two. I don't see what the problem is. Other animals have moved without a fuss.' Edward tilted his antlers towards the small skulk of foxes several leaps away, who had gathered at the edge of the woodland to wait for the sun to set. 'And your friends are being very cooperative.'

'That's because you've told them a load of scat about how great the cemetery is,' Vince said, the copper fur on his back bristling. He'd had every intention of talking this through civilly with the stag, but his temper had other ideas. Just like last time.

'The cemetery is perfectly fine – there's trees all around, and there'll be more rats for you to eat there.' Edward clenched his jaw.

'Because it's right next to the town! There are people everywhere! It's not like there's no room here for all of us. You just don't want to have to share the best spot with us.'

'Hardly,' Edward snorted.

The spring sun was low, the sky now washed with pink, but the lake still glittered as the fish gulped at the surface, water boatmen disappearing into their gaping mouths. Now was the time the frogs began to clamber up the rocks and sit in the soft, warm dusk, licking flies from the air to fill their spongy bellies. Vince had learned to hunt here. His father showed him how to catch frogs, lying low in the grass and pouncing on the fattest, slowest ones. On the odd occasions Vince thought about his own future cubs, the lake and the woodlands beside it were always the setting for his daydreams.

Vince stopped pacing and sat on his haunches, golden eyes narrowed. 'If the cemetery is so stinking great, why don't the deer move there?'

'Don't be ridiculous. We need to be near water. Can you imagine having to trek back and forth out in the open like that? Just wandering about exposed all the time?'

'But it's fine for us?' Vince barked, unmoved by the stag's statuesque appearance.

'Exactly.' Edward stamped his hoof and a cloud of dust billowed between his glossy russet forelegs. 'Look, we're different animals, Vince. You know that. Foxes, rabbits, squirrels, you're fine near the town. You're underground all day and you can come to the lake at night. We deer, we need shelter, lots of grass, more space to run. Our woodland is getting too crowded and the pond near us is far too small.'

'Rat scat. You just think you're better than us. Always have. You think you can push everyone in this park around. Or get them on your side with bribes. Now you come over here all, "Ooh! We fancy a bit of this lake action actually, so get out of the way or get an antler up the backside," yeah?'

Edward lowered his head and turned an oil-black eye to the fox. 'You'd better be quiet, *vermin*.' The deer's voice rumbled through the air between the two animals. 'You know why we're in charge. You think any old animal can organise Park Watch? Keep you all safe? This place is *nothing* without us.'

'It was fine before you became Head Stag,' Vince said.

'Your parents told you that, I suppose? Yes, well, that doesn't surprise me. And they clearly passed on their unruly nature to their offspring. Time to grow up, don't you agree, Vince? You will move to the cemetery with the other foxes, and that's the end of it.'

Vince rose onto all four paws, stretched his snout towards Edward's and bared his fangs. 'What happens if I say no?' he growled.

'We will destroy your den tomorrow morning' – the deer lifted his head high – 'whether you are in it or not.'

'How dare you!' Vince said. 'My grandparents dug this den. It's been my family's for ten seasons.'

'Your call.' Edward turned his towering frame away from the fox with a swish of his tail.

Vince wouldn't be able to stop them. His teeth and claws could do some damage to one, two even, but they would be no match against a mass of dagger-like antlers and sharp, solid hooves. The other foxes wouldn't risk helping. Not this time, anyway. This wasn't another petty disagreement about noise, or digging in the wrong place, and they had their own homes and families to think of. Plus, they were getting tired of his constant arguments with Edward and the other deer. Just shut up and do what he says for once, they said. Why fight over every little thing? Relax and enjoy being safe.

How could he relax? Do what Edward says or have his skull kicked in. Not much of a choice. Think for yourself. That's what his parents taught him. But what else could he do? Leave? No mammal had left Richmond Park in countless seasons. Even the birds came back after migrating for winter. It just wasn't done. That didn't mean he couldn't, though.

Before his better judgement could stop him, Vince yelled up at the deer's backside. 'I'd rather leave the park altogether than stay here with *you*.'

Scat. Did I mean that?

Edward sighed and circled back to face Vince. 'Leave? Really, Vince? Have you ever heard the phrase "cutting off your nose to spite your face"? The humans say it. It means you—'

'I know what it means,' Vince spat.

'Very well,' Edward continued. 'Look, we are in charge. We always have been and we always will be, that's just the way it is here. But I'm not your enemy, Vince. This park is a wonderful place where we can all live together in safety, where humans respect us and take care of us. But there are rules. Just follow the rules like everyone else and you can stay. The last thing we want is to drive anyone away. Be serious, Vince. Do you really want to leave this place and live among humans? Dodging their cars, being kept awake by their incessant noise, eating their leftovers out of bins? Especially after what happened to your father.'

My father would never have put up with this.

'I'd rather eat their leftovers than ponce around posing for photos like one of their desperate pets.'

Edward snorted and stomped a hoof. 'Watch your mouth, fox!'

Vince's lips curled into a smile. 'Have you ever heard the phrase, "in for a penny, in for a pound"? He held his paws to his head like two extra ears, and waggled his toes. 'Ooh, look at my beautiful antlers! Please, human, please take a picture!' Edward reared onto his hind legs and Vince leapt backwards. A yelp escaped the fox's mouth as the deer's glossy black hooves thumped into the dirt, missing his brush by a hair.

'I'll aim for your head next time,' Edward roared, then whispered under his breath, 'Like father like son.'

Before Vince could reply, Edward was already dashing away through the trees. The other foxes had heard the noise and were looking over at Vince, frowning.

Vince exhaled slowly. 'Hmm, that went well,' he muttered to himself.

Despite having a full belly, Vince couldn't sleep. His night of hunting had been marred by Edward, and the prospect of wandering around in the daylight to look for a new home had put him on edge. The frogs in his stomach would be his last fresh ones for a while, and these dark early morning hours one last chance to rest before his eviction.

I've made my bed, now I have to lie in it. There's another nice human saying for you, Edward. The irony has not gone unnoticed, either.

'Are you in there?' A soft voice called from the den entrance. It was Sophie, the only fox he simultaneously did and did not want to speak to.

'No,' Vince mumbled.

Sophie made her way down to the main chamber, where twisted tree roots supported the dry earth ceiling. Vince was curled underneath, the voluminous thickness of his brush covering his snout.

'We were wondering if you'd changed your mind,' Sophie said, sitting back on her haunches.

Vince sighed into his pillow of fur. 'As soon as the sun comes up, Edward will arrive with the herd and destroy my home. He hasn't left me much choice, has he?'

'Why are you being so stubborn? Come to the cemetery with the rest of us. They'll let you stay if you just apologise.'

'No thanks.' Vince shifted his weight and buried his face deeper into his tail.

'You're being ridiculous. There's loads of space, more trees, you can have a den twice the size of this one. Plus, the deer have said we can hunt the birds on the outskirts.'

Vince lifted his head and peered at Sophie over his brush. 'Oh, the *deer* have said, have they? How kind of them! Do the *deer* tell you where you can drop your *scat* as well?' he snarled.

Sophie paused for a moment, blinked, then whispered, 'There's no need to be like that. We're just worried. As much as you hate the deer – and don't get me wrong, you know I hate them too – you have to admit that it's safe here, right? Edward wants what's best for the park, and for everyone. He may be a pain in the backside about it sometimes, but you have to look at the bigger picture. The humans come to the park to see all of us animals. We're like a show. As soon as you leave the cast, you'll be just another pest.'

'Open your eyes, Soph. The deer already treat us like pests. At least out there I'll be a pest who can do whatever he wants. No one telling me what time I can hunt, what I can and can't eat, when to be quiet, how big my den can be…'

She thrust her snout forward. 'You're exaggerating, like you always do. Don't you understand that you could get hit by a car, or shot, or attacked by a city fox…?'

'I know. I don't care.'

'How can you not care?'

'You don't understand. My grandparents built this den when they first arrived here, my parents lived in it their whole lives, and now it's mine. Ten seasons.' Vince uncurled and lifted himself onto his paws. 'Except it's not mine, is it? It was never mine, or my parents', or my grandparents'. As long as my den is in this park, the deer own it. They own everything. One deer decides he wants a new tree to scratch his backside on and *boom*, we have to move.'

'We all have to make sacrifices, Vince, that's how it works.'

'They're full of scat, Sophie. How can you not see that? All those excuses about their pond being too small, it's lies. They just saw something they wanted and now they're taking it.'

Sophie looked down at her paws. 'Maybe that's just the price we have to pay to live in safety.'

Vince laughed. 'You think this is the only park in London?'

'No. But it's the biggest. It's the *safest*.'

'How do you know that? Because those jumped-up twig-heads told you?'

Sophie widened her yellow eyes. 'Because... It just *is*. Everyone knows that.'

Vince started to pace back and forth – as much as he could in the confined space. 'My parents told me about the park my grandparents were born in. A big, safe park just like this. Except more like how it *used* to be, before Edward. No one in charge telling anyone what to do. My father talked about going back there once, but then he died...'

'So why did your grandparents travel here, if this other park was so brilliant?'

'I don't know, they never said. Maybe my grandparents didn't tell them. But it was normal back then, wasn't it? You wanted a change of scenery, you just went somewhere else. Animals could come and go. You must have heard the stories. Why stay in one place for ever when you can explore? But the point is, Richmond Park used to be the same, until Edward became head of the herd. My mother said he changed everything, made all these new Park Watch rules...'

'I'm not disagreeing, but you know what older generations are like... Always going on about how great things used to be... Not all rules are bad, you know. They make things safe. Make sure there's enough food to go around. They stop all the city animals from coming in too, don't forget that. Do you really want to live somewhere where any old fox off the street can come and make a den next to yours?'

'Ugh, you sound just like them.' Vince turned, sunk onto the soil and curled his tail around himself once more. 'I'm leaving, and that's the end of it.'

'Fine. I would have come with you, if things had been different. You know I—'

'Don't, Sophie. There's no point.'

'Goodbye, Vince.' Sophie sighed, then whispered, 'I'll miss you,' before slinking back through the tunnel and disappearing into the cold night.

'I'll miss you too,' Vince breathed to himself.

He must have eventually fallen asleep, because the tramping of hooves above his head startled Vince awake. He got up, looked around at the comfy chamber and sighed. Familiar constellations of shallow lines, made when his grandparents' claws had scraped the curved walls, hung over him as they had for the entire five seasons of his life. He'd only heard stories about them, but the marks they'd left on the earth were a constant reminder of the new life they started here in Richmond Park. When he was a cub, it had always been a happy story, but Edward had slowly leached the joy from it, and now the marks themselves would soon be gone too.

As he padded through his tunnel towards the blinding spring sunshine, the booming voices of the deer grew louder.

'... don't know what he thinks he's playing at...'

'... won't last a day in the city...'

'... gone too far this time...'

Vince shielded his eyes with a paw and took in the surrounding herd as he exited the only home he'd ever known for the last time. He forced a smile, despite his knotted stomach. 'Calm down, I'm out, I'm out.'

'You look cheerful, considering,' Edward said. 'Have you decided to accept our offer?' The rest of the herd were behind him, watching Vince closely with narrowed eyes.

'Nope. Just happy to be rid of the lot of you, to be honest.' A few leaps away the rest of the foxes, Sophie included, had gathered at the edge of the trees.

Another strained goodbye with Sophie was the last thing he wanted this morning, but he tried to appear optimistic in front of the herd. 'I'd best say goodbye to my friends then, before you crush my skull with your fat hoof, eh, Edward?' As he turned away from the deer, Vince heard Edward snort before instructing the herd to destroy his den. Head high, ears up, Vince padded towards his friends as the hooves and antlers began to grind into the earth. His family's home for ten seasons, gone in a few blinks. It took all his strength to not howl with grief.

'We'll miss you,' said Alice, who was one of Sophie's friends.

'You can still stay,' Marge, an older vixen, added. 'Just come to the cemetery with us.'

The platitudes were genuine, but Vince was a nuisance, and they all knew it.

'Nah, I think I'd finally like to find the place where my grand-parents came from. Besides, I don't think the deer want me here any-more.' Vince looked over his shoulder at the herd. They were making light work of his den, using their antlers to collapse the ceiling of the tunnel, then pushing the loose soil into the chamber. There was now a deep gouge in the earth, soil strewn for leaps in all directions, radiat-ing from the line the tunnel had followed just moments before. Vince blinked, stalling the tears for a few more moments. He wouldn't give the deer the satisfaction of seeing him cry.

'Please just stay, Vince,' Sophie said. 'You've made your point.'

Vince locked eyes with the vixen. 'Is that what you think of me, Sophie? You think I'd risk my life, everything my family built, just to make a point?'

'That's not what I meant, I—'

'Save it.' Vince shot a glance to her mate, Jake, who was sitting at the back of the group, washing his paws. 'Enjoy your new home, both of you.'

Jake looked up at him, but said nothing.

Vince continued, 'I wish I could stay here, I really do, but when something feels right, or wrong, you have to do what you have to do. I hope you can understand that one day.'

Sophie, whose muzzle was now buried in Jake's fur, began to sob quietly, while Jake himself only frowned before wrapping a protective tail around his precious vixen.

Vince tried to ignore the lump that had risen in his throat and the salty sting pricking his eyes.

'Goodbye, everyone,' he whispered, then quickly turned and ran.

He ran north, away from his old friends and the vixen he'd once loved, the trees and the lake, the deer and his den. He was as unaccustomed to the warm morning sun as the smattering of birds, squirrels and humans he passed were unaccustomed to seeing a fox tearing across the open park in broad daylight. Luckily, they were far enough away that they couldn't see the torrent of tears seeping into his fur.

It wasn't long before Vince reached the edge of the park, where a chain-link fence marked the north boundary. On the other side a strip of oak and sweet chestnut woodland stretched westwards, bordering the cemetery that his friends would soon be calling home sweet home. To the east and the north, the trees thinned out to make way for rows of large human houses.

When he was a tiny cub, his father would sneak out to forage in the gardens. No doubt Edward quickly put a stop to that. After his father's death, Vince's mother became more protective, making him promise to stay in the park and not even approach the fence. Neither his grandparents' park nor their journey from it was ever mentioned again.

Even after his mother died he honoured his promise, but always wondered what he was missing. Now he could finally discover what no one else in the park dared to. He hoped she would understand.

But first, rest. His emotions were still raging. Everything he cared about was either gone or may as well have been, and he had no plan other than to get the hell out of Richmond Park and away from the deer. He didn't even know where the next nearest park was, let alone where his grandparents had travelled from before he was born. It was north of the big river, he knew that much, but his parents had never told him the name. Perhaps they didn't know it themselves. A good sleep would help clear his head. Plus, it was daylight. There would be humans everywhere.

Finding a gap in the fence, he squeezed through and made his way into the trees. Above him, grey squirrels leapt from branch to branch and chased each other up and down the thick trunks. After a brief search, Vince found a particularly large tree with broad, twisting roots growing at the base where he could safely curl up unnoticed for the day. A thorough sniff of the surrounding ground confirmed that no other foxes had claimed this patch. Good to go, he wrapped himself in his tail and settled in for a few hours' kip.

2

'Scrrraaaack-ack-ack-ack-ack-ack!'

What… ugh… Goddamn birds.

Vince slowly peeled open his eyelids and looked around for the source of the irritation. It was dusk, the sky deep orange and navy, the trees around him almost silhouettes.

Breakfast time.

His stomach growled so loudly he almost mistook it for another fox. Unfurling himself, he set about finding something to eat. He could worry about directions later.

Head to the ground, he sniffed around for anything that would pass for a meal. His nose led him to small log, which he rolled over with his snout to reveal a wriggling pile of beetles and worms. Vince prepared himself. Although not unfamiliar with such a meal, frogs were his go-to diet. A bird was a rare treat, back when his parents were still around, before Edward started to crack down on everyone.

The birds bring humans to the park, Edward would always say. Humans help the park, apparently. The nicer the park, the more humans that visit and the better the animals will be looked after. Give and take. That was the lecture he used to give the foxes every now and again. Of course, more humans meant more attention for the deer. And the more attention they got, the more power they had. A vicious circle.

'Scrrraaaack-ack-ack-ack!'

'Shut up!' he muttered to himself.

Stinking parakeets. Always shrieking. At least leaving means I can get away from that racket.

Vince sniffed the insects once more before scooping a few into his jaws. He crunched the tiny bulbous creatures between his teeth and swallowed the gritty mouthful. He shuddered.

A nice plump bird would go down very nicely right now.

'ScrrraAAAAAACK!'

'Shut *up*!' Vince called to the hidden owner of the noise.

'Vince?'

'Who's there?' Vince jumped to his feet and looked up into the trees.

'Thank goodness! I thought I'd missed you!'

'Who is that? Where are you?' Vince craned his head back and forth, trying to locate the bird, but the blanket of thick, spring leaves obscured his view.

'It's meeeeeee!' The bird emerged atop a high branch.

Vince sighed. Not a parakeet, but a magpie. Bird calls were never his forte, but he blamed his still-half-asleep brain for not recognising her voice sooner. 'Rita? What the hell? Did you follow me? And please stop squawking, it's very annoying.'

He wouldn't have described Rita as a friend, more of an irritating acquaintance. She'd built her first nest in the woodland near Vince's den when his parents were still alive and never moved, so they'd been neighbours his whole life. He'd explained to her – repeatedly – that her singing, if you could call it that, was very much *not* appreciated, but her love of music transcended her courtesy. And her common sense. Luckily, Vince's underground sleeping habits meant he avoided most of the din, but he'd heard the blackbirds complain about her after she insisted on joining their choir and drowned out their songs with her tuneless chattering.

Rita's metallic feathers glittered in the evening light as she hopped from her branch and flew to the ground in front of Vince. 'Sorry! I was just looking for you. Been looking all day. Was just having a little practice before I went to bed. I'm so glad I found you! I thought you might have already left the park and then I would have had to look in *all* the gardens and that would have taken *ages* and—'

'Rita, shush. Why were you looking for me?' Vince sat and rubbed his sleepy eyes with a paw.

'I want to come with you,' Rita said as she hopped from foot to foot, her long tail bobbing up and down excitedly.

'What? No.' He stood up and stared down at her.

'Why?'

'Because.'

'That's not a reason.'

'Why do you want to come? I don't even know where I'm going.'

'I want to travel with you. See London. Have an adventure!'

'I'm not going on an adventure. I'm just looking for my grand-parents' old home.'

'Sounds like an adventure to me. Come on, I've spent too many seasons in this place. There's nothing for me here and I'm getting old… I want to see the city! Fly to new places and taste new food and hear new birds!'

'I'm not stopping you.'

'It'll be better with two of us. Just imagine the songs I'll sing! A sheltered park bird like me, experiencing all that the big city has to offer, accompanying a freedom-fighter fox on his quest for a new life in his ancestral homeland!'

Vince sighed. 'I'm not a freedom fighter. And I'm really not good company. Besides, I could eat you, you know. Just turn around one day and CHOMP! Haven't eaten a tasty bird in a while, thanks to the deer…'

Rita laughed. 'You wouldn't do that.'

'Oh?'

'We're friends!'

'No, we're not.'

Rita's face fell. 'Neighbours, then. Or, we were.'

'And?'

Rita blinked. 'And… I can help you,' she said.

Vince sighed again. She could definitely help him. She could tell him what was in each direction, where the nearest place to sleep was, if any humans were near… He could put up with her. Maybe. If she stayed quiet.

'Who says I need help?' he replied.

'You're just going to wander about, are you? Bumping into humans and rivers and roads and train tracks…'

'Train tracks?'

'Yes. Lots.'

Vince knew all about trains. Huge, rumbling metal carriages that don't stop for anything in their way, especially small, furry animals. He'd heard stories that they weren't even controlled by humans. That's why they ran on rails instead of roads.

'And you know where the train tracks are? And the big river?'

'Well…' The magpie poked at the ground with one of her claws. 'No. Not all of them. But I can. I will! I'll fly ahead of you every day and tell you which way to go and warn you about things. I've been exploring today already, when I was looking for you. I can help you. *Please* let me come with you.'

I'm going to regret this…

'Do what you like.' Vince sniffed and began to walk off.

'Really? Oh, wonderful! Scraaaaaaaaack!' Rita screeched as she hopped alongside him, flapping furiously to keep up with his long strides.

'On three conditions.' He stopped dead and stared into her inky eyes. 'You can come with me, and I'll promise not to eat you, if – and *only* if – number one, you help me find my grandparents' park; number two, you keep me out of danger; and number three… You. Absolutely. Do. Not. Sing. While. I. Am. Asleep.'

'I'm sorry, I just got overexcited!' Rita flapped her wings and hopped in a circle. 'I'll try to be quieter. I hope you don't mind the odd sing-song, though. I don't want to get out of practice.'

Vince continued on towards the edge of the trees. Rita flapped a few leaps ahead, then settled on the ground and waited for him to catch up. It was easier than hopping beside him. 'We're going to have a great time! The Fox and the Magpie! Vince and Rita! The Famous Travelling Duo of Richmond Park! Scraaaaaaack!'

Vince winced. 'You know I'm nocturnal, right? We're not going to get very far if we don't travel at the same time.'

'Of course. I'll adapt!'

Vince smiled through clenched jaws. 'Well, I'm awake now, so, which way? All I know is that my grandparents came from north of the river, but right now I could do with getting as far away from here as possible.'

Rita explained how she had seen some big green areas to the north-east, in the middle of the city. She would take a better look in the morning, but for now it seemed like his best option. She flew past Vince again and rested on a low branch while he strode through the long grass below.

He looked up as he passed below her. 'Just to be clear, Rita, I don't want adventures. I want to find my grandparents' park, dig out a den, eat, sleep and maybe do a bit of frolicking about. No drama, okay?'

'Ha! Drama is your middle name. I've heard all the arguments you've had with Edward over the seasons.'

'That wasn't my fault. He made it his business to piss me off.'

'And you lost your temper every time.'

'Shut up.'

'There you go again,' she called from the branch, Vince now a short way ahead of her.

The pair continued in silence for a while before arriving at the tall brick wall that marked the north edge of the dense woodland. On the other side were a path, a road and some houses. What lay beyond that, neither of them knew for sure.

'Well, this is it,' Vince said. 'The big wide world.' He tipped back onto his haunches and sprang upwards. His front claws grasped the top as his back feet found purchase on the rough bricks, propelling his slim body onto the top of the wall with little effort. 'Are you absolutely sure you want to come?'

'Yes.' Rita grinned and flew up to join him on the wall. 'Adventure awaits! Scraaaaack-ack-ack-ack!'

Vince rolled his eyes. 'After you.'

The evening was quiet and the pair made good progress zig-zagging through the house-flanked streets. Vince padded along the path, pausing momentarily to look up at a tall, red cylinder with a thin slot near the top, and wonder what on earth the humans used it for. Rita glided from tree to tree, chattering constantly as she waited for him to catch up.

The first few cars that roared past sent Vince slinking away into nearby gardens, or behind less terrifying, static versions of the same metal monsters that dotted the street, but after a while he'd started to get used to them. If he stuck to the path that ran alongside where the cars were, he would be safe. Plus, Rita was always nearby yelling at him to hurry up, which somehow calmed his nerves. Or distracted him from them, at least.

Every now and again, though, Rita would quieten before disappearing off into the dark sky, leaving Vince alone. The street lights that lined the roads – and the absence of them – made a rudimentary map that helped the magpie locate nearby areas of grass and trees. Once she'd got her bearings, she returned to Vince and they continued on their adjusted course.

The bark of a dog echoed from a back garden up ahead and Vince's ears flattened instinctively. They'd only left the safety of the woodland a short while ago, but with all the harsh noises and no cosy den to return to, he felt exposed and on edge.

'We'll need to find somewhere I can sleep without being seen. I don't want any hassle from humans,' Vince said to Rita, who was now hopping along the pavement in front of him.

'Already?' she replied.

'We've got all the time in the world; might as well take it slow,' Vince said.

And I don't like it out here.

'Sure!' she chirped. 'I saw the perfect place just now.'

'Good. I'll need food as well.'

'We've got hours of darkness left yet, don't you worry your little paws.'

'My paws are not little,' he grumbled.

They approached a place where several tall lamp posts cast their yellow glow onto rows of gleaming metal bars that traversed the road they were on. The bars were sunk into the surface of the tarmac so that cars could cross over them. Long red-and-white-striped poles reached upwards on either side.

After surveying the situation, Rita shouted from the air, 'Right, just across here. Still a few houses about on the left. But you should be able to find… Vince?' Vince had retreated several leaps and ducked behind a tree. 'Vince?'

Rita flew back along the road until she caught sight of him peering around the tree's thick trunk at what lay ahead.

'Are they…?' Vince whispered.

'Are they what? Train tracks?' Rita landed next to him.

'Thought so. Scat.' He exhaled slowly. The stories Vince's mother had told him had always scared him, but he'd never expected to actually see a train, let alone go near one. After she'd died, he'd all but dismissed the threat of human vehicles; he'd grown up in Richmond Park, after all, with no intention of going into the city. Now that he was within sniffing distance of the metal rails, the stories came flooding back.

'It's okay. It's night-time. Trains don't run at night-time. I don't think,' Rita said.

'You don't *think*?' He looked down at Rita, his eyes wide with fear.

'I don't know. I'm not nocturnal. But neither are humans. There are fewer cars at night, so there probably are fewer trains too.'

'Fewer is not none,' Vince snapped.

'Well, I haven't heard any, have you?'

'I… I don't know.' Vince edged out from behind the tree, eyes locked on the tracks. 'Go and investigate.'

'What are you so scared of? You can run across in half a blink.'

'That's easy for you to say, you don't have to go near them. We definitely can't go around them somehow? Or just stop here for now?'

'I don't think we can go round. They seem to stretch for a long way… There might be a bridge somewhere, I suppose, but I'd have to go and look. If you wait here—'

'No!' Vince barked and Rita jumped back, startled. 'I mean, no. It's fine. Stay here. Please,' Vince said.

'Okay, okay, don't worry.' Rita stretched a comforting wing towards the fox. 'We could rest in the small park over the way until tomorrow.'

'But we'll just be delaying the inevitable, right? And there could be more trains then, you reckon. Might as well get it over with.' Vince's fear was turning to embarrassment, despite Rita's understanding. 'Go and have a look and make sure it's safe. But don't go too far. Stay where I can see you.'

'Okay,' Rita said, before flapping to the nearest lamp post. She looked both ways along the tracks, then flew across to a lamp on the far side. 'It's fine. Come on,' she called.

Vince approached the rails cautiously, head snapping back and forth with each step. 'How do you know which way it will come?'

'We don't, I guess. But there isn't anything coming. Listen.'

Vince listened. Beneath the rustling of the leaves above him, a low rumble vibrated in his ears. 'I hear something. Sounds like thunder. Far away.'

'I can't see anything. Maybe it is thunder? Just come on! You could be across by now!'

Rita was right. He was being ridiculous.

'And trains *definitely* don't run at night?' he called up to her.

'I didn't say that, I said there were *fewer*. But even if there *was* a train coming, you'd still be able to run across in time. Come on!' She hopped from foot to foot.

It's fine. Dad was out during the day. He was always taking risks like that…

'Okay. Count me down. From three,' he shouted.

Was that rumbling getting louder? He squeezed his eyes shut and took a deep breath.

No. You're being ridiculous.

'Three…' Rita began.

Just my imagination…

'Two…'

…but it's getting louder.

A horn blared, vibrating the air around them both. Orange lights flashed out of nowhere. The red–and–white poles juddered as they fell horizontal and thumped into position to block the way. The road on the far side taunted him through the gap beneath.

Scat. What do I do?

Scat.

Scaaaaat.

Vince hurled himself under the barrier.

'No! Vince! Stop!' Rita screeched.

As his front paws touched the road on the other side of the tracks, he half opened his eyes. The glare of the street lights dazzled him, doubled by the reflections from the train hurtling towards him. His back legs followed his front and pounded onto the tarmac. The horn sounded again and noise coursed through Vince's body. A warm rush of air tugged at his tail, dragging it sideways. Vince stumbled, but kept his footing, as the demon-eyed metal hulk cruised past.

'You did it! Well done!' Rita cheered as Vince sprinted past her into the near darkness. 'Wait!' She flapped after him, barely keeping up as he tore along the road.

Vince's heart pounded in his ears and chest. He had to get far away. Quickly.

In his peripheral vision a building flew by. A car park. Tall metal fences. He raced onwards, gaze locked ahead. Lamp posts. A flash of scarlet and white. One of his paws landed on something cold. Then trees. Bushes. The road narrowed. More bushes. The cold air stung his eyes and burned his throat, but he ran on.

'Vince!'

He darted to the right and disappeared into the undergrowth, leaving the brambles rustling behind him. Rita dived into the trees, following his noisy trail of snapping twigs and paws on leaves.

'Vince!' Rita called. 'It's okay! Slow down!'

The trees gave way to a wide expanse of grass and Vince slowed to a trot. He panted, tongue lolling from his jaws. Rita swooped down and landed in front of him.

'Vince! Are you okay? You just shot off like a grasshopper!'

'I'll be fine. I just... I'm fine.' Vince let his back legs collapse underneath him as he gasped for air. He looked around at the park he'd brought them to. 'Where are we?'

'A park. Small one. Not where I had in mind, but it'll do I suppose.'

'Is there somewhere else nearby?'

'Yes, but you need to rest. Let's go back into the trees and...'

'No. I'm fine. We've hardly gone anywhere. Come on, let's keep going.' He hauled himself off the ground.

'Okay, but in a bit. Let's have a rest now, yes? You've had a fright. You need to calm down.'

'I AM CALM,' Vince barked. Rita flinched at his outburst, hopping a few steps backwards. 'Sorry. I didn't mean to shout at you. I'm just... I don't like trains. Because...' He pawed at the grass in front of him. '...I just don't.'

Rita tilted her small head. 'I understand.'

Vince managed a smile, despite the tightness in his chest. She was right, he did need a rest. His nerves were shredded. Rita started to hop towards the trees and said, 'Let's find somewhere to relax for a bit, hmm?'

Vince followed in silence, his breathing steadying. The pair reached the edge of the park and slipped through the long grass. The air was slightly warmer under the tree canopy. Vince looked around for a spot to lie down. A quick nap would help him forget the train and focus on what lay ahead.

Rita flapped up into a tree. 'Well, this looks alright. Will you be okay down there? That was quite the near miss! And I can't believe you crossed the second set of tracks without even stopping!'

Vince's eyes widened. 'What do you mean, the second set of tracks?'

'There was another set. Parallel, a stone's throw from the first. I was going to tell you after you'd crossed the first but I didn't want you to get scared and turn back to the park.'

His head spun. The cold metal on his paw. The red and white.

He looked at the ground, towards the direction of the tracks, over to the field. Everywhere but at Rita.

Another set of tracks. She didn't say anything… I could've run straight into another train.

'You lied to me.'

'What? No…'

'You tricked me,' he snarled.

'No, Vince. I was trying to help. Honestly. I—'

'You couldn't bear the thought of me turning back. You said it was fine to cross! Risked my life just so you could carry on with your stinking adventure?'

'No! I didn't know you would bolt off like that. And it's fine, anyway. You're safe! You're overreacting.'

'Am I? I agreed to let you come with me on the promise that you would help me and keep me safe, and you're leading me into the path of trains.'

'Vince, you know I would never do that. You're my friend. I'm sorry for not telling you about the other tracks. I didn't hear anything. If I had, you know I would have said so.'

'Liar,' Vince growled.

'You're tired. Why don't you get some sleep and we can talk after, yes? Find some food too. That'll help. I'll wake you when the moon starts to fall, okay?'

'Don't bother.' Vince turned and trotted away, then slunk under the cover of a nearby bush, the white flash of his tail the last to disappear.

Edward was dozing in the woods, close to Vince's old den, when Jake approached him. Edward always slept at night, as he liked to be awake when the humans visited the park so he could soak up as much admiration as possible, but it did not take much to rouse him.

'Sorry to disturb you, Edward. Can I have a word?' whispered Jake.

'Of course.' Edward rose to his feet, towering over the fox. 'Is there something wrong?' He was usually courteous. At first, anyway.

It was really only Vince who rankled him, but Edward was definitely one animal Jake didn't want to get on the bad side of.

'Not exactly,' Jake said. 'It's Sophie. She won't stop crying. And she hasn't eaten or slept since Vince left… She's too tired to hunt now. I'm really worried about her.'

'Can't keep your vixen happy, eh?' Edward sneered.

The deer was obviously saving some of his courtesy for another occasion. Jake refused to let Edward get to him. He had come for Sophie's sake, and the thought of her in tears back in the den was enough to make sure he wouldn't leave without getting what he wanted.

'She just wants to know that he'll be okay,' Jake replied.

'And you?'

'You know Vince and I never saw eye to eye, but he means a lot to Sophie, and I don't like seeing her so upset.'

'Oh, how very heart–warming. So, what would you like *me* to do, exactly?'

'Send a bird to check on him, maybe give him a message? Just tell him we're thinking of him, and that he can still come back. We won't think any less of him. But if not, just to let us know that he's okay.'

Edward snorted. 'Who says he can come back?'

'Oh, come on, Edward. You've already destroyed his den. If he wants to come back and live in the cemetery, then what difference does it make to you?'

'You're a decent fox, Jake. More decent than Vince ever was. I suppose that's why Sophie chose you in the end.'

Jake didn't reply. Edward would take some convincing to do him a favour, and mind games were the stag's speciality.

Edward continued with a sly smile. 'If he comes back – if I *let him* come back – then who's to say Sophie won't go back to him? You really want to take that risk?'

'She wouldn't do that. Vince and Sophie are just friends now. Like you said, she chose me.'

'True. But she'll always have feelings for him. You know that, surely? Anyone can tell you that.'

'Okay, fine. I admit, I don't particularly want him back here.'

Edward's smile widened across his dark face. An admission of Jake's real feelings towards Vince was clearly what he wanted to hear. 'Ah, I knew you hated him, deep down. I don't blame you.'

Jake sighed. Edward's penchant for drama was wearying. 'Hate is a strong word. Will you send a bird or not?'

'I'll send Kara to check on him, but Vince can't come back to Richmond Park.'

'Fine.'

'And you'll obviously need to do something for me.'

Jake knew Edward would want something in return. That was how it worked. 'Such as?'

'Oh, I don't know… Letting me know the comings and goings of the cemetery, perhaps?'

'Spy on my friends, you mean?' It was a higher price than he'd expected. He did his best to hide his trepidation.

'No, just keep an eye on them. And if anyone steps out of line, you come and tell me. They don't need to know. One of the owls does it in the woodlands, some of the does from our herd check the perimeter every evening… It's how Park Watch works. Now that you lot have relocated, I'll need an extra pair of eyes. It's really not a big deal.'

'Not for you.'

The pair stood in silence for a long blink. If Sophie found out… But what else could he do? He had nothing to offer the birds in return for a favour. It had to be Edward.

'Two full moons, then you find someone else,' Jake said, finally.

'Four.'

'Two.'

'Three, or no bird. Do we have a deal?'

Jake sighed. 'Do I have a choice?'

'Of course, but it depends how much you want this message sent to Vince.'

Vince wasn't the issue, Sophie was, but it was only temporary.

Worth it to put her mind at rest. 'Then I suppose we have a deal. But if this gets back to anyone…'

'Do your job and it won't. If you even think about keeping anything from me, I'll have you and that vixen of yours exiled from Richmond Park so fast your fur will fall off,' Edward said.

Jake turned to leave. Despite the deal, he was relieved. The foxes tended to stick to the rules, so his new position as Chief Fox-Snitcher would hopefully not involve much disloyalty. Plus, it was for Sophie. She was his only priority.

'Oh, and Jake?' Edward called after him.

Jake looked over his shoulder at the deer.

Edward laughed. 'If you need some advice on how to keep your female happy, then let me know.'

Jake narrowed his eyes, then turned back, fur bristling. Without a word, he headed in the direction of the cemetery, where Sophie awaited him – and any news of Vince – in their newly dug den.

Rita hopped around the base of a hawthorn, pecking off caterpillars among the small white flowers. Half an hour had passed since Vince stormed off, but she wasn't worried about him disappearing. After their argument, she'd stealthily followed him and watched as he'd curled up under a prickly holly bush. She'd seen enough of his tantrums over the last few seasons to know that he always sulked for a while afterwards. It was worth putting up with, though. For the company. She stayed nearby so she could hear him when he eventually decided to emerge.

After swallowing one last beakful, she'd settled on a low branch to preen her feathers when a rustling from behind alerted her senses. Too big for a mouse or rat. Definitely not a bird.

The creature let out a deep guttural grunt. A white pointed snout with a black mushroom nose appeared, methodically snuffling at the ground. Close behind, and very much attached, was the unmistakable black-and-white-striped head of a badger. Its large body followed, lumbering along slowly and awkwardly, as if its four short legs couldn't quite decide how to work together. The wiry grey fur covering the creature was patchy in places, and one of its ears had seen better days.

Rita let out the breath she'd been unaware of holding. A badger was no threat to her. Not that Rita was a particularly nervous bird – she was more of a predator than most.

'Hello there!' she called down. He might know the surrounding area well enough to give them a few directions.

'Uh...What's that Sid hears? Show yourselves!' he spluttered, twisting his small head back and forth.

'Up here.'

The badger looked up. 'Oh, hello. A single pie-bird? Curious. Not from around here, you're not.' It was less of a question and more of a statement to himself.

'No. Just passing through. But you are, I take it?'

'Here and there. Sometimes there, but mostly here,' he said.

'Ah, good. Maybe you can help us?'

'Who is *us*? You appear charmless, lonely bird!'

'My friend is sleeping over there. He's a fox.' She pointed her wing in the direction of the holly bush. 'Vince, he's called. I'm Rita.'

'Very good, very good. I'm Sidney or Sid, whichever suits your beak.' Sid sniffed at the ground absentmindedly, then looked up sharply and continued. 'A fox, Sid heard you say?'

Rita nodded.

'Sid finds this interesting. Most remarkable indeed. And you are... *friends* with the red-furred mammal?'

'Yes. Sort of. Well, he's angry at me right now. But he'll be alright soon. I think. I hope.'

'Oh, I suppose it was yourselves quarrelling earlier, then? My, my, what exciting drama unfolded before Sid! Such interest Sid has in your personal existences!'

'Um... Really?' Rita replied.

'No. Very not quiet, you were. Woke old Sid up, you did. *Very* not quiet, indeed.'

'Sorry. I was trying to stop him getting too scared. He doesn't like trains. But he thought... Well, I don't know... He thought I tricked him. To stop him from going back home. But he got frightened and lost his temper.'

'Scared of trains? Whose ears ever did hear of a fox scared of trains? These fresh litters… Pfft.' He shook his head. 'Well, no matter to Sid. Help you if I can, I will, I suppose. What can Sid do for you?'

'We're looking for a park. The one Vince's grandparents came from. It's north of here, apparently. We don't know what it's called, though.'

'Northwards, the pie-bird says?' Sid frowned. 'Well, Sid's not left these woods in many seasons. Sid's directions may not be of any purpose to yourselves now. New roads popping up all over the situation… Why do the furless ones need so many? All this journeying around… Here, there… It's all the same anyway, if you ask Sid. Where are you from, pie-bird? If you don't mind Sid asking?'

Rita fluttered down to Sid's level. 'Richmond Park.'

'What's that now? Sid knows that name. Close by, is it? Why would you leave?'

Rita explained about Edward and the deer. 'It was okay for me, I suppose, but Vince had had enough. I think he's pretty brave, standing up for what he believes in. And he left his vixen. Well, she's not his vixen any more, but he still cares about her. Don't tell him I told you that.'

'Deer you say? Hmm… Met some of those I have, perhaps. Or not. Hard to remember, now. But Sid knows something, indeed. You fresh-litters don't comprehend the good life. Standing up for what he believes in? A fool's errand. Your red-furred mammal is unwise. A few rules might help arrange these woods, if you ask Sid. Bush-tailed-climbers keeping me up all sunshines. Small beasts stealing my food. Speaking of such…' The badger lifted his head and peered over the top of Rita. 'Is that your red-furred companion?'

Vince was several trees away, rolling a small log with his snout. The pair watched from afar as he pawed at the newly revealed ground and then guzzled down a mouthful of what Rita presumed were insects. Vince coughed and bared his teeth in a grimace, then shook his ears. Rita couldn't help but giggle.

Sid shouted at Vince, 'I was conserving those actually, but Sid supposes you may have a few.'

'Oh, er, sorry,' Vince replied, startled. 'I didn't realise they belonged to someone.'

'No trouble, red-furred Vince.' Sid plodded towards him, but Rita held back, worried Vince might still be angry with her. 'My, my, you certainly appear as a park creature should to Sid's eyes. Such a glossy coat!'

'Um, thanks. I suppose you've met Rita, then?'

'Oh no, the legend of your adventure has spread far-long among the creatures of this woodland!'

'Really?'

'No. Sid just met your pie-bird friend.' Sid waved a paw towards Rita.

'Oh. We're not friends.' Vince's stomach growled and he looked at the ground. 'Anyway, I should go. I need to find some food before I—'

Now that her cover was blown, Rita seized her chance to make amends and hopped towards them. 'I can take you to where there's lots of frogs.' If there's one thing that would get him back on her side, it was the promise of an amphibian-based meal.

'No thanks.' Vince turned away and began to head off into the trees.

'Wrong way!' Rita called.

'You don't know where I'm going,' Vince shouted back.

'Hang on!' Sid barked. 'Sid thinks you should listen to the pie-bird.'

Vince stopped and faced them both. 'With all due respect, this is none of your business.'

Sid ignored Vince and turned to Rita. 'Grumpy fellow, your red-furred friend, isn't he?'

'He is indeed,' Rita replied to Sid.

'I can hear you,' Vince said.

'I know you're going the wrong way,' Rita said. 'And I know

you'd rather eat frogs than beetles.' She flapped into the air and swooped in front of the fox, attempting to block his way.

'Beetles, frogs, magpies. I'm not fussy.' Vince weaved around her.

Rita flew up to a branch ahead of him. 'I know you're angry with me. I'm sorry about the train tracks. I'm *really* sorry. But this was just a silly misunderstanding. You don't need to punish yourself.'

Vince ignored her and continued on through the undergrowth. Rita flapped behind, keeping close on his tail, then Sid started to follow them both with slow, laboured steps. Vince's pace quickened, while Rita began to zig-zag through the mesh of branches above to keep up.

Rita settled on a high bough. 'Okay, fine. You don't want me around. I get it. But you're going back the way we came. You'll reach the train tracks again if you keep going.'

Vince stopped dead and blinked up at the bird. 'Really?'

'Really,' Rita said.

Sid bellowed from behind them, 'Turn your ears to your pie-bird friend, you ungrateful mammal!'

The long grass behind Vince parted and badger trudged through, the saggy fur under his chin wobbling.

'Can you please mind your own business?' Vince snapped.

'This is Sid's home and you just swallowed half of Sid's dinner, so my business I'm making it. Your pie-bird friend is correct about the frogs, and the train tracks. Sid has heard about the wetlands. Many green-hoppers there indeed, so I'm told. Never been myself, no. Or have I? I can't quite remember…'

'Wetlands?' Vince said, turning to look at Sid, then at Rita. 'In the city?'

'Yes. Wetlands,' Rita replied. 'Look, I know I'm not your friend. But I like you. I want to help you.'

Once again, Vince's belly rumbled noisily. He collapsed on his haunches, defeated by his own hunger. 'Fine,' he said. 'Just tell me which direction this wetlands place is. I'll find my own way.'

Rita pointed her wing behind them. 'It's this way. Although I'm heading there myself, so you might as well follow me.'

'Whatever.' Vince made an about-turn, then stopped as he came face-to-face with Sid, who had finally caught them up. 'Oh, uh, thanks for the food, by the way. Sorry for snapping at you,' Vince mumbled.

Sid furrowed his furry brow. 'No trouble, red-furred Vince. However, it's not Sid you should be delivering your apology to.'

Vince looked at the ground between his front paws.

'These fresh litters, I don't know…' Sid shrugged his hefty shoulders. 'Well, be having fun, both of you. Sid believes yourselves to be most peculiar to be leaving Richmond Park, however I suppose Sid is too old now, for all this nonsense, indeed.' He began to sniff at the ground, as if he had forgotten where he was, then suddenly remembering, lifted his head. 'Wait… Wasn't that…? Hmm…No. Never to be minding. Like a dandelion, Sid's memory is. Good luck to you.'

'Thanks.' Rita smiled warmly at Sid, then turned to Vince. 'So, you're coming with me?'

'I'm going this way. If you are too, then I suppose I can't stop you.'

'You could always eat me.' Rita laughed, then flew ahead to a low branch and waited for Vince to catch up. Their previous travelling routine quickly re-established.

'True,' Vince replied. 'You're in luck though, because I'm in the mood for frogs.'

As Edward lounged in the long grass, he watched Kara approach high in the jet-black sky. The dark chestnut heart of feathers that outlined her ghostly face was unmistakable. He stood up as gracefully as any deer could, straightening his back legs to lift his rear end and then resting on his forelegs, before extending them one at a time. The barn owl swooped down and, with a few deft beats of her grey and ochre wings, landed gracefully in front of the deer.

'You're late. I sent for you an hour ago,' Edward said.

'Things to do, mice to eat,' Kara said with a shrug. 'Heard you need a message sent.'

'Not quite,' Edward replied. 'I need you to find Vince. I need you to make sure he doesn't get to where he's going.'

'Right, and I'm s'posed to do that *how*, exactly?' Kara asked, then began preening the long flight feathers on one of her wings.

'Find some animal – a dog, another fox or something – and tell them there's a home for them here if they get rid of Vince.'

'You mean kill him.' The owl paused her primping and blinked her large eyes at Edward.

'Exactly,' he replied. The thought had entered Edward's mind as soon as Vince left the previous morning, but Jake's request had cemented it.

'Why bother? He's already gone.'

'His death will be a warning to everyone here. They need to be reminded that the city is dangerous and that Richmond Park is the best home they'll ever have. I have little doubt that Vince will fail on his own, but I'm not risking it. I can't have him sending messages back, encouraging others to flout the rules or leave or… worse. Park Watch would fall apart. I've spent seasons making this park what it is and I won't have that flea-ridden creature ruin it for me.'

Kara spotted another ruffled feather. She dragged her pointed beak along it and the fine barbs bounced into pristine alignment. 'What's in it for me?'

'You can hunt near the golf course. Where all the big rats are. Twice a week.'

'Rats? Is that it? Make it four times a week, and two rabbits per moon.'

'Three times a week, and *one* rabbit per moon,' Edward said with a grunt. 'But you have to be discreet about it. That's my final offer. And I want Vince sorted as soon as possible. No dilly-dallying.'

'Would I?' she trilled innocently. 'You have yourself a deal, Mister Deer. You know which way he went?'

'North. He won't have got far, though. I doubt he's crossed the river yet, but check the bridges and ask around. You'll find him. Wouldn't be surprised if he's already got himself killed. A soft park fox like him won't last long in the city.' Edward laughed. 'Don't let me down, Kara.'

'Wherever he's going, he won't make it, don't worry.' Kara stretched her wings and turned away from the deer. 'Nice doing business with you,' she said over her shoulder, before a couple of wing-beats lifted her small frame off the ground. Straightening her legs back under her speckled tail feathers, she spiralled upwards, before disappearing into the darkness.

The rabbits won't thank me for that.

But he could always blame one of those trespassing hawks that conveniently popped up every now and again, when he needed them to. He would vow to defend them from the malicious murderer, then do another deal with Kara so the rabbit deaths stopped, leaving Edward looking like the hero. Yes, with Vince dead thanks to the dangerous city and another deadly intruder seen off, his constituents would soon feel safer than ever.

3

After Rita chirped a goodbye to Sid, the badger beckoned her towards him. 'Look after your red-furred friend. Sid can see you are a caring pie-bird, but that one is an angry creature. It is a most peculiar situation, but Sid believes you can locate the old-litter's sleeping place. But watch out for the two-legged ones. Dangerous, they are. Sid remembers that, at least.'

Rita thanked him, although his warning seemed unnecessary. Of course humans could be dangerous. Every animal knew that. She shrugged and wished him well, before leading Vince in the direction of the wetlands.

It was a short walk from where they'd met Sid, across a few small fields separated by paths. The last field they crossed appeared to be used by humans for their play. There were white lines painted on the ground, the grass was cut uncomfortably short and trees were scarce. Vince hurried across it, eager to get out of the open space and gorge himself on the frogs Rita had promised him.

The fox was sceptical, though. Not that he didn't believe her, but he couldn't understand why the humans could possibly want a bunch of great big ponds with no grass. In Richmond Park they ate picnics, played games, ran, let their dogs loose from their leads... But he couldn't argue with the sign he'd seen as they turned up the path. Dark green with white human writing. He couldn't read it, of course, but the white silhouettes of two geese above it were obvious even to his eyes. Geese meant water. Water meant frogs.

'This is it! Scrraaaaack-ack-ack!' Rita sang.

'Please stop that,' Vince said through clenched teeth. Despite Sid's harsh words, he still hadn't gathered the courage to apologise to Rita and her squawking wasn't improving his motivation to do so.

'No. You're not asleep. That was your rule. No singing while you're asleep. You're not asleep, so I'm singing,' she replied, before launching into a particularly loud bout of chattering. 'SCRRAACK! SCRAAACK-ACK-ACK!'

Vince bubbled with envy for humans, who could walk and hold their hands over their ears at the same time. He flattened his own ears to his head, but it made little difference.

The pair passed over a bridge spanning a small pond before arriving at a large pale-brick building dotted with windows and dark wooden doors. A high slatted wooden fence stretched left and right, butting up against the building, with no apparent gates or gaps. Apart from a small paved area in front of the building, it was surrounded by thick greenery and flowers. Vince imagined it in daylight: insects buzzing, frogs plopping into the water, birds chirping among the plants.

'If this is the outside, it must be amazing inside,' Vince said, thinking out loud. 'I'll bet the fence goes all the way round. The humans must have to go through the building to get in. If they're this restricted, then it must be even more exclusive than Richmond Park.'

'Looks fancy,' Rita squawked.

'Mmm,' Vince replied, then wandered off to look for a way in.

'I'll fly over. See if there's anyone inside who can help.' Rita flapped away before Vince could respond.

Vince padded up to the fence and sniffed along the bottom, among the flower beds. A fox had been here before. Not recently, but there was definitely a lingering scent. A female. He followed it along the wood panels, then stopped, overcome with a desire to mark his own scent on the wood. As he did so, he thought back to the last time he'd had to mark his territory. Although his den back in the park was his and his alone, the pack had an understanding to never encroach on anyone else's space. Even Jake, who was far from Vince's biggest fan, respected his den. It was only the deer who didn't. When he was a cub, Vince's parents had taught him about marking territory, and how foxes outside the park would try to one-up each other to claim the best areas, but it wasn't until he was older, and his parents were gone, that he was forced to claim the den for his own. Even then, he'd never fully understood why he had to do it. He'd grown up in a safe community where even enemies respected one another, but this instinct, to mark his territory, ran deep.

He continued along the fence as it turned a right angle, the unfamiliar scent leading him further and further from the building.

If anyone knows a way through this fence, a fox does.

His intuition was right. The scent intensified as the covering bushes disappeared, making way for a road and a large gate made of the same wooden slats as the fence. A thick metal chain hung from the middle, locking the two halves together, but it didn't matter to Vince. The bottom edge of the fence was a couple of paws' width higher than the surface of the road, giving him – or any other fox – room to squeeze underneath. A smattering of red hairs caught on the wood left him in no doubt.

Belly flat to the ground, Vince gripped the solid concrete as best he could and pushed himself through the crack with his powerful hind legs. He shook his ears and looked around. His paws remained on hard ground, and the fence doubled back on itself, forming an enclosed square, with another gate, identical to the one he'd just navigated, directly in front of him. A large human truck sat in the far corner, along with a pile of boxes and some rubbish bins. The back of the brick building sat to his right, making up the fourth side of the square. Unsurprisingly, the area was devoid of ponds and frogs, but over the far fence he could see the tops of tall trees, leaves rustling invitingly. He grinned.

He hurried through the concrete area, ears up and eyes forward, then – just as he reached the second gate – Rita appeared from behind the fence and perched on top of it. 'You found it! Good. Come on, come on! Quick!' she chattered, before disappearing as quickly as she'd arrived.

Vince quickly slid under the gate and was met on the other side by Rita hopping gleefully in the middle of a round, paved area. 'Look at it all! Isn't it lovely?'

Vince took it all in. Paths snaked around small, pristine grassy areas dotted with picnic benches and irregular shaped ponds, glossy lily pads floating serenely on their surfaces. It was blissfully quiet. The only things breaking the silence were the water lapping at the banks and the reeds rustling in the breeze.

'It looks great.' He smiled at Rita, the stress of his journey so far all but forgotten. 'I'm dying for some dinner, there'd better be some frogs in one of these ponds.' He leapt over the fence with ease and made his way down the bank to the shallow water, Rita following close behind. Vince scanned for shadows under the surface. 'Be quiet, or you'll scare them off,' he whispered, crouching low, ears up.

They remained motionless, Rita watching Vince intently, for half a minute or so. Suddenly, Vince's ears twitched and he sprang forward, his forelegs piercing the mirror of water, droplets spraying in all directions. Rita jumped back, protecting her feathers, as Vince dragged a squirming, dark-green frog from the pool, which was now murky from the disturbed silt. The frog croaked a protest in rudimentary water-language from under Vince's paw. 'No! Away, fox!' Vince lowered his head to consume his long-awaited prize, when a piercing scream tore through the air.

'Arreeeee! Eeoo! Arreeeee! Eeoo!'

Vince jumped, showering water around them both once again as he stumbled in the shallows. The frog made its escape and disappeared into the water with a plop. 'What on earth was that?'

'Arreeeee! Who's there?' the voice screeched. 'Danger! Danger!'

'We're sorry, we didn't mean to intrude,' Rita called into the dark. 'We were just looking for some food and somewhere to sleep for the day.'

'Thought you could eat my eggs, did you?' A vast, grey bird appeared out of the darkness and, after clocking them, cried, 'Fox! Magpie! DANGER! ARREEEEE!' The bird spun in a circle and shook her enormous wings wildly.

They had never seen or heard anything like her. She was ash grey, as tall as Vince, her huge, clawed feet and angry face both the same shade of vivid pink. The comical tuft of dark feathers protruding from the back of her head did not lessen the impact of her curved, razor-sharp beak.

'Calm down!' Vince began. 'We're sorry, we didn't realise—'

The bird stopped spinning and lunged at Vince. In a flail of feathers, she jabbed her pointed beak into the flesh of his cheek.

'Ouch! *Mother Nature!*' Vince raised a paw to his bleeding face.

Rita beat her wings, ready to retaliate, when the bird shrieked again. 'Felipe! Felipe! Get over here! Danger!'

Vince searched the area for whoever she was calling to but saw only two otters in the distance, their dark-brown fur slick with water. They crouched, avoiding his gaze, and looked at each other worriedly.

Vince's stomach lurched. Rita trembled beside him and whispered, 'I shouldn't have brought us here. I'm so sorry. Come on, Vince, run...'

'No! ARREEEEE!' The bird lunged again and ripped at the fur on Vince's neck.

'Argh! Stop!' Vince pulled back and bared his fangs, ready to pounce, when another ear-splitting scream pierced his eardrums.

'Arreeeee! Eeoo! Arreeeee! Eeoo!'

A bird of the same species, but larger – Felipe, presumably – hurtled across the grass and collided with Vince in a maelstrom of feathers. Vince tumbled onto his back, shielding his face as the birds pecked at him with their keen beaks. Something stabbed at his ribs, puncturing his skin, as their claws tore away clumps of fur from his belly and legs.

Vince lashed out with his claws where he could, but the birds were quick, working as a team, striking instantly at any unprotected patch of his face.

Rita tried to get close. She flapped above the writhing animals and swiped with her small talons and beak as best she could, but she was too small to fend them off. One well-aimed bite from either of them and she'd be done for.

'Rita!' Vince howled desperately.

Just then, a deep voice boomed from the air. 'Gabriela! Felipe! What are you doing? This behaviour is completely unacceptable!'

A gust of air from a vast pair of ghost-white wings rustled the birds' already dishevelled feathers, and they retreated. Rita scrabbled across the grass to Vince. 'Are you okay?' she asked.

'Ugh… I'll… be fine,' he groaned, pulling himself to his feet.

They looked over at the new arrival. A swan. Twice as big as the grey-and-pink birds, with a wingspan longer than Vince himself, nose to tail. His bright-orange beak was not sharp, but his long snaking neck was pure muscle. Vince didn't fancy his chances. Vince pushed Rita behind him with a wounded paw. 'Go,' he whispered. 'Fly away, now!'

'No, I'm not leaving you here.' She dodged his paw and flapped onto his head, gripping his short hair with her talons.

'Ow! What are you doing? Get off!' He shook his head and Rita fell to the floor with a stumble. Vince instantly regretted it, but she tidied her feathers and hopped in front of him without a word.

'You have my most sincere apologies,' the swan began. His deep voice was gentle, but it didn't relax Vince. 'My name is Oswald, I oversee everything here, and Gabriela and her mate have not acted according to the rules of this residence.'

'They're trespassing!' Gabriela screeched from behind Oswald. 'Trying to steal eggs!'

'We weren't!' Vince snapped at Gabriela, then addressed the swan. 'If you just show us the quickest way out, we'll be on our way.' He lifted his foreleg to lick his grazes.

'Unfortunately, I can't allow that, I'm afraid. Not yet, anyway. Our rules state that trespassers must be detained until the vote.' Not waiting for a response, he yelled at the top of his voice. 'Gentlemen!'

From behind Oswald, two geese and one more swan trotted out of the bushes. The second swan was as imposing as Oswald and the geese only slightly less so, with their sinister uniform of jet black necks and feet, white chests and grey wings.

Over by the fence, the otters had not moved or spoken a word, but were now quickly retreating.

'Now, Gabriela, Felipe, you know that's not how we do things here. Get away home now and I'll pop by in the morning to check you're okay. Save it for after the vote next time, eh?' Oswald smiled.

The two grey-and-pink birds clucked their annoyance and left, disappearing in the direction from which they arrived.

'Come on, lads, you know what to do,' Oswald said to his newly arrived friends.

Honking impatiently, the three birds moved in. Their huge webbed feet flapped on the grass, long necks extended haughtily. They gathered either side of Oswald and formed a semi-circle around Vince and Rita. Vince flattened his ears and took a step back, his hind legs slipping down the bank towards the water. He was an adequate swimmer, for a fox, but four water birds – huge ones at that – would have no trouble stopping him.

'What… what are you doing?' Vince barked.

'All transgressions must be dealt with in the appropriate manner, and punished accordingly,' one of the geese said. 'This is how we do things in the wetlands, and it's worked very well for us thus far.'

They're worse than the deer!

'This is ridiculous!' Rita flapped.

'Well, you're obviously free to go, madam,' the other goose said. 'Never in the history of the wetlands have we detained a bird, even an outsider land bird such as yourself. I doubt we could if we tried. But if you insist, then we can put you with your… ahem… friend.' He waved his enormous wing towards Vince.

'Well, I'm not leaving,' she replied, her tiny face twisted into a grimace.

'Rita, no! Just go. You don't need to stay here. Go and find help or something,' Vince pleaded.

Oswald shook his head. 'That would not be wise, madam. The animals you see here are just a small percentage of the inhabitants of the wetlands, and we take trespassing very seriously. Any animals you bring back will be dealt with swiftly, by the full force of our community. We don't want to hurt you, sir. Just come with us, and we can sort this out in a reasonable manner.'

'You said something about a vote, right? Like a trial?' Vince asked. He'd done nothing wrong. Not really. They might just let him go free.

'Of course. We are civilised, you know. The community will decide what happens to you.'

Vince growled under his breath, but with nowhere to run and no hope of fighting the birds alone, he relented. 'Fine.'

'Excellent. Roger, Frank? You want to do the honours this time?' The two geese stepped forward and waddled towards Vince.

'What are you doing?' Rita squawked. 'If you hurt him, I'll—'

Roger and Frank honked loudly at Rita before grasping Vince's scruff and tail between their strong beaks. Vince snarled, but didn't resist.

'Right, this way!' Oswald said, much too cheerily for Vince's liking, and the pair of geese led him away, flanked by the two enormous swans. Rita kept close to Vince, hopping uncertainly among the birds' flat, wide feet.

After a long walk across the grass and along a winding path, the birds dragged Vince into the foliage, emerging on the other side at the bank of an expanse of water so large that Vince couldn't see the other side. The scent of fresh fish was too much to bear and Vince groaned, wondering if his meagre mouthful of Sid's beetles would wind up being his last meal.

Vince remained on the bank, held tightly by the geese, as the swans descended into the water and paddled out towards the middle of the deep lake. They returned quickly, pushing a square, wooden platform with their broad chests. Oswald honked an order to Vince to get on, and he did as he was told, stepping into the shallows then stumbling as he clambered onto the unstable surface. Rita followed, her tiny weight making no difference to the balance. The four birds gathered on one edge of the platform and pushed it away from the bank, towards the dark depths of the centre of the lake.

'You'll remain here while we make arrangements and inform everyone,' Oswald said.

Vince paced back and forth, sniffing the platform, desperately inspecting every crevice in the wood. For what, he didn't know. 'And how long will that take?'

Oswald replied, 'Should all be sorted by tomorrow evening. We like to get things done as soon as possible, but we are largely diurnal birds by nature, you understand. My colleagues will ensure you don't try to leave in the meantime. And there will be additional security on the shore, just so you know.'

A fox trapped by birds. If his friends back in the park knew, they would never let him live it down. 'And what happens if I'm found guilty? Those grey-and-pink things tear me apart?'

'That will be decided by the jury,' Oswald said. 'Sometimes we let nature take its course, but yes, the Screamers occasionally assist with punishment protocols.'

'Screamers? Is that what they're called? Mother help me…' Vince stopped pacing.

'Yes. Southern Screamers, brought here from South America by the humans. Never been myself. Heard the weather's lovely.'

Vince was too exhausted and starving to listen any more. He lay down on the rough wood and began to clean his wounds.

Of all the animals he'd expected to come across, a bunch of water birds were the last he'd imagine could outwit him. They were slow on land. Doddery. Powerful, but not terribly smart. And in darkness too… If he'd just been more careful, quieter, quicker, he could have made it out safely. He was a fox, after all. Sneaking was meant to be his speciality.

Oswald directed Frank and Roger to stay behind on the water and guard Vince, while he and the other swan swam back to the shore and waddled into the bushes. Perhaps to get a bit more sleep before sunrise but, more likely, to guard the bank, ready to attack if necessary.

Vince turned to Rita, a lump in his throat. 'What do you think he meant by "let nature take its course"? Do you think they'd just leave me on here to die? I don't know what's worse. Screamers or starvation.'

'Don't worry,' Rita said softly. 'Everything will be okay. I'm sure.'

'You're *sure* are you, Rita? Really? Because to me, it looks like I either have to stay here and face some kind of vote where Mother knows what will happen to me, or try to escape and be drowned by geese or attacked by those...' He waved a paw towards the bank. '...*Screamer things* back on land. That's if I don't starve to death on this *stinking* piece of wood first.'

Rita drew a black-and-white wing over her head. 'I'm so sorry. I shouldn't have brought you here.' She began to sob. 'It's all my fault. No wonder you hate me. First the train tracks, now this. I've ruined your adventure...'

Vince softened his voice. 'It's not your fault, you didn't know. And, hey, what happened to "everything will be okay"?'

'Quiet!' Frank honked from the water. Vince shot him a look.

'I'll try to find help,' Rita whispered through her feathers, sniffling between words. 'I can be back at Richmond Park by morning.'

'No, Rita. You heard what Oswald said,' Vince whispered back. 'Anyway, who's going to come and help me? The foxes?' He shook his head. 'Even if they all came – which they wouldn't – it sounds like they'd be way outnumbered. And what are they going to do? Swim all the way out here? You saw what those two grey birds did to me. I won't risk the others getting ripped apart or drowned. I just have to face this trial and suffer the consequences.'

Rita sighed. 'You're probably right. I'm sorry.'

'Listen, just try to rest. We'll be able to think more clearly after some sleep. I'm going to try to nap while it's still dark. Mother knows how I'm going to sleep during the day on this stupid thing, right out in the open.'

'Quiet, both of you!' Roger tutted. 'What's a goose got to do to get some peace around here.'

Rita scowled at the goose and lowered her voice further. 'Okay, sleep well. And I am truly sorry. I promise I'll never get you into trouble again.' She lowered herself onto the wood a little way away from Vince and tucked her head under her iridescent blue-black feathers.

Vince curled his tail around his battered body and wished her a goodnight. He watched through his brush as Rita quickly fell into a deep slumber, her tiny chest rising and falling with her breath. The smallest of chirps whistled from her beak each time she exhaled, which brought a smile to Vince's face. For a short while he stared at her, the gentle bobbing of the floating platform and tranquil sound of water lapping at its edges serving as both an unwanted reminder of his imprisonment and a soothing lullaby. With eyelids dropping and the throbbing pain in his sides and legs fading, he drifted away. Back to Richmond Park, back to his den, and back to Sophie.

Kara settled on a branch and gulped down the lifeless mouse she'd plucked from the ground moments ago. A small reward to herself for her good work so far. After she'd departed Richmond Park, a tabby cat pointed her down the road Vince had travelled and told her of the chattering magpie tagging along. At the side of the road a quivering vole, urged by the grip of Kara's talons on her back, confessed to seeing him approach the train tracks, but hid before she saw which way he went, scared she might end up his next meal. Kara let her go in return for the information, but made a mental note of the location of her burrow, planning to stop on her way back to Richmond Park for a vole-sized snack.

Kara would have to up her fee. Edward didn't say anything about a magpie. Vince was close by, though, she was certain. If someone could give her some proper information, she could track him down before daylight, maybe even organise an ambush too. Job done in one night! If that wasn't worth an extra rabbit...

Down below, a badger snuffled in the undergrowth, muttering to himself. 'These small beasts, always stealing my supper. I don't know...'

Kara called down to him. 'Hey, you!'

'Uh... what's that? Sid hears another visitor?'

'You seen a fox around here?'

Sid looked up at the owl 'Ah! A moon-faced bird! What a dark heart you have!'

'Excuse me?'

'Around your face. A dark heart of feathers.'

'Oh, yeah. I asked you about a fox...'

'A fox, have I seen?' Sid cocked his head and stared intently at a nearby log for several blinks, before looking back up at the owl and replying, 'Maybe Sid has, maybe Sid hasn't. Many red-furred mammals I have met over the moons. One is very much like another.'

'Have you or haven't you? I need to find him.'

'Why?'

'None of your business.'

'Then Sid has *not*.' The badger shrugged and continued on.

'Hang on!' Kara stepped from the branch and glided across to a lower one in front of Sid. '*Another* visitor, you said just now… You *have* seen him, haven't you? His name is Vince.'

'No bells does that ring in Sid's ears.'

'Alright, fine, a magpie, then?'

'A single pie-bird? Alone? Well, such a sight Sid's eyes would never forget! But perhaps… Hmm, let Sid think…' He furrowed his brow.

'I really don't have time for this,' Kara muttered.

'Well, no creature *has* time, moon-faced bird. Time is no one's. Time cannot be held in paws or claws, nor hidden underground, nor eaten with beak or jaws. Sid knows this, and you should do well to learn, pale-feathered one. You park dwellers are most unwise, it seems. Most unwise indeed.'

'How do you know I'm from a park?' Kara tilted her round head almost horizontally. 'You *did* meet them. Tell me which way they went.'

Sid's ears drooped. 'Ah, the moon-faced bird is correct. Alas, Sid has said too many words, yet again. Botheration.' He let out a sigh and shook his head. A moment later, his ears perked up again and he blinked at the owl. 'Sid has decided he must return to bed.' He started to drag his cumbersome body away from Kara as fast as his stumpy legs could manage, ducking under a bramble in an attempt to prevent her from following.

'Stop right there!' Kara shrieked from the tree.

Sid looked over his shoulder at her. 'You, moon-faced bird, are rude. And old Sid does not help rude birds, he does not.'

Kara sneered. 'Maybe there's something I can do for you? A favour? There must be something you need.'

Sid ignored her and carried on nosing his way through the thick leaves.

Crazy old idiot. Fine, have it your way, badger, she thought as she spotted the entrance to his sett and flapped down to it. Sid emerged from the thorny bush and she waited for him to get closer before lunging at him. Her talons briefly seized his snout, leaving short stripes of raw pink flesh as he shook her off. He didn't seem to notice, and retaliated with a surprisingly swift swipe of his paw, but she dodged it by a whisker.

'Get out of Sid's way.' Sid snapped his teeth in her direction before ploughing ahead, his bulk simply too much for her to compete with, despite her fierce agility. 'What exactly does the moon-faced bird think she will do, Sid wonders. Follow me underground? Sid doesn't think so. I may be old, but still in working order, my claws and teeth are. Be gone now, rude bird.' He sniffed at the opening of his sett, then ducked inside.

He was right, of course. She could follow him, no problem, but then he would have the advantage, and having a wing torn off by a senile badger was not her idea of a nice evening, nor would it help her find the fox. A different approach was called for.

She hopped back to the sett, lowered her head close to the entrance, and shrieked down into the chamber. 'Hreeeeek! Hreeeeek!'

'Quiet, bird!' the badger's voice yelled from within.

'Sorry, am I bothering you?' she said sweetly, before another, 'HREEEEEEEK!'

Around her, mice dived through the grass, desperately searching for cover, while birds fled the trees. Unchallenged, Kara's screams filled every cranny of the woodland.

'Be gone, bird, I said! Off with you!'

Kara pictured the trembling badger, paws over his small ears, and cackled, then continued the harassment. 'HREEEEEK! I CAN KEEP THIS UP ALL NIGHT,' she shouted. 'HREEK HREEK! HREE-

EEEEEK! TELL ME WHERE THE FOX WENT AND I'LL STOP! HREEEEEEEK!'

Sid poked his head from the hole. 'Mother Nature, please! Alright, noisy bird, you've beaten Sid. Now quiet!'

'The fox?'

'South, back home, the red-furred one and his friend went. The red-furred one loves another. Could not be without her, he said. That's all Sid knows. Never left these woodlands, Sid hasn't.'

'Back to Richmond Park? Are you sure?'

'Oh, yes. The pie-bird convinced him. Too many dangers. Return to his true love, she said he should.'

'Hmm, he did have a thing with that Sophie, didn't he?' Kara said to herself, then addressed the badger again. 'I didn't see him on my way here. If you're lying to me…'

'Why would Sid lie? Sid does not know these creatures. They appeared, ate Sid's food and left. No regard for Sid, these creatures had. It matters not to me what the moon-faced bird wants. Perhaps the red-furred one was hiding. Perhaps a different route, to avoid some unknown danger. Sid does not know. Sid only knows what he has told the moon-faced bird.'

'Alright, alright, enough of your jabbering, badger. But if I find out you've lied to me, I'll make sure you get more than sore ears, do you understand?'

'Sid thinks the moon-faced bird is rude. Goodbye to you.' Without another word, Sid faded away into the dark sett.

Kara still had a few hours before sunrise. If the badger was telling the truth and Vince was heading back, she had to get to him before he reached the park. Who knew whether Edward would hold up his end of the bargain if the fox turned up unharmed. But if the badger was lying, she'd find out quickly. There weren't that many routes, and there were other animals she could extract information from. She flapped into the air and turned south, gliding back over the trees she'd passed before, her eyes scanning the ground for red fur or black-and-white wings.

Something slapped onto the wood behind Vince, droplets dashing his rear. He dragged one eye open. The sky was painted with a wash of purples and pinks, the sun peeking over the horizon. Turning to identify the noise, he found a fish thrashing on the edge of the platform. Vince jumped up, reached out a paw and slammed the writhing creature firmly against the wood. On the water's surface, a trail of bubbles erupted, a dark shape underneath zipping towards the shore, its long tail swaying back and forth.

Strange…

On the other side of the platform, the geese police were asleep, their long necks doubled back to face their tails, black heads resting between their wide, grey wings as they bobbed on the water.

'Rita…' Vince whispered. 'Rita?'

She was gone.

He looked towards the bank, then squinted at the sky. No sign. He pulled the fish towards him and took a bite. It was the best thing he'd tasted in a long time, despite the situation.

'What's that? Heeeooonk!' Roger extended his periscope neck and glared at Vince, who had his back to him on edge of the platform. 'What are you doing, fox?'

'I was just stretching my legs and slipped. This thing's wobbly, you know.'

'Hmmm… well, just as long as you weren't thinking of trying to escape. You wouldn't be the first, let me tell you, but never in the history of the wetlands have we had an escaped convict, no sir.'

'Do you memorise those lines?' Vince said. 'Like, do you all stand in a line and recite them?'

'I… I don't know what you mean.' The goose puffed his chest.

Frank chipped in, 'Hey! Just stay still and be quiet, or we'll—'

'What? What will you do? Bring those Screamer birds over here to have another go at me? Pah!' Vince snorted, acutely aware that his temper was flaring but ignoring it. His ego had taken a battering the previous night and he needed a pick-me-up. And it just so happened that he had a couple of geese on hand to taunt.

'They'd enjoy that, I'm sure, eh, Frank? Heeeeonk! Best security guards we got here. They'd attack a tree if we told them it was after their eggs! HEEEOOONK!' Roger tipped his head back and flapped his wings, hooting with laughter at his apparently hilarious joke.

'Keep it down, Roger. We're on duty,' Frank said.

'Oh, shut up. Oswald can't hear us out here.'

'No, but he's trusted us to watch the fox, so you should take it seriously.'

Roger rolled his eyes. 'I *do* take it seriously, but that doesn't mean I can't make a joke, does it? It's not like there's any other fun to have around here.'

'You sound like a gosling. Just do your job and be quiet,' Frank said.

'Oh dear, do I sense some unhappiness in the ranks?' Vince asked.

'I won't tell you again, fox.' Frank flapped his wings and kicked his feet, sending a wave towards the platform. Vince dug his claws into the wood as it undulated wildly underneath him.

'Whoa! Okay, okay! I'm shutting up. Please, carry on with your pointless posturing.' Vince waited for the platform to settle and curled up on the wood.

Idiot birds.

Birds…

Rita.

Vince looked over his shoulder towards the distant trees back on land. Maybe Rita was hiding, watching the water birds, waiting for them to show some kind of vulnerability. Or maybe she had ignored his pleas and flown back to Richmond Park. If Sophie came…

Sophie won't come. Don't be stupid, Vince.

All he could do was wait, but that was easier said than done; Rita was gone and he didn't know where, or if she was coming back. His stomach still burned with hunger and the bloody cuts strewn across his skin throbbed with his heartbeat. Plus, he had to get through a whole day of trying to sleep in the uncomfortable sun. If forced to swim for his life later, he wondered if he would be able to summon the energy to make it back to land, let alone escape the wetlands completely.

It was almost impossible to sleep through the day. The sun was too bright and warm, beating down on Vince's unwalled prison from high in the robins'-egg sky, and the geese honked loudly to one another intermittently in what he was sure was a deliberate attempt to keep him awake. Humans arrived too; the playful shouts of the younger ones were high-pitched and carried across the lake. Earlier on he'd barked to signal their attention, but he was too far out to be seen, and the geese threatened to hold his head under the water if he tried it again.

He must have dozed off at some point, though, because he woke to an orange sky and cool air around him. The platform rocked lazily as he rose to his paws and gathered his bearings. He was ravenous, aching inside and out. The unknown animal's gift of a fish had briefly calmed him, but Rita's absence kept his anxiety gently simmering.

'I see your friend's disappeared,' Frank said, flapping his wings before briefly dipping his head under the water. Droplets cascaded down his long black neck and plopped back into the lake. 'Just as well. Not much point in an outsider bird waiting around here, if you ask me.'

'Well, no one did,' Vince said, his heart sinking as Rita's absence hit him once more. 'How long do I have to wait for this vote, then?'

'Just sit still and shut up.'

'At least tell me how it works. Will I have a chance to defend myself?'

'You'll find out soon enough – here's the security team now,' the goose said as Oswald and the other swan from the night before glided across the water towards them. Following behind in a perfect arrow formation were seven more swans and geese, wings arched over their backs, heads held high, eyes locked on to Vince. As they arrived, the newer birds waited while the two swans exchanged pleasantries with Roger and Frank, intermittently dipping their heads under the cool water to refresh themselves. On the bank, an enormous crowd of birds gathered, their hubbub of calls a faint hum from out on the lake.

'It's nearly time, fox,' Oswald said.

'My name is Vince,' he replied, standing.

'It doesn't matter. Come on, team.' Four of the newer birds circled the platform, lined up along the back edge and pushed it towards the bank. It tilted, the front almost rising out of the water, causing Vince to stumble.

The journey took a minute or two, and the chattering from the bank grew louder as they approached. The whole of the wetlands had arrived to watch, it seemed. Vince crouched low, ears flat.

The birds stopped pushing and the platform slowed to a halt, still some way from the bank. The bottom of the lake remained indistinguishable, but now he could swim the distance, if he had to. As they saw him arrive, the birds on the bank began to surge forward into the water; swans, geese, ducks, coots and grebes of all species and sizes, along with the infamous Screamers, Felipe and Gabriela. They filled the pond, leaving a strip of open water a couple of leaps wide between themselves and Vince. The platform rocked wildly as the birds stirred up the water with their paddle-like feet. Dark excitement buzzed through the air.

On the bank, all the resident non-water birds remained. Among them, a crowd of squirrels, rabbits, mice, rats and four otters, two large and two small. Vince's eyes rested on the otters for a few blinks, as he tried to make out their expressions. It had to be one of them who'd brought him the fish, but why? Their faces, so far away, gave him no clue.

He searched the crowd for Rita, knowing full well she wouldn't be among the residents. He was right. Hundreds of small birds chirped and whistled from the bank – blackbirds, starlings, tits, finches, sparrows – but not a single magpie among them. A tiny part of him still hoped she had gone back to fetch Sophie. Any of his friends. Even Jake. But he doubted Mother Nature was in a wish-granting mood.

Six of Oswald's team fanned out, circling the platform, while the head swan himself paddled to the front and faced the crowd. A hush fell over the wetlands like a heavy blanket of snow.

'Good evening. You all know why we're here. Last night, this mammal was found trespassing and in direct breach of the laws of the wetlands. As leader of the elected security team, I ask you to listen to the evidence provided by the witnesses and the mammal himself, then make a decision regarding his guilt. Following this, a punishment will be decided by the panel of representatives of the wetlands, chosen by the security team earlier today.' He gestured to a small group of birds to his right who had separated themselves from the others. Three ducks, a goose, two grebes, a swan and a cormorant.

Row upon row of small feathered heads nodded enthusiastically, a low babble rising from the carpet of feathers undulating on the water. At the back, Vince could just about make out the otters, sitting on their haunches, stretching their long bodies to see over the throng. Some of the squirrels had left the group and climbed a tree to get a better view. Rabbits hopped on the spot or piggy-backed one another.

They all want me dead.

'Right! Let's get started!' Oswald shouted. 'Our first witness is Gabriela. Please swim forward, Gaby.'

She did as instructed, the rest of the water birds parting to create a path for her.

'Gabriela, please tell everyone what happened last night.' Oswald smiled at the crowd.

'Eet was the middle of ze night – very dark – and I heard a noise. Eet was a bird squawking, but I didn't recognise eet. Then I heard another voice. Eet was zis mammal here.' She twisted her neck and pointed her beak at Vince.

A chorus of boos rose from the birds at the very front, some flapping their huge wings and hissing menacingly. Vince balanced on his hind legs and peered over their long necks. The otters were looking at each other, shaking their heads solemnly. Frowning, Vince sat back down.

'Ee was trying to steal my eggs!' Gabriela continued. 'Heem and zat magpie! They just walked right een!'

The boos grew louder.

'Calm down, everyone, calm down,' Oswald said. 'Please continue, Gaby.'

'I was so scared! I thought ze fox would try to keel me after eating my eggs. Ee was barking at me, and ze magpie was scratching me with her talons. I… I paneeked. I pecked heem, and I hurt heem, but I was so scared! I deedn't mean to!'

'Are you saying you lashed out at the fox in self-defence?' Oswald said calmly, but loud enough for everyone to hear.

'Yes. I'm very sorry. I know I should have let ze security team deal weeth eet, I just…' Gabriela began to sob.

'It's okay, Gaby. No one's blaming you. Anyone would have done the same in your situation.'

A murmur of agreement emanated from the water birds.

'What in Mother's Name…?' Vince said to himself.

Oswald continued. 'And Felipe came to your aid, is that correct?' he asked, reaching a comforting wing around Gabriela.

'Yes,' she sniffed.

Oswald called Felipe to the front and he obliged, settling next to his mate and offering yet more sympathy for her fictional hardship. Oswald asked Felipe to tell the crowd what he saw.

'Eet was dark and I was sleeping, but I heard Gaby scream and woke up straight away. I rushed to where I heard ze noise and found ze fox barking at her, threatening to keel her, and ze magpie was attacking her face.'

Vince jumped to his feet. 'That's not true! They're lying!'

The lakeside roared with noise. Feathers flew in all directions as the birds flapped in outrage.

'How dare he!'

'Disgusting behaviour!'

'Expect nothing less from a *mammal*.'

The platform lurched as the commotion sent waves swelling towards it. Vince dug his claws into the wood. Despite everything, he kept shouting: 'I don't even like eggs! I just wanted some frogs! I'm sorry for trespassing, I really am, but I would never hurt anyone, I promise you. Neither would Rita.'

Oswald calmed the crowd and glared at Vince. 'Well, I think we've heard enough. The fox clearly has no respect for our way of life. Shall we move on to the vote?'

'*What?*' Vince yelled. 'What about the other witnesses? The otters? They were there! They saw those birds attack *me*. Rita was protecting me! She barely touched them!'

A collective gasp seemed to freeze the air. The birds looked around as Vince scanned the bank desperately for the otters, but they were gone.

'Ahem. Let me get this straight.' Oswald looked at Vince. 'Are *you* – an *outsider* and a *fox* –' he spat out the words like mouldy bread crusts, then turned back to the crowd '– accusing Gabriela and Felipe – two *upstanding* members of this *community* – of a crime against yourself?'

The birds erupted into boos once more.

'Er… I…' Vince floundered. Hundreds of accusatory faces glared at him from the water, their jeers jostling his thoughts.

'We will *not* tolerate this insolence from a *mammal*. And I don't know why you're expecting the otters to help. They have no part in this process. They're here to watch, that's all.'

'I… I don't understand…' Vince said.

Oswald shook his head sternly. 'There is a hierarchy. Water birds, land birds, mammals. Any respectable animal would know this.'

'What? That's ridiculous! And how could I possibly know that?' Vince said. 'Is that why you're taking Gabriela and Felipe's words as truth? Because they're water birds? I don't even get to defend myself?'

'Ridiculous, is it? Maybe out there –' Oswald pointed a wing towards the outer fence '– you *creatures* run wild, doing whatever you please. In here, we have a system. A system that has worked for count-less seasons.'

'And what do the mammals think of this *system?*'

'The mammals here are safe and looked after by the humans, just as previous generations were. That's the way it's always been.'

'At what cost? Silence? Cowering in the corner while you order them around? How are they any better off than me?'

'Let me remind you that you are the one on trial here, fox. All residents here are free to do as they wish, within the rules set out by those who first dwelled here, our ancestors, who believed – quite rightly – that no animal should pass in or out of these fences, especially *your* kind. And you would have had a chance to say your piece, if you'd remained quiet and waited your turn. Now, I fear, a vote would be a waste of time. You have proven yourself to be disrespectful and a menace to our community. The panel shall commence with deciding your punishment.'

'That's not fair! I demand to give my evidence!'

'That's not for you to decide,' the swan said. 'Now be quiet or—'

'I left my home because of a bully like you,' Vince interrupted. 'But at least where I'm from the rules applied to everyone. Mammals and birds. We were all in it together.' Vince couldn't believe he was defending Edward, but he persisted. 'I made a mistake. I broke your rules and I'm sorry, and I respect your right to punish me however you want, but shouldn't I get the same trial that any bird would? Shouldn't I get to tell my side of the story?'

Oswald's face was pure fury, but Vince carried on. 'I get it. You want to show me – all mammals – how powerful you are. That we can't mess with you. Trust me, I get it. But the fact is, I did nothing to their eggs and *they* attacked *me*!' He pointed to the Screamers. 'And you'd rather believe their lies than my truth, because they're water birds and I'm not. That doesn't make you powerful. It makes you wrong. And it makes you worse than any mammal I've ever met.'

The lake was silent. Birds stared up at Vince from the water, shaking their heads, or looked to Oswald for a response. Oswald waited a few blinks, then began. 'Typical mammal, trying to turn everything round on us. Whether you are guilty or not, you've now disrupted this whole affair. You could have let Felipe speak, said your piece and let the residents vote based on all the evidence, as is customary. You speak of power, as if it is not you mammals who have it, who crave it, who have *always* craved it. You think you own the ground you walk on just because you have sharp teeth and long claws. Well, they mean nothing here. This is a democracy, and now the panel will decide your punishment. As you are clearly in favour of fairness, surely you will not dispute their right to choose the most appropriate death for you?'

'You've already decided that I'm guilty! What about the residents' vote? The otters' evidence? You won't even give your own community a choice! All we've heard is lies from those birds!'

'Again, we hear your accusations against the witnesses! This anarchy will not stand!'

'This is rat scat!' Vince barked over the heads of the birds bobbing in the waves. 'Rabbits, squirrels! Aren't you sick of this?'

'SILENCE!' Oswald honked, flapping violently. The other water birds did the same.

'Blackbirds! Sparrows! Where are your representatives on the panel? Aren't you part of this community too? Or is it just the biggest and strongest who get a say? Do you really think that's fair?' He raised his voice, but it was drowned out by the water birds' heckling. He stepped towards the front of the platform. 'You think this is *democracy?*'

'Stay where you are, fox! I mean it!' The security team closed in on the platform.

'His name is VINCE! SCRRRRRAAAAAACK!' Rita's shriek pierced the air. She emerged from within the dense leaves of a nearby tree and soared high above the mass of birds. In her talons, she clutched something white and round.

'Arreeeee! My egg! She's got my egg! ARREEEEE!' Gabriela screamed and flapped hysterically, launching a spray of water over Oswald.

'Let him go, or I'll drop it,' Rita called from the air as she circled the bank, her long tail outstretched behind her, shimmering green in the dusky moonlight.

'No! No!' Gabriela flapped furiously and pedalled at the water as she tried to make her way to the bank. Felipe followed, squeezing through the packed rows of geese, swans and ducks.

'Stop her! Someone fly up and stop her!' Oswald shouted.

A horde of water birds beat their wings, but there was no room for their near-horizontal take-offs. The shallows were a frenzy of feathers. Swans knocked ducks sideways with their massive wings, the ducks angrily nipping at the swans' flanks with their blunt beaks in retaliation.

On the bank, the land birds simply watched and smiled as Rita zipped across the shadowy sky. Probably fearing retribution, the squirrels, rabbits, mice and rats had already fled.

Gabriela finally made it to shore. The small land birds flitted away in an instant as she barrelled across the grass.

'No! Rita!' Vince yelled.

Gabriela sprang into the air and beat her wings desperately, but tumbled back to the earth.

Oswald honked at his colleagues surrounding Vince. 'Do something! You know her wings are clipped!'

The birds looked at each other, then at Vince, then back at Oswald.

The ineptitude of his team had worn away the last of Oswald's already thin patience. 'I'll stay with the fox, you two get the magpie, the rest of you calm everyone down. GO!'

The birds split up. Two geese turned away from the bank and made their long take-off, running along the water's surface as if it were solid ground beneath their webbed feet. Eventually, their broad wings lifted them into the air and they circled around, soaring over Vince and towards the bank.

The remaining security paddled into the throng. Arguments had broken out; some birds had left the water and were trying to settle Gaby and Felipe. The team honked loudly, calling for everyone to compose themselves.

Oswald remained, his dark marble eyes fixed on Vince. 'Don't think for one second that you're going to get away with this, fox,' he spat. 'You move one inch and I'll drown you myself.'

Vince said nothing. His eyes followed Rita. She whirled in large circles above the entire rabble, unable to land on any branch due to the egg tightly gripped in her feet. She seemed to be slowing, her wingbeats laboured, sinking lower to the ground with every loop.

'Rita!' Vince called. 'Be careful!'

Still she soared. The two Screamers hopped helplessly below her, air rushing uselessly through their clipped wings. The two geese approached like arrows, streamlined beaks and sleek, white bodies ripping through the sky. Rita turned her small head and looked at Vince, her tiny black eyes glittering.

'SCRAAAACK-ACK-ACK-ACK!' she sang, as her talons opened.

The skirmish in the water ceased. A hundred birds – including Oswald – turned in an instant to witness the egg fall to earth and splatter on the patchy grass. Gabriela screamed.

Vince's gaze was locked on Rita, all thoughts of escape long gone. The magpie forced her final drops of strength into her wings, and careered into a tree, leaves quivering in her wake. The geese were close behind. Their bulky bodies slammed into the treetop with a flurry of feathers and leaves. They struggled and honked, the branches creaking as their flat webbed feet grasped and slipped on the smooth bark, but their sheer size and the density of the branches kept them suspended aloft. Rita was utterly lost in the tangle.

'Rita!' Vince called again as the front of platform rose out of the water. 'What the—' The back end sunk into the dark pond. He staggered backwards, scrabbling at the wood with his front claws as his rear end splashed into the water. Oswald heard Vince's shouts and turned. He opened his beak to signal the rest of the team, but the honks turned to muffled whispers as Vince was dragged under the surface and icy water filled his ears.

Sophie found Edward in the copse of trees near the lake – Vince's former territory – settling down to sleep in the grass. She looked sadly at the ruined earth before addressing the deer.

'Edward, can I have a word?'

Edward sighed melodramatically. 'Can't it wait until morning?'

She took a deep breath. 'I'll make it quick. Jake said you agreed to send a bird after Vince. Shouldn't we have heard something by now? It's been a whole night and day. I'm worried, I can't sleep... I just need to know that he's okay.'

'I am aware of your feelings towards your *friend*, which is why I sent Kara. And a fat lot of thanks I've got for it too,' he snorted.

'You sent *Kara*?' Sophie said.

'Of course. She's the best hunter in Richmond Park. If anyone can find a fox out there, she can.'

'She's a rat's backside.'

'A rat's backside who will get the job done,' Edward said.

'Have you forgotten what she did? When she dug up all the rats we were storing and ate them all herself?'

'And didn't I sort that out for you?'

'Yes, but...'

Edward turned away from Sophie. He dropped his forelegs to the ground, then bent his back legs before lowering his body to the grass with a thump. 'Will that be all?' he said.

'What if Vince is in danger? What if he needs our help? Will she try to help him?' Sophie said to the back of Edward's head.

Edward slowly turned to face her as he spoke. His voice was calm, but irritation laced the silence in between his words. 'Kara's instructions were to find him and report back. You forget, Sophie, that Vince left of his own accord, and as he is no longer a resident of Richmond Park, his welfare is not my concern. Unless you make it my concern, of course.'

'A bribe, you mean,' Sophie said.

'A deal. But call it whatever you want. Help doesn't come for free. You should know that by now.' Edward smirked.

'No thanks. You've already got enough idiots doing your bidding. I'll wait for Kara,' Sophie said before turning away.

'So true,' Edward replied, still smirking, but Sophie was already gone; a rufous blur tearing across the open park.

4

Small paws gripped the fur on Vince's back and sharp teeth clenched his scruff and tail. He squirmed as he was hauled through the water, twisting and kicking, but the teeth and claws held firm. The moments rolled by like days and nights. His lungs burned. The urge to gasp for air was overpowering, but he held on.

Eyes clamped shut, he concentrated on the muted noise fading fast behind him. The creatures were obviously taking him somewhere, and not trying to drown him. He stopped resisting, letting his body go limp.

The jaws around his tail jerked and released their grip, but the rest didn't budge. A sharp pain ripped through his flank. Instinctively, he kicked out, but the animals clamped down harder and swam onwards. Lungs now empty, he bucked and wrestled, clawing his way to the surface. The animals yielded, pushing him upwards. His snout broke the surface and he gulped down lungfuls of air, wheezing, as he beat his paws against the waves. Otters – four of them – emerged around him, their small heads like round, mossy rocks. They had dragged him away from the bank and the birds, towards the middle of the lake.

Then Vince saw the bird. A cormorant. Black, slick like oil, riding low in the water. It dived.

'Quick!' one of the otters shouted. 'Follow us!'

Vince pedalled his front legs frenetically – the only way he knew how to swim – but found little resistance, his tail and back legs trailing uselessly behind him. His whole body ached and his right hind leg throbbed, but he moved as fast as his paws could manage. The otters were swifter, winding their way through the water with their undulating tails. They made it a few leaps before realising Vince couldn't keep up, then turned back to help him.

A strong beak grabbed the brush of his tail and jerked him down, submerging his head. He thrashed, kicking with his back legs and reaching for his attacker with his front, but the bird was agile. It let go, and zig-zagged away.

Vince resurfaced, gasping, and the otters arrived at his side. 'We've got to get to land,' one of them panted. Two of them each grabbed a front leg and the other two supported his sides. Again, they began to drag him, this time on the water's surface, their tails blurred as they whipped back and forth. Despite the pain, Vince pedalled his back legs. With the extra force, they seemed to motor across the pond. He took a deep breath. There was no way that bird had given up.

His instinct was right. The cormorant grabbed him again, higher up his tail this time. Another beak closed around his foot. Backup had arrived. Together the birds wrenched him towards the depths, thrusting against the water with their powerful wings and webbed feet. The otters pulled back, paddling upwards. Vince was caught in the middle. A fox tug-of-war.

Vince twisted and snapped at the birds, missing by inches. He tried again, throwing the otters off, and grazed a wing with his teeth. A bundle of black feathers hung in the water, but the cormorants held fast, pulling him backwards, further and further down into the darkness. A shelf of mud rose up underneath him. Black rocks jutted at all angles like daggers. His chest raged with pain. The air in his lungs was almost gone. One last chance. He bent forward, head towards his tail, and lunged. His jaws slammed shut onto the bird, fangs sinking into the soft flesh above its tail. With a deft twist of his neck, he wrenched it free and cast it away into the obscurity of the deep water, a trail of crimson blood dispersing behind it.

Horror in its eyes, the other cormorant darted away before Vince could make another move, but it made no difference. The last fizz of Vince's oxygen had gone. Reaching his front paws towards the pale orange light shimmering above him, he pulled his hind legs towards him and kicked back one last time. The dappled sun faded. His muscles relaxed. Water rushed over his tongue and down his airway, filling his crumpled, empty lungs.

Inside the fence the animals had dispersed and returned to their homes but, high among the trees, the land birds and squirrels whispered to one another about the fox and the magpie. They had never seen a mammal escape the platform, nor seen Oswald angrier. They worried for the otters, and the repercussions their actions might have on all of them.

Below, water birds paced the undergrowth, stomping down the long grass and weeds with their flat feet, no doubt searching for signs of the fox. A feeding pair of rabbits, disturbed by a goose, darted away and hid under a nearby bramble.

'Get back to your burrows,' the goose honked, then tilted his beak upwards. 'And stop that noise up there!'

'No rules against talking,' one of the squirrels squeaked.

The goose puffed his chest out and continued on his search for traces of Vince. A bird laughed, and several others joined in. The rabbits crept back to their feeding spot and looked up at the squirrels overhead. Flashing a smile, not caring whether the goose heard or not, the squirrel shouted down to the rabbits, 'They can't put us all on the platform.'

The rabbits grinned at each other.

'Push again! Nearly there!'

The empty darkness embraced Vince like a cool, mossy blanket. His limbs were numb, the voices around him distant and foggy.

'One more time! Come on… Come on…'

Tiny paws pounded his tender ribcage. 'Vince! Wake up!' A faint voice pierced the fog, like a thorn through skin. 'You're not dead. I know you're not dead.'

A fiery pain roared through his chest. The safety of the darkness unfurled from around him, a throbbing swelling in his leg. The breeze nipped at the peck wounds that peppered his wet fur.

The paws thumped again, again, again, the pain rising with each heavy beat.

No… Just leave me.

'I saw him move! I did! Keep going!'

As the hammering on his chest continued, his mind drifted back. The cormorants, the swans, the platform on the water. Sid, the train tracks, Richmond Park. It felt like a season – a lifetime – ago, yet it had only been two nights. He'd barely gone anywhere, seen anything of the world.

Thump, thump, thump… His ribs ached, his bones longed for silence and rest, but something wanted him alive. Thump, thump… But he had so far to go, still. How could he make it now?

'Wake up! Yes! You can do it!'

Only half voluntarily, Vince relented. His jaws fell open and he gasped. His chest and stomach heaved and he vomited over the damp grass, watery bile stinging his nostrils and throat. He opened his eyes and blinked away the stream of tears. The four otters sat around him, smiling and clapping their wet paws together.

Not dead.

Drowned. Wounded. Homeless. Lost… But not dead.

Now that they were all on land, Vince could see they were a family. Two adults and two pups, a male and female of each. He took a few rasping breaths as one of the smaller otters stroked his flank, then rolled onto his front, facing them.

'Wh… Where…' he croaked.

'Just outside the fence. We can't hang around too long, though,' the young male otter replied, looking around nervously. 'Security will be searching for us. We shouldn't be out here.'

Vince blinked at his new surroundings. They had brought him – dragged him, probably; wet blades of grass still clung to his filthy fur – to the edge of a long dirt path where the familiar fence divided the tall, dense trees of the wetlands' perimeter from the short grass where they now crouched. He slowly pulled himself upright and coughed deeply, his lungs a mass of brambles in his chest.

'You need to find somewhere to hide and rest,' the mother otter said. 'You can't outrun them like this. They won't look out here, none of us ever come past the fence.'

Vince looked down at the bloody wound on his back leg where

the cormorant had ripped his flesh away. 'Why are you helping me?' he said, each jagged word catching in the rawness of his throat.

The father explained, 'The little ones saw what happened with the Screamers. We know you didn't do anything wrong. We don't normally get involved, but—'

'We heard the security team talking,' the mother interjected. 'They had no intention of letting you go free, even with a proper vote. It makes us so angry, the way they treat you... Us.' She shook her head. 'We wish we could help you more, but...' She trailed off and looked towards the fence.

'Why can't you leave?' Vince said.

'Where can we go? The city isn't the place for otters,' the father said. 'And it's okay, really. The humans take care of us, there's always food. It's clean and safe, no cats or dogs running around after dark. It's hard to leave somewhere like this, you know? The votes don't really affect the residents too much, it's more of a power trip for the water birds. It's just...' He paused and sighed. 'Hard. We feel responsible, you know? Season after season, we have to stay here and watch mammals get... get drowned, or... or...'

'Don't upset yourself, darling. Let's try to forget about it for now.' The female nuzzled her mate and smiled sadly.

'I understand, and it's not your fault. I came from somewhere a bit like this. If there's anything I can do...' Vince said.

'You've done more than enough. What you said up on the platform...'

The young female grinned. 'It was so great! Everything's going to change! No more mean swan bossing us around!'

'Calm down, sweetie,' the father said. 'It might not be that easy. Oswald has been in charge for a long time, but Vince has started something good, I'm sure.'

'Well, that's something.' Vince coughed again and shook his damp fur. 'Thank you. For saving me.'

'Well, you should thank your magpie friend. If she hadn't—'

Rita.

He'd almost forgotten. His empty stomach heaved with guilt and dread. 'Rita. Is she okay? Where is she?' he said.

The otters looked at each other, then back to him. 'We don't know.'

'I have to go back. I have to find her.' Vince turned and sniffed at the fence, searching for the way through.

'The security team will be looking for you,' said the young male pup. 'And you need to rest your leg.'

'What if she's in danger? She saved me, I need to save her.'

'She'll be okay,' the pup said. 'Birds always—'

'Shut *up*! Don't you *dare* compare her to *those* birds!' Vince snarled.

The pup backed away into his mother's arms.

'Oh, Mother Nature, I'm so sorry,' Vince said. 'I'm just worried. I didn't mean to…'

'It's okay, we know you care about her, but he's right. There will be security everywhere. In your state, you won't make it out of the trees before they've got you back on that platform, if the Screamers don't finish you off first,' the father said.

Vince paced back and forth along the fence, limping as his wounded leg failed to hold his weight. 'I know, but… I just can't leave her,' he said.

In his mind's eye, he watched again as Rita flew in circles, energy drained, then slammed into the tree, the geese so close behind. A tired and injured magpie wouldn't last a night and day alone, especially with the Screamers out for revenge. And what was the point of trying to find his grandparents' park if she wasn't there with him? How could he live in peace anywhere now, knowing what it had cost?

'What if she's hurt and can't fly? What if she's hiding somewhere, waiting for me? I *have* to go back.'

'Vince, please listen to us,' the father said. 'You don't even know if she's hurt, you're just thinking the worst and getting yourself all worked up. If she's okay, then she'll come and find you. If not, then, well, you've got nothing to gain by going back in.'

'What do you mean?' Vince stared at the otter, tears in his eyes.

'I mean, there's no point you both getting killed.'

'If it means saving Rita, then I'll risk it. I can't find a new home without her. I won't.'

'You're not thinking straight.'

The otter was right, of course. Vince knew that. If one of them was going to go looking for the other, Rita would be quicker and cover more ground. She would know that, and she wouldn't hang around in there if she didn't have to. And Vince could barely walk, let alone run or fight.

As Vince opened his mouth to reply, a chilling scream reverberated through the night air.

'Arreeeee! Eeoo! Arreeeee! Eeoo!'

The animals looked at each other. 'That's Felipe. He's not far. You need to leave, Vince,' the mother said.

'What about you?' he asked.

'We'll be fine. We'll find somewhere to hide until morning. We know where the humans are likely to find us when they do their morning checks, so they'll take us straight back to our pond and we won't have to worry about running into security.'

'And after that?'

'Who knows – but we're residents, so they won't kill us. The humans wouldn't let that happen. Hopefully your speech will have made a difference, though. We'll just have to wait and see.'

He looked to each of the otters in turn. 'I really can't thank you all enough. You know, we're trying to find a new home, a place where everyone is free. You're welcome to come with me... With us.'

'Thank you, but we can't leave our home. We've got the pups to think about. They'll be safer here than out in the city, despite all this. I'm sure everything will be okay.' Her words reassured her pups, but the mother otter's grave face gave away her uncertainty.

Vince felt awful. Who knew what those birds would do to the family, but at least they had the humans on their side, and their community, broken though it was. Unlike them, Rita was an outsider, and now she'd actually committed the crime they'd first been accused of.

What chance did she stand? He looked at the fence again as another shriek boomed from the trees on the other side. Felipe was much closer.

Vince shivered. He could almost feel their rigid beaks ripping at his fur again. 'Okay, well, I think I need to run.'

The otters wished Vince good luck and they all exchanged good-byes as he turned to leave. His wounded leg was stiff and throbbed as he forced it to move with the other three. Glancing back, he watched as they scurried back along the fence, low to the ground, almost invisible against the wood panels. Felipe screeched, now mere leaps away, and the trees quivered in response. Vince returned his attention to the path, flattened his ears and ran as fast as his broken body would allow.

Kara woke with the moonrise, still hacked off. She had wasted most of the previous evening on a wild goose chase, making it all the way back to Richmond Park before realising the badger had lied. She'd even checked the whole perimeter again in case she'd missed the fox approaching. Once she was sure he was nowhere around, she only had time to make it back to the badger's woodland before sunrise. It was her own fault, though. She had been complacent. From now on, she would double-check her sources. At least Edward hadn't spotted her. He was probably already getting impatient and thinking about sending someone else. Over her dead body. Those rabbits were hers. She had to find Vince tonight.

As the orange sky melted away to inky blue, she preened her feathers one by one. The chattering of the diurnal birds dwindled until the only sounds were the distant hum of the human road and the rustling of mice in the long grass. Several of the latter made an excellent breakfast, and now that her belly was full, her search for the fox and the magpie could resume. The badger would probably be surfacing soon too, but, despite her threat, he was not her priority.

She took off from the tree and sailed noiselessly northwards on her ghostly wings. The fox would probably have crossed the bridge that Edward mentioned by now, but that just meant he would be easier to find. North of the river meant fewer trees, more roads and more street lamps. She wasn't worried. It was rare that a creature slipped from her grasp.

Below, paths carved their way through closely packed trees and irregular ponds like a slow worm. A solid expanse of water shimmered to the east, pockets of birds sleeping at the edges. The whole area was fenced off. Paradise, if you liked that sort of thing.

If that fox didn't show his face there, then I'm a spineless hedgehog.

She spiralled down, then fluttered onto a branch overlooking a patch of grass where a swan, a goose and a cormorant were arguing.

'How could you let him get away?' the swan shouted at the cormorant, stamping his large orange foot.

'He killed Ash! What was I s'posed to do?' the cormorant replied.

'Tear him apart! Like the boss ordered you to!' the goose said.

'He was too strong! If there had been more of us...'

The goose shook his head. 'You couldn't even bring back one of the otters for questioning. Not good enough, Cole.'

'My instructions were to stop the fox, Frank. No one said nothing about the otters. Besides, they'll be back, then we can question them. And we cut up the fox's leg pretty bad. He won't get far.'

'Stop squabbling. We'll find him,' the swan said. 'And there's still the magpie. Steve said her wing was damaged. She might not have made it past the fence. I've got some of the team on the case. Hopefully they'll find her body, then we can avoid the hassle of trying a land bird.'

Kara smiled. They were here. And recently. Vince might not have even made it to the bridge.

'So, what do we do about the fox, then?' Frank said.

'He was heading north with the otters. I heard that they hid in the trees, where it's too dense for most of us to fly, but someone else said they'd made it outside,' Cole said.

'Outside the fence? Are you sure?' the swan said.

'Yeah, but like I said, they'll be back. They wouldn't last past high-moon out there,' Cole said.

'The fox will, though.' The swan frowned. 'Injured or not, he's an outsider. And that's exactly why we can't let him get too far. If he tells anyone about this place…'

'They will be queuing up to get in, right, boss?' Frank said.

'What? Er, yes, exactly,' the swan said, nodding. 'Protecting this community is our top priority. We'll track him down if it means chasing him halfway across the city. Frank, I want you to take three of your strongest north. Find the fox and kill him at all costs. I don't want you back here until he's dead, understand?'

'Ah, erm, past the fence?' Frank said.

'That's what I said.'

'Right. It's just… We have never been, like, outside the wetlands before. You always said—'

'Yes, well, there's a first time for everything, isn't there? Unless you don't think you're up to it? I can get someone else, if you—'

'No, no! I'll do it. No problem, boss. And how do we kill him? We can't drown him if there's no water…'

'I'm sure the best four members of my security team can deal with an injured fox. Ambush him. Peck his skull in. Scat on him until he suffocates. I don't care how you do it, just do it.'

'Ah, right. Will do, boss.' Frank turned and ran, then launched his bulk swiftly into the air with a few precise flaps. He commanded his team below with a honk as he sailed over their heads. Within moments, three more geese joined him in the air. Kara's workload had just lightened. Now, she just had to follow the geese and make sure they did their jobs. She could pop back on the way home to find out what had happened to the magpie, and finish her off herself if necessary. Easy-peasy.

Kara jumped from the tree and soared over the swan and cormorant who were still talking below, then, with a casual flick of her tail, altered her path northwards. Some way from the birds, three ducks foraged in the reeds below. Circling a few times, she snatched glimpses through the patches in the tree canopy, which was enough to notice the black-and-white bird sprawled in the undergrowth a mere leap or two away from them. If the magpie wasn't already dead, it soon would be. Perfect.

She twisted in the air, resuming her northerly course. Distance and darkness had turned the solid, uncompromising geese into tiny, black claw marks torn into the dusky sky. Climbing higher with each soft wingbeat, the breeze assisting her, Kara kept the birds firmly in sight. She would be there when they found Vince, she would watch them kill him, and then she would claim her reward from Edward without ruffling a single feather.

Vince veered off the path, away from the fence and the wetlands, and ran through a stand of trees. Beyond them lay a small area of neatly mown grass, then another tall fence. He scrabbled up the trunk of an overhanging tree, tiptoed along a branch, then dropped down onto the grass on the other side with a soft thud, wincing as his injured leg almost buckled beneath him. A trace scent of the vixen once again whispered at his nostrils. He shook his ears and pushed it out of his mind. No need to mark his own scent again; he wouldn't be staying long.

Perfect rectangles of earth lay in organised rows, the odd little wooden hut dotted around. What were the rectangles for? Human-made, obviously, but looking closer he could see this was where they grew food. He needed somewhere to hide, somewhere the water birds couldn't see him if they did decide to go beyond their borders. But if he was to survive the night, he needed something to eat. It would no doubt be a while before he would taste a frog again, so Vince prepared himself for an unappetising meal of raw vegetables or, worse, worms.

If Rita was here she'd fly off and find us something juicy.

He padded quickly through the neat patches of soil, sniffing each as he went, but there was little on offer. Row upon row of tiny shoots poked out of the earth, their leaves barely the size of ladybirds; not worth the bother of digging up. Eventually a slightly more promising patch presented itself, where green globes of cabbage and cauliflower, bigger than his own head, sat stoutly on the surface.

Ugh, gross. But there's nothing else.

Vince checked behind him and overhead. Safe, for now. He settled down beside the largest of the cabbages and got to work, tearing

off chunks of leaves with his teeth and swallowing before the bitter-
ness could fully reach his tongue. It was hardly tasty, but it was food
and it would keep him going until dawn, when he could make a break
for it and hopefully lose any pursuers.

As he swallowed his third mouthful, a whiff of something deli-
ciously salty caught the attention of his nose. Leaving the cabbage in
tatters, he followed his snout to a nearby allotment, half of which was
covered with small vegetable sprouts and the other half with a large
pen made of wood and wire. The back of the pen housed a wooden
hutch but, save for a few brown-and-white feathers, the entire thing
was empty.

That's not what I can smell.

He circled the pen, pausing at the back, where the wooden slats
of the hutch were covered by long, uncut grass and thick bushes. The
smell was overwhelming. Fish, perhaps? But how? Vince investigated
with his snout and tentatively pawed at the ground, before finding
the source of the odour. It was fish alright. Large chunks of pink-and-
silver flesh lay in the grass, the edges flat and neat – clearly cut by
humans. He poked a piece with his paw.

Seems alright.

There were no other animals about. At least, none that he could
see or hear.

*I guess some humans just leave food out for animals. Like they feed the
otters in the wetlands, or the birds in their gardens.*

He bit a small piece from one of the chunks and held it on his
tongue for a moment before swallowing.

Not as fresh as usual, but still good.

One by one he devoured the bitesize portions, his confidence
growing with every bite. Warm and heavy in his belly, they reminded
him of the balmy summer evenings spent fishing for frogs with
Sophie back in Richmond Park. He smiled, almost forgetting where
he was and the events of the last couple of nights.

The last few remnants of fish lay deep in the long grass, underneath the thick, waxy leaves of the bushes. Belly to the ground, he
crawled towards them, nose guiding him.

As his snout reached the nearest morsel, the ground shifted and a deafening clang rang through his ears. He went to turn and run, but thick wire surrounded him on all sides, wedging him in. He reversed, but found his backside pressed against a metal door, which had slammed shut behind him.

SCAT!

A trap.

He thrashed his tail and clawed at the wire, but the cage was solid and heavy. How could he have missed it? Even camouflaged with grass and leaves, he should have seen it. The fish was bait. Of course it was. How could he have been so stupid?

He howled as loud as his raw lungs could manage. 'RAOOOOOOOWL!'

Closing his eyes, he tried to forget that the sides of the cage were a mere paw's width away from his snout and sides. He counted slowly to four as he drew breath into his lungs, held it for four counts, then four more as he exhaled. His mother had taught him the calming trick when he was a cub, putting it to good use after his father was killed. She'd woken him in the middle of the day, so he knew immediately something was wrong. A train, she'd said. He'd stayed out too early. The sun had been rising and the humans were up and about, their cars and trains already moving. He'd always enjoyed sunny mornings, she told Vince, watching the sunrise and exploring in the first few hours of soft daylight. The humans weren't to blame, she said. They meant him no harm. He'd just been in the wrong place at the wrong time.

Vince believed her. The humans looked after them in the park, after all. They were different creatures – noisy with strange customs – but he had never had any reason to think they wished animals any ill will before.

Now, cramped in a cage hidden by a human with the sole intent of catching a fox, he realised that his life in Richmond Park had been more sheltered than he'd thought. Humans created spaces for animals – Richmond Park, the wetlands – but mostly for themselves. Edward was right. They liked to look at the deer and the otters, listen to the birds, catch rare glimpses of foxes and badgers, but only when and where it suited them. It helped them forget their indoor lives. Novelties. Out here, he was no more than a pest, waiting to be trapped. He howled helplessly once more through the bars of the cage. 'RAOOOOOOOWL!'

In the distance, from high above, a goose bellowed across the allotments. 'Hooooooonk!'

No. Not now.

More geese joined in as they flew closer. Three, maybe four in all. Vince craned his neck, the bars pressing deep into his head, but it wasn't enough. He whimpered, twisting his bruised body back and forth, metal pinning him in on both sides. Panic set in. He scrabbled uselessly at the grass poking through the bars.

Had they heard his howl? Why had he done that?

The geese blared their warnings as they descended. Vince heard the rustling feathers of their outsize wings as they settled on the grass several leaps away, in the direction of his discarded cabbage. They began to speak, Vince only just able to hear but recognising two of the voices from his time on the platform.

'I don't like this, Frank. Not one bit,' Roger said.

'Listen, it's fine. Oswald wouldn't have sent us out here if he didn't think it was necessary,' Frank replied.

'But what about all the stuff he told us about? The evil mammals? And the humans?' another voice said.

'It's night-time, you idiots, there aren't any humans around. We're just here to kill the fox. See anything suspicious, then stay away, alright? We won't be here long.'

The geese all honked in agreement.

'Spread out, guys,' Frank said. 'Roger, you go that way. Donna, you go there, towards those bushes, and Jules, over there. The fox might be hiding, or he might have already gone, but look for paw prints, or see if you can smell blood or anything else that might help us track him. The sooner we kill him, the quicker we can go back home.'

The geese plodded off in different directions.

If they find me, they'll kill me. Or leave me to die in this trap. If they don't find me, I'll die in this trap anyway.

To his left, a pair of flat feet trudged through the grass. Vince stiffened.

Pull yourself together. You're a fox, you can outsmart a goose.

If he could just convince the goose to let him out, somehow…

He began to bark softly. 'Wroof wroof! Wrrrooooof!'

'Wha… huh?' Donna said, stopping still.

Vince barked again, this time louder. 'Wrrooooof!'

'Ah!' The goose plodded towards him.

Vince's body was rigid with nerves.

'Guys! I think I've found him!' Donna called. 'Get over here.'

Vince turned his ears to listen as the four birds closed in on his position. He groaned. Four of them would be a tough fight, if they even let him out. As the geese's flapping footsteps grew closer, Vince jumped as the bushes around him rustled and a flash of dark orange slipped past in the corner of his eye. It was no goose; his nose told him that.

A silky voice addressed the birds. 'Good evening, can I help you?' Vince couldn't see her, but the vixen's scent was unmistakable. Despite its softness, her voice had an edge to it that cut deep into Vince's gut. She had seen him. She was helping him. She had to be.

'Keep your distance, everyone. I'll deal with this,' Frank said, as if the vixen wasn't there, before replying to her. 'Ah, erm, good evening. We're looking for a fox actually. Male. He has a wound on his leg. My colleague here must have, ah, mistaken you for him.'

'My bad. I'm told I sound like one of those humans' car horns when I'm hungry,' the vixen said. 'This fox you're after… He in trouble or something?'

'Very much so!' Roger said. 'Wanted for trespassing. He's on the run! We're—'

'Quiet, Roger,' Frank hissed.

'Trespassing? You must be from the wetlands, then…' the vixen said. 'What a place, eh? I've heard all about those big lakes. Wow, the frogs I would eat if I could get myself in there, I tell you…'

'Yes, well. That's not your concern. Have you seen the fox or not?' Frank said.

'I've seen a lot of foxes tonight, to be honest. So, you geese are in charge, then? How exciting! I never thought I'd get to meet the leaders of the wetlands. My friends are going to be so jealous!'

'Ahem, well, not exactly…' Frank said.

'Oswald's in charge, really. He's our boss,' Jules said, before adding. 'He's a swan.'

'One swan? Well, now, that is interesting,' the vixen said. 'You know… No, I probably shouldn't say. I mean, I suppose it doesn't *really* matter who's making the rules, right? Of course, I'm only a fox, so what do I know?'

'What are you talking about?' Frank said.

'Oh, nothing, it's just we all assumed it was the geese who were giving the orders over there. Now, don't get me wrong, I've got nothing against swans, but in my experience, geese are proper team players. Swans, not so much. And then I find you lot out here tracking down a trespasser, you know, getting scat done, teamwork… That's what leaders do. Setting an example.'

'Erm…' Frank said. 'I don't—'

'Look, you're the ones putting yourselves in danger by being out here, and your boss – Oswald, was it? – he's where? In his comfy nest, sleeping? Having a nice relaxing swim? I just hope you guys are appreciated, that's all I'm saying.'

'Appreciated?' Roger said.

'Sure. Some extra food here, a nicer nesting spot there. That's what being at the top of the food chain's all about, right?'

Vince held his breath as the geese's silence filled the air. Whether she meant to help him or not, the vixen was clearly smart. If only he'd tried harder to outwit the birds when he was on the platform. If he hadn't lost his temper at the trial… Vince blinked away the thoughts. This was no time to wallow.

'We… We don't get that… Do we, Roger?' said Jules.

'No… No, we don't,' Roger replied.

Frank interrupted. 'Stop this pointless prattle right now. We're here to do a job. Oswald chose us to serve on the security team because of our strength, bravery and loyalty. It's our responsibility to serve our community. Appreciation has nothing to do with it.'

'Well,' the vixen began, 'if you look at it that way, I *suppose* responsibility and respect is its own reward for a lifetime of servitude. Whatever works for you guys, I guess. Personally, if I was spending my nights hunting mammals with the potential to tear my head off, I'd want the best view of the lake and first dibs on food each morning, but that's just me.'

The birds fell quiet again. Damn, she was good.

Donna broke the silence. 'She's right, you know.'

'Uh huh,' Jules agreed.

'No! Shut up!' Frank said. 'It's not like that... It's... He's...'

'Oh dear, did I say something wrong?' Vince detected a smirk in the vixen's voice.

'I don't know why we never thought about it before,' Roger said. 'Risking our lives all this time, and what for? Not even a thank you! Oswald is the one who's always telling us how dangerous it is outside the fence, but when he wants something done, he sends us out here anyway. He doesn't even care if we get killed, does he?'

'It's... It's not about *caring*... It's about—' Frank began, before Donna interrupted.

'Find the fox *at all costs*, you said! That means us! He gets to make *all* the rules. It's not fair, is it, guys? You know what? I think us geese *would* be better leaders.'

'We should definitely bring this up at the next security briefing,' Roger said.

'No! Let's go back and tell him right now. We can get the other geese on our side first,' Donna said.

'I cannot believe I'm hearing this! We are here to kill the fox! We are not leaving here until he is dead, do you understand?' Frank said.

'Listen,' the vixen interrupted. 'Clearly, I've touched a nerve, and I think it's best that you have a talk with your boss. I'll keep an eye out for this fox, but honestly, he's probably dead by now anyway. There's traps and cars and whatnot all around here. You know what?

I thought I smelled blood earlier. That's what brought me here, before I ran into you. I bet he's not far. If I find him, I'll keep him here, then you guys could come back and do whatever it is you need to do.'

'We can't trust an outsider, and we can't go back without the fox, I'm sorry,' Frank said.

Indignant groans rose from the other three birds.

'Guys, I don't know what this Oswald has told you about us non-wetlanders, but I promise you we're all perfectly nice,' the vixen said. 'I just wanted to help you out, one animal to another, but I understand if that's not how things are done over your way.'

'See! She's not horrible like Oswald says! Who knows what else he's lied about! Like the vixen said, the fox is probably dead by now anyway. Let's just tell Oswald we found his body and leave it at that – it's not like he's going to come back. We're sick of this. Aren't you?' Roger said to Frank.

'This is not about *us*, it is about the *community*. How do you think Oswald is going to react to this insolence? We simply cannot return without the fox's body. I will not be held responsible otherwise, do you understand?'

'Fine. We're going to speak to Oswald, aren't we? Come on, Donna, Jules.' The three geese beat their wings as they made their run-up along the grass, in the direction of the wetlands.

'Wait! Get back here. NOW!' Frank yelled at their backsides as they took off into the dark sky, leaving him alone – almost – with the vixen.

Sophie and Jake weaved through the mottled gravestones of the cemetery, the moon overhead lightly cloaked in silver clouds.

'Get the *job done*. That's what he said, Jake,' Sophie said. Edward's words had been playing on her mind ever since their conversation.

'And?' Jake said.

'Don't you think that sounds odd?'

'Not really. You know Edward – he likes to ponce things up. Wants to sound important.'

'I suppose,' Sophie said. 'It was the way he said it, though... Made it sound like something bad.'

'I think you're reading too much into it, Soph.'

'Maybe.' A tiny, brown ball zipped across their path. Sophie chased it, ducking behind a gravestone and emerging almost instantly with a lifeless mouse in her jaws. She gulped it down. 'He tried to get me to do a deal with him too. Help doesn't come for free... Blah blah blah.' She held her paws up to her head, mimicking antlers. 'What did he ask you to do in return for sending Kara, by the way? You never told me.'

'Oh, just some food collecting a couple of times a week for the herd. You know how lazy they are – can't be bothered to find their own acorns.'

'Yeah, lazy twig-heads. I just worry, you know? I think Edward's pride was dented. I don't think he actually thought Vince would leave. Maybe he's worried that people won't respect him now and he needs to make some kind of statement.'

'Hmm, maybe,' Jake said absentmindedly as he nosed a loose pile of earth.

'Are you listening to me?'

'Yes!'

'Then what did I just say?'

Jake looked at her and smiled. 'That you think Edward is worried that he's lost our respect and wants to make a statement. See, I'm not such a terrible mate, am I?'

Sophie narrowed her eyes, returning his smile. 'You've got dirt on your nose.' She bounded behind a bush, giggling.

'Get back here!' Jake circled the bush from the other direction.

Sophie lifted her eyes to meet his. 'No, you're alright, I suppose.' She smiled as she wriggled her backside, whipping her tail left to right, then pounced on him, gently batting his snout with a paw.

Jake rolled over, all four legs in the air, and laughed. 'You have beaten me, oh strong, powerful vixen! Please, make my death quick and painless! I beg you!'

Sophie pinned him to the ground, her front paws pressing on his white chest. 'Your death will be long and agonising if you don't back me up on this. I know Edward's not telling us everything. Maybe it's nothing, but I have a weird feeling.'

'You know I'll always back you up. I'll ask around later. Maybe someone else has heard something,' he said, still upside down.

Sophie reached over and nuzzled him. 'Thank you. Now, please catch me a nice big rat. I'm starving.'

'Of course, oh brilliant, beautiful vixen!' Jake rolled away and jumped to his feet. 'Oh wise, wonderful vixen!' He ran off, zig-zagging through the tall, mossy headstones. 'Oh enchanting, excellent vixen!'

Sophie cocked her head as she watched him frolicking around the cemetery like a lunatic, knowing he was only doing it to make her laugh. Her happiness was the reason he did most things. Vince had loved her, had been kind to her, but Vince always came first to Vince. His arguments with Edward and the other deer had ruined more evenings than she could count. Jake was different. He never raised his voice. His displays of daftness were infrequent but no less sincere than his steadfast earnestness. Everything he did was for her.

'You'll never catch anything if you keep that dreadful noise up!' she called as she followed him.

Jake reached a tree with an ancient stone slab resting against its trunk. Sophie watched as he crouched, waved his tail, then thrust his head and forepaws into the triangular tunnel. He struggled for a few blinks but then pulled out a rat, brown and plump. He presented it to Sophie with a grin across his cobweb-draped face.

'Nope.' Sophie smiled at him. 'Not terrible at all.'

Frank paced back and forth in front of the vixen, the rest of his team now almost out of sight. 'Mother Nature! They're in for a shock when they get back. Oswald is not one to take any subordination lightly.' Frank was almost talking to himself. 'What am I going to do now? Even if I find him somehow, I can't kill a fox alone. I'll have to go back with them.'

'No, this is perfect!' the vixen said. 'You get to be the hero now! I can help you.'

'You would help me kill one of your own? I, uh…'

'Sure, why not? I don't know him, and you say he's a trespasser, so who am I to argue? Maybe you can do something for me, as a thank you.'

Vince tensed. She wasn't on his side. Unless she was messing with the goose? She'd got rid of three of them and Frank was ready to leave. Why hadn't she let him?

'Oh?' Frank said.

'Oh, I don't know… five nights in the wetlands, as many frogs as I can eat?'

'Ah, I see Oswald was right about the animals out here. No community spirit. Always wanting something,' he tutted. 'Anyway, Oswald simply would not allow it. We have strict rules about outsiders, particularly those with four legs. No offence. I, uh, really should be getting ba—'

'Come on, where are those famous goose guts?' the vixen interrupted. 'Don't you want to tell your boss that you found and killed the fox? You'll be a hero! Oswald'll put you first in line for the humans' bread-crusts for this.' Frank protested, but the vixen carried on. 'Listen, Frank, I do something for you, you do something for me – how is that not community spirit? Your friends have abandoned you and I'm offering you help. All I'm asking is a few nights of safety and some decent meals. It's hard, living on the streets, you know. You're not going to make me beg, are you, Frank?'

She oozed charm. Vince was transfixed, despite not being able to see her. There were worse ways to die than at the teeth of such a brazen, captivating creature.

Frank sighed. 'I can't promise anything, you understand? But if you kill the fox and help me bring his body back to the wetlands, then I'll see what I can arrange with Oswald.'

'No problem. You're trustworthy, I can tell. Right, I definitely smelled him around here somewhere.' Vince heard the vixen's feet padding towards him. 'Yep, some blood over here – fresh too. But listen, if he's not dead then he might still be dangerous, so you'd better leave this to me, alright?'

'Um, okay. And you can keep him under control, yes? Not that I can't, you understand, just that you're better equipped...'

'Of course. Wait there. He could have been listening this whole time, waiting to pounce.'

The bushes rustled, then parted, and the red-and-white face of the vixen appeared on the other side of the bars. Her eyes were light green, like almost-turned autumn leaves. She sniffed the cage and Vince. 'How hurt are you?' she whispered. Her smell was intoxicating.

'Huh?' Vince replied.

She rolled her eyes. 'Can you stand? Walk?'

'Er, just about.'

'Good. Play along.'

'Okay, er... What do I—'

Before he could finish, she disappeared from the bushes and called to Frank. 'Believe it or not, he's here, stuck in a trap. Half dead – won't be too much trouble but we'll have to let him out to finish him off, so I'll need your help. Unless you'd rather just leave him here...'

'Well I never. He was right here this whole time?' Frank said. 'But no, I can't risk him escaping somehow and making his way back to the wetlands. I need him dead.'

'Of course. Follow me.' The vixen entered the bushes again, then circled the cage until she was behind Vince. The goose was close behind; Vince could feel the warmth from its massive bulk. He closed his eyes, rested his head against the bars and let his tail go limp in an attempt to look as pathetic as the vixen was making him out to be.

Mother Nature help me.

The vixen spoke to the goose. 'Okay, I need you to pull back that catch there on the top. Do you see it? Then I'll lift the door with my snout at the same time. Hopefully he'll cooperate. You can grab him so he doesn't escape, right?'

'Certainly,' Frank replied.

Above Vince, the goose's beak clanged against the bars, then came a creaking as the vixen forced the door upwards against its strong spring.

The pressure on his tail relented and Vince began to reverse. The bottom edge of the cage door scraped along his spine, then a beak seized his tail. Vince growled under his breath and continued backwards until his front paws, shoulders and head were free and the door sprang shut again with a deafening clang. Before he could stretch his aching muscles, the goose yanked him backwards. Vince stumbled. His instinct screamed at him to fight but the vixen paced back and forth in front of him, her piercing eyes locked onto his for the second time, silently warning him to remain still, or else.

Whose side is she on?

Vince braced himself, ready to dodge her jaws and run – dragging the goose along with him if necessary.

'Thank you, Frank. You can release him now. I don't think he's going to be any trouble.'

'Aah hoo ure?' Frank muttered, his beak full of fur.

'I'm sure,' she replied, with the briefest of winks.

Was that at me or the goose? ME OR THE GOOSE?

Frank released Vince's tail and retreated a few steps. Vince quickly stepped to the side, forming a triangle with the two animals so he could keep them both in sight.

'Now!' the vixen barked as she sprang towards the goose, soaring through the air as if on her own pair of invisible wings. Frank honked in terror, puffed out his broad, white chest and extended his wings to vicious points. The vixen's paws grazed the wall of feathers. Her wide jaws followed but missed his slender neck as he snapped it away. She was quick to react, twisting her own head and clamping her teeth onto his thick shoulder.

Frank's eyes bulged as he jabbed his beak towards her face. He missed, then tried again, striking her above the eye, then the temple. She began to bleed. She bit deeper, harder, but he was too large, his muscles too strong. She couldn't adjust her grip to finish him off without him breaking free.

Her eyes flickered to Vince, wide with desperation. He stood frozen, staring uselessly, before he finally realised that she was, indeed, on his side. He jumped into the fray and snapped at the goose's head as it darted between the two foxes, dealing jab after jab. Vince retreated, panting, his vision a blur. His damaged leg gave way underneath him as he watched the vixen wrestle with the huge bird.

Frank escaped her grip, deafening them with his shrieks, and began to run. He flapped, but one wing flopped uselessly at his side, his shoulder pouring with dark blood.

'Help me, for Mother's sake,' the vixen barked in between gasps of air as she chased the goose down.

Vince clambered to his feet, head spinning, and ran. He reached them in a moment, but the vixen had already pinned the goose to the ground. She sunk her teeth into his neck and the allotments fell silent as Frank's head flopped to the ground, blood pouring into the grass.

'Mother Nature. What the…' Vince shook his head as he dragged his gaze from the goose's lifeless body to the vixen. All he saw was blood. It covered her muzzle and chest, the white of her fur replaced with dark crimson. Her right eye was half closed from the blood that streamed from the beak-wound above it and pooled in the corner by her snout. Vince's heart thumped in his chest and ears and his legs shook from the adrenaline coursing through him.

'You're welcome,' the vixen said flatly.

'Scat. I mean… Thank you. But…' He shook his head again and his leg collapsed once more. He let himself fall this time.

'That was—' the vixen began.

'Horrifying?' Vince said.

'I was going for brilliant. Maybe cunning. Both, really.'

'Oh. And I was—'

'Useless.' The vixen laughed, then wiped the blood from her eye with a paw. In any other situation, he would have smiled at the way her long tail shook with her chuckling, but he was too exhausted.

'Yeah.' He sighed and dropped his chin to the ground, between his front legs. 'I'm really sorry. Are you okay?'

'I'm fine. I'm Laurie, by the way.'

'I'm Vince. Thank you again. I don't know what I would've done if you hadn't shown up.'

'Died, I expect.' She laughed again. 'Starved and shrivelled in that cage over there. Or been made into a nice human coat.'

Vince looked at her, horrified.

'What? It's true. Sorry.' She shrugged. 'You're no city fox, are you?'

'Is it that obvious?' Vince mumbled.

'Yep. All those scratches are fresh. You'd be rather pristine if it wasn't for those.'

'Oh.' He looked down at his battered forelegs. 'Screamers. From the wetlands. Do you—'

'I know them well. Only from afar, of course. Cravings got the better of you, eh?' She nodded towards the trap.

'Yeah. I've never seen one of those before. Where I'm from, humans don't trap foxes. I'll be more careful now, though. Thank you.'

'Ha, don't thank me too much – that trap was for me. Polished off those chickens a few nights ago. Human obviously isn't too impressed. Frogs are nicer, to be honest, but they're few and far between out here.' She sat down and began to groom her tail, apparently unbothered by the swathe of red covering her front.

Vince raised his eyebrows.

'Don't look so shocked. You'll need to toughen up if you want to live in the city. I've escaped more traps and dodged more cars than you've seen full moons.'

As her words sunk in, Vince looked past the bloodstains and took her in, completely, for the first time. Her dusty dark-brown fur was patchy in places, her ears badly torn, her tail thin and sparse. Scars dotted her bloodstained legs, chest and face. She was like no fox he'd ever seen before.

'I'm no pretty countryside vixen, I know,' Laurie said. 'But I'm alive. Which is more than you would be if I hadn't got rid of those geese. Anyone else would've just left you for dead. Anyway, I should get back to my bins. Smelled some good fried chicken, but it's probably gone now. Ho hum.' She turned to leave.

'I'm sorry, I didn't mean anything... I was just...' Vince said. 'You look fine to me. I mean... You look nice. Great. Not that it matters, of course. But...' He trailed off.

'Ha, thanks, and no, it doesn't matter.' She faced him and smiled, then turned away again.

'Wait!' he called after her. She couldn't leave. Not this quickly.

Laurie stopped and looked over her shoulder.

'Is there anything I can do to repay you?' Vince asked, standing up.

'Nah, I like to do a good deed every now and then. Us city animals have to watch each other's backs – we don't always have humans on our side.'

'Right.' Life out here was certainly different.

'Plus, winding up geese is fun. They are *beyond* stupid.'

'I'd noticed.' He couldn't help but glance at Frank's lifeless body again. He'd seen dead animals before, of course, but they were always food and never killed quite so viciously. If this was what Richmond Park had been sheltering him from, a tiny part of him wished to go back to blissful ignorance. Vince continued, 'He was going to leave with the others. Why did you keep him here?'

'To help me open your cage,' Laurie said.

'You couldn't have gone and got a friend to help? I mean—'

'Who says I have friends? And, I'm sorry, but are you upset that I killed a *goose*? A goose who was ready to do you in for absolutely no reason? Unless you did more than trespass... but that's none of my business.'

'I didn't. And I'm not upset, I'm just...'

'Just what?'

'I don't know. He was willing to make a deal with you...'

'That *deal* was to make sure he trusted me, nothing more. But, whatever. Listen, you've obviously been through a lot and I was happy to help you, but now I'm hacked off. That goose pecked the scat out of me and it turns out I risked my life to save a stinking poo-dle.'

'I am not a poodle!' Vince was not entirely sure what a poodle was, but he definitely did not want to be thought of as one.

'And not that you care, but I just turned those puffed-up chickens against their leader, for which a thousand stinking animals in there should thank me, but whatever,' Laurie snorted.

'Screw you! What do you know about that place?' Vince snarled, his energy returning with his temper. 'Did they put you up on a plat-form in the middle of the lake and starve you? Did they try to drown you?'

'No, because I'm not stupid enough to get caught. And what kind of fox won't kill a couple of geese if he has to? Did you just sit and lick your backside the whole time, like you did just now?'

'That's not fair,' Vince said with a thrash of his tail.

'Isn't it? I asked you if you were going to help and you said yes, then I let you out and you do nothing.' She walked towards him. 'You let that bird attack me.'

'You asked me if I could *stand* and *walk*, which I *can*. You said nothing about killing him.'

'It was kind of *implied*.'

'Ugh.' Vince turned away. Tears of anger burned his eyes and there was no way he was going to let her see them.

'Well, if there's nothing else then I'll be on my way. Things to do, animals to see, you know how it is,' Laurie said. 'Good luck. You're going to need it.'

Vince blinked and faced her again. Another animal he'd driven away with his temper. But, Mother Nature, she was infuriating. 'Lis-ten, I'm sorry…'

'You can eat that if you want,' Laurie said, ignoring him and nodding to the dead goose. Vince frowned, but said nothing. Laurie began to trot away, then looked over her shoulder through the dark-ness, her green eyes flashing as they caught the moonlight. She grinned as she called to him. 'I prefer frogs anyway.'

5

Laurie's whisper of a tail followed her like a ghost as she bounded effortlessly over the allotments and disappeared through a set of tall metal gates. Part of Vince wanted to call out to her again, chase her, but his anger and exhaustion overruled him. His attempted apology hung in the air, ignored. No way was he adding to his embarrassment. Plus, she owed *him* an apology or two. Who did she think she was, talking to him like some kind of wetlands know-it-all?

Vince shivered as the silence struck him. He needed to leave. Those geese might come back, or Oswald himself, and if they found Frank's body... Well, that wouldn't help his case. Going back to the wetlands was out of the question. Hours had passed. If Rita was alive, she would have found him by now. He pushed the thought aside.

Screw the wetlands. Screw Laurie. Screw Edward. Screw all of this.

Get out of here. That's what he had to do. As far away as possible. North of the river. That's where he was supposed to be going, wasn't it? The city? He could come back, maybe. When things calmed down. He couldn't think about that now. He just had to put distance between him and those birds.

Vince took one last look at Frank's mutilated corpse – his black eyes turning milky, staring nowhere – and headed towards the gates. His leg throbbed as he limped through the rows of vegetables. Each shed he passed promised warmth and safety within its walls, but the padlocks on the doors sneered at him menacingly, reminding him of the humans who owned them. The same humans who had scattered the fish and hidden the trap.

Laurie's words circled his mind.

Good luck. You're going to need it.

He squeezed through the black bars of the gate and his legs carried him aimlessly onwards. The road was busy with cars, but with his eyes and ears forward their roaring engines quickly turned to background noise. After a while he reached a bridge. Thick cables hung vertically, uniformly spaced along two horizontal beams suspended between two leaf-green arches, which ushered cars underneath their ornate towers. A path ran alongside so that walking humans – and foxes – could cross separately from the traffic.

The moon was high and the buzz of the city coaxed him further north, but he could go no further. His desire to get as far away as possible from the wetlands had carried him this far, but now, seeing London's famous river properly for the first time, he felt dangerously unqualified to cross it.

I'm no city fox.

Those were Laurie's words too, and she was right.

The thoughts flooded in. Clawing at his brain – above the pain of his injured leg, the fresh bout of hunger creeping up on him and the humans and animals doing everything they could to kill him – was Rita. She had been his eyes. Without her, he had no idea where he was going. No idea if he'd accidentally stumble across more train tracks or into another trap.

He thought of the geese. Their size, their strength, compared to a magpie, was immense. Not forgetting the swan. The Screamers. The cormorants. Even the ducks. If she was injured and couldn't fly, she had no chance.

Then again, just because she hadn't turned up at the allotments didn't mean she was dead… She could still be there, hiding, hurt and waiting to be rescued. But he knew that was just wishful thinking, his brain doing its best to ignore the truth and ease his guilt.

He covered his face with his paws. He didn't know what to do, but the facts turned his stomach. Rita had saved his life and he had left her behind. And his first worry? Getting lost. Selfishness squeezed his gut, forcing the half-digested fish up into his throat. He swallowed, disgusted with himself.

All she wanted was to see the city, tag along for the ride, and because of me she didn't even make it across the river.

Vince's eyes brimmed with tears. If he'd never left Richmond

Park, she wouldn't have either, and then she'd still be flapping and squawking at his side. Why did he have to be so stubborn?

He backed up off the bridge and headed immediately left, where a path and row of trees lined the river bank. There were no humans around; anywhere would do. Finding a thin tree with a curtain of leafy branches, he nestled into the dirt and curled his tail around himself. Tears spilled onto his cheeks. Eyes closed, he sobbed as the cars rumbled over the bridge, the moon sinking behind the city's skyline.

A set of tiny claws pulled on Vince's ear, then scrabbled on the tree bark above him. The owner of the claws yelled down from the branches with a shrill voice. 'Excuse me!'

Vince sighed, got up and peered up into the leaves. In the elbow of two boughs a grey squirrel clasped its front paws in front of its dusty white chest.

'Hello,' Vince said with as much energy as he could muster.

'You're probably wondering why I'm not scared of you. The answer is that I saw you limp over here and then I heard you crying, so it's logical to assume that you are probably too tired to chase me up a tree,' the squirrel said.

'Logical indeed.' She wasn't wrong, but he didn't like to eat squirrels anyway. Too bony. But she didn't know that. 'That's quite an assumption.'

She shrugged. 'I'm faster than you up a tree and I'm smaller so I can climb higher.'

'Can't argue with that, I suppose.'

'Anyway, please be quiet. I'm trying to sleep.' She pointed to a tangle of twigs higher up the tree that formed her drey.

Vince started to mutter an apology, but the squirrel interrupted. 'Why are you upset? Are you lost?'

'Lost? Uh, technically, yes, I suppose so. But I'm upset because my friend—'

'I can give you directions. Where are you going? That's north, south, east, west.' She pointed as she spoke.

'I know which way is north, thank you,' Vince said as politely as possible. 'I was just having a rest.'

'You said you were lost.' The squirrel blinked her jet-black eyes, the rest of her face unchanging.

'Well, I don't know where I *am*, but I'm going north, across the river.'

'Then you should have said that in the first place.'

Vince sighed. 'Sorry. Anyway, I'm going to stay here for a while, if that's okay. I'll be quiet. I need to have a rest and think about some things.'

'Think? I can help. I'm good at thinking.'

'Er, thanks. This is kind of personal, though. I don't think you'll be able to help.'

'You'd be surprised. Most animals think about silly things.'

'Well, this isn't silly,' Vince said sternly.

'I bet it is.'

Vince flattened his ears. 'It is NOT.'

The squirrel didn't flinch, but blinked again. 'Then tell me.'

Rita had been persistent when she first insisted on joining him, but this was another level. Vince conceded – to shut her up more than anything else – and told the squirrel about Richmond Park, the wetlands and Rita.

When he had finished, the squirrel sniffed. 'I knew it would be silly. You can't go back, so you have to go forward. Easy.'

'It's not that simple.'

'Isn't it? Your friend's current condition and location are unknown and her actions are beyond your control. You have three choices. Return to the wetlands, which is out of the question because probability suggests you'll be killed, stay here and wait for her to find you, which is illogical for the aforementioned reasons, or go forward towards your destination.'

Vince frowned. Of course it made sense when put like that, but it didn't ease his guilt, anger, or sadness.

'There is another option,' the squirrel continued. 'Go back home to Richmond Park. Travel a different way. You could almost certainly make it back safely, if you are logical about it.'

Back home. Back to Sophie and the others. Compared to the wetlands, it seemed almost perfect. Almost logical. So what if Edward was in charge? The cemetery wasn't that bad...

But it wasn't his home. Not anymore. His den was gone, Edward would make his life hell and Sophie was with Jake now. There was nothing left go back for.

'I can't,' Vince said.

The squirrel shrugged. 'So, carry on then. If your original objective was to find this park, then there's no reason to quit now.'

'But I'm not from the city. I don't know what I'm doing. I've already messed so many things up...'

'On the contrary. You're here, aren't you?'

'Yes, but—'

'Your wounds are temporary. As long as you don't make the same mistakes again, there's no reason you can't survive here. But if you haven't learned anything, then maybe you should go home. The city is no place for stupid animals. Are you stupid?'

Vince blinked. 'No.'

'Then keep going.'

Rita had wanted an adventure; if she couldn't have one, he would do it for her. A small smile spread across his face. 'You're right. But it's not just about finding the park anymore. It's about doing all the things Rita wanted to do. Seeing the city, experiencing new things...'

The squirrel began washing her tail, thoroughly bored by Vince's epiphany.

He didn't care. He was no less upset about Rita, but he knew now that he couldn't give up. His grandparents' park was out there somewhere. It might even be just around the next corner... All he had to do was keep going. And there was so much to see in the meantime. He could do this. No more moping, no more stupid mistakes, no more being a poodle... whatever that meant.

Keep going, prove Edward wrong, prove Laurie wrong, and make Rita proud.

Vince thanked the strange squirrel and went to leave, as her main concern seemed to be going back to bed. After a few steps, though, she called after him, 'I told you I was good at thinking, didn't I?'

Vince left the squirrel to return to her slumber and wondered if every animal who woke her received the same matter-of-fact treatment or whether it was just the ones who bothered her with their emotional self-loathing.

Tired as he was, beside an open path was no place for a fox to sleep through the day, and the sun wasn't due up for hours anyway. The plan was simple: keep going.

Vince peered through the latticed metal barrier as he crossed the bridge, marvelling at the inky river beneath him. It smelled salty, like the fish that had lured him into the trap, but refreshing. Then he spotted them; curled up asleep on a metal walkway extending into the water from the bank was a small flock of geese. He pressed his ears against his head and quickened his pace.

They were nothing but strangers, of course, simply sleeping in the place they slept every night, but Vince ran all the same. He passed under the second green arch, which signalled that he'd almost reached the other side, but it wasn't until the rushing water below changed to solid concrete that he began to relax.

He looked over his shoulder at the trees that lined the bank he'd been on moments before, their mossy outlines undulating in the wind. Almost exactly the same shade of green as the bridge. Now, greeting him on the north side of the great river, was a line of brown brick buildings, their square, white windows grinning unsettling welcomes.

Up ahead, the road split into two and a huge concrete structure ran from east to west, blocking out the lower part of the sky. Cars whizzed over it, but it was raised up on thick pillars with an empty, concrete area beneath it. He waited for a break in traffic, then dashed across. It was safe from humans, but exposed; the street-level road circled the entire area.

Mother Nature, why do they need to travel in circles?

Ahead, high on a black pole, a green light flicked to red and the traffic slowed to a halt. The lights changed again, and the cars moved away. When the red light appeared once more, Vince took his chance, weaving around the warm, humming cars as fast as he could manage.

His back paws landed on the path as the cars roared away, a hot draught pulling at his tail. The smell was metallic, the air gritty in his eyes and lungs. A few steps away, a narrow path led him away from the busy roads. On his right, a vacant car park and a tall building; to his left, a neat row of small houses.

He exhaled slowly as the noise from the road faded and a pungent scent wafted through the air.

Bins.

It was time to see if old human food matched up to fresh frogs. He wasn't confident, but as long as it was edible and he didn't get trapped in anything, he would consider it a success.

There was no shortage of choice; each house on the street had at least one bin in its tiny garden. One in particular, though, caught Vince's nose. Meaty, but somehow sweet, and very fresh. It was piled high, the lid precariously balanced on top of a black plastic bag, which bulged over the sides.

He approached it cautiously, still aware that this was new territory, but jumped the low fence with no trouble. After a quick look around, confident he was alone, he grabbed the bag in his teeth and pulled. The bin toppled over, spilling the contents across the wet gravel. Another quick tear of the bag opened a hole wide enough for his snout to inspect the goodies inside. Jackpot!

With his paw, he ripped the bag further, dragging out three small, brightly coloured cardboard boxes, each filled with the meaty remains of a bird, and strips of potatoes covered in a red, sticky substance. He devoured it. The potatoes were oily and strangely sugary, and some of the meat had a thick, crunchy coating, which was much too strong for him, but it was the most satisfying thing he'd eaten since leaving Richmond Park. He licked every scrap of flesh off the bones and pushed his nose into the corners of each box until he had consumed every morsel, then sat back on his haunches and surveyed his accomplishment.

'Anything good?' a voice spoke from the darkness.

Vince spun around and crouched low, tail waving warily. 'Who's there?'

'Only me.' From the darkness of the house's sheltered doorway a pair of luminous eyes gleamed at him. Four stout legs and a long tail emerged from the gloom. Black as a crow, the largest, roundest cat Vince had ever beheld cocked his head and began to wash his paws.

Vince relaxed slightly, but remained on his feet. 'Are these your bins?'

'Aye. Well, technically they belong to my human, but don't let that stop you.' The cat chuckled.

Vince introduced himself, the cat doing likewise. 'Socks is my usual name,' he said.

'Socks? Like the things they put on their feet?' Vince lifted a paw.

'It's meant to be funny.'

'Right.' Vince raised an eyebrow.

'I also go by Bernard. That's from a nice couple up on Hammer-smith Grove. And this other family calls me Shadow. But the less said about that the better.'

'I see,' Vince said, thoroughly confused.

'But Socks is fine.'

'Um, great, nice to meet you. You don't happen to know of any big parks around here by any chance?' said Vince.

'Big parks? Ain't none in my patch, sorry. Got some small ones. Tiny, really. Better described as greens than parks. No big'uns, though, I'm afraid.'

'Your patch?' Vince asked.

'Indeed. Official Feline Administrator, Hammersmith branch. From the flyover to Goldhawk Road, the Town Hall to Barons Court, that's all me. Any questions, problems, or aggravations in my patch, you come to me and I'll sort you out. Any further and you'll need to speak to one of my associates.'

Vince had no idea where any of those places were but, Socks

being a domestic cat, he guessed they weren't particularly far. 'You don't know much of London, then?'

'Afraid not. I'm no stray. A strictly three-household cat, me. Well, four, if you count the chicken shop, but that's a food-only relationship. Nothing serious. Anyway, I digress… You off somewhere nice?'

Vince, still not entirely sure whether the cat was insane or a genius, replied, 'I'm trying to find the park my grandparents came from. All I know is that it's north of the river, which I suppose could be anywhere, really.'

'I see. As I said, not my patch.'

'Well, thanks anyway…'

'*But…*' Socks continued. 'It is my duty to help any animal who requires assistance within my jurisdiction, and I might just know a few animals who are more well-travelled than myself. Follow me.'

The cat leapt down the steps and onto a thin fence, surprisingly gracefully given his size, but it wasn't until Socks dropped onto the path almost soundlessly and began to wander away that Vince saw the extent of him. From nose to tail, the cat was almost as long as Vince. A hefty black barrel held aloft by thick, sturdy legs and wide paws that could flatten the most menacing of rats. Cats and foxes generally kept a mutually respectable distance, but Vince got the feeling this feline could easily hold his own against any animal that might try its luck.

Vince followed Socks over the fence and together they strode to the end of the row of houses, out onto a wide street, busy with cars and humans. Vince waited uneasily at the corner as a couple of nearby humans pointed at him. One of them reached into his coat and pulled out a small rectangular object.

'What's that thing?' Vince asked.

'It's called a phone. They use them to take pictures. It's like a memory, but they can look at it over and over again. There are moving ones, too – they show them to each other. My human does it.'

'They won't… Shoot me?'

'Shoot you? You ain't even from the city at all, are you?' Socks laughed.

'No,' Vince said, embarrassed to have been identified as an out-of-towner again so quickly.

'Well, there ain't any guns here. Humans are alright, mostly. Any trouble, give them a warning. Get up close, that scares them. They want to get bitten as much as you want to get shot. And you know to stay away from the cars, I expect? They won't slow down for you here. A few of my associates learned that the hard way.'

Vince nodded. If all the animals in the city were as friendly as this one, his journey might actually be easy. They stepped out onto the joining path, Socks leading Vince to the right. More bins stood at regular intervals, their contents overflowing onto the pavement, but the stench wafting from them was sickly and turned Vince's stomach. Socks looked this way and that, pausing every now and again to shake his thick fur. He seemed oblivious to the humans who staggered around them, shouting and staring, but Vince couldn't help being wary.

Eventually, the pavement ended and the road extended in all directions like the veins on a leaf. Cars droned around them and faces peered through the foggy glass, eyes wide at the sight of a fox and an enormous cat taking a casual stroll together.

'Ah, over there!' Socks bounded away and – flouting his own advice – dashed across the road, escaping the wheel of a car by a whisker. Vince once again waited for a suitable gap, then followed at a more leisurely pace.

A tall, brown brick building with a facade of huge glass windows towered over them, but at ground level several shops were set further back, the building overhanging to provide a shelter of sorts from the majority of the wandering humans, and any potential rain. Vince was glad to be somewhere where the humans were not, but a frown spread across his face as he saw the animal Socks had brought him to meet.

Jake lay on the long grass, licking earthworm juice from his lips. A few paces away, Sophie foraged in the bushes with two of her vixen friends, Alice and Marge. He listened as they gossiped, hating himself for doing so.

'I rather like it over here, you know. Not the same as the old den, of course, but it is quiet, and the food is exquisite,' Alice said.

'True. I do miss my little place by the big oak, though,' Marge, the oldest of the three, said. 'I'm not sure I like being on the edge of the park, so close to the houses.'

'Ah, but it has its benefits. Shall I let you in on a little secret, ladies?' Alice said, lowering her voice. Jake pricked his ears. 'There's a tabby cat a couple of streets away who can get things for us.'

'What kind of things?' Sophie said.

'Food. The kind we can't get here. Human food. Chicken. Bacon.'

Jake's stomach turned and he instinctively checked for deer over his shoulder. He'd have to tell Edward. Wouldn't he?

'Bacon? I've never had it. Is it any good?' Marge said.

'Good? It's better than anything you've ever had before, I can tell you that.'

Marge's interest was piqued. 'And this cat… It just brings it to us?'

'Yeah,' Alice said. 'You just arrange a time and place to meet, then give him a rat in return.'

Sophie frowned. 'Do you think that's a good idea?'

Alice shrugged. 'No harm, is there? I have what he wants, he has what I want.'

'I would quite like to try some of this bacon stuff…' Marge piped up.

'What about the deer? If they knew you were giving away the park's rats to outsiders…'

Alice sniffed. 'So what? What are they going to do?'

'You saw what they did to Vince's den, Alice,' Sophie said. 'And all he did was refuse to move. Edward could kick you out completely.'

'Maybe, but you know what I think?' Alice whispered. 'Vince leaving has put the wind up him. Edward, I mean. He's been on edge ever since he left. Like, really distracted. A squirrel told me he was scraping his antlers on the same tree from sunrise until midday. He's too worried about more animals leaving to be bothered with a bit of bartering.'

Sophie pulled a face, then shook her head, but Jake knew Sophie suspected similar. Alice was prone to exaggeration, but if others had noticed the same thing…

'Either way, you should stop. It's too risky,' Sophie said.

Alice rolled her eyes. 'No one said you had to get involved, Soph. I promise I'll be careful, okay?'

'Fine. Just don't come crying to me when the deer trample you to death.'

'As if,' Alice laughed.

Sophie made to leave as Marge nudged Alice with a paw. 'So… When do you think I can get some of this bacon?'

Sophie shook her head again and padded away. Jake rose to his paws and followed her, a knot now fully formed in his stomach. If he'd known the foxes were going to start breaking rules, he would never have agreed to Edward's shady deal. Keeping it to himself was an option, but if Edward found out, Sophie would be at risk as well as himself. Could he downplay it? Put all the blame on the cat some-how? Whatever his decision, he needed to make it by sunrise, when he was due to meet Edward for his first report.

'Alright, Laurie? This is Vince,' Socks said to the vixen before setting his backside on the paving slabs to wash his ears.

'Well, well, well, the poodle returns.' Laurie pulled her snout from a greasy paper bag and sat up. The blood on her chest was now a faded pink.

Vince rolled his eyes, then met her gaze and instantly regretted it. Being made fun of was one thing, but being made fun of by the owner of those eyes was completely another.

'Didn't expect to see you over this way so quickly. Couldn't keep away, eh?' Laurie smiled.

'You wish.' Heading north had brought him straight into her ter-ritory. But if she knew the location of a potential park, he could prob-ably put up with her for a bit longer.

'You two know each other?' Socks said.

'We met, briefly,' Laurie said to Socks. She didn't elaborate about the trap. That was something.

'Right... Well, Vince needs some directions. Thought you might be able to assist, since you're the most well-travelled among us?'

'I see.' Laurie's smile stretched into a mischievous grin, her eyes glittering to match. 'And what could possibly top your lovely visit to the wetlands and that relaxing stopover in the allotments? How about a leisurely swim in the Thames? Or a day dodging buses on Oxford Street? Oh, I know! You want to go for a nice ride on the Underground!' She laughed, then a serious tone cut through her voice. 'There might be some other vixens about who wouldn't mind risking their lives for you, but once is enough for me, thanks.'

Vince's stomach churned with embarrassment and anger, but he pushed it aside and lifted his chin. 'If you're going to be like that, I'll find my own way.' He moved to leave, but Socks blocked his way.

'Hang on! I can't let you go wandering about without any idea where you're going. I have a reputation to maintain.'

Vince spoke to Socks, ignoring Laurie, forcing politeness through his rage. 'I promise you, I will have only good things to say about you to any animal who may ask, but if *she* is going to be like *that*, then I'll go on alone, thanks. Nice meeting you.' Once again, Vince tried to weave around the huge cat, but the furry barricade held his position.

Socks looked at them both in turn. 'Laurie, stop being such a bitch, pardon my language, and Vince, grow yourself a pair. She's only messing with you.'

'Good advice, but I think I'll leave you two to it.' Vince started to push his way past the cat, who eventually relented out of politeness. 'Thanks again for all your help,' Vince called to Socks over his shoulder.

'Hang on... Wait! Vince!' Socks shouted, then hissed something at Laurie, too quiet for Vince to hear. She whispered an inaudible reply, and Socks hissed again.

Vince carried on, weighing up which direction to take, but, after a few blinks, Laurie appeared at his side.

'What can I do for you?' he said as nonchalantly as possible.

'I think we both know it's the other way round.'

'You're full of yourself, you know that, don't you?' Vince snapped. He strode onwards.

'I was only joking you know. You shouldn't take things so personally,' Laurie said.

Vince snorted.

'Do you want my help or not?' Laurie said.

'Not.'

'Look, Socks will never forgive me if I don't give you directions. Can you just tell me where you're going? I'll never hear the end of it otherwise.'

'Wow, you sure know how to make a fox feel special,' he said.

'I already saved your life once, don't forget.'

'So much for all that scat about good deeds and city animals looking out for each other.'

'Technically, you're not a city animal, but listen, I…'

He broke into a run and Laurie fell behind. He would find his way without her. If Socks was anything to go by, there were plenty of animals out here that would help him. If he found one of them tonight, he could be there by tomorrow; grass under his paws, rats to chase, birds in the—

Birds.

He must have stopped running, because Laurie's voice echoed through the still air and into his ears. 'You okay?'

Vince sighed. This was exactly what Rita had wanted to see. The busy streets, the animals. She and Socks would have got on like moss on a tree.

'I'm fine.'

'I would tell you to stop being so stubborn, but it's not advice I've ever taken myself.' Laurie's voice was closer this time.

Vince sensed her green eyes blinking at him as she approached his side once more. He recalled Sophie's frustration with him the night before he left. Stubborn and ridiculous, she'd called him. She'd failed to mention his temper that night, but she'd said it enough times before that it didn't need repeating.

And what would Rita say if she were here? Probably the same thing.

There *were* animals who would help him, and one of them was sitting next to him. She wasn't rainbows and sunshine, but she was better than no one.

Vince blinked back his tears. 'I'm looking for a park, and all I know is that it's big and north of the river.'

Laurie smiled. 'Well, let's see… Hyde Park is the closest to here and it's pretty big. Nice stretch of water. There's a couple of small parks next door, but they're not what you're after. Very busy. Good for a night, but not long term. That's all I know, really; I don't go much beyond Hyde Park these days.'

'Thank you. Hyde Park it is, I guess. If it's not the one, I'll get more directions from there.'

'Good idea. There's a few folk there who will help you. Are you sure you're okay? You seem—'

'I'm fine, really.'

Laurie shrugged. 'Okay, if you're sure. Well, it's straight along this road. Keep going this way and you'll get there before morning, easy. When you get to the Tube station, you're nearly there. It's the one with the red-and-blue circle signs. You'll know it when you see it.'

'Right.' Vince committed her words to memory, then added, 'Can I ask you something?'

Laurie nodded.

'Why don't you live in one of the parks, you know, permanently?'

'I could, I suppose, but I prefer not to stay in one place too long.'

'But where do you sleep?'

'Here and there,' Laurie said. 'There's an empty shop on the high street that way, and I found a nice new shed in a back garden the other day. Might check that out again.'

'Isn't it tiring, having to move all the time?'

She shrugged again. 'I'm used to it.'

'I just don't understand why anyone would choose a noisy, concrete street full of humans over a quiet open space with trees and grass.'

'Look, you might want peace and quiet and stability, but I like the noise and freedom. It's exciting. There's food everywhere. I get to hang out with animals I'd never get to hang out with in a park. Like Socks.'

Vince couldn't argue, but the thought of having to find a new place to sleep every few nights filled him with dread.

'But it's so dangerous here. What about the cars?'

'Vince, come on! Don't make me call you the P-word again…'

Vince sighed. He wasn't going to convince her that catching frogs in a quiet park was better than rummaging in bins by a road, and he wasn't sure why he was trying. She had only helped him because Socks told her to. And in the allotments she'd seemed more interested in winding up the geese than saving his life. Although she had asked if he was okay… But that was really just basic manners.

When she spoke again, though, all traces of sympathy were gone. 'Well, good luck. I guess I'll see you around.' Laurie blinked, turned away and started to hurry back towards the busy junction where Socks was still waiting.

This was it. Rita had helped him get this far, and Laurie's directions would get him further still, but from now on he would be alone. There was no way he was letting Laurie leave with a perfunctory 'see you around', though.

'Wait!' he yelled, with no idea what the next words out of his mouth would be.

She stopped and faced him, cocking her head.

She might not care about him, but she would sure as Mother Nature remember him.

He blurted out the words before his brain had a chance to kick in. 'What's a poodle?'

Laurie cackled, her tail shaking uncontrollably. 'Are you serious?'

Vince went to speak, but the words stuck in his throat.

'Why don't you find out and tell me next time we meet.' Laurie winked. The same wink she'd given him back at the allotments. Except, unlike at the allotments, this time he knew exactly who it was aimed at.

From a window ledge above the shops, Kara watched Vince pad down the long road, away from the vixen. 'Perfect,' she whispered under her breath, although it was far from it. If those geese hadn't been so incompetent, she would be halfway home by now. Idiots. All of them. Never send a water bird – or four – to do the work of a raptor.

No matter. She knew where Vince was going now, and, Mother Nature, she'd earned it. Listening to them blather on, pretending to hate each other, would have been tedious for any animal, let alone one who wanted to be done with this as soon as possible.

Anyway, it would be a quick journey, if that vixen was to be believed. She straightened out a windswept feather, opened her pristine wings and was about to set off after Vince, when a voice echoed from below.

'Hello up there!' It was that busybody cat. 'You don't look familiar. Can we help with anything?'

'No, I'm fine, thank you,' she called down. They'd seen her. Damn.

'You have some stunning feathers, if you don't mind me saying. Very dark and unusual.'

'Thanks,' Kara said. 'I should get go—'

The cat interrupted, 'We don't get a lot of owls around here, especially your kind. Apologies if that sounds... Er, where are you from, out of interest?'

Too many questions. She had to get away, but was wary of seeming suspicious. If they doubted anything she said, and saw her follow Vince, they might go after him and ruin her plan. A slight risk, but a risk all the same, and she'd come too far to fail now. 'A park. Quite far away. I'm just passing through. I really need to be on my way, thanks.' She went to open her wings, but the cat started to speak again.

'Oh, really? Do you know a lot of the city? Our friend – he just left, you might have seen him? – is looking for a park. Maybe you can help?'

The vixen added, 'He's going north, but I only know Hyde Park really.'

'Oh, which way did he go? I'll give him a shout on my way past if you like,' Kara said in her cheeriest voice. She could feel her energy draining with every word. Being nice was hard.

The vixen smiled. 'He went that way, towards Hyde Park. It's a bit of a walk but he won't have got far. You'll easily catch him up.'

Catch him up, overtake him, and beat him there. With enough time to find an animal, make a deal, and finish the job.

'Okay, great. Well, I'll be off then.' Kara stretched her wings once again, but this time the cat didn't stop her.

'Thank you so much,' the cat said. 'And if you have any questions, problems, or aggravations, do let me know. It's my duty to help any animal who requires assistance within my jurisdiction.'

'I'll bear that in mind.' Kara flapped away, circling upwards, before heading down the road. An annoying little delay, but at least they hadn't suspected anything. It wouldn't be long now until she was back in her roost, munching on a juicy Richmond Park rabbit. She could taste them already.

Vince made his way down the long road, measuring his progress by the street lights. His head throbbed from their yellow glow, but he ignored it. Hyde Park would be dark and quiet. Hopefully.

Tall buildings flanked the road and, in place of the occasional paving slab, gaunt trees waited in the dark for the sun to return and warm their leaves. The cars had thinned out, one or two buzzing by every now and again, and the humans had all but disappeared.

A drop of water tapped him on the nose. Clouds had rolled across the sky, poised to burst. At his feet, tiny dark spots materialised, multiplying across the concrete as he traipsed onwards. Vince pulled his ears back and lowered his head.

Not stopping yet. Not until I get to Hyde Park.

The rain grew heavier. Fat droplets plummeted from above and, with dull *thwacks*, bombarded him like a squadron of angry bumble-bees. Still he walked, trying to keep his destination at the front of his mind.

His last words to Laurie gnawed at his stomach. So much for her making fun of him; his question about the poodle had all but given her a ready-made punchline. He wouldn't care so much if he thought she was gone for good, but her final words…

And that wink…

She could have just been winding him up, though. Based on her attitude up to that point, it was more than likely.

He shook the vixen out of his head and focused on the pavement. The ground was slick with rain, the orange of the lights reflecting back up at him from between his paws.

Keep going.

He repeated his new mantra over and over as the rain pummelled him. His fur was sodden and water dripped from the tip of his snout and tail, but it would take more than a downpour to stop him.

Keep going. Keep going.

Up ahead, above the glass shop fronts, two red-and-blue signs jutted from the building wall. Circular, just as Laurie had described. Stretching between them, a wide semi-circular window like the fanned tail of a bird, and a longer sign in the same blue. At ground level, the doorway was blocked off with a latticed metal gate. What had she called it? A *Tube* station? What did *that* mean? It didn't matter. He wasn't staying. He passed under the signs with little more than an upward glance.

Not far now.

The rain carried on, and so did Vince.

The rain had driven most of Hyde Park's animals back to the nooks and crannies they called home, but desperate rats still scurried along the path edges. Apart from their skerfuffling, and the raindrops slapping on the leaves, the park was quiet.

Perched on the back of a bench, Kara explained the deal to a triplet of foxes. Two females and a male, with matching slender frames and oversized ears. Despite living in the park, their fur was grimy, with bare patches across their legs and faces, not unlike that vixen Vince had spoken to. They obviously roamed outside the boundaries more often than not. They narrowed their amber eyes at the owl as she finished speaking.

'So, if we kill this fox, we can come and live in Richmond Park?' Bailey, one of the females, said.

'Like, for ever?' Bonnie, her sister, added.

'Yep,' Kara said, dragging a long feather through her beak.

'What's the catch?' said their brother, whose name was Blake.

'No catch. If you make it there, then you can stay. You have my word.'

'And it's as good as everyone says? Safe? Lots of food?' Bonnie said.

'Oh, it's better. And I happen to be very close friends with the deer in charge, so anything you want, I can get.'

'And how do we know we can trust you?' Bailey said.

Kara shrugged. 'You don't. Take it or leave it.'

Blake and Bailey started to speak together. 'We—'

Bonnie held up a paw to silence her siblings. 'Deal.'

'I'll hang around until I'm satisfied you've held up your end of the bargain, but then I'm heading home. You can make your own way there.'

The foxes nodded and Kara flapped up to a higher branch, glad of a rest. They seemed capable. Smaller than average, but definitely more street-smart than the geese, although that wasn't difficult. Regardless, there were three of them. Even a fox bigger than Vince couldn't beat those odds.

Kara eyed a rat sniffing at a morsel beneath a litter bin. She silently dropped from the tree, wings open, talons out. The rat froze. Kara swooped. In an instant she snatched it from the ground before flapping effortlessly back up to her perch.

The rat shrieked, pleading for its life, and squeezed its black eyes shut. Kara grasped its throat with her beak and tore it open. The rat fell still, blood seeping into the coarse fur on its breast. She ripped off a chunk of flesh, tipped her head back and swallowed it whole.

She remained in the tree for a while, eating her prize as the rain pattered around her. Below, the foxes headed out into the wet night and made their way towards the corner of the park where Vince was most likely to appear. Kara wondered if Edward's promise of a home to whoever killed Vince actually would stretch to three foxes. The other residents would hardly jump for joy when this lot showed up, demanding their share of the space and food in the hallowed grounds of Richmond Park. Not that it was her problem. As long as she got her rabbits, she couldn't give a hoot.

Laurie shook the last of the rain from her fur as she approached the tall fence that separated her from the wetlands. Now that the rain had eased off and Vince was on his way, it was business as usual.

She heard a barrage of voices, which grew louder as she slipped through the fence and slunk through the nettles. She'd only come for a quick nosey to see if those geese had given that swan his marching orders – she'd been denied the food here for too long – but there was clearly an altercation of some kind going on and she wasn't about to miss it.

Honks, chirrups and squeals filled the air as she arrived at her usual hiding spot: a thick tree with low-hanging branches that looked out over the water. She jumped up and balanced on a limb, camouflaged by the leaves. Any slight movement or noise would usually have alerted security, but that wouldn't be a problem this time.

Every animal in the wetlands cheered and chattered on the bank. Nearest the water were the mammals – squirrels, rats, rabbits, otters – all watching with delight as five geese and the two Screamers held Oswald on the wooden platform. The platform she'd seen from a distance too many times. She thought of Vince up there. How on earth had he escaped?

Roger the goose waddled forward from the bank and the hubbub died down. He addressed the crowd.

'Animals of the wetlands! Oswald has been brought here, in front of you all, to account for his behaviour! There will be no witnesses this time, because every one of you – every one of *us* – is a victim of this animal's wrongdoing!'

A cheer erupted. Water birds, songbirds and mammals hopped together on the grass, flashing delighted smiles to one another. Wings embraced furry bodies and paws patted the backs of feathered heads. In all the times she'd perched in this tree and watched the trials of the foxes and other mammals out on that lake, Laurie had never seen anything like it. One swan. That's all it had taken to turn these animals against each other. And to unite them...

'The foxes were right!' Roger continued. 'Vince showed us that we are equal. We do not have to be friends, but we should respect each other, and work *together* to keep our community safe. The vixen showed me that no animal has the right to be in charge here, especially one as cowardly as Oswald!'

More noise rose like flames from the bank, angrier this time, cheers morphed into hisses. Oswald struggled and honked, but the birds held him firm in their beaks.

Laurie couldn't help but smile. Vince had started this, somehow, and she had finished it. Or pushed it in the right direction, at least.

A cluster of voices murmured below Laurie. She looked down from her branch. Five small shapes twitched in the thick nettles. Young animals, she guessed. No real threat to her.

'Hey!' she called down to them.

The nettles rustled as three goslings and two tiny otters craned their necks. 'Hey yourself,' a gosling replied.

'Who are you?' the young male otter asked.

'I'm Laurie. Just wanted to see what all the noise was about.'

'Oh. It's Oswald. Everyone is fed up with him,' the female said.

'Yeah. He wasn't very nice to me and my sister,' the first otter said.

'Or our parents,' one of the goslings added.

'They told us to go back to bed, but we want to see what happens,' said another.

'I see,' Laurie said. Then her curiosity got the better of her. 'Say, do any of you remember seeing a fox called Vince up on that platform? Maybe last night?'

'You know Vince? Is he okay?' one of the otters squealed.

'He's fine! How did he escape this place?' Laurie asked.

'We helped him. Us and our parents. We pulled him through the water to the bank,' the otter replied. 'He killed Ash, the cormorant. Vince was very brave. And he told us about how unfair it all is here.'

Laurie nodded. Had she underestimated Vince? He had stood on the water and faced those birds, even killed one of them, while she only ever cowered in the trees and watched the trials from afar. She was more of a poodle than him. Not that it mattered now. He was gone, off to find his new home. He didn't want to live on the streets and eat leftovers from bins, and she couldn't really blame him. He was over-sensitive – most park animals were – but she might have taken her jokes a *bit* too far.

'*Boys don't like being called names, Laurie. Especially not by girls,*' Laurie's mother had said.

'*It's not my fault they're all pathetic runts,*' Laurie had replied.

'*Language! And you'll never find a mate if you spend all your time hanging around that ridiculous cat.*'

'*Leave Socks alone! And who says I want to find a mate?*'

Laurie shook the memories from her head as the first otter broke her train of thought. 'Did he find Rita?' he asked.

'Rita? Who's that?' Vince hadn't mentioned a mate. Laurie's stomach lurched unexpectedly.

'His friend. A magpie. They came here together.'

'A magpie? Oh, no. He didn't mention her.' Laurie relaxed a little, then instantly felt ridiculous. 'What happened?'

'She distracted the geese so he could escape, but then flew into the trees and the birds came after her. No one saw what happened. Vince had to leave quickly. He didn't have time to look for her.'

'Daddy said she was killed,' one of the goslings said sadly.

'Oh, I'm so sorry,' Laurie said. Maybe that was why Vince had gone so quiet.

Another of the tiny birds piped up. '*My* daddy said she wasn't killed. *He* said the ducks were too scared to follow her out of the fence, so they had to lie to Oswald about it, so there!'

'What? Really?' Laurie said, looking to each of them.

The goslings looked at each other and shrugged.

The otters frowned, then one said, 'If she made it out of the fence then she might be alright. But we weren't here, and when we got back inside everyone was shouting and flapping around.'

'No one tells us anything! It's so unfair!' the other otter added, slapping her thick tail on the ground.

'Do you know where she was last seen?' Laurie said.

'Over there.' A gosling pointed a small, downy wing through the trees to Laurie's right. 'By the fence.'

'Thanks.' Laurie looked out over the pond. The birds were still grappling with the swan on the platform while Roger made his impassioned speech. They would soon drown him, or worse, but Laurie didn't care about Oswald. She slid down the tree and bounded through the weeds.

If Rita was alive, she would find her. If she wasn't, the least she could do was discover what had happened to her. Vince would want to know, and for some reason, Laurie wanted to be the one to tell him.

Vince arrived at the entrance to Hyde Park just in time. The rain had stopped, but his fur was still damp and his legs ached like never before.

He'd barely stopped moving since leaving the wetlands, not counting the time spent in the trap – which he didn't.

He crossed the road and headed for the gate. Beside it stood two scarlet boxes, just taller and wider than a human, small columns of windows on three sides. Vince peered through as he went by. Inside one, a human slept, slumped against the glass. His hands and face were filthy and holes littered his drab clothing.

All these buildings I've passed and he'd rather sleep in there?

The black metal gate was locked, but – as always – the bars were widely spaced. As he squeezed through, reassuring scents hit his nose. Wet grass, earthy and crisp, muddled with an abundance of rats, birds and squirrels. Less reassuring, though, was the smell of foxes.

They were close by. He kept his head and ears high, scanning the area. Once again he was trespassing but it wasn't mating season; there was no way his own kind would bother with much more than a few angry barks, as long as he left sharpish.

He headed deeper into the park but as he reached a fork in the path a deep growl rumbled from the shadow of a nearby tree. Vince turned his ears towards the noise.

'Stop right there,' a female voice said.

'I'm just passing through,' Vince said. 'I don't want any trouble.'

'Neither do we,' another voice said from the opposite side.

A third – male this time – surprised him from behind. 'We're hoping to get this done without much trouble at all, *Vince*.'

'Huh?' Vince spun around, coming face-to-face with a male fox. The two vixens closed in from his left and right. 'How do you know—'

The male bared his teeth and lunged but Vince leapt sideways, paws landing on the damp grass. He turned to run but one of the females cut him off, her back arched, tail whipping back and forth. The other two moved in, backing him into a tree.

He was bigger than all of them but it was three against one.

And I guess a civil conversation is out of the question... What won't they be expecting?

They crept closer, ears up, snouts aimed like arrows. He

retreated, the space between him and the tree shrank with every step until the claws on his back feet scratched on the roots.

Yes.

But, wait. Not yet.

One of the vixens pounced, claws razoring towards his face; the other two went low, dagger-like teeth aimed at his forelegs and chest.

Vince jumped backwards, twisted in the air and sunk his claws into the rough tree. His front paw found a foothold in a knot of the bark and he pulled his back legs up towards his belly, bracing them against the wood. For a split second he hung from the trunk as the foxes below snapped their teeth on the empty space his body had occupied moments before. Uncoiling like a snake, he pushed off with all four legs, sailing over their heads and landing behind them. A burst of pain erupted across his sore leg as the foxes snarled, already half turned towards him.

'Get him!' one of them shouted as Vince sprinted away across the grass. Adrenaline coursed through him, blocking the pain from his leg, as he weaved through the trees. The foxes' threatening barks thundered over him. They were on his tail and the park was unfamiliar to him. They had the edge.

A path appeared under his feet and he tore down it. In the corner of his eye he saw a pointed spire stretching to the clouds and a brief flash of gold, then it was gone again. He ran on. The park was unending, with nowhere to hide. Behind him, more claws than he could count drummed on the hard ground, but they were no longer as close. The foxes might have known every inch of the park but Vince was quicker. His legs were a little longer, his lungs a little bigger, his body a little fitter. Not by much, but enough. The lead vixen was falling behind, panting as she galloped, the others to her rear doing the same.

The path curved to the left and he followed it, drawing on every ounce of his chicken-fuelled energy. Littering the grass, countless holes punctured the earth: the tell-tale signs of a rabbit warren. His panicked brain briefly considered diving into one but quickly dismissed the idea. No rabbit was stupid enough to dig a burrow large enough for a fox to squeeze into.

His breathing grew shallow and his leg screamed, stiffening every few strides. He couldn't let it ruin his pace. The foxes barked again but Vince saved his breath. He could shake them off. He just had to keep going.

'He's too fast!' one of the rear foxes yelled.

'He's gotta get tired some time!' the lead female replied.

Not before you.

Vince focused on his burning lungs, counting in his head, timing his breaths to his footfalls. Blood poured from his leg wound as his heart pumped double-time, but he ignored it. On his left, a red-brick building sat behind a tall, sculptural structure formed of large hollow blocks. It would have been the perfect hiding place if it were some other animal chasing him, but the foxes would smell him wherever he hid.

The strange sculpture-building disappeared behind him. The foxes were slowing – four or five leaps behind him now – their barks ceased as they panted deep, rasping mouthfuls of air. He was flagging too. Lungs on fire, his leg was giving up, turning his steady stride into a jerking lollop. Suddenly, a fresh scent filled his nostrils.

If that's what I think it is…

Wincing from the pain, he forced his leg back into formation and sucked up the last drop of his energy reserves. His feet pounded the rough ground, driving him forward. The gap between him and his pursuers lengthened, inch by inch. Up ahead, a large overhanging tree obscured the way. His nose told him to carry on, the rest of his body obeyed and the leaves sailed over his head. Then the path ended.

A hard-left turn back into the centre of the park or a gate through to a road on the right? He took the latter, skidding on the wet concrete as he altered direction and bounded over the metal spikes. The surprise lost him a second and the foxes gained some ground, but the smell gave him hope. It was stronger now.

Just as Laurie said.

Water.

Lots of it. The grass and trees fell away, revealing the dark expanse of a lake, stretching unbroken to his left and right. The road transformed into a bridge, a flat stone handrail on each side held aloft by a long line of stout pillars. Through the gaps, Vince snatched glimpses of the green-brown algae carpeting the lake's gently rippling surface. Along the water's edge, a path tunnelled at right angles through the first arch of the bridge. There was no way to reach it directly without a leg-breaking jump or back-tracking into the park, where the path had split off. The lake was his only chance.

Now halfway across the bridge, Vince focused on the water and the thick, stagnant algae blooms. He was loath to become acquainted with it and he hadn't been expecting such a long drop, but it was the only way he could potentially lose them. Of course, they might simply follow him and tear him apart in the water but, if they were like most foxes, unless there was a guaranteed meal they wouldn't waste their energy. That said, they had just chased him almost a mile across a park for no apparent reason, so Vince was less than confident in his own half-formed plan.

Slowing down so he didn't slip, he leapt onto the handrail and looked over his shoulder. His assailants had already hurdled the gate and were about to reach the bridge, their jaws wide, saliva dangling from their lolling pink tongues. They looked exhausted but far from defeated. Whatever their reason for wanting him dead, it must have been a good one.

'Get him! He's… going… to…' the lead fox yelled through gasps of air. They upped their pace for a final sprint, three sets of gleaming teeth bared.

Vince took a deep breath, closed his eyes and jumped.

Laurie scrabbled at the tangled foliage and thrust her snout towards the damp earth beneath. The rain had washed away any scents she might have picked up but there was no doubt birds had been there. They'd trampled a path through the weeds, which ended suddenly near the fence. Laurie investigated, nosing through the broken stems and flattened leaves, until she found it. A feather. Black, with the faintest shimmering hint of electric blue, a wedge of white carved across one side. From the wing of a magpie.

Laurie searched for more, for blood, for anything else, but the single feather was the only hint of Rita. Had she got away or been taken by the water birds and killed somewhere else? Laurie had no way of knowing without asking more animals for information but now wasn't the time. The ruckus over by the water was reaching its climax, the swan's panicked honks now almost drowned out by the crowd's wild exhortations that he should drown. Just because those goslings were friendly didn't mean everyone else was… yet. She was still an outsider, after all. If Rita was alive – and had half a brain – she would have got out of there at the earliest opportunity. Laurie could come back later and ask around, when things had died down a bit.

She found another gap in the fence and squeezed through, then started to make her way home. As she strode along the dirt track, a noise from her left caught her attention. She stopped dead and listened.

'Aaauuuuuck!' The feeble wail came from the long grass. Laurie's head whipped around and she spotted the dark shape instantly. It moaned again.

'Hello?' Laurie ran to it. Sprawled in the grass, with one wing tucked up against her white belly and the other splayed out to her side, it was unmistakably a magpie. All over, her feathers were ruffled and torn. 'Rita?'

The bird slowly opened one eye and let out a short, rasping breath, before murmuring, 'Vi… Vin…'

'Vince is fine, don't worry. I'm going to help you, don't move.' Laurie scooped Rita up in her jaws and clutched her as gently as possible, her pointed teeth resting on the bird's soft back. Rita's long green tail swung forlornly as Laurie began to jog.

Laurie didn't know if she could save Rita but if anyone would know what to do, Socks would. It was a long way to carry her, but she couldn't leave Vince's friend injured and alone.

So Laurie ran, careful not to bite down on her passenger, through the allotments and across the green bridge. Several times Laurie stopped to set Rita down for a few blinks, readjusting her grip and easing her aching jaw muscles. Rita held on. Her shallow breaths barely stirred her chest and, when faint moans escaped her beak every now and then, Laurie wondered if the pain might be too much, but the bird was stronger than she looked.

Eventually, they made it to the end of the street where Socks's primary home was situated. He wasn't anywhere to be seen, so Laurie placed Rita on the pavement between her front paws and yowled at the top of her lungs.

'SOCKS! SO-OOOOOOOCKS!'

Moments later he appeared, a crispy lump of chicken clasped tightly in his mouth. He dropped it as he saw Rita. 'Eh up, what's all this, then?'

'This is Rita, Vince's friend. She's hurt. We need to help her, but I don't know—'

'Bring her this way. Quick!' Socks spun around and ran towards the house, his stout legs a blur beneath him. Laurie lifted Rita again and followed, hurrying up the garden path to the front door, where Socks waited. 'Put her down on the step, then go and hide,' he said.

Laurie did as Socks instructed, ducking behind the bin at the end of the garden. Socks began to mew and scratch at the door. Peering around the bin, Laurie kept her eyes on Rita. The magpie's life was in Socks's paws now and, judging by his attempts to get someone to open the door, she suspected it would soon be in a pair of human hands, too.

It was risky. The humans could just leave her on the step to die. Or finish her off. But it was their only option; animals weren't equipped – or predisposed – to save one another's lives unless they were related. To help, sure, if there was no predator–prey issue but a half-dead bird to Laurie usually meant a nice, fresher-than-usual dinner.

Socks's whining had grown unbearably loud. Finally, Laurie heard the sound of footsteps and the half-moon window above the door flickered from black nothingness to the orange glow of a bulb. The door opened to reveal a man, his legs bare, covered neck to knees in a fluffy, blue material, with another strip of fabric pulling it tight at his waist. The fur sprouting from his head and his chin was light brown flecked with grey but it was much sparser on his lower legs and feet.

He yelled, 'Socks! What the hell are you doing? It's three in the bloody morning! What have you got there? Oh, Jesus Christ.' He crouched down and inspected Rita, then looked at Socks, who had retreated to the path. 'Was this you? Bad cat.'

He nudged Rita with the back of his hand and she responded with a brief jerk and the quietest of caws. He smiled, took a deep breath, then exhaled with a puff of his mostly furless cheeks. 'Why do you do this to me, Socks?'

He cupped his long fingers underneath Rita's body, then lifted her, cradling her to his chest. He stepped back into the house then smiled again as he looked at Socks. 'You coming inside, you bird-bothering bugger?' Socks bounded up the steps, turning to wink at Laurie before slinking through the man's legs and into the warm hall-way. The man turned away, whisking Rita from Laurie's view, then pushed the door closed with his heel.

Laurie stared at the door for a while, knowing full well it was futile. All she could do now was wait.

7

The freezing water hit Vince like a brick wall. The impact forced the air from his lungs and slimy weeds enveloped his body. Water filled his nostrils, burning the back of his throat, but he fought the urge to take a breath and held his head under. All four legs whirling, he swivelled in the water and began to pull himself towards the arch of the bridge. Algae had wrapped around his legs, shackling him to the spot, but he kicked and thrashed, loosening it just enough to get away. Heading for the shadow of the arch, he swam until his empty lungs could take no more. He pushed his snout to the surface and gulped a mouthful of air. His eyes followed and blinked away the droplets, then his stomach lurched. He hadn't reached shelter. The foxes' eyes flashed through the darkness above him, peering down from the balustrade.

'We should go back,' the male fox said. 'He's gonna swim to the path down there.'

'There's no time! Blake, jump in and get him!' The lead female jabbed the male with her nose.

'Me? Why not you?' Blake replied.

'Because I'm older and I'm telling you to.'

'You're a *minute* older, Bonnie, and you can't tell me what to do.'

Finally, Vince reached the dark cavern of the bridge's arch. They could no longer see him, but stopping for a rest was not an option. The path was waiting, and the foxes wouldn't argue for long.

'Come on, Blake, get over the other side – he's getting away! If we don't get our den in Richmond Park because of you, I'll tear *your* head off instead,' the other female said.

A den in Richmond Park?

'Alright, Bailey, fine. Just let me catch my—'

'No! NOW!' Bonnie growled. She must have bitten Blake, because he yelped and barked in retaliation. Vince took his chance, pedalling his legs, snout pointed towards the path. The gnashing of teeth from above echoed through the arch as he ploughed through the water.

'He's there!' Bailey yelled through the noise of the scuffle.

'Scat! Quick…' Bonnie said.

'Wha— No! NO! AAARRROOOOWL!' Blake smacked into the water behind Vince, sending a shower of droplets cascading over his face. A surge of water followed, rolling over the back of Vince's head and into his ears and eyes. He spluttered and his legs lost momentum but the expanding waves from the fox's impact propelled him in the direction of the path.

Blake surfaced, coughing and gasping for air. 'You *runts!*'

'What are you waiting for? Get him!' his sisters shouted from the bridge.

Vince reached the edge, slapped his wet paws onto the path and hauled himself out of the water. After a quick, instinctive shake of his sopping fur, he began to run. His pelt bristled in the cold air but, combined with the icy water, it helped numb his leg wound.

Vince wasn't a keen swimmer – even less so now, after the wetlands – but his penchant for frogs meant he'd taken his share of dips in the Richmond Park ponds. In contrast, Blake splashed wildly in the water, as if his paws were the only part of him that had ever been submerged before.

After tonight, I'm never going near the water again.

'You useless mongrel! Quick, let's get on the path. We can catch him up.' Bonnie's voice faded as Vince upped his pace and sprinted away.

Rita woke up in darkness. The ceiling and walls were low and close. A quick peck told her they were made of thick cardboard. It was warm, though. Toasty, in fact. The air outside was still, so she concluded that she must be inside a human's house. In the corner of the box was a tiny dish of seeds and another of water. Her belly was flat against a carpet of spongy material which, she decided then and there, if she ever got the chance to build another nest, she would definitely try to procure from somewhere.

Whoever had put her in the box obviously didn't mean her any harm. She'd been around long enough to know that if a human wanted a bird dead, they shot it. Over and done with before they even realised, assuming they were a good aim. No, she was safe, wherever she was.

She moved to sit up and winced as her muscles protested but managed to get onto her feet. Good. Sore, but not broken. She stretched her wings tentatively and pain ripped through her left side, from shoulder to stomach.

'Ack!' she croaked falteringly, sinking back down into the soft material.

Then someone called her name. 'Rita?' The voice was faint. She would have put it down to her imagination if it hadn't called again. 'Rita?'

'Hello?' she shouted, her voice dulled by the thick cardboard.

'You're alive!' The voice was louder this time, but still muffled. Rita suspected something else was in between her and the creature.

'I am! Who are you and how do you know my name?'

'I'm Socks, Official Feline Administrator of the Hammersmith area. It is my duty to help any animal who requires assistance within my jurisdiction.' After the introduction, he explained his encounter with Vince, and how Laurie had found her.

'Vince got out of the wetlands? That's amazing! I can't wait to see him again!' Rita's excitement about Vince had eclipsed any thoughts about her own situation, but she paused for a moment to reflect, her chattering echoless in the stale air. She continued, 'Feline Administrator? So, you're a cat... Am I in your human's house?'

'Aye. I took a chance on him looking after you. He's a nice guy, loves animals. Once you're fit and well, it shouldn't be too hard to find Vince. He was on his way to Hyde Park. Although that owl may have given him new directions, so—'

'An owl?' said Rita.

'Yes. Barn variety. Female. Very odd to see a bird like that around here, to be honest. Not particularly social, but seemed nice enough. She said she was from a park.'

Rita questioned Socks about the owl, but he didn't know much else. She might just have been feeling extra wary after the wetlands, but something felt wrong.

'Unusual markings, though,' Socks added. 'Very dark—'

'—heart around her face?'

'Yes! How did you know?'

'It's Kara.'

Why would she come looking for Vince? She doesn't care about him... But she obviously didn't want Socks to know... Unless someone else sent her? Sophie? She wouldn't trust Kara, surely? Maybe Edward? But why? And why so secretive?

Rita hopped frantically. 'Something's not right. I don't know what, but if it involves Kara then it can't be good. We have to find Vince.'

'Right, I'll—' Socks was cut off by footsteps above them. 'He's awake.'

'Can you get me out of here?'

'Shouldn't you rest? You looked pretty banged-up...'

The footsteps grew louder.

'I can walk. I'll be fine. Or you can carry me. I need to see Vince.'

'Alright, if—'

'Socks! Stop winding up the bird! If you can't be quiet then you're going outside,' the human said from the other side of the door.

Rita heard the scraping of Socks's claws on the wood, then a pitiful mew. The man's voice was stern. 'No! Birds are not for playing with! You're scaring the poor little fella.'

Fella? Hmph.

The door opened and, with a click, pinpricks of light appeared all around her from tiny holes pierced in the cardboard. Through them she saw the outline of the man moving across the room, a large, black cat in his arms.

'Scraaaaaack! No!' She knew screaming wouldn't help, but she couldn't do nothing.

The man moved his face close to the box. 'Shhhh… It's okay, little bird, the scary cat is going away now…'

'Put me down, stupid human! I don't want to hurt her!' Socks must have lashed out and wriggled from his grip, because the man screamed and sucked air through his teeth.

'Ow! Get back here you little—'

Socks leapt from the floor, his paws landing softly next to Rita's box. His silhouette moved across the pinholes until he was behind her. 'There's something on the top holding it shut. Get ready!' said Socks. He pushed and the box slid across the counter.

Rita wobbled and water spilled from the dish, soaking into the bedding. 'It's moving! Keep going!' she called.

'No you don't!' The man leaned over the box, briefly blocking out what little light could make it through, and suddenly it ceased to move. Socks's shadow was gone.

'It's nearly there. Push, Rita!' Socks wailed from the man's arms.

Rita used all the strength in her legs to propel herself into the side of the box. Her head made contact with the cardboard and she fell backwards, dazed from the impact.

'That's it! Once more!' Socks yelled, further away now.

'Shush, Socks! You're scaring the poor thing. Out you go.'

A door opened and thin blasts of cold air rushed through the holes, ruffling Rita's feathers.

She threw herself against the box once more. It fell. The bottom became the wall as it revolved in the air. The water dish and now-sodden blanket tumbled around her, coming to an abrupt stop as the whole thing hit the smooth, hard floor. Whatever was on top of the box smashed and the folded flaps that formed the roof loosened, a sliver of light beaming through the corner as they parted.

'Shit!' The man rushed over. The air was still cold, which meant the door was still open. Rita thrust her beak into the opening and pushed. Her head emerged and she scrabbled at the cardboard with her needle-like claws. Too smooth – she couldn't get enough purchase. Socks was keeping the door open, half in, half out, watching helplessly.

Kneeling, the man covered Rita's head with his smooth, pink hand and tried to push her back inside. She jabbed with her beak and a berry of blood erupted from his palm. He recoiled and fell sideways, steadying himself with his other hand.

Rita pushed and scraped again. One toe punctured the cardboard. It was enough. Shoulders, chest, wings... She screamed as she dragged her injured wing through the narrow gap, then tumbled onto the floor. The man made for the door, but on his knees he was slow and awkward. Rita found her feet and hopped across the tiles, ducking underneath Socks's chest before collapsing onto the concrete path. Socks turned and grabbed her gently in his mouth, the door clicking shut behind them.

The path hugged the entire length of the lake, then curved around the end to follow it back in the opposite direction. Vince carried on straight. The foxes were no longer in earshot, but whether they'd given up or not he wasn't about to assume.

They'd let one of their secrets slip back on the bridge, though. They'd been promised a home in Richmond Park. And the only animal who could do that was Edward. He must have sent someone to follow him. Vince hadn't noticed anyone, but a bird would have been near impossible to spot, if it was sneaky enough.

But why would Edward want me dead?

Whatever the reason, he could dwell on it later. His fur was still damp and the pain had crept back into his leg, forcing him to slow down as he crossed the grass, but the edge of the park was in sight. Beyond the boundary, the maze of roads and densely packed buildings was just as unfamiliar to him, but they promised hiding places in abundance.

He looked over his shoulder. No sign of the foxes. They could be near, though. Still chasing, drawing closer every second as his pain and exhaustion threatened to overwhelm him. But he couldn't run anymore. He needed somewhere to hide. Preferably somewhere that didn't involve getting wet.

He jogged onwards, gritting his teeth as the searing ache spread to the rest of his limbs, and was soon greeted by two tall, silver gates. The bars were twisted into ornate shapes and looming between them, fashioned from the gleaming metal, were two animals he didn't quite recognise; a white horse with a long, golden pointed horn, and an oversized cat with a halo of fur. He passed through the gate, careful not to snag his tail on the thin coils of metal and wondered whether the creatures actually existed. He knew so little about the city; the thought that animals he'd never seen, or even heard of, could actually be real terrified him.

The roads were all but empty now, but there were so many and they intersected so haphazardly that Vince had no idea where to begin. Instead, he decided to trust his instincts and limped straight across towards the towering buildings, trying not to think about a huge horned mare appearing over the top and impaling him on its spike.

That would be just my luck.

Passing a multitude of multicoloured signs adorned with all manner of lines and markings, he reached the closest building and followed the path round to the back, into the grey labyrinth of the city. He turned left down a narrow street, then right onto another. Every few paces, streets branched off like twigs on a tree. All was quiet. There were few bins for rats to forage in and no trees for birds to nest in, which was fine by him. He retraced his footsteps a couple of times so his scent would take any pursuer in circles. If the foxes *were* following him, there was no way they'd find him now.

High above the street where Vince walked, Kara settled on a black metal rail in front of a window and cursed under her breath. First the geese, then the foxes. Useless.

Blake had eventually climbed out of the lake, shivering and whimpering, but the shock of the fall combined with his exhaustion meant he barely reached a jog before he collapsed in a soggy heap. His sisters were more determined but their detour back around to join the path drained what was left of their energy. They slowed to a walk, barked one last futile warning at Vince, then gave up.

They'd come close, but Vince was more cunning than Kara had realised. If she could have taken Vince down herself, she would have. Her speed and hunting instinct were second to none, but it was her size that was the problem. As much as she hated to admit it, she needed help.

Down below, Vince zig-zagged through the streets, sniffing at doors and pawing at piles of boxes. Hopefully he'd find somewhere to rest and stay put for a while. Enough time for her to find the foxes again.

Kara flitted silently from railing to windowsill to lamp post, eyes never leaving the wandering fox below. She yawned, wondering if she'd get back to Richmond Park before the next moon, when Vince finally finished his endless inspections and settled on a resting spot. Midway along a row of shops was a building-sized construction site, hidden from the pavement by tall wooden boards. Cut straight into the wood was the outline of a door, but a heavy chain and padlock kept it flush. Four large plastic bins sat in a row on the path in front. Vince jumped onto one and, from there, onto the edge of the narrow boards, then dropped onto a tall pile of rubble behind, then to the dirt floor below. He yelped as he landed, clearly in pain. After a few more sniffs and a quick lick of his wounded leg, he curled up against the neighbouring building wall behind a pile of wooden planks.

Kara waited a few moments in case he changed his mind but he quickly fell asleep. Perfect. She was bored of chasing him and wanted this over and done with. She flapped away and headed back to Hyde Park where the foxes were waiting, gathering their strength.

8

Socks carried Rita to the high street, where they found Laurie about to duck behind a loose board into the empty shop she sometimes called home. The vixen listened as Rita explained her suspicions about Kara.

'What can an owl do on her own, though?' Laurie said. 'She could just be keeping an eye on him.'

'Maybe, but Rita's worried, and I feel terrible… I'm supposed to be vigilant about suspicious goings-on around here. I can't believe I trusted her,' Socks said. 'We should check on him, just to be sure.'

'We both did. We weren't to know,' Laurie said. 'And it's your job to help strangers.'

'I know, but if anything happens to Vince now, I'll never forgive myself,' Socks said. 'You'll have to run on ahead, Laurie. Rita can't fly yet and I'll just slow you down. You can track him better anyway. We'll catch up with you.'

'Me? Oh, yeah, of course.' Laurie tried to settle her scattered thoughts. She'd assumed reuniting Rita and Vince would be simple. It hadn't occurred to her that she might have to help Vince out of trouble *again*. But Socks felt responsible, and she had to do whatever she could to ease his guilt. 'How will you find me?'

'Leave a trail in the grass. Scratch some marks?' Socks said. 'The human ones, you know, on the signs? The ones that point the way.'

'Yes, I think I know the ones. Okay, well, hopefully there's nothing to worry about anyway,' Laurie said.

Socks couldn't manage a smile. 'Mmm, hopefully.'

'Please find him, Laurie,' Rita said.

Laurie nodded, then turned away and began to run.

'Good luck!' Socks called after her. 'We'll be right behind you.'

Laurie pointed her ears forward and tore along the high

street towards the junction, before heading along the road she'd directed Vince down only hours ago. How had she become embroiled in this fox's drama so quickly? A good deed here and there, sure, but this was above and beyond anything she'd helped Socks with before. Hopefully this was all just a misunderstanding and they could get back to normal as soon as possible.

The rain had formed deep puddles in the pavements, soaking her paws as she galloped through them. The sunrise was only an hour away and cars were creeping back onto the roads. Tinny chirps from the keenest of the morning birds rang like alarms from the trees and bushes. Laurie ignored all of it. She ran as fast as she could, eager to put Socks's and Rita's minds at rest, until she reached the outer fence of Hyde Park.

She slipped through the railings and crept along the path, ears twitching at each leaf-rustle and twig-snap. Every few paces she stopped to scrape the human sign into the dirt, hoping Socks would remember what the angular lines meant. She cocked her head as she finished one of them. It made sense, sort of. Not like the long strings of symbols they used, which were incomprehensible.

She wanted to shout for Vince, but stopped herself. The owl was obviously a good deal smarter than the geese, so if she was spotted, talking her way out of it might not be an option this time. Padding through the park, she did her best to look inconspicuous. Then something caught her nose. Blood. She lowered her snout to the ground and sniffed at a dark wet patch of it, scouring the path for a trail. The scent was muddled.

Foxes.

A couple more blood droplets led her further, but seemed to stop.

That's good...

... isn't it?

She followed the smell past a statue and then north, towards the bridge over the Serpentine. He'd come this way, she was sure of it, but so had these other foxes. Were they working for the owl, or just looking for a fight?

Eventually, she reached the bridge, where, halfway across, the scents disappeared. She slowly turned, sniffed the handrails on either side, then peered over the edge into the water. She didn't know what she expected to see – Vince's bloated corpse, perhaps – but breathed a sigh of relief when only her distant, shimmering reflection stared back at her from between the clumps of algae.

She walked back the way she'd come, ears and nose primed for the next clue, when a distant murmur echoed across the expanse of grass to her left. She stopped dead and turned her ears towards the noise. The muttering continued, then a sharp laugh burst through the still air, making her jump.

Foxes.

A path snaked its way across to the voices, but enough trees lined it so that she could sneak up undetected. Animals could come and go as they pleased here, so her scent wouldn't be suspicious if she kept hidden. She scratched another pointed arrow-mark into the dirt and skulked through the shadows, the laughter growing louder.

'… And your face when you were trying to swim… So ridiculous!' a vixen said.

'Terrified!' another female chuckled. 'Like one of those little Chihuahuas!'

'Shut up, both of you!' a male fox whined. 'And if you push me in again, I'll tear both your tails off.'

'Ha, sure you will,' the first female said.

Laurie stopped and lowered her belly to the ground, keeping her breathing light, just in case.

'Anyway, thanks to you we won't get our fancy den in Richmond Park,' the female continued.

'You heard the owl. She's going to find Vince and come back,' the male said.

'Yeah, she says that, but I bet she's gone and found someone else to do the job. Someone who isn't a bug-eyed human-dog.'

Richmond Park… The owl… The job… Bingo! And Vince is okay. Or not dead, at least.

The feeling of relief surprised her but she pushed it to the back of her mind. Now, she just had to wait for Kara to get back, find out where Vince was, then beat the foxes to him. As long as Kara *did* come back. If she didn't, then Laurie might have to employ some more of her conversational skills on the foxes.

Closer now, she could just about see them lounging on the edge of the human-built circular river. They lapped lazily at the bubbling water as it flowed around the loop. The triplets. She'd seen them hanging around once or twice before on previous visits but had never spoken to them. They were scrawny and immature, more concerned about tussling with one another and being noisy than anything else, but the owl's offer was obviously too good to resist.

Laurie settled down under the nearest bushes and watched them for a few moments, then, like a ghoulish apparition, the owl appeared in the distance. She swooped down to a spindly sapling nearby and called to the foxes. They ran over, whispering excitedly to each other.

'I've found him. I'll take you there now and we can have this done before sunrise,' Kara said.

'Can't we wait until tomorrow? I'm beyond tired,' Blake said through a yawn.

'Do it now or the deal's off,' Kara snapped.

'Don't listen to him. We'll do it,' Bonnie said, shooting her brother a stern look.

'Right, follow me then.' Kara flapped away without another word.

Damn.

The owl had given no clue to Vince's whereabouts. She wouldn't be able to beat them there.

Laurie waited until they were suitably far away before sneaking after them, darting from tree to tree to stay as concealed as possible, leaving hastily scraped markings in the grass as she went. The owl led them all the way out of the park, through the tall silver gate and across the wide road. Laurie hung back as they crossed, then dashed to a patch of grass that separated the two directions of traffic as they disappeared behind the buildings on the other side. She marked another arrow, then looked back at the gates. Would Socks know to cross? She couldn't worry about that, though. She had to get to Vince.

She checked for cars, then negotiated the rest of the road before following the foxes' route into the backstreets. They were already out of sight, hidden among the multitude of crisscrossing thoroughfares, but she dropped her snout to the ground and quickly found their scent trail. The three of them together would be more than enough for Socks to sniff out too, if her directions were good enough to get him there.

Laurie scurried through the narrow roads, ducking behind bins and buildings when she got too close for comfort. Eventually Kara settled on the edge of a tall wooden board that concealed what Laurie assumed to be a building site. Laurie remained at the end of the street, peering around the corner.

'He's in there, sleeping behind the pile of wood,' Kara said, her voice low.

'Right, that means be *quiet*.' Bailey prodded Blake with a paw.

'Get on with it. The sun's nearly up, I want to get back to my roost,' Kara whispered sharply.

Laurie pictured Vince curled up inside, worn out from the previous ambush, the three foxes attacking him unawares. He had no chance this time.

The foxes jumped onto the bins and then, one by one, onto the edge of the board, before disappearing behind it. Kara rotated her head halfway to watch them below.

Laurie bolted from her position and tore down the street. 'VINCE!' She bounded onto the bins and straight over the hoarding. She landed hard and skidded across the sandy dirt. 'VINCE!'

The foxes – almost at Vince's sleeping spot – turned to see what had caused the noise. Their faces grimaced with confusion as they saw Laurie pulling herself to her feet.

'Who are *you?*' Bonnie shouted.

'Never mind her, just kill Vince!' Kara screeched, flapping on her perch.

Laurie howled. 'Raooowl! Vince! Wake up! If you're there, wake up! RUN!' The foxes looked up at the frantic owl, then at Laurie, then faced the wood pile. Blake was closest to the stack and poised to dive behind it when Vince's head appeared from the darkness.

'*Laurie?*' He looked around, blinking as he emerged from his hiding place.

'Run!' Laurie yelled.

Before Vince could move, Blake arched his back and snarled, his lips curling away from his teeth. Vince did the same, looming over the smaller fox, fur bristling. In an instant, they each reared back on their hind legs, jaws wide, and pushed their paws into the other's chest.

Laurie rushed towards them but Bailey intercepted, gekkering loudly. She lunged at Laurie's neck. Laurie twisted away, stumbling, then sprang back. The pair of vixens grappled with each other as Bonnie crept around to the side of Vince and her brother. Vince shoved Blake hard and he hit the ground, rolling onto his back in the dirt. Bonnie pounced before Vince could regain his balance and bit down viciously on the fleshy scruff of his neck.

Vince yelped. Laurie wrenched herself from Bailey's grip and dashed towards him but Bailey was quick, seizing Laurie's tail between her teeth, pulling her backwards. Blake got to his feet and joined Bonnie, swiping his claws across Vince's face before baring his incisors and driving them into his throat. Vince screamed.

'NO!' Laurie dug her claws into the dirt, dragging herself forward and Bailey along with her, but Vince was just out of reach. Blood dripped from his neck onto the pale, dusty ground. Bonnie clung on still, Vince too hampered by Blake to shake her from his back.

Laurie kicked back with her hind leg, landing a glancing blow to Bailey's face. As the vixen lost her grip, Laurie leapt forward, slamming her paws down on Bonnie's back and sinking her teeth into the side of the younger fox's scrawny neck. Bonnie howled and let go of Vince, Laurie's weight dragging her to the floor. Her mouth full of fur and flesh, Laurie kept hold. She couldn't break her neck like she would a rabbit's – Bonnie was too heavy – but if she could just hold on...

Now with one less assailant to deal with, Vince lashed out with his paw and struck Blake hard enough to dislodge him. Vince staggered backwards, gasping for air, but Blake reacted immediately. He aimed for Vince's neck again and grabbed it between his fangs. Vince's eyes bulged as Blake's teeth crushed his windpipe.

Bonnie gurgled between Laurie's jaws, lungs nearly empty, as Bailey approached from behind and clamped down on Laurie's tail again. She yanked Laurie backwards, but Laurie's jaws didn't budge from Bonnie's neck. Releasing her tail, Bailey tried Laurie's back leg instead. Teeth squealed against bone. Laurie squeezed her eyes shut and a growl of pain rumbled from the corners of her full mouth.

Bonnie's air finally ran out. Her eyes rolled back into their sockets and the dead weight of her body dragged Laurie to the ground as she collapsed. Laurie let go and Bonnie's head thumped into the dirt. The grip on Laurie's tail slackened as Bailey realised what had happened. Laurie quickly pulled her leg free.

'No! What have you done?!' Bailey shoved Laurie aside and nuzzled her sister's lifeless body. The male released Vince's throat and rushed over to join her. Vince's legs buckled. He slumped onto his side into the dirt, breath rasping through his open mouth, his heaving chest wet with blood.

'Vince!' Laurie limped over as quickly as she could, sank to the floor next to him and nudged his head with hers. He whimpered as blood dribbled from four deep punctures on his neck; two on the side, two under his chin. She licked the wounds, desperately trying to stem the flow.

Behind her, Bailey wailed to her brother. 'Is she...?'

'I don't know... I...' Blake stuttered.

Laurie ignored them. If one fox had to die, fine. But not Vince. 'Come on, Vince, get up. Please.'

'Laur…' Vince's eyes closed.

'No, Vince! You are not allowed to die! I came all this way for you…' Laurie half shouted.

He said nothing. His breathing slowed.

'No! Wake up!' Again, Laurie frantically lapped at the blood seeping from his neck. 'Wake up!' she yelled into his ear. 'You can't die. Not now. WAKE UP!' She nuzzled him fiercely, a sob catching in her throat. 'I'm sorry I called you a poodle.' She sniffed and buried her head in his side. 'I'm the poodle. I'm so stupid. I told that *stinking* owl where you went. It's my fault. I'm so sorry.'

Laurie lifted her head and turned towards the hoarding. Kara was still there. She'd watched the whole scene unfold.

The sky was turning berry-pink as the sun stirred from its sleepy hideaway, but Jake didn't notice. The rats he'd consumed that night were threatening to make an appearance again and, as he walked, he swallowed hard to keep them down where they should be. Edward would be waiting by the pond for him and he still hadn't decided whether he should mention Alice's transgression.

Betraying his friends was one thing, but lying to Sophie was far worse. It ate him up inside, but he couldn't let her find out exactly what he'd agreed to. Her mood had improved instantly when she'd found out Edward was sending a message to Vince and it wasn't worth ruining that to ease his own guilt.

On top of everything, another question plagued his mind: what was Edward planning? Alice seemed to think he was agitated too. It could be nothing, but if there was any chance Edward was screwing him on their deal, Jake wanted to know about it.

Edward was awake and already chewing on his breakfast of nuts – gathered, no doubt, by some other lowly creature stupid enough to try to bargain with him. He looked up as Jake approached. 'You have an update for me?'

'Yes. But I want you to tell me something too,' Jake said.

Edward snorted. Steam clouded from his nostrils and dissipated into the cold morning air. 'I think you may have misunderstood our agreement. I send Vince a message, then you report any misdeeds to me. That's it.'

'I'm aware of our deal. I just get the feeling you're not telling me the whole truth, and I don't like being messed around.'

Edward smiled. 'The truth about what? Look, if you're going to listen to every bit of idle prattle you hear…'

'So, there's no *job*? Kara's just sending Vince a message… That's all, yes?'

'What else would she be doing?'

'I don't know, I—'

Edward moved towards Jake, chest puffed, and spoke slowly. 'Listen, fox, you are on very thin ice. Do you really want our relation-ship to sour? This arrangement is beneficial to both of us, remember, so just keep your head down and do your job, okay?'

Jake wanted to tell Edward that they had no relationship. That the deal was a one-off. That his lack of denial and thinly veiled threats only made him sound more guilty. But – terrified of what the deer might do to him and Sophie – he simply nod-ded. Pathetically.

'So,' Edward continued, twisting his neck to scratch his side with an antler. 'Anything to report?'

'Uh, yes… I…' Jake swallowed again. 'A cat. On the outskirts. He's offering human food in exchange for rats.'

Edward stopped scratching and glared at Jake. 'To whom?'

'Animals.'

'Don't get smart with me, vermin.' Edward lowered his head and aimed his antlers towards the fox. 'Who is it? Foxes? Which ones?'

'I don't—'

Edward lunged, jabbing with the hard spikes of his antlers. Jake leapt out of the way, a whisker's width from being impaled.

'WHO?' Edward roared.

'Alice!' Jake yelled, breathless, then whispered the name again, 'Alice.'

'Thank you.' Edward smiled. 'You can go now.'

Jake narrowed his eyes and thrashed his tail, a low growl rippling from his lips. Edward stared, his muscles taut under his short, glossy coat.

There was no point. Jake exhaled, then stepped back, dropping his tail between his legs. He turned and walked away. His ears twitched as Edward's deep laugh thundered through the air behind him.

The contents of Jake's stomach rose into his throat again.

This was bad. Very bad.

But his den awaited, Sophie curled up inside, ready to sleep the day away. Would she dream of Vince? She had loved him once. Jake didn't blame her for caring about him still. Her compassion was what he loved about her the most. But among the lies, the betrayal, the fear, another feeling – dormant until now – sparked into life.

Jealousy.

Even a thousand leaps away, Vince had Sophie's attention. Why was Jake doing all this? Because he loved Sophie and wanted to make her happy? Or because, deep down, he still wanted – needed – to prove to her that he was the better fox. But how could he? Vince had made the ultimate gesture, standing up to Edward, making his mark on the park – and Sophie – for ever, leaving Jake to pick up the pieces. And a right mess he was making of that.

Sophie had chosen Jake because he was sweet and generous and reliable, which Vince was not. But now he was just a coward and a traitor. A coward and a traitor who loved her more than anything in the world, but who didn't deserve her.

Vince may have been unreliable and stubborn, with the temper of a hungry crow, but he was not a coward, and he was definitely not a traitor.

'*You…*' Laurie spat the word at Kara.

Bailey moved her gaze from her sister's body to the owl. Tears streamed from her yellow eyes. 'She's dead. This is your fault. You didn't tell us he had a mate. That's a whole different situation. We would never have agreed...' She trailed off.

'You didn't ask. And what am I, your mother? It's not my fault if you can't handle yourselves. Anyway, looks like Vince is dead too, so the deal still stands. Look at it this way, there'll be more room for the two of you.'

'Screw you!' Bailey ran across the building site towards Kara, teeth bared. Kara arranged herself for take-off, crouching and stretching her long wings. Bailey jumped onto the pile of rubble as Kara flapped, her talons leaving the perch. The vixen pulled herself up onto the edge of the board, found her balance, then leapt out over the building site, paws outstretched towards the owl.

Kara flapped, gaining height above the other foxes, but Bailey clapped her paws together, catching Kara's tail feathers between them. Kara squawked as Bailey dragged her to the ground, landing awkwardly and skidding across the dirt. Bailey went to bite her but Kara lashed out with her talons, scraping long, red welts across Bailey's cheek. As Bailey recoiled, Kara pulled away with a furious beat of her wings, leaving the fox in the dust with nothing but three tail feathers.

Laurie filled with anger as Kara vanished over the buildings. The orange sky glowed through the empty stripe in her tail, but it gave her little solace as she turned back to face Vince's body, prone in the dirt. Behind her, blood oozed from the deep scratches on Bailey's cheek, but her expression was blank. She walked over to her brother and dead sister, slumping in the dirt next to them.

Laurie ignored them. She'd killed the vixen to defend Vince. He was just minding his own business, trying to get somewhere, and they'd attacked him – all three of them – for their own gain. They deserved everything they got. They remained in silence for a while until Laurie's ears picked up the shuffling of paws behind her. She quickly rose to her feet and turned around. Blake was marching towards her, teeth bared. 'Someone has to pay for this,' he growled.

'Blake, come on, no...' Bailey shouted from beside her sister's body.

'You want to kill me too? Bring it on,' Laurie snarled and snapped the air with her teeth. Another fight was the last thing she wanted, but if Blake thought she was just going to sit and let him rip her apart, he had another thing coming.

Blake stopped in his tracks, obviously not expecting her to retaliate. He shook his head and grunted.

'Stop it, Blake,' Bailey said. 'Killing her won't help.'

'Nope.' Laurie went back to Vince's side. 'No reward for killing me. You'll just have to make do with your fancy new home, I'm afraid.'

'We won't go there now,' Bailey said.

'Like I care where you go,' Laurie spat. 'Except out of my face.'

'Leave her alone,' Blake snapped. 'We didn't know—'

'Didn't know what? That killing an innocent fox three-against-one wouldn't be quite so easy for you?' Laurie said. 'You're only sorry because your sister is dead. If I hadn't turned up, you'd all be scampering off to Richmond Park now, happy as moles in holes.' The two foxes looked away. 'Exactly,' Laurie finished, before turning her attention back to Vince.

Laurie held her ear against Vince's chest. His heartbeat was barely discernible. She nuzzled him again but his head lolled, heavy and unresponsive. He smelled of pond water and grass, a scent so incongruous with their dusty surroundings that it made Laurie feel even worse.

'Come on, Vince. Help me out here. I don't know what to do!' She let out a pitiful howl. She couldn't leave him. The sun was already peeking over the horizon, which meant the humans would be arriving soon. Perhaps they could help him, like Socks's owner helped Rita. But he was a fox, not a bird. In his state, they'd more than likely just finish him off.

'Vince, you have to hang on,' she pleaded. 'You can get through this. Rita's alive, you know. She's coming to find you. You can still find your park together.'

A brief flicker of his eyelids, a twitch of his tail...

She held her breath.

He fell still.

9

The sky above the building site was aglow with lilac, pink and orange, the sun's early morning greeting burning the clouds away to wisps. Despite the approaching daylight, Laurie remained at Vince's side, babbling softly into his ear.

He was fading in and out of consciousness, but the mention of Rita had stirred him enough to give her hope. The rise and fall of his chest was almost imperceptible, but it was there. She had cleaned his wounds as best she could and the blood had stalled, crusts now beginning to form around the small perforations in his neck. A few blinks longer in Blake's grip and he would have suffocated. Like Bonnie. He'd lost a lot of blood, though, and the fight had drained the very last of his strength. But if she could just keep him from drifting away…

Bailey and Blake had gone. They'd sat with Bonnie for a while, quietly grieving together, before saying their final goodbyes and leaving her body where it lay. Humans buried their dead with a tall stone slab – creating the cemeteries that gave the animals some of their safest, quietest homes – but other animals had their own rituals. Rabbits prayed that their departed would go into the afterlife, an endless field of grass, to be cared for eternally by Frith, their sun god. Foxes, like many animals, had no afterlife or god – Mother Nature was not a god, but the earth itself – and believed only that the dead returned to the earth, to be reborn into the world as Mother Nature saw fit. Once Bonnie turned to dust, she could become grass or air, an acorn or frogspawn. That was why animals killed only to eat, or defend themselves or their family. Their ancestors were a part of everything around them.

Generations of stories didn't stop some from forgetting, or ignoring, that, though. Selfishness was a new trait, learned from humans who took what they wanted from nature without giving anything in return, and passed down as young grew up around the busy city, where cars, trains, traps and meaningless slaughter taught them that they had to do whatever it took to survive.

The triplets were perhaps the worst of the afflicted, as if a diseased blood coursed through their veins. The swan at the wetlands too, confused by the humans' artificial barrier, driven to destroy anything that threatened his sanctuary. Laurie was not immune, either. That was why she'd killed Frank. Not for nourishment, or safety, but to prove her strength to a stranger. A stranger she'd thought weak for protesting at the death of a harmless goose. A stranger who, she now realised, was stronger than her in every way.

That stranger was now beside her, taking what might be his final breaths, someone who, in the short time she'd known him, had shown nothing but compassion to the animals around him. Even those out to kill him.

Yet, he was the one suffering, not her.

She spoke to him as he floated just beyond consciousness, telling him of how she'd found Rita, how the geese had returned to the wetlands to bring Oswald's leadership to an end. She told him she'd met the otters and heard about his trial and his speech, and witnessed their joy at knowing he was alive. She recounted the trap in the allotments, embellishing the story with danger, exaggerating the geese's nasal honks, as though she were telling it to a pack of cubs before bedtime.

Finally, as he lay motionless in the dirt, she described their meeting in Hammersmith. Then, after giggling – despite everything – when remembering his bewilderment of poodles, she began to tell him more than the bare facts.

'I'm sorry, Vince. I didn't know what you'd been through, with the water birds and everything, but that's no excuse. I wanted to help you, but... I couldn't admit that I was being a stubborn bitch. I couldn't because I'm... Well, I'm awful, and...' The words caught in her throat. She sniffed, chest heaving. '... And I helped that owl too, and now... Oh, I'm so sorry, Vince. This is all my fault.' A solitary tear fell onto his bloodstained fur.

Suddenly, his front paw twitched.

Laurie jumped up. 'Vince!'

'Lau…' he breathed.

'Yes, Vince! Yes! Wake up! Come on, that's it!'

He opened his eyes and blinked as the pale sunlight hit his wide pupils. 'Laurie…' He coughed, then winced from the pain.

'It's okay, don't speak. Don't move. Just… Just don't die.'

'I… won't…'

'Mother Nature, you're okay! You're going to be okay!' Laurie danced beside him.

'Rita…?'

'She's fine. Well, she's hurt, but she's with Socks.'

'You…' Vince coughed.

'Me?'

'… Came to… find me.'

'Um, yeah.' She looked at her paws. 'But this was my fault. I told the owl where—'

Vince shushed her. She protested, but he silenced her with a sharp, 'Shut up.'

Laurie wasn't used to being told to be quiet, but she obeyed. If Vince asked her to pop to Oxford Street to ask a human for a fresh bag of fried chicken, she probably would. 'Can you get up? It's morning. The humans will probably arrive soon.'

'I… I don't…' He tried to stand, but fell back with a yelp as his body resisted.

'Okay, stay still. I'll figure something out.' She looked around at the building site. If she could move him to somewhere more hidden, they could wait it out for a night or two until he'd got some strength back. 'I'm going to drag you behind the wood pile. We can hide there until tonight, okay?'

'Uh huh.' Vince closed his eyes again and bared his teeth in pain.

'Stay with me, Vince. You've just got to power through, okay? Can you do that?'

Vince moved his head in the smallest of nods.

Laurie circled him and gently clenched the scruff of his neck in her teeth. She was about to pull when her ears pricked. Claws scraping on wood. She gently let go of Vince before searching for the source of the noise. Sitting on the edge of the hoarding, a bedraggled Rita clinging to his back, was Socks.

Socks cocked his head. 'What did we miss?'

'Vince!' Rita squawked and hopped from Socks's back, fluttering clumsily to the ground. Vince opened his eyes and managed a weak smile. He never imagined he'd be so glad to hear her shrill voice.

Her joy at seeing him shone from her tiny black eyes, eclipsing the slight grimace as she tucked her wing back. 'Vince! Are you okay?' Her face dropped when she saw the blood, and she scuttled towards him. 'Oh… Oh no! What's happened?'

'I'm… fine…' he murmured. 'I'm… happy to… see you.'

'Me too.' She stroked his paw gently with her beak and smiled. The feathers around her head were dishevelled and she held one wing awkwardly, a long black-and-white flight feather hanging loose. Tears split her shimmering green tail.

'Your wing…' Vince whispered.

'Oh, it's nothing a bit of preening won't fix. I'll tell you later.'

Socks jumped down from the boards and joined them. 'Who did this to him?'

Laurie nodded to Bonnie's body. 'Her and two others. They've gone, don't worry.'

'What about Kara?' Rita said.

'She made a deal with them. A home in your park in return for killing Vince.'

Rita paused, thinking. 'But, why?'

Laurie shrugged. 'I don't know, but right now we need to move Vince before the humans come. Over there.' Laurie pointed her paw.

'I think… I… Help me up…' Vince panted. His neck throbbed with pain he'd never thought possible, but he wanted to walk the few steps. Maybe it was his pride, but he didn't care.

Socks ran over and pushed his head under Vince's shoulder. Laurie did the same further down his back and together, under Rita's meticulous supervision, they lifted Vince to his feet. His back legs gave way almost immediately, but Laurie was quick to help him up again, hoisting him from under his belly with her head.

Slowly, the four of them made their way to the dark alcove behind the wood pile. It was a tight squeeze for the four animals, but they were just about hidden; Rita nestled on Vince's back, Laurie and Socks either side, keeping watch at both ends. There they all waited, resting, but a combination of the pain and Edward's unknown motives kept Vince awake for a while.

Why kill me when I've already left? Is he scared I might come back? But why? I'm no threat to him. Does he know something that I don't? About my grandparents' park?

Eventually, exhaustion caught up with him and dragged his eyes closed. Outside, the workmen arrived and the sun arced slowly over the city, burning down on the dusty, bloodstained ground.

Kara was exhausted, but her first port of call on arriving back at Richmond Park was Edward. Her job was done and she wanted her reward. She found him grazing in the cool shadow of the trees by the lake. Settling on a branch above, she shouted to him. 'Oi! Edward!'

Edward swallowed his mouthful of grass before looking up and replying. 'Ah, I was wondering where you'd got to. Everything went to plan, I hope?' He nodded to her patchy tail feathers.

'Course. Took a while to find him, but he's been dealt with. Oh, and make room for two more residents.'

'*Two?* I didn't say you could invite the whole of London.'

'Don't be dramatic. Two tiny foxes, that's all. Would have been three, but things got a bit... heated.' She explained about the foxes and the fight.

'Well, what's two more vermin in the cemetery, eh?' Edward laughed.

'So... my rabbits?'

'Yes, yes. Three times a week at the golf course, and one rabbit per moon, as agreed.' He bent down to nibble at the grass again.

'Didn't we say *two* rabbits per moon?' Kara cocked her round head.

Edward's head shot up. He stared straight at her. 'You know full well we did not.'

'Yeah, alright, worth a try.'

Edward sniffed. 'Don't be squawking about this to anyone, Kara. Be discreet. I can't have the warren on my back. You know what they're like when they're upset; thousands of the stupid, furry little bastards squeaking at me all night…'

'My beak is sealed.' Kara smiled.

'And Jake has been sticking his snout in,' Edward said. 'I doubt he'll be asking any more questions, but whatever you do, stay away from the foxes, okay? I don't need any more hassle.'

Things had been kicking off in her absence, it seemed. Not her problem. Her work for Edward was done, and any allegiance she had with him was over. Until the next time.

'You got it. Right, well, I'm off to bed. Smell ya later.' She flapped away, not waiting for a response, her beak watering at the thought of the tender rabbit – her first in seasons – she would taste that evening.

After a full day of ceaseless noise, the building site ground to halt. Confined in the stuffy space between the wall and the woodpile, Vince and Rita slept fitfully through the drilling and hammering, regaining their strength, with Laurie and Socks taking it in turns to snatch an hour here and there where they could. More importantly, the wood had been left where it was, leaving them concealed until the last human left, locking them inside with a twist of his jangling keys.

Vince opened his eyes and yawned, then grimaced as the movement pulled at the still-raw wounds on his throat.

'All clear, guys,' Laurie said, then looked at Vince. 'Do you think you can walk, or should we stay here a while longer?'

'I'll be okay.' Vince uncurled and the four of them made their way out into the open air. The sky was a deep red, the sun low behind the buildings. Socks stretched, backside in the air, and set to cleaning his paws as Rita ran her beak through her dishevelled feathers. Laurie kept her eyes on Vince as he hobbled across the dirt, testing his tender muscles. His wounds throbbed painfully as he straightened each limb in turn. 'I'm fine, see?' He smiled at her.

'You don't look fine,' Laurie said, frowning.

'Well, I don't want to hang around here.'

'You don't think Hyde Park was the right park?' Laurie said.

'No. I mean… I don't know, but I don't think so. It's surrounded by all these big buildings, and there's a long road running through it… I admit I only saw it briefly, but there weren't many trees. It didn't feel like much of a sanctuary.'

'Okay, well, I doubt I can convince you to rest, can I? So, let's just take it slow, yeah?'

'You're coming with us?' Vince plopped his rear end down in the dust and widened his eyes. Rita hopped over to his side.

'I… Uh…' Laurie looked at her paws for a second, then back at him. 'I just thought you might need some help. Finding your park… That's all. I'm sure Socks would help too, but he probably needs to get back…'

'That's very kind of you, Laurie,' Socks said. 'All this was my fault, after all. I would love to come along, but duty calls, I'm afraid. Laurie's the next best thing!'

Laurie dropped her head, hiding an embarrassed smile.

Vince might have been half unconscious at the time, but the things Laurie had said as he lay bleeding were slowly emerging from the fog in his brain. Did she actually care about him? Or was she just helping him for Socks's sake? Either way, he was glad she was tagging along. He'd seen a glimpse of her softer side, and was curious to know the extent of it.

'What do you think, Rita? Room for one more?' Vince said.

'Hmm, maybe. Does she mind me singing?' Rita replied.

'I don't know, let's ask her. Laurie, do you mind Rita's singing?'

Laurie pulled a puzzled face. 'Um… no?'

'Welcome to the gang!' Rita squawked.

Vince laughed. 'You might regret that.'

'Oh, it can't be that bad. And just so we're clear, I'm not saying I'll hang around at your park or anything. I just want to make sure you get there okay so Socks will stop feeling guilty.'

'Of course. Your empty shop and greasy human food are far too good,' Vince said sardonically.

Laurie smiled. 'Exactly.'

'If you two are finished with your attempts to appear coy, then I'll be getting back to my patch,' Socks said. 'Mother knows what kind of chaos my being away will have caused.'

Vince and Rita thanked Socks and said their goodbyes. Just before turning to leave, he faced Laurie. 'And you better come and visit, you hear?'

'I'll be back soon. Don't worry,' she replied.

'Aye, sure.' He winked, then turned and leapt gracefully onto the pile of rubble. 'Oh, I nearly forgot!' he called back to them. 'Any problems, ask for the nearest Official Feline Administrator – they'll be able to help you.'

Socks jumped onto the hoarding. His eyes flashed at them one last time before he dropped down onto the street behind, a chorus of goodbyes echoing in his wake.

'Right, let's get going,' Vince said as he followed Socks's pawsteps to the rubble pile. Getting over the tall wooden boards would be painful, but once he was back on the streets, he could take it easy. Especially now there were three of them.

He hopped up onto the pile, squeezing his eyes shut and holding in a yowl as pain erupted in his neck and side.

'Careful. Take it slow, yeah?' Laurie shouted.

The hoarding was next. He gathered his strength and jumped, grasping with his paws on the thin edge, then slid down to the street. Panting, he sat on the pavement and licked his wounds while he waited for the others. They weren't far behind. The hoarding wobbled behind him as Laurie launched herself from it, Rita clutching the fur on her back. She landed softly next to Vince.

'Right, which way?' Laurie said.

Vince looked to Rita, forgetting her injured wing.

'I can't fly yet. I'm sorry,' Rita said, then added, 'Later maybe. It already feels much better than it did.'

'Not to worry. We'll just head away from Hyde Park and ask directions as soon as we can,' Vince said.

Vince began to walk and Laurie sidled up next to him, Rita clinging tightly to her scruff with her thin black talons. Vince looked sideways at the vixen. Words rattled around his head. He wanted to tell her how grateful he was for her help. That he didn't blame her for what happened. That he didn't think she was awful. Not completely, anyway. But who knew how she would react? She'd only poured her heart out because she thought he was almost dead. He didn't want to embarrass her, especially with Rita listening over their shoulders.

He sighed and forced out the only words he could manage. 'Thank you.'

'You're welcome,' Laurie replied. She opened her mouth to add something, but Rita interrupted.

'It's so good to be back together, isn't it, Vince? I think I'll write a song to commemorate the occasion...' She belted out a few eardrum-destroying notes.

Laurie winced.

'Told you.' Vince smiled. 'You can always turn around and go back home.'

'Nah, I'm good.' Laurie smiled back.

10

Tall buildings flanked every street Vince, Laurie and Rita turned down. Without a bird's-eye view, they were lost. His instincts told him which way was north, but without a destination they would just be wandering aimlessly. Vince wasn't worried, though. All they needed was to find one animal who knew the area. And finding out that Edward didn't want him to reach his destination made him even more determined to do so.

Now, with the foxes gone and Kara no longer following his every move, his memories of Richmond Park, his den and Sophie, were fading away with them. Helped too – in no small part – by Laurie's return.

The three of them weaved through the city, in no particular direction but keeping Hyde Park firmly behind them. They stuck close to the buildings, remaining in the shadows and slinking behind bins and piles of cardboard boxes where they could. Vince's wounds nagged at him, and his pace was slower than normal, but he pushed through it as best he could. Humans gathered on corners and under awnings, drinks and phones in hands, but apart from the odd pointed finger and hastily snapped photograph, they made little effort to interfere.

As they walked, Laurie chuckled as Rita told her about Vince's encounter with the train and his subsequent tantrum.

'Stop exaggerating,' Vince said. 'I was a bit annoyed, that's all.'

Rita cackled from Laurie's back. 'You went off in a huff! You—'

'Shut *up*! Anyway, you seem to have perked up, Rita, why don't you test your wing?'

'You're just trying to get rid of me.'

'Yep.'

Rita puffed her chest feathers, but relented. Laurie stopped and lowered herself to the ground so Rita could disembark. She hopped onto the pavement and slowly stretched her wings.

'Hmm, not too bad. Bit of exercise might help.' She flapped ahead keeping low to the ground, landing every couple of leaps for few quick hops before fluttering further down an empty alleyway.

'Vince, can I ask you something?' Laurie said.

'Sure.'

'What if this park doesn't exist?'

'What do you mean?' Vince asked.

'What if it's gone? Or it's not the same as it was when your grandparents lived there? What if it *was* Hyde Park, but it's changed so much that it's not the safe, quiet place you're looking for anymore?'

'Then I'll find somewhere else. Somewhere better.'

'But what if there is nowhere better? What if Richmond Park is the best park in London, like everyone says it is?'

'Trust me, it's not.'

'You don't know that! Where have you been? The wetlands, Hyde Park... Were they better? You have to admit, Vince, it doesn't look likely, does it?'

'There has to be a better place, Laurie.'

'Why does there? This might be all there is.'

Vince stopped walking and stared into Laurie's eyes. 'Because I refuse to accept that the best we can hope for is living under another animal's rules, or fearing for our lives every day.'

Laurie blinked.

Vince continued. 'I will keep going until I find somewhere where I can live my life my own way, and if I don't find it, then I guess I'll be looking until I die.' Vince tore his eyes away from Laurie's and started to walk off in the direction Rita had hopped.

Laurie said nothing as she hurried after him, quickly returning to his side. They walked in silence for a few moments, watching Rita – now venturing much higher – flap clumsily from lamp post to lamp post up ahead.

After a while, Laurie took a deep breath. 'I've never lived like that,' she said.

'Huh?' Vince said.

'I never lived under anyone's rules, or feared for my life.'

They locked eyes. It hadn't occurred to him that freedom didn't automatically mean peace, quiet and open space. He'd dismissed her chaotic lifestyle, but maybe it had the potential to be everything he wanted? Laurie seemed happy enough.

Rita disappeared down another road, her loud and tuneless song fading as she explored balconies and window ledges.

Vince gazed up at the imposing buildings, then down at the dirty grey street.

No frogs here, that's for sure.

Laurie broke his train of thought. 'I suppose it's hard for you to understand. I was born in the city. I can't imagine living anywhere else,' she said.

'I do understand,' Vince said, then added absentmindedly, 'Where do you catch frogs?'

'Frogs?' Laurie replied.

'Uh, back at the allotments... You said you preferred frogs. Where do you find them?'

'Garden ponds. Human ones. There's a few about, if you know where to look. Why?'

Vince looked at his paws. 'Oh, I was just thinking about frogs. I used to catch them with... Uh, back home. I didn't realise you could get them out in the city.'

'Thinking about staying out here, then?' Laurie said.

'No. Maybe. Why? Do you want me to?' Vince replied.

'What? Why would *I* want you to?'

'I... Sorry, I just...'

'I mean, if you wanted—' Laurie began.

'SCRRAAAAACK!' Rita hopped towards them.

Thank Mother.

'What are you two chattering about?' Rita said. 'Never mind. I spoke to a very nice pigeon who says there's a little green square over the road. Come on!' Without waiting for a reply, she hopped a short way and turned back to face them. 'COME ON!'

'Well, at least she's feeling better,' Vince said.

Jake fidgeted in the dry leaves that lined the sleeping chamber of his den. He'd barely slept, running the conversations with Edward over and over in his head, contemplating what to do next. Conclusions were just out of reach, though, and every option seemed worse than the last.

Sophie had woken at dusk as usual and gone out to find breakfast. Jake wearily pulled himself to his feet and made his way through the tunnel, towards the dim light. A bit of hunting would take his mind off things. Maybe.

But hunting would have to wait. Across the cemetery, Sophie ran towards him. 'Jake!'

As he ran to meet her, the tear-stained fur around her eyes became apparent. 'Soph! What's wrong?'

Her voice was hoarse from exertion, but between gulps of air she managed to get the words out. 'Alice is gone.'

The words passed through him, sinking into his belly like a rock. 'What do you mean, "*gone*"?'

'Her den is smashed in. I've looked everywhere. There's some blood... Not much, but...' she sobbed.

'I... I don't understand...' Jake knew exactly what had happened, but the lies flowed from his mouth. Alice's death was his doing. The truth would destroy Sophie as well as him.

'It must have been because of the stuff with the cat... Edward must have found out somehow,' Sophie said.

'Sophie, you don't know that. It could have been an animal from outside... Another fox or a human's dog...' Jake said.

'Another fox? Are you serious? Her den is ruined. There are *hoof marks in the dirt*. It was the *deer*, Jake.'

'Okay, okay... Just... Calm down. Let me talk to Edward.'

'Don't tell me to calm down. My friend is dead,' Sophie snarled. 'If anyone's going to talk to Edward it's going to be me.'

'No!' The word slipped out before he could think. 'I... I just don't want you getting hurt. If it was Edward, he might think you're involved too. Please, Sophie. Let me talk to him. You're too upset right now. If you march over there and start accusing him, who knows what he'll do.'

Sophie narrowed her eyes at him and let out a long breath through her nostrils. 'Fine.'

'Thank you. I'll go first thing in the morning.'

'No, you'll go *now*,' Sophie snapped.

'He'll be asleep, Soph. It'll be better to wait until morning so he's in a better mood. You know what he's like.'

'Well, you do, apparently.' Sophie blinked back fresh tears. 'I'm going to find some food. Don't follow me.' She turned and padded away, quickly upping her pace to a sprint. Without a backward glance she disappeared into the gravestones.

Jake sank to the ground. Everything was spiralling out of control. Alice's blood was on his paws for the rest of his life and the lies would only continue. If he came clean now, Sophie would never speak to him again, and who knew what Edward might do. He could live with her hating him, though, if she was safe. But the only way to keep her safe now was to do what Edward wanted, and pray to Mother Nature that she didn't break any rules.

The square was set neatly into the surrounding buildings, a tiny haven circled by a ring of trees among the towering offices and busy roads. It was empty of humans, despite the many benches that offered them rest from their bipedal existences. As always, black railings ran around its periphery, a locked gate on each side. Night-time had transformed it into the animals' domain.

Rita raced ahead, flapping into a tree, while Vince and Laurie approached tentatively. There was no way they were risking another attack, especially with Vince still recovering. Muttering and squeaks of laughter emanated from within the small square's boundary. Vince relaxed slightly. Whoever was in there, they weren't foxes.

'Hello?' Rita squawked.

The laugher stopped and a small sing-song voice followed the silence. 'Hellooo?'

'Are you friendly?'

'Subtle, Rita,' Vince whispered.

'Friendly? Ha! That depends!' another voice said.

'On what?' Rita said.

'Whether *you* are,' the voice said.

'We are definitely friendly,' Rita said.

'Then so are we, darling. Come on in!'

Vince whispered to Laurie, 'What if it's a trap?'

'Nah. They sound rodenty. What are they going to do? Nibble us to death? Come on.' Laurie headed for the railings.

'Maybe. If there's a hundred of them…' Vince mumbled under his breath, then followed obediently.

Laurie squeezed through the bars, made her way past the trees and up a small flight of steps. She sniffed her way over to the animals as Rita sailed down to join her. Vince wasn't far behind and, although cautious of the strangers, was keen to appear in control of the situation. He arrived and sat down next to his friends as he took in the animals and his new surroundings.

He was surprised to find that, at the centre, hidden slightly by a low wall and the benches, the square was not grassy but paved. Large sections were filled with dirt and flowers, with strange stone carvings of half-finished human bodies dotted between. Vince could imagine the humans enjoying it, but he wasn't sure if he was.

Three brown rats were sitting on one of the benches, an array of leftover food strewn across the wooden slats and the floor beneath. Prey animals, usually, but this was their patch, and Vince was more interested in getting directions than a meal.

Vince lifted his chin and did his best to sound authoritative. 'Hello there. I'm Vince, and this is Rita and Laurie.'

As soon as the first rat spoke, though, he realised he could drop the pretence. 'Ooh, two foxes and a magpie! That's, like, totally new! I'm George, but you can call me G. This is Jonny and Ra-Ra.'

Ra-Ra? We're definitely a long way from Richmond Park now…

'Nice to meet you. Do you live around here?' Vince asked.

'Yeah, Soho's where we usually hang out. It's got the best snacks, y'know?' G gestured to the piles of crumbs around them.

'Yeah, like, we had *the best* burrito yesterday. What was it, Jonny? Pulled pork? That's right. Oh, the guacamole was a-maz-*ing*,' Ra-Ra said, her whiskers dancing as she spoke.

'I literally *died*, it was so good,' Jonny added, waving his tiny paws dramatically.

'You look remarkably healthy, considering…' Laurie said, and was met with blank stares. 'So… anyway, we're just passing through and wondered if you could give us directions? We're looking for a park.'

'A park, eh? Interesting. Never seen the appeal myself,' Jonny said. 'Not a whole lot going on, y'know? The last park I visited – just seeing a friend, of course – didn't even have a Pret.' He paused for a reaction.

Silence.

'A *Pret*,' he repeated.

'What's a Pret?' Rita asked.

The rats glanced at each other, mouths open.

'A place where humans get food,' Laurie said. 'There's one near the street where I live.'

'Oh, so you're a foodie yourself?' Ra-Ra said.

'I, er, eat food, yes,' Laurie said, confused.

'Ha! Well, sweetie, we all *eat* food, but do you *love* food?'

'I… I suppose I like food a… normal amount?' Laurie's words came out as a question, despite them not forming one.

'I see. Well, we are a bit more *into* food, you see. Yes, darlings! Food should be a joy, a delight, an *experience*,' Jonny said.

'I really like caterpillars,' Rita said, almost thinking out loud. 'I guess picking them off the bushes is kind of a joy.'

The rats' faces contorted in unison. '*Caterpillars?*' G said. 'We're talking about *gourmet* food. Flavours and textures to tantalise your taste buds, smells to rouse the nostrils, colours your eyes can feast on; a riot of pleasure for all the senses!'

'I mean, have you really never tasted balsamic caramelised onion hummus with sourdough pitta bread?' Ra-Ra said. '*Divine.*'

'I have no idea what any of those words mean,' Vince said.

'I usually just stick to chicken,' Laurie said.

'Ugh, not that awful fried stuff, I hope. So bad for you, sweetie. Do you have a sweet tooth? What about coconut, stem ginger and dark chocolate macaroons? Melt-in-the-mouth.'

'Gluten free, too,' Jonny chimed in.

'But… this is all leftovers, right? You get it all from bins?' Laurie said.

'Of course. We're rats,' G said.

Laurie shot the others a smirk.

'Judge all you like, sweetheart, we gotta get our kicks from somewhere.' Ra-Ra stuck her nose in the air. 'Old human food is the only thing we know is safe, so we might as well enjoy it. Every few steps there's poison or bait for a trap.'

Vince nodded. 'I was caught in one. I'd be dead if Laurie hadn't helped me.'

'Yeah, well, when rats go in, they don't come out,' G said. 'And that ain't even half of it. You think the humans hate *you*? Just yesterday we heard news of a friend… Eleven babies too… I mean, she shouldn't have made her nest in the pocket of an apron, but still… Oh, it's too dreadful to even think about.' G covered his eyes with his tiny paws.

Ra-Ra shuffled over and gave G a friendly pat on the shoulder.

'That's terrible, we're sorry,' Rita said. 'Couldn't you move, though? Away from the humans?'

G dropped his paws from his face and snorted. 'And give up this food? No way, blue jay.'

'Very well,' Vince said. 'Listen, we should get going. Can you give us directions to a park?'

'Sure thing, darling,' Jonny said. 'Nearest park is Hyde Park, thataway.' The rat pointed left, the way they'd come. 'Or north is Regent's Park. Just follow Regent Street all the way up. Clue's in the name.'

Vince's eyes followed Jonny's pink paw through the trees and could just about make out the gap between the tall buildings. He and Rita exchanged a smile.

G, seeing their faces light up, asked, 'The one you're looking for?'

'Maybe,' Vince said, before adding, 'Hopefully.'

'Wonderful! Glad we could help. Would you like to stick around? We were just about to have dessert... Pistachio and raspberry sponge cake. Although I'm not sure how much there will be to go around...' Ra-Ra said.

Vince politely declined, admitting that it would be wasted on them, and they said their goodbyes. The three rats waved as the group departed the square.

'They were...' Vince began.

'... Interesting,' Laurie finished.

'Rats of Soho, so *into* their food, hummus and cake, it tastes so good!' Rita sang.

'*Food* and *good* don't rhyme,' Vince said.

'Yes they do! Foo-*ood*, goo-*ood*.'

'Well, when you say them like that, then yeah,' Vince said.

'They totally rhyme, Rita. Don't listen to him.' Laurie gave her a friendly nudge with her paw.

'Thank you, Laurie. You know, I was worried about you coming along with us, but I think we'll get along just fine,' Rita said.

'I think so too.' Laurie flashed a grin at Vince. 'Hear that? She likes me better than you. Jealous?' Laurie stuck out her tongue.

'No,' Vince mumbled as the three of them emerged onto a bisecting street. Humans strode and staggered along the pavements, some slumped against the shop fronts. Yelling and singing rang through the stale evening air. He realised then, despite its size, just how much of a sanctuary from the hustle and bustle the square was. But it was not his park, so leaving it behind was the easiest decision he'd made so far.

Rita hopped ahead of Vince and Laurie, investigating every nook and cranny with her inquisitive beak. They turned up another narrow street, which was quieter, but not by much. Heading north, they walked quickly but clung to the edge, their bodies almost pressed up against the walls. They proceeded largely undisturbed, though, as the humans went about their evening revelry. Four legs being faster than two, they found that by the time the humans had spotted them and attempted to take a picture or – optimistically – bent down to pat them on the head, they were already long gone. Socks was right, it seemed; humans *did* like foxes. Most of them, anyway.

Up ahead, something caught Vince's eye. A sign hung above a doorway, black with white writing that he couldn't understand, but it was the picture that made him hurry towards it. Another cat – blood red this time – with long fur around its neck.

What are these things?

Laurie crept up beside him. 'What are you looking at?'

'Do you know what these weird cats mean?' Vince said, raising a paw towards the sign.

Laurie shrugged. 'They all have different ones, these types of buildings. Cats, horses, human heads with gold hats on… It's where the humans go to drink together. Like how animals go to a pond, I guess.'

Vince shook his head carefully, so as not to worsen his wound. 'I don't know… There was a big cat on the gate at Hyde Park, now this one. They both have that fur on the neck. That can't be a coincidence, can it?'

'Maybe not, but they're hardly going to be helpful to us, are they? Come on, let's get a move on. We've got a park to find.' She smiled at him, then added, 'And the sooner we find it, the sooner I can go home.'

Vince nodded and pushed his thoughts about the strange cats aside. She was probably right about them not being helpful.

They made it to the end of the street then turned left, as the rats had instructed. Regent Street was much wider. Cars and tall, red buses tore down the centre, like a pulsing vein in the city's chest.

Rita had grown tired from her constant hopping, so she scrambled onto Laurie's back to rest her legs. Vince wasn't entirely convinced she wasn't simply enjoying having someone new to chatter to, but couldn't really blame her. He probably hadn't been the fun travelling companion she had been expecting.

From the vixen's back, Rita stared open-mouthed as they walked. On either side of the road, shop windows stretching almost to the sky reflected the fiery lights of the cars back onto them. Fake, faceless humans stood motionless behind the glass, their purpose unfathomable to the animals. Strung high across the road, colossal rectangular sheets, emblazoned with bright colours and human words, fluttered in the breeze from the traffic below.

Through the humming parade of cars, Rita pointed at a resplendent building, four enormous arched windows ran from edge to edge and glowed from inside with pristine orange light, like the dawn sun. Burning bright white within each arch was a simple depiction of a piece of fruit. Rita asked Laurie what it was all about, but she shook her head, replying that she had no idea, and that humans were just really, really weird.

It wasn't a long walk, and eventually they reached a huge crossroads, where traffic came to a standstill to let the humans pass. The intersecting road was equally fear-inducing in its size, humans crawling its length like ants in both directions. Vince shook it off. A busy street was nothing but a mild irritation after all he'd been through. Plus, there was not a train in sight.

The humans were clearly fascinated, though, as they waited among them on the pavement, too close for comfort. One particularly loud man reached out a smooth hand towards Laurie, who reacted with a swift, warning snap of her teeth, followed by a growl so menacing, even Vince recoiled a little. The man snatched back his hand and yelled, his friends laughing and dragging him away.

The lights above changed from green to red and the crowd jostled forward, but Vince and Laurie, with Rita in tow, darted in front and began to run, eager to leave the mass of humans behind. Halfway across, another swarm of humans marched towards them, heading for the opposite pavement. Vince and Laurie circled them, ignoring the turned heads and garbled shouts from their furless faces.

The foxes reached the other side and continued their dash towards quieter territory. Regent Street seemed never-ending, but at least this side of the crossroads was less popular. Onwards they walked, the humans petering out until the pavements were empty, with much of the noisy hum of the city behind them, and the odd car trundling along the road to their left.

Rita took the opportunity to fill the relative silence with her own voice. 'This is so great. *So* great. Isn't it, Vince? You, me and Laurie. The Famous Travelling Trio! Animals will tell stories about us one day, I bet. Maybe even humans!'

'We're hardly famous, Rita,' Vince said.

'Oh, I don't know...' Laurie said. 'Everyone in the wetlands seems to know you.' Vince turned to her, about to speak, but she beat him to it. 'Listen, Vince, I know what they did to you... I'm sorry for—'

'It's okay. I heard some of what you said when I was unconscious. You know I don't blame you or Socks for any of this, right? You weren't to know who Kara was. And I don't think you're awful. At least, no more awful than me.'

'She's *definitely* not more awful than you,' Rita chirped from Laurie's back.

They all laughed. 'Anyway,' Vince said, 'let's forget about all that. Let's just concentrate on getting to Regent's Park.'

Laurie smiled, eyes twinkling under the street lights.

'Will you really not stay there with us, Laurie?' Rita asked sadly.

'I can't leave Socks,' Laurie replied.

'You two must be very close,' Vince said.

'We are. I owe him everything.'

'Would you stay with us otherwise?' Rita said.

'Rita!' Vince shot her a look.

'What? It's hypothetical.'

Laurie laughed. 'I don't know. Hypotheticals are pointless. Anyway, if you're so keen to hang out with me, why don't you come and live in Hammersmith?'

Rita looked at Vince. Vince turned back to the path ahead.

'Hypothetically, if we don't find my grandparents' park, then there's a possibility that I'll consider it.'

'Really?' Laurie stopped walking.

Vince stopped too, then turned to face her. 'It's a last resort, obviously, but...'

'Right. Well, let's hope it doesn't come to that, then. But, just so you know, if you're *forced* to live on the streets, I'd be happy to teach you the basics. How to stay safe and stuff, y'know?' Laurie said.

The more she talked about it, the more he came around to the idea. Laurie's company might make up for the shortage of frogs. It would be nice to hunt with another fox again. After Sophie left him, the pack in Richmond Park ignored him most of the time. Sophie was always the more popular one, and Vince's spats with Edward didn't help.

'But let's find your park first, eh?' Laurie added with a smile.

Kara's stomach grumbled as she scanned the grass below her tree hollow. The sun had set and several rabbits grazed in the distance but, closer, a small brown nose emerged from the warren entrance. It sniffed the air, then two tawny ears popped out, tall and alert.

'Perfect,' Kara said to herself.

The rabbit lolloped out onto the grass. Kara waited. Too close to the warren and it would dive straight back in. It lowered its head to nibble on the blades, ears turned outwards.

'Come on, come on,' Kara whispered.

Others had come above ground now, but they were scattered widely across the warren's multiple openings. The youngster was alone. It inched across the grass, cautious hops punctuated by brief upright surveillances. Eventually, it settled into feeding, ears laid flat against its soft, round body. Young, exposed and inexperienced; an easy catch.

Kara jumped, soaring silently towards the rabbit. She approached it from behind, where she would be spotted too late – if at all – for the rabbit to get away.

Stretching her legs and spreading her talons, she dived. She grasped the rabbit's back and it squealed in terror, thrashing with its small but powerful back legs. The other rabbits stood up, ears and noses alert. One thumped the ground with its hind leg and yelled, 'Danger!'

Flapping hard, Kara lifted the baby off the ground. Its squeaks echoed across the park and the rabbits on the ground fled, their white tails flashing like lightning as they vanished into the warren.

The rabbit kicked and struggled, but Kara's grip was deadly. She squeezed her prey, puncturing its neck with her claws, and the rabbit screamed out one last time before falling limp. She sailed back to her hollow and with one foot holding the rabbit steady, tore off a chunk with her beak. She closed her eyes as she gulped it down, savouring the taste of the rich meat.

Finding Vince had been gruelling, and had almost killed her, but she'd already forgotten the whole thing. The rabbits alone were worth the effort, but, forbidden from hunting them for countless seasons, the other owls would be sick with jealously if they found out she was entitled to one every moon. And even though she had to keep it to herself, knowing it made the prize even sweeter.

11

Rita hopped back from the junction she'd been exploring. 'It's up ahead! Come on, you two! Nearly there!'

They crossed the final road. Despite the pain, Vince raced ahead, twitching with nervous excitement. This could be the place he was looking for. A dense hedge bordered Regent's Park, which served its purpose keeping humans out when the gates were closed, but did little to stop the three animals.

Inside, the park looked no different from any of the others. The grass was short, trees were sparse and trimmed to form bubbles of leaves on top of largely branchless trunks, and the smooth grey paths led in obvious directions; left, right and straight on. Nature, as curated by humans.

Once he'd taken in the slightly disappointing surroundings, Vince lowered his snout and sniffed the soft grass. A multitude of scents – both familiar and new – filled his nostrils. His heart sank further when the sickly aroma of rotten human food made its way from the nearby bins to his nose, but he kept going, hoping that this entrance area would lead him into the wide-open spaces, trees and fresh frogs that he was desperate for.

Laurie padded across the neatly mown grass to the nearest bin. She rocked back on her haunches and pawed at the debris inside, pulling out a triangular container made of cardboard and plastic. She nosed at the bready remnants inside. 'Hey, I think those rats would be pretty pleased with this, what d'you reckon?'

Vince ignored her and looked back and forth down each path. 'Do you think there's any water here? A lake or something?'

Laurie shrugged. 'Can't smell anything. Let's keep walking.' She picked up the morsel of sandwich and chewed it down before heading off.

They took the middle path and headed deeper into the park. The grass opened out to their left, but on their right, another long, thick hedge divided it from whatever lay beyond. In the corner by the hedge, a neat collection of trees formed a cosy-looking hideaway.

'Well, this is pretty nice,' Rita said as she investigated the hedge, picking off several bugs with lightning speed.

Vince looked around, concern spreading across his face.

'What's wrong?' Laurie asked.

'Nothing. It's just... not what I expected.' He sat down, deflated.

'It's not your grandparents' park?'

'I don't think so. It could be, but... I don't know. It's not how my parents described it. It feels wrong. Too... organised. Too human.'

'But how do you know if you've never been there? And, like I said before, maybe it's changed... it's been so many seasons since they were here.'

'I know, you're right. And we've only seen this small part. Maybe it gets better?'

'Maybe. Come on, let's have a proper look.' Laurie started to pad away, then looked back over her shoulder, her green eyes glittering. 'Race you to those trees.'

Before Vince could reply, she was sprinting away, tail waving behind her.

'Hey! Get back here, you!' Vince gave chase, but his body protested and forced him to shamble along at about half his usual speed.

Laurie's chuckle carried on the air as she dashed along the path, then ducked behind the first tree she reached.

'I may be slow, but you can't hide from me! I'll sniff you out!' Vince yelled.

Laurie's tail waggled from behind the thin trunk, beckoning him over. He caught up and crept towards her, low to the ground, but once he was just a whisker away, she darted to the next tree.

'What are you waiting for? I'm over here!' she shouted from the shadows.

Vince smirked, his heart pounding. His injuries were screaming at him, but he was having far too much fun. 'First fox to get pounced on is a poodle!' he replied, inching forward, backside in the air.

'Then start curling your fur, Vince, because— AAARGH!'

'Laurie!' He ran towards her scream. Another trap? Had something attacked her?

No, no, no …

Vince arrived at her side. '*Mother Nature!*' Laurie said through clenched teeth. 'Auuugh.' She was slouched on her flank, head curled around, licking her back paw furiously. 'What is it? Are you okay?'

'I trod on something,' she said between licks.

'Oh, thank Mother,' Vince sighed. 'I thought you were in actual trouble.'

'It *hurts*,' Laurie snapped.

'Sorry, yes, I'm sure it does. Let me see.' He crouched down to inspect the damage.

'Get off! I'm fine.' She screwed her nose up and got to her paws.

'Well, if you're fine, then stop complaining.' Without thinking, he nudged her neck gently with his snout. When she didn't pull away, his stomach fluttered. He swallowed. 'What did you stand on?'

'I don't know.' Laurie searched the ground.

A small voice squeaked from behind the tree. 'Um, that might have been me. Sorry.'

'Who's there?' Laurie put her snout to the grass and made her way around to the back of the tree, Vince close behind. When she saw the bristly beast at her feet, she jumped back in alarm. 'What the…?'

'It's just a hedgehog, Laurie,' Vince said.

'A what?' Laurie's eyes were wide.

'Hedge. Hog. You've really never seen one?'

'No. Why is it all covered in *thorns*?'

Vince snorted with laughter. 'Ha! Who's the poodle *now*?'

Laurie gave him a stern stare and he cut his laughter short before turning back to the hedgehog. 'Hello, I'm sorry about Laurie, she's lived a very sheltered life.' He introduced himself and Rita, waving his paw towards where they'd left her foraging in the hedge.

'Um, very nice to meet you both. I'm Arthur. I'm really sorry about your, um, paw.'

'Oh, don't worry about it.' Laurie sat down and gave her paw another lick, while keeping her eyes firmly on the hedgehog.

Rita flapped over. 'Did I hear my name?'

'Yes, I was just telling Arthur about you,' Vince said, then flashed a mocking smile at Laurie, before adding, 'He's a *hedgehog*.'

'Well, obviously,' Rita said.

Laurie glared at Vince again. He had no doubt that she would get her revenge, somehow, but it was worth it after all the poodle comments she'd made to him.

'I was just, um, looking for worms,' Arthur continued. 'Do you live nearby? I don't think I've seen you before.'

'No, we're adventurers!' Rita said. 'We've come a long way across London, looking for a park.'

'Oh, how exciting!'

'Can you tell us about this place? How big is it? Is there any water?' Vince asked.

'Oh, um, I don't know… I don't get out much. Not at all in fact. I'd say it's big, yes, but I have nothing to compare it to really. There is a lake, though. Penelope knows more about this stuff, but she's not here right now. She's a heron, and she lives at the zoo.'

'Zoo?' Vince said.

'Penelope says it's where all the really rare animals live. And animals from really far away, too. She lives there with these tall pink birds and these other birds that swim like fish, and she says there are giant cats.'

'*Giant cats?*' Vince looked at Rita, who was wide-eyed with intrigue. 'Do they have fur, like all around their necks?'

'I don't know. The road runs all the way around this corner of the park, so I've never been,' Arthur said.

'Do you know when Penelope will be—'

'Wait, you've *never* crossed the road?' Laurie interrupted. 'They really aren't that bad.'

'Not for you, maybe,' Arthur said, his spines bristling. 'They're very dangerous for hedgehogs.'

'Well, perhaps, but they're much safer at night. You just—' Laurie began.

'There are cars at night too! Don't tell me there aren't cars, because there are!' Arthur said.

'But, it's different for hedgehogs, obviously,' Vince stared at Laurie, willing her with his eyes to be more tactful, and annoyed that she'd changed the subject.

'Is it?' Laurie said, obviously not getting the message, or purposefully ignoring it.

'Yes. They curl into balls,' Vince said.

'What? Why?' Laurie frowned.

'Self-defence,' Arthur said.

'Against *cars*?'

'No, it's—' Arthur said.

'I'm so sorry,' Vince said. 'Laurie's from the city, she doesn't understand—'

Everyone remained silent. Arthur looked at Laurie, who looked at Vince, who looked at his paws. Rita looked at the sky, but it wasn't clear if she'd been listening or not.

'Um, some of us tried to cross, but no one ever made it,' Arthur said. 'Most panicked and turned back, some got squashed. Then my family decided a few seasons back that it wasn't worth it and we all stopped trying. I'm the only one left now.'

'It's *just you*?' Laurie said.

Arthur nodded. 'Bad winter.'

'That's terrible. I'm so sorry,' Vince said.

'But if you're the last hedgehog, that means when you… When you're gone…' Laurie said.

'Yes.' Arthur nodded again. 'But it's fine. Don't worry about me.'

'But you could be the last hedgehog north of the river! We can't just leave you here,' Laurie said.

'Um, what do you suggest?' Arthur said. 'I don't want to be a bother.'

'We could help you cross the road, for a start. There might be other hedgehogs out there somewhere.'

'Oh, no...' Arthur took a step backwards. 'It's fine, honestly. Please don't go to any trouble for me. And Penelope has looked, she couldn't find any.'

'Laurie, maybe we should leave him to it? He clearly doesn't want our help,' Vince said, eager to speak to the heron about the park, and potentially meet one of the giant, hairy cats that the humans adorned their city with.

'Of course he does, he's just being polite.' Laurie looked at Arthur. 'Right?'

'Um, well, it *would* be nice to see somewhere new... Just a quick walk, then straight back here? Only if you don't mind...'

Vince hadn't anticipated picking up another animal on the way, particularly a slow one, and he was itching to find out if this was his park or not. 'What about Penelope? Can we speak to her once we help you cross?'

'She'll be at the zoo now, sleeping. It's north of here, just across the road, apparently,' Arthur said.

'We can kill two birds with one stone,' Laurie said, then turned to a frowning Rita. 'Pardon the expression. Shall we get going, then?'

Vince nodded. Plenty of animals had helped him since he'd left Richmond Park, so one favour for a lonely hedgehog really was the least he could do. He wished he didn't feel so annoyed about it, but he felt so close to his goal that he couldn't help but want to run on ahead, to meet the heron as soon as he possibly could.

Arthur, after a little encouragement from Rita, was happy to lead the way and the three of them followed the hedgehog as he waddled slowly northwards. Vince did his best to hide his frustration at Arthur's painfully slow pace, remembering that without Arthur, he wouldn't know about Penelope or the zoo. And at least it made a change from being chased.

After a short while the group reached the road. A thick hedge bordered the grass area, cutting it off from the long stretch of flat tarmac.

The other side, too, was hidden by an equally imposing hedge, and if Arthur hadn't been so relatively laid-back about the whole thing, Vince might have actually felt nervous. Bats flitted overhead, obviously unperturbed by the danger beneath them. Right before reaching the kerb, Arthur stopped dead and looked up at Laurie expectantly.

'Can you hang on to my back, or do you want to walk? You can go between us,' Laurie said.

'Um, between, please.'

Vince sighed under his breath, but immediately felt guilty. He tried to push his impatience to the back of his mind and focus on the task at hand.

He and Laurie positioned themselves either side of the hedgehog, their flanks just touching, forming an eight-legged roof over the tiny creature. 'Ready? We'll go slow,' Laurie said.

'What about cars?' Arthur said.

'No cars, look.' Laurie gestured in both directions. The road was silent. 'But if one comes, we'll protect you, I promise. You just have to go for it, no hesitating, and no going backwards.'

Laurie counted down from three and stepped into the road alongside Vince, with the hedgehog shuffling along beneath them. Rita hopped to the other side, cheering encouragement to Arthur as his tiny legs moved as fast as they could. Vince's ears twitched. An engine hummed in the distance.

'Quickly, Arthur,' he said.

'A car? Oh no!' Before Vince could stop him, Arthur tucked his nose into his belly, morphing himself into a ball of spines.

'What are you doing?' Laurie shrieked. 'Keep going!'

Further down the road, the trees lit up from the white beams of the approaching car. Arthur remained where he was, quivering.

'Move!' Laurie shouted, but Arthur remained frozen.

'That's not helping,' Rita said. 'He's terrified.'

'He'll be dead if he doesn't move,' Vince said.

A sharp blast from the car's horn made the foxes jump and Arthur curl even tighter. The headlights were on them.

'Hurry!' Rita yelled from the pavement.

'Run, Laurie!' Vince lowered his head, pushed his nose under-neath Arthur and thrust him forward with a flick of his snout.

The car horn sounded again; a drawn-out blast. The air vibrated from the droning engine as the car sailed towards them. Arthur grunted as he rolled to a halt in the middle of the wide road. Vince ran towards him. Another honk from the horn boomed through Vince's ears. The car was almost on top of them. There was no time. Vince threw himself onto Arthur and curled around him, fighting the urge to recoil as spikes pierced his belly. He clamped his eyes shut. The car swerved around them, tyres squealing, before the engine let out a roar and the metal machine cruised away.

Despite a successful hunting session, Sophie ambled back to her den feeling empty. Jake would be waiting for her, and she had no idea what she wanted to say to him, or if she even wanted to see him.

He was only looking out for her, trying to keep her safe, but she couldn't help but resent him for it. She didn't need him to fight all her battles. She should think herself lucky, though. At least she had a mate who cared about her.

The den entrance was set back in the trees, a short distance from a row of crumbling gravestones. She stopped at the graves, blinking as angry tears threatened to spill from her eyes again.

She took a deep breath and walked towards the entrance, but as she went to duck inside a voice called from across the cemetery behind her. 'Hello?'

She turned and saw two foxes approaching. They were small and wiry, their fur pitted with scars. One of them – the vixen – bore a fresh wound across her face. They were clearly not locals.

'We don't want any trouble,' the male said cautiously.

'We're looking for someone,' the female said.

'If the deer spot me talking to you, I'm dead,' Sophie said. Usually she would've helped them without a second thought. But things were different now. 'You should leave.'

'Kara. A barn owl. Do you know where we can find her?' the female said, ignoring her.

'How do you know Kara?' Sophie said.

'She came to our park. Asked us to kill a fox for her...' the male said.

'Mother Nature.' Sophie's stomach lurched. She took a deep breath, trying not to think the worst. 'Vince... Is... Is he okay? I'll *strangle* that bird.'

The two foxes looked at each other nervously.

'No... Tell me he's not...' Sophie squeezed her eyes shut, her knees buckling.

'We're sorry. Our sister died too... There was a fight and...' The female trailed off.

Sophie looked up at the black sky, blinking through the tears. Dead. She didn't want to believe it – Why would Edward go to the trouble of killing Vince when he was already gone? – but after Alice's murder, this was the least surprising news of the day. As she opened her eyes and stared at the foxes, angry tears fell. But now they were tinged with grief too. She should've killed the scrawny creatures right there, right then, but what was the point? It wouldn't have made her feel any better. And they seemed cooperative. Maybe she could use them to prove Edward's guilt?

'We know it was wrong. We didn't think...' the female looked at her paws, choking back her own tears.

Sophie ignored the vixen's sadness, her anger taking over.

'Save your tears, *bitch*,' Sophie screamed. 'Just tell me what Kara promised you in return?'

'A home in Richmond Park,' the male said.

Sophie laughed hysterically. 'Lucky you! She told you all about it, did she? How safe we all are? How *happy*?'

The male looked stunned, but waited for his sister to respond.

'We don't want to stay, not now,' the female said. 'We just want to find the owl and get her back for what happened to Bonnie.'

'Good, because you're about as welcome here as dog scat. I'm going to see Edward. He's the one who sent her and I'm very keen to hear his thoughts on all this. Kara's tree is not far from where he sleeps. You're welcome to tear her apart. Saves me a job.'

The foxes nodded, embarrassed. Sophie turned and faced the entrance to her den. 'Jake! Jake, if you're in there, get out here *right now!*'

A few blinks later, Jake crawled from the den and did his best to stifle a yawn as he saw Sophie's steely expression, followed by the strangers behind her. 'What's wrong? Who are they?'

'Vince is dead.' Her voice cracked as she said the words, but she composed herself. 'Edward sent Kara to have him killed. I'm going to go and have a word with him, and yes, I know he'll be asleep, but I'm going anyway. I want to know why. It doesn't make any sense.'

'I, uh…' Jake spluttered. 'Are you sure that's… a good idea?'

'What in Mother's name is *wrong* with you, Jake?' Sophie snapped. 'First Alice, now Vince… Do you want me to just ignore what Edward is doing? Because I won't sit by and let him get away with this and, frankly, I don't know how you can either.'

'I want Edward to pay for what he's done, of course I do, I'm just thinking of you, Soph. If you got hurt, or worse, I don't know what I'd do. I couldn't bear it.' Jake walked towards her. 'I'm sorry about Vince. Honestly, I am. He was a decent fox.'

'He was.' Sophie turned away. 'Are you coming, then? Because I really need you there, Jake. I need you to back me up on this.'

'Yes, of course.' Jake moved to her side.

Together, Sophie and Jake began to walk towards the trees which separated the cemetery from the main park. The other foxes followed behind. Sophie told them to tell her what had happened and they obliged, fearing her anger. They explained everything, from Kara's first appearance at Hyde Park to her quick departure after Bailey's attempt to grab her. Sophie listened in silence, reacting only with a fierce furrowing of her brow as they explained how they'd left Vince in the building site with another vixen.

'We're all just Edward's little playthings,' Sophie said to herself. Jake tried to comfort her but she batted him away.

The four of them continued across the expanse of the park in silence, the moon glowing overhead. Edward would be asleep, but Sophie wasn't about to let courtesy get in the way of finding out the truth. Edward may make the rules, but now, as far as she was concerned, the winner was the animal left standing at the end of the game.

'Vince! Arthur! Are you okay?' Laurie shouted from the kerb, then ran into the road.

He uncoiled himself and hissed through his teeth. 'Yes. Ouch.' He sat back on his haunches and licked his sore belly.

Arthur stayed where he was. Laurie tapped him gently with the back of her paw. 'Come on, all clear. You need to move before another car comes.'

'Um…' His tiny body muffled his words. Finally, he relented and unfurled, still shaking with fear. 'Thank you, Vince. I'm really sorry.'

'No problem,' he said through gritted teeth.

'I couldn't help it… I… I tried…'

Vince managed a smile. 'I know, sorry. You did great. Well done.'

Vince and Laurie escorted Arthur across the remainder of the road. Rita squawked 'Bravo!' as he made it up the low kerb on the other side.

'I did it!' he said. 'I can't believe I crossed the road!'

'I can't believe I just wrapped myself around a hedgehog on purpose,' Vince said.

Laurie laughed.

'Onwards!' Rita said.

'Um, this way, I guess?' Arthur started off down the path alongside the road until they reached another leading into the grassy area. Their pace was slow, as he sniffed and investigated nearly every inch of the ground in front of him. Following his nose north they passed under a shroud of trees, emerging at a roundabout of sorts, a pointed fountain marking the convergence of several routes. Arthur circled around it, leading them straight on. They walked for a little while, then Vince's ears pricked.

'Can you hear that?' he said.

'Bird calls,' Laurie replied. 'But not the usual ones.'

'Oh, we must be almost there then,' Arthur said.

'How are you feeling, Rita? Think you can go and investigate now?' Vince said.

Rita gingerly stretched her wings. 'I think so.' She hopped away and flapped clumsily, feet briefly leaving the path, before tumbling back down to earth in a flurry of feathers. 'Whoops! Almost. Let's pretend that was a practice run.' She shook her tail and tried again. After a few strong wingbeats, she made it into the air.

She disappeared over the trees, but returned a minute or so later with a loud squawk. 'This way! Come on!'

Arthur veered off the path to the left and waddled across the grass in her direction, the foxes close behind.

A metal fence, disguised by bushes growing around it, appeared to mark the boundary of the zoo. The hedgehog nosed his way under, pushing aside the loose leaves, as Vince and Laurie found a less camouflaged area and squeezed through the bare vertical railings.

Rita was already on the other side, pecking spiders from a pile of loose logs. 'Through these trees, come on!' she said, flitting away again.

Tired of waiting, Vince stepped over the hedgehog and followed Rita out into the open where a wide concrete path met his paws. He stopped and took it all in.

Apart from the intermittent cries of some unknown birds, the zoo was silent. Smells bombarded his nose; raw meat, fresh fish, the musk of countless mammals, scat. Too many to distinguish and some completely new.

To his right, a long wire-mesh cage ran alongside the path. It was taller than a shed, but not quite building height. Trees loomed over the back edge of it. Inside, plants and bushes covered the floor and bare, mostly branchless tree trunks jutted from the ground. It looked pleasant enough, and it was certainly spacious, but Vince couldn't help but compare it to the trap in the allotments.

Laurie emerged from the bushes with Arthur and they joined Vince on the path. 'What is that?' Laurie blinked at the huge cage.

'They're for animals. Penelope says there's hundreds of animals here – maybe thousands – and they're all kept in things like that, so they can't get out,' Arthur said.

'Wait, so the giant cats are in these too?' Vince said.

'Probably,' Arthur replied.

'I thought they'd be roaming around,' Vince said. 'Free.'

'Oh, no. The humans keep them in these enclosures for safety,' Arthur said. 'Penelope can leave when she wants because they don't care about her. Herons aren't special, apparently.'

'Special?' Laurie said.

'Some animals are from far, far away. Some are, um… What's the word? En… Endangered. Yes. That means there aren't many of them left.'

'So the humans are protecting them?' Vince said.

'I suppose so. Penelope knows more than me. We might be able to find her. She lives with the tall pink birds.'

'So, what's in this enclosure?' Rita hopped towards the cage and yelled through the mesh. 'Hello?'

A voice screeched back at her from inside. 'Be quiet! We're trying to sleep!' Towards the back, two large yellow-and-blue birds were perched on a thin branch. Tails as long as their bodies, and of an equally electric blue, pointed at the ground. Green feathers fringed their black-and-white-striped faces and their heads lolled on their shoulders, eyes closed. Vince had never seen anything like them. Despite his disappointment at the enclosures, their vibrant, exotic feathers made him even more excited to meet the giant cat he'd seen plastered over the city.

Vince called up to the birds. 'Sorry to disturb you. Could you just tell us where the giant cats might be? Or the tall pink birds?'

'How would we know anything about cats? Some pink birds over there, behind you. Now, go away!' The birds flapped from their branch and soared the length of the cage, landing on another perch at the far end. They turned their heads away and quickly resumed sleeping.

'How rude,' Rita said.

Vince turned around. Across from the cage, beyond a couple of slender trees, were some railings. Beyond that, he hoped, the tall pink birds. It was then he realised, the blue-and-yellow birds could only see what was directly in front of their enclosure. A wave of pity swept over him.

'Let's go and see these pink birds,' Vince said. 'There doesn't seem to be a cage over there.'

They followed the path to the railings which, it turned out, were bordering a small pond. On the closest bank, a flock of huge white birds slept. Their extraordinarily long orangey-pink beaks rested on their plump necks, pointing forward like blades. Wide, orange, webbed feet peeked out from under their bellies. Vince's heart raced. Water birds. Even sound asleep, they looked menacing. They could, he was sure, swallow him whole. Occupying the opposite bank were, undoubtedly, the tall, pink birds Arthur had been talking about, also asleep. Nestled on the edge of the flock, standing on one thin yellow leg, was a grey heron.

'Penelope!' Arthur squeaked. 'It's me! It's Arthur!'

'Eh?' Penelope opened one eye. 'Who'sat?'

'It's Arthur! Over here!'

'Arfur?' she said. 'What the...' She lowered her other leg and waded across the water, through a cloud of buzzing midges, then carefully through the sleeping birds, to greet them. She bent down and peered through the railings. 'Well I never! What you doin' 'ere, little spike?'

'I came to see you. This is Vince, Laurie and Rita. They helped me cross the road.'

'Well, well, well... Aren't you the brave adventurer, eh?'

Arthur giggled. 'Vince is looking for a park, and I thought you might be able to help, but he wants to see the big cat first. The one with all the fur around its neck.'

'The lion? He'll be asleep, but I'm sure he won't mind saying hello.'

'Lion,' Vince whispered to himself. It sounded grand. Majestic. Vince trembled at the thought of meeting him, unable to imagine a real-life cat bigger than Socks. 'What are those, behind you? Are they... dangerous?'

Penelope looked over her shoulder. 'Pelicans? No, not unless you're a fish,' she laughed.

'So, they just stay in the pond, then?' Vince said, trying not to show just how uneasy he was.

'Yeah, they can't fly. Flamingos neither. That's the pink'uns over there.' She pointed with her beak. 'If they're not in a cage, the humans cut their feathers.'

'What?' Rita said, eyes wide.

'So they don't escape,' Penelope said, shrugging. 'Ain't much point in a zoo if all the animals can leave.'

'Don't they mind?' Rita said.

'They don't know any different. Been here their whole lives.'

Rita looked shocked. If this was how the birds were living, what would the humans be doing to the lion? Vince's eagerness to see the big cat was diminishing, but his curiosity overruled. 'Can we see the lion?' he asked Penelope.

'Follow me.' Penelope stretched her long, grey wings, leapt into the air and flapped slowly over their heads. She circled back around, then headed off to the left.

The group followed along the path, eventually reaching a tall stone archway with a pair of yellow gates underneath, where Penelope had perched. She jumped to the ground and led them through a brightly coloured passageway; yellow, pink, orange and blue assaulting them from every direction.

More images of the cats caught Vince's eye, looming large on the garish tiled walls. He recognised the musty scent of cat that hung in the still air, but it was different this time. Smoky and exotic, and much more pungent. Like a thousand house cats gathering around a fire. He was so close.

'Here we go.' Penelope pointed to a huge window up ahead on their left.

Vince rushed over, propped his paws on the ledge below and pushed his wet nose against the glass. Sand covered the floor of the enclosure, with tufts of dry grass sprouting in rows among bare trees, rocks and human–built wooden structures. Vince frowned. 'Where? I can't see anything.'

'At the back.'

Vince squinted, then held his breath as the indistinct shapes in the distance came together in front of his eyes. Legs, paws, tails and noses. Three of the biggest cats he'd ever seen, golden brown, asleep and camouflaged on the sand underneath a thick tree trunk. Instinctively, he took a step from the window and exhaled slowly. Despite being awestruck, he couldn't help but notice that they didn't look like the pictures.

'Where's the fur around their necks?' he asked.

'Oh, only Ajadi has that. And it's called a mane,' Penelope said. 'He's the male. Usually on his own somewhere.' Penelope led Vince away, out of the passage and back into the open air, where the path opened out into a circular area. One side was walled, the other looked out over the enclosure. No glass this time, but instead, a thick, metal mesh divided them from the lions. In front of the mesh, a railing prevented humans from getting close.

Vince leapt over the rail with no trouble, but couldn't see another lion. Behind him, Laurie, Rita and Arthur arrived. Rita flapped over to join Vince, while Laurie waited with Arthur on the other side of the railing. Vince looked expectantly at Penelope.

'Ajadi!' Penelope shouted. 'Got some animals wanna meet you; come and say hello!'

A deep, rumbling growl thundered through the air. Grass crunched as the lion trudged through the tussocks, still nowhere to be seen. Finally, from their right, Ajadi came into view. Vince stared in awe at the magnificent animal. The images on the gate and the sign had not done him justice. One stomp of his paw would have crushed Rita, if she'd sat still long enough. Huge, round ears poked from the golden crown of fur around his neck. His tail, thick as rope, swished lazily as his jaws opened in a cavernous yawn. Jet-black lips curled back from a set of dagger-like teeth. The lion could have bitten Vince's head clean off, if not for the mesh. The smell grew stronger and Vince's heart pounded in his chest and ears. Half of him was transfixed, the other half wanted to sprint clean out of the zoo.

'Sorry, did we wake you?' Penelope asked the lion.

'Yes, but it's fine. Never get more than an hour at a time, these days.' Ajadi's voice was deeper than any Vince had ever heard, and his accent unfamiliar.

Penelope introduced Vince and the others to Ajadi, and vice versa. The lion nodded at them in turn, smiling through his obvious tiredness.

'Nice to meet you all. What brings you here?' he said.

So in awe of the beast in front of him, Vince almost couldn't reply. After a blink or two he managed to force his words out. 'We were on our way to find a park and ran into Arthur here. He told us about this place, so we thought we'd take a quick detour. It's nothing like where we're from.'

'And where are you from?'

'Richmond Park,' Vince said.

'Is that far? You look like you've seen a bit of action.' Ajadi nodded to the gashes on Vince's neck.

'Quite far. We've been travelling for a while, but Arthur says the animals here are from even further away.'

The lion sighed. 'That's true. I was born in Germany, then I lived in Canada with my brother for many seasons, then they moved me here.'

'The humans did?' Vince said.

'Yes. I wouldn't have minded, but they sent my brother off somewhere else. I doubt I'll ever see him again.'

'Oh, I'm so sorry,' Vince said, realising now why he looked so sullen. He tried to imagine himself being carted around in boxes, made to live inside a cage where he could barely run. Or Rita, stuck in one place, unable able to see anything except what was in front of her. 'But at least you have those females for company I suppose,' Vince added.

'Pfft.' The lion shook his mane. 'Idiots. All three of them. It's ridiculous. The humans put me in here, no doubt expecting me to…

Well, you know… with these dull, fatuous creatures. Honestly, I've had more enjoyable conversations with the flies on my dung.'

'That's… unfortunate,' Vince commiserated. 'But the humans seem to think a lot of you. There are pictures of you everywhere. Even in the city. Did you know?'

'Of course I don't know. Can't you see *this*?' Ajadi slammed his huge paw against the mesh. Vince and the others flinched as the rattle echoed through the zoo. 'What the humans think and what the humans do are two very different things.'

'Ajadi, don't be a grump. He's trying to be nice,' Penelope said.

'It's okay. You're right. It makes no sense,' Vince said.

Laurie spoke from behind the fence. 'Maybe we should get going, Vince? Ajadi probably doesn't want us bothering him all night.'

'Oh, stay if you like, it's no fur off my mane. I'm sorry if I've not been as exciting or interesting as you were expecting.' Ajadi sighed.

'Don't be ridiculous, you're the first lion we've ever met! There was no way you could have disappointed us,' Vince said. 'But Laurie's right, we should let you sleep.'

'Fair enough. Where did you say you were going again?'

'Not sure. Perhaps I'll stay in Regent's Park. It seems nice enough. Or maybe in Hammersmith, where Laurie's from.'

'You don't sound convinced.'

Vince shrugged and explained about his grandparents' park.

'Listen,' Ajadi began, 'I may be the most disappointing lion in the world, and I know practically nothing about anything outside this cage, but will you take one piece of advice?'

'Of course.'

Ajadi moved his face towards the mesh, so close that Vince could feel the damp heat escaping the lion's jaws. Ajadi's expression changed to one of fierce resolve, but his tone was laced with sadness. 'Never stop looking for your park. *Never.* If you know it exists, then it does.'

'But how—'

'I have lived my whole life in these cages – I was born in one, and I'll die in one – but I *know* there's a place out there somewhere where

I am meant to be. Somewhere with no walls, where I can chase and kill my own food, and lie in the hot sun. I know this place is far away – don't ask me how – but if I had any opportunity at all, I'd get out of here and run east. I'd run as far as I could. I would never make it, but I could at least die knowing I tried.'

'East? You think that's where you're from?' Vince said.

'I know it is. Like I said, don't ask me how. The humans gave me a name from this place, but that's all I know of it. Except what I see when I sleep, and what I feel pulling at my heart when I am awake. It is a constant ache in my chest. An emptiness that will never be filled by anything the humans can give me in here. Do you feel the same about your park?'

Vince thought for a second. Did he? After leaving the allotments, he'd certainly felt something driving him northwards. And when Laurie had suggested that maybe his park didn't exist, he'd refused to accept it. He'd considered going back to Hammersmith if they failed, but was that what he really wanted? He imagined them huddled in the corner of a dank, empty shop, munching on scraps of greasy chicken meat.

Do I feel the same as Ajadi?

Vince opened his mouth and the words tumbled out. 'I think so, yes.'

'Then go and find it.'

Vince looked over his shoulder at Laurie, then turned back to the lion and gave the smallest of nods.

'Right, well, I'll get off to bed then. Nice to meet you all.' With a whip of his tail, Ajadi turned to leave.

'Thank you. You've helped more than you know,' Vince said. 'It was truly an honour to meet you.'

'If you say so. You're welcome,' Ajadi muttered as he sauntered away across the enclosure.

A lump formed in Vince's throat. He'd been so excited to meet the lion, the signs around the city making him out to be important in some way, but the zoo confused him. If the humans loved lions so much, why had they taken him away from his brother? Kept him in this small enclosure with three females he detested?

'Penelope?' Vince asked. 'Is it right what Arthur said, that there aren't many lions?'

'Yep. That's why Ajadi's here. To keep him safe and encourage him to father some cubs.'

Vince shook his head. 'So, they don't care if he's happy? They just want more lions?'

'Oh, they do care. They want to make more lions, and Ajadi's happiness depends on that. It's just hard for them to understand what he feels. A lot of the animals here are very happy.'

'Oh.' Vince thought better of arguing, since he'd known about the zoo for all of an hour and Penelope was clearly more understanding of the humans' intentions. Perhaps that came from her unique position of being fed by them, despite being the only animal here that could leave.

If the humans really cared, then the animals would be free. Isn't a shorter, happier life better than a longer, miserable one? I bet Ajadi would think so.

'So, you're looking for a park...' Penelope said.

'Yes, maybe you can help us?' Vince explained about his grandparents' park, and how he wasn't sure that Regent's Park was the one.

'Well, if Regent's Park ain't what you're after, then I might know a place. It's north. About as north as you can get, really, before you're not in London anymore. Straight up.'

'What's it like?'

'I've never been, so don't take my word for it, but I know a crow what lives there. It's bigger than this place, from the sounds of it. Not far, either. Big lakes, a ton of trees. Loads of foxes. Right up your alley, I reckon. Won't be hard to find.'

A shiver of excitement passed over him. This could be it.

'And it's straight north from here?' Vince asked.

'Yup. As the crow flies. Literally.'

Don't get your hopes up. Don't get your hopes up.

Vince couldn't help grinning at Rita, who hopped from foot to foot on the railing, a smile spread across her black beak.

'Looks like that's our next stop then, after we take this one back home.' Laurie smiled down at Arthur, who was grinning from ear to ear, then looked back up to Penelope. 'Are there really no other hedgehogs anywhere?'

Penelope shook her head. 'Not in London. Regent's Park was the only place.'

'Um, actually, I've been thinking...' Arthur squeaked. 'About what the lion said.'

'Oh?' Laurie cocked her head.

'I'd like to go with you. If you don't mind, of course. Every night I see the same hedge, the same patch of grass... It's as bad as being in a cage, like Ajadi. If I am the last hedgehog, I'd at least like to see as much of the world as I can.'

Laurie looked at Vince. 'What d'you reckon? Room for one more?'

If Arthur felt something similar to him and Ajadi, and wanted to see what else lay beyond the hedges and roads that had kept him prisoner his whole life, then Vince couldn't bear to leave him. The little hedgehog had had a taste of freedom, and his appetite would only grow. If he didn't go with them now he might eventually leave some other time, without any help. If his reaction to the car was anything to go by, he wouldn't last very long without them. He might have been impatient, but Vince still had a conscience. 'Sure,' Vince said, 'and it'll be useful to have an expert worm hunter on the team.'

Arthur grinned.

'I always knew there was a little explorer in you.' Penelope bent her long legs to give the small hedgehog a friendly nudge with her beak.

'Right then,' Laurie said. 'North? Are you coming too, Penelope?'

'I'll tag along, make sure you get there okay,' Penelope replied.

'What's this park called?' Rita said, as the group set off towards the north edge of the zoo.

'Hampstead Heath,' Penelope said.

'Hampstead Heath,' Vince said to himself, a smile stretching across his snout.

12

After leaving the zoo through the north fence, Penelope led the way towards Hampstead Heath from the air, with Rita keeping Arthur company on the ground. Vince and Laurie ambled behind.

Laurie hadn't said anything about their new destination, so he assumed that she still wanted to head back to Hammersmith whenever they found it. Part of him was happy to avoid the subject, but he'd definitely felt something between them earlier, when she'd trodden on Arthur, and since she hadn't recoiled when he'd touched her, he also assumed she felt it too. That was two too many assumptions for him, but there was one thing he was sure of: he wanted her to stay.

But what if he was wrong and she didn't share his feelings? Had he exaggerated it in his head? Best to wait until he was sure, and if he was going to be humiliated, he'd rather the others weren't around.

Instead, Vince turned his ears to Rita as she chatted to Arthur about their recent travels. He laughed along, despite not being part of the conversation. Anything to avoid talking to Laurie, who was walking so close to him he could feel the swish of her tail on his back legs. Laurie, being Laurie, saw right through him.

There was a brief lull in Rita's chatter and Laurie didn't waste any time. 'I suppose after what Ajadi said you definitely won't be coming back to Hammersmith?'

There was no getting away from it, and the truth was all he had.

'Actually, I was hoping you might stay.'

'At the park?' Laurie said, with a hint of sadness in her voice.

'Well, with us. Wherever we end up.'

'Us?' Laurie cocked her head and smiled.

'Me and Rita,' Vince replied, then added quickly, 'And Arthur, of course.'

Laurie looked down between her paws. 'I can't leave Socks. He's my best friend. He's the only friend I've ever had.'

'Until now.' Vince smiled at her, but she didn't return it. 'I can understand. I only left Richmond Park because there was nothing there for me anymore. My parents are dead and Sophie—'

'Who's Sophie?'

Vince had forgotten that the topic hadn't arisen before. He stuttered, unsure how to answer, but Laurie interjected with a laugh. 'She was your mate, right?'

'Yeah. We fell out, though. It was stupid and she's with someone else now. But that's not important. We weren't right for each other,' Vince said.

Laurie gave a small nod. Vince sighed. He'd wondered if he'd ever find another mate, but never imagined he'd have to compete for a vixen's heart with a house cat. He faced forward, avoiding her eyes. There was no way he could say what he wanted to say if he caught even a glimpse of them. He took a deep breath and the words tumbled into the air. 'If you decide to go back home – if it's what you really want – then I won't stop you, but I like you, Laurie. A lot. And I'd really love it if you stayed.'

He forced his head to turn and face her, his stomach dropping when he saw the sadness in her eyes. He dreaded her next words.

'I can't,' she said, 'I'm sorry,' before quickening her pace to join Arthur and Rita up ahead.

Vince was left alone, staring, as she joined in with the end of a joke, her tail shaking along with her chuckles.

To Sophie's surprise, Edward was already awake when the four foxes arrived at the lake. He looked less than happy about it, though, shaking his head wearily at the rabbit in front of him.

'I *am* listening to you, but I'm telling you it was that hawk,' Edward said. 'You know, the one from last year? He comes back every year to try his luck hunting here. I'll send one of my team to keep watch for the next few mornings and evenings.'

The rabbit frowned. 'Okay, but several of us saw what happened and it didn't look like a hawk. It was white. Like an owl.'

Edward smiled. 'You *know* the owls aren't allowed to hunt rabbits. Of course, we can't rule out a non-resident owl. Either way, one of my team will sort it, okay?'

'Thank you, Edward,' the rabbit said, before hopping away.

Sophie would bet a week's rats that it was no hawk. It had to be Kara. She obviously didn't do Edward's dirty work for free. Not that Sophie expected her to, but it was good to know what Edward's end of the bargain was.

A few other deer slept close by, which made her anxious, but she had to hold it together. She'd never stood up to Edward like this before, but she'd watched Vince do it enough times to know that the deer's bark was worse than his bite, and he was usually too proud to call for help, especially against a bunch of vermin like them. Plus, Jake was with her, and if things got really heated, she could run. Besides, she only wanted to ask him some questions.

Blake and Bailey held back as she marched up to Edward, Jake by her side. Her voice quivered as she began to speak, but she thought of Vince and pushed through her fear. 'Good evening, Edward. We've got some visitors to see you, and something alarming has come to our attention.'

'Get back to the cemetery, fox. Whatever it is can wait until morning.'

'But look, *intruders!*' She waved a paw at Blake and Bailey. 'Aren't you going to trample their skulls? Don't you want to know why they're here?'

Edward sighed. 'Not particularly, but I suppose you're going to tell me anyway?'

'It seems Kara promised them a home,' Sophie said.

'Is that all? Yes, Kara may have done that. You know, you aren't aware of everything that goes on around here, so there's no reason to get all worked up every time a new resident arrives. There's plenty of room.'

'On the contrary. I don't give a flying squirrel who lives here.

It's just that we haven't had new residents from outside in seasons, so naturally I was interested to know how they managed to wangle an invitation. As it turns out, you sent them to kill Vince,' Sophie said flatly.

Edward's eyes grew wide, but his voice was calm. 'That's not strictly true.'

'Don't split hairs!' Sophie barked. 'You didn't send Kara to give Vince a message like we asked, you sent her to hire a pack of murderers.'

'Okay, okay, you've got me.' Edward shrugged. 'What difference does it make to you?'

'He was our friend, you *runt*.'

Edward's face contorted into a frown as he turned to Jake. 'Are you really going to let her speak to me like that?'

Jake opened his mouth to respond but Sophie cut him off. 'But the question, Edward, is what difference does it make to *you*? Because from my point of view, the answer seems to be none.'

'Well, I weeded out a bad apple from the foxes, so there's that. Makes a bit of room for our new arrivals.' Edward smiled.

'We don't want to stay here anyway,' Bailey said from behind Sophie.

'Then, by all means, please leave. The fewer of you the better.'

'Stop avoiding the question. Vince was already gone; you could have left him alone. Was it just for fun? For your own amusement? Because I never had you down as gratuitously cruel, Edward. Strict, yes, but you always have your reasons, don't you?'

'You know me so well, Sophie. It's just a shame you don't know Jake as well as you thought?'

'What?' Sophie said.

'Edward, please…' Jake said.

Sophie looked at her mate. His pleading eyes were fixed on Edward. 'What is he talking about, Jake?'

Edward carried on. 'I'm simply saying, perhaps someone else wanted Vince dead too. Someone who wanted to make sure he never came back, someone who was scared his vixen might stray to her old flame...'

'That's not true!' Jake said.

Edward ignored Jake and spoke directly to Sophie. 'You know how jealous he is. You know how much he hates... sorry... *hated* Vince.'

'Shut up,' Sophie said.

'I don't hate Vince,' Jake said.

'No? Oh, perhaps I'm getting confused. But I'm sure I remember something... During one of our little chats, wasn't it? But there have been so many now, haven't there? It really is hard to keep track. What was it you said, again, Jake? That you *didn't particularly want him back here?*'

'I... You're twisting my words...'

'Am I?' Edward cocked his head.

Jake's eyes were wide and wet. 'Sophie, it wasn't like that, I promise. Please don't listen to him...'

Sophie took a step back, away from Jake, shaking her head in bewilderment. 'Twisting your words? So, you did say *something*, then? And how many *chats* have you had? What have you been talking about?'

Before Jake could reply, Edward replied with a smirk. 'Oh, just business. Jake kindly volunteered himself for Park Watch duties. Surveillance, mostly.'

'No...' Sophie dragged her gaze from Edward to Jake, who could only stare at the floor. 'Tell me he's lying, Jake.'

Jake squeezed his eyes closed. 'I'm so sorry, Sophie.' He looked up at her and blinked. Tears welled in his eyes. 'I promise I didn't mean for any of this to happen. I only wanted to make you happy, to send a message to Vince, and then to keep you safe, but it... It got out of control... I'm so sorry.'

Something had felt wrong when he'd convinced her not to go and see Edward, but she never imagined he was working for him. 'You spied on us? Oh, Mother Nature, *you* were the one who told Edward about Alice? You lied to my face! How *could* you?'

'I only agreed because I know how much Vince meant to you. I never wanted him dead, I swear. I wanted you to be happy again and I thought it would be okay… It was only temporary… But then Alice… He blackmailed me. He threatened to hurt *you*…'

'Why didn't you tell me straight away?' Sophie whispered. 'We could have handled it together.'

'I'm sorry, Sophie. Please listen—'

Sophie snorted and turned away, hiding her own onslaught of tears. Blake and Bailey were a few leaps away now, unsure whether to stay or leave them to it. 'Your words don't mean *scat* to me anymore, Jake.'

Vince had let her down more times than she could count. Not showing up when they'd arranged to meet. Forgetting to catch her any rats when it was his turn to hunt. But he'd never lied to her. Not once.

Jake moved towards her. 'Sophie…'

Sophie spun to face him and pushed her snout close to his, almost touching. Lowering her voice, she growled, 'Alice and Vince are both dead. My friends. Both dead because of *you*.'

Edward's voice rumbled over them. 'If you two don't mind, I'd quite like to get some sleep.'

Sophie quickly turned and bared her teeth at Edward. Looking pleased with himself, Edward took a step towards her, stamping his hoof in the dirt. Her heart pounded in her ears. *Retreat*, her instincts screamed at her, but she took a deep breath and held her ground. If Vince were here, he'd tell Edward exactly what he thought of him. He was never scared of the deer. Sadness and anger exploded in her chest. Edward had taken Vince away from her. He'd taken Alice away from her. Now he was taking Jake away from her. She couldn't let Edward have the last word.

She walked right up to him, close enough to receive a hoof to the head, if Edward decided on it.

'Sophie, stop! What are you doing?' Jake said.

'Be careful!' Bailey shouted.

She ignored them. 'You…' she began, her legs trembling

beneath her, '...are a lying, manipulative, twig-headed, dung-eating, human-pet. And you can avoid my questions all you like, but the residents of this park will soon learn the truth about you.' She turned to leave and the others quickly followed.

'What exactly do you think you're going to do, fox?' Edward boomed after them. 'You better watch your backs.' Edward snorted as he settled down on the grass then curled his neck around to rest his head on his flank. Sophie spun her head and watched him close his eyes, before yelling as loud as she could.

'And your antlers look like *scat*.'

The journey towards Hampstead Heath was uneventful. The roads were almost empty, and Arthur, with his new-found bravery, curled up only a few times. They passed through a smaller grassy area, skirting around a steep hill, taking their time to enjoy the relative silence. After the grass ended, houses spread in every direction. Penelope landed briefly to tell them that it was nothing but houses from there to the heath. Their route would be twisty and indirect, but following the paths was easier and safer than trying to leap fences and avoid the humans' dogs.

Vince had joined Laurie, Rita and Arthur, and they walked as a foursome at Arthur's pace. The tiny hedgehog could be surprisingly speedy when he wanted to be, although he did need fairly frequent rests. Vince was glad of the breaks, though, as his injuries were still bothering him.

As they walked, Arthur was full of questions for Vince. How far had he come? What was the scariest thing that had happened to him? Had he eaten any good worms? Rita grew tired of hopping and went back to perching on the back of Laurie's neck. As Vince dutifully responded to Arthur's endless inquisition, Laurie hurried ahead, eager to speak to Rita alone.

'Can I ask you something?' Laurie said.

'Sure,' Rita replied over Laurie's shoulder.

'If you had to choose between your best friend, who you'd

known your whole life, and someone who you might want to be your mate, but you weren't really sure, which would you choose?'

'I think you're asking the wrong bird. I've never had either.' Rita laughed. 'What would Socks want you to do?'

'Socks? Oh, I don't know. He's always joking about me finding a mate and leaving him, but I never in a thousand seasons thought I would.'

'So you *do* want Vince to be your mate?' Rita jumped down from Laurie's back to peck a beetle from the pavement, then quickly flapped back up and grasped Laurie's fur in her talons again.

'Maybe. I mean, he's nice…'

'Stubborn, though. And grumpy,' Rita said. Her voice was serious but Laurie could tell she was smiling. 'Really quite grumpy, to be honest.'

Laurie laughed. 'That's true. But I've been called worse in my time.'

'I think you know what you want to do, Laurie. You just want me to give you permission. Which is odd, because I didn't have you down as a fox who needed permission from anyone to do anything.'

Rita was right, of course. Ajadi's speech had had an impact on Laurie too. It was a battle between her head and her heart, but when she thought about spending the rest of her nights with Vince, she filled with warmth. She just wanted someone to tell her that leaving Socks behind was okay. That Socks would be fine without her. Not that it would help her feel any less guilty, or upset.

'I'd miss him so much, though,' Laurie said. 'There's not been a day since we met that I haven't spoken to him. He's the main reason I wanted to help Vince.'

'But Vince was the reason you helped *me*, right?'

Rita was right again. Laurie nodded.

'I don't think any of us really knows how you feel,' Rita said. 'I had no friends in Richmond Park, Arthur was all alone and Vince had lost everything… But you know what? You can always go back. It's a long way, but why not stay with Vince for a while and see how you feel? You've got nothing to lose. And if you decide to stay, we can send messages back to Socks. Go and visit him. It doesn't have to be one or the other.'

'Hmm, I suppose that could work. It doesn't seem fair, though. I don't want Vince to get his hopes up.'

'Laurie, I know almost nothing about males, and even less about foxes...' Rita paused. 'But I think it's probably already too late for that.'

Laurie let out a snort as she tried to hold in her laugher, worried that Vince might hear and interrupt. After composing herself, she moved the subject away from her own dilemma. 'What about you, Rita? Are you excited about Hampstead Heath? Do you think it's *the one*?'

'I hope so. I'm excited for Vince. I just want him to be happy.'

'Of course, but what about *you*? There might be some magpies there. Aren't you looking forward to meeting new birds?'

'Not really,' Rita said.

'Oh, come on, not even a nice male? One who likes singing as much as you...' Laurie wriggled her backside to rouse Rita into a response. It didn't work.

'No,' Rita said.

'Oh.' Laurie had never seen or heard Rita on any setting other than 'absurdly cheerful'. She'd obviously hit a nerve. 'Sorry. I didn't mean to be rude...'

'It's okay. I'm just not used to talking about myself, I suppose,' Rita said. 'No one's ever asked about me before. Or cared.'

'Until I met you and Vince, no one ever cared about me either. Except Socks. The only reason I brought it up is because I thought magpies always lived in pairs. Mated for life, you know?'

'Some do, some don't. There are sometimes flocks of us who don't pair up. If there's not enough trees to build nests.'

'There weren't enough trees in Richmond Park?'

'I didn't say that. You know what? I don't really want to talk about me at all. I'm going to fly up with Penelope.'

Before Laurie could respond, Rita unfurled her talons and disappeared from Laurie's back. She flapped overhead, climbing higher until she was a mere speck in the sky. Laurie frowned. She'd clearly said something wrong, but what?

'Just over this bridge,' Penelope called from the air.

Laurie's back was once again Rita's resting place, their previous truncated conversation apparently forgotten, as Laurie ambled beside Vince and Arthur. It had been a slow journey, but a mercifully quiet one, with most of the local animals keeping their distance from the strange group.

Vince's heart was pounding. This could be the one. His grand-parents' park.

They crossed the final road – Arthur announcing his complete lack of curling up, followed by cheers from everyone else – and made their way onto the bridge that Penelope was now perched on the edge of.

Vince had assumed the bridge spanned a river, but a glance through the handrails on either side told him different. Train tracks.

He froze, heart racing – this time with fear. He was far above the rails. Even if a train came by, he'd be perfectly safe. Despite repeating the fact over in his mind, it didn't seem to slow the hammering in his chest. 'You didn't say there were train tracks,' he said to nobody in particular.

'Just look straight ahead. Focus on the trees,' Rita said.

Vince did as he was told and locked his eyes on the trees at the end of the bridge. His legs moved slowly towards them, his brain focusing on the park beyond. The rest of them followed, whispering encouragement. He was horribly embarrassed, but remembering how Laurie had been scared of Arthur made him feel a bit better.

The clank of metal on metal turned his ears. His stomach lurched at the faraway humming of an engine. The wounds on his neck threatened to explode, such was the pressure of the blood surging through his veins, powered by his relentless pounding heart. 'No, no, no...'

'It's okay, it can't hurt you,' Rita said. 'It's all the way down there, and we're all the way up here.'

Vince's legs moved him into reverse and he stared wide-eyed through the handrails as the train trundled closer. Pure fear flushed away his embarrassment and he staggered backwards until he was clear of the bridge, then collapsed onto his belly. His friends approached, Laurie's face bearing a sympathetic – if somewhat exasperated – smile.

'After everything that's happened, you're scared to walk over a bridge?' Laurie said.

Behind them, the train sailed past with a hum, then faded again as the tracks led it away to its unknown destination.

Vince looked at Penelope. 'Is there another way in?'

'Mother Nature, pull yourself together, Vince!' Laurie grabbed the scruff of his neck between her jaws and dragged him to his feet. He cried out, more in protest than actual pain, and wrenched himself from her grip.

'Okay, okay, I get it! I'm pathetic!' he barked.

'No one said you were pathetic.' Rita shot Laurie a look, who responded with a 'who, me?' expression.

'Do you think you can go across now? The train's gone. We'll help you,' Rita said.

'Maybe. I think so. Just… don't rush me, okay?' Vince replied.

Rita and Penelope flew to the other side of the bridge and perched on the handrail. Arthur began to scuttle across. 'Come on, Vince! You can do it!'

'I'll be right behind you, okay?' Laurie whispered.

Vince's fear was fading, but the embarrassment was creeping back in.

'Can… Can you go across first?' Vince said to Laurie.

'Nope. Off you go.' She nodded towards the others.

Vince took a deep breath and began to walk. A car engine roared some way away and he stopped, front paw poised in the air. His ears twitched and the hair on his back bristled. Something nudged his back leg. He turned and Laurie's green eyes flashed at him.

'Go on! You're doing great!' She smiled.

He carried on, the others cheering with every step, like new parents encouraging a cub to pounce or howl for the first time.

A siren blared behind him. Adrenaline filled his body and he went to turn, but Laurie grabbed his tail between her teeth. 'Don't even think about it,' she said, her mouth full of fur. She didn't let go, even when he started to walk again. Vince wasn't sure which was worse, feeling like a new-born cub, or like a dog on a lead.

Holding his breath, he focused his gaze on the ground in front of him. Paw by paw, he made his way across, Laurie tugging at his tail whenever he paused for longer than a blink.

Finally, he reached the other side and exhaled. Rita, Arthur and Penelope cheered. Laurie released him. 'Thank me later, poodle,' she winked. If it had been anyone else he would have taken a swipe at her.

'Next time, you'll be *riding* the train!' Rita said.

Vince shivered at the thought. 'Let's just get to the park. I need a lie down.'

Rita sang as the group headed to the entrance, where the trees parted for the path. 'A home for Vince across the tracks, trees tall and grasslands wide, a magpie flutters overhead, a vixen by his side.'

Laurie turned away, trying to conceal a smile.

'Shh!' Vince hissed at Rita, then after a moment added, 'At least that one rhymed.'

Vince looked towards Penelope. 'Is this it? Are we here?'

'Yup. Hampstead Heath,' she said. 'I don't know my way around, mind you, but you'll soon get your bearings. Listen, I really should be getting back. I'm not usually nocturnal, you know.'

The animals thanked her, and Arthur said a tearful goodbye, promising to send her a message soon. Penelope bent her long legs and jumped into the air, before beating her great wings and soaring away.

Vince turned back to the path in front of him, which split out three ways, with a building nestled in the left-most fork. He began to walk along the middle path, which looked like it would lead into the middle of the park, rather than along the edges like the two others.

'Are you coming, you lot?' he shouted over his shoulder.

'Yes!' Rita flapped over to him.

'How does it feel?' Laurie asked as she joined him, Arthur trotting alongside.

'Good, I think. Yes. Definitely good.' Vince twisted his head back and forth, taking in everything.

As the path curved around the building, an enormous expanse of grass opened out in front of them. Thickets of plump, green trees huddled together in the distance, where a thin path ran. Beyond that, more grass, more trees and who knew what else? Penelope said there were ponds, but at that moment, he didn't even care. It was what he couldn't see that filled him with happiness. No neatly clipped hedges. No perfectly symmetrical flower beds. No roads. No railings. Just wide, open space.

'Want to run?' Laurie said.

'More than anything,' Vince replied.

'Go on, then.' She nudged him with her snout and bared her teeth in a grin.

Vince returned her smile, trying to forget that she would soon be heading back to her home on the noisy streets.

'Not without you.' He nudged her back, then took off across the grass, as fast as his aching body would allow. She chased him, caught up and bounded beside him, and together they raced through the park that – as the moments went by – felt more and more like his home.

As they ran, Vince's worries dissipated into the air, and the pain of his injuries wasn't far behind. He pounced, pinning Laurie to the ground and pressing his snout gently into her neck. She laughed as she rolled from under him, then leapt up and did the same to him, being extra careful to avoid his sore spots. The last fox he'd tussled with had been Sophie, a season ago, but it felt like longer. It felt like for ever. This was not just a different park but a different world. He shivered as the thick grass tickled his back and the cold night breeze whipped at his fur, but inside he was warm. He was happy. This was the place. And this was the vixen.

'What are you thinking about?' Laurie said.

'What do you think?' he said, pushing her off with his hind feet. She landed on all fours and crouched low, tail wagging.

'Oh, I don't know... Me?' She screwed her face up and stuck her tongue between her front fangs.

'Yes.' He matched her pose, belly to the floor. 'But specifically, what I will do when I have to say goodbye to you for ever.' Without her, there would be a void – in the park, and inside him – but he was asking her to give up everything... He sunk to the ground, ears drooping.

Laurie relaxed, letting her weight fall onto the grass. 'Well, I've been thinking...'

Vince's ears perked up.

'I've become rather fond of Rita and Arthur. Laurie's voice was flat, but her eyes glittered. 'So, I think I can probably put up with you for a little while longer.'

'I see. And how long is a little while?' Vince matched her tone. She could tease him all she liked, he didn't care anymore. She was staying and he felt like his heart might burst out of his chest.

'Oh, I don't know... Until I get fed up with you, probably. You seem to have a habit of getting into trouble, and I'd really like a quiet life, y'know? And if you ever upset me, Socks will have every cat in London over here to tear you to pieces, understand?' Her mouth began to curl up at the edges.

'Oh, and there I was thinking you could look after yourself...' Vince began to pull himself to his feet. 'Perhaps I've made a terrible mistake?' He grinned.

Laurie stood up. 'Says the fox who's scared of bridges.'

'Actually, I'm scared of *trains*,' Vince leapt towards her, rearing up on his hind legs. Laurie did the same and they stood together, paws on chests, for a second, before collapsing onto the grass in a fit of giggles. Vince leaned in and licked the fur on Laurie's neck. She moved her snout towards his and their noses touched, her green eyes meeting his yellow ones.

'Sorry to interrupt...' Rita's voice came from the ground beside them. Rolling their eyes at each other, they found their feet and shook the loose grass from their fur. '…but someone wants to speak to you. Well, us. All of us.'

'Who?' Vince said.

'A pigeon. She's back there. Where we came in.'

The three of them made their way over, arriving to find an animated Arthur telling a speckled grey pigeon about his incredible brave journey from Regent's Park. She nodded along, smiling in all the right places.

'…and I only curled up twice. Maybe, um, three times. Definitely not more than five… Isn't that right, Vince?'

'That's right.' He smiled at the pigeon. 'Hi, I'm Vince and this is Laurie. I see you've met Arthur, the bravest member of our team.'

The pigeon spoke with a clarity that Vince had never heard before, not even in Richmond Park. As though each word was special, and deserved nothing less than to be pronounced perfectly. 'I have indeed, and what a surprise to see a hedgehog! You must have come a long way… Anyway, we'll have plenty of time to get to know one another. Let me start off by saying what a pleasure it is to meet you all, my dears, and to welcome you to Hampstead Heath. My name is Theresa.'

'Thank you, it's really beautiful here,' Vince replied, unconsciously smartening his own speech to match. 'Are you… In charge here? Or…' Vince felt himself tense. He realised it might no longer be the utopia his parents had described, but if it turned out that one animal made all the rules, he didn't think he could bear it.

'Oh, dear me, no!' She let out a friendly, but restrained, laugh. 'I'm just the Welcome Officer. All new arrivals are greeted by me. Any day, any time.'

'Oh, how nice!' Rita said.

Vince relaxed as Theresa went on to describe the heath, pointing her wing in various directions whenever she mentioned a landmark. It seemed everything he'd heard was true. The heath was enormous, with more open space and trees than he'd imagined, and no single species had more power than any other.

'Well, it makes a change from the other places we've been,' Vince said.

'Indeed. We're very proud of our park. We all work hard to make it as lovely as possible. It wasn't always this way, though. Things were very different before the Solstice Riot. You may have heard of it?'

'No,' Vince said. 'A *riot*? Really?'

'Yes. The deer used to control this park,' Theresa explained. 'Everything was fine for a long while, but over time they became more and more obsessed with power, making new rules every day, punishing those who broke them with injury or death. The residents were too scared to leave their homes, except to hunt, and even then they were restricted to what the deer told them they could eat. It was dreadful.'

Vince's mouth hung open. He couldn't believe it. The same thing here as back in Richmond Park. 'But, it's okay now, right?'

'Oh, yes. The deer eventually took it too far. It was the start of winter and they'd restricted hunting and gathering to such an extent that animals were starving, dying from the cold. Can you imagine? Enough was enough, then. The foxes stood up to them first. Some were killed in the process, and the deer cracked down even harder, but other species – who now had little to lose – quickly followed suit and eventually the whole park gathered together to confront the deer. There was a stand-off, and although the deer were strong, the resistance had the sheer numbers. The deer had no chance. A doe was killed – one can't imagine how brutal it must have been – and the deer finally accepted defeat, realising they could no longer control everyone.'

'And you remember this? When did it all happen?' Vince said, his eyes wide.

'Oh no, my dear, this was seasons ago. But everyone here knows the story. It's passed down to our children and grandchildren. It's important to us that every new generation knows about the past, so we don't let it happen again.'

Vince's mind raced. Were his grandparents here when the riot started? Were they two of the foxes who instigated it? That must have been why they left.

Vince was eager to know more. 'Are there any animals still alive who remember the riot?'

'Just a few of the older deer. They keep themselves to themselves now, understandably.'

Vince shook his head. 'If the animals at Richmond Park heard about this, they…'

Then it clicked.

Vince turned to his friends. 'That's why Edward wanted me dead. Somehow he knew about Hampstead Heath, about the riot and how it had stripped the deer of their power, and he knew that if I made it here, I would find out too.'

'He was scared you would come back and tell the others,' Rita added, her eyes wide.

'Or send a message back. Which is exactly what I'm going to do,' Vince said.

Theresa raised a wing. 'Sorry to interrupt, but are you actually wanting to stay? It's just that there are some things we need to confirm before we can officially welcome you as residents, and I'm not really the nocturnal type. You're welcome to come back any time if you have business to attend to outside.'

Laurie jumped in before Vince could speak. 'No, we definitely want to stay.' She turned to Vince. 'Let's get settled here tonight and we'll send a message back first thing tomorrow. I don't know about you but I'm exhausted, and you've waited this long. Try to enjoy your new home before you start any more trouble, okay?' She smiled.

Vince nodded. 'You're right.'

'Glad to hear it! Now, on to the boring bit, I'm afraid,' Theresa cooed. 'Boring, but very important. I'll need to take some details from all of you, so we can match and assign you to the most suitable area.'

'Assign us? What do you mean?' Vince's stomach lurched.

'Oh, it's nothing to worry about, my dear. Everyone has a designated area. There are eleven in total, all very lovely, but I won't bore you with the details now. That's where you'll build your den, your nest, whatever, and sleep, but you are free to go wherever you like the rest of the time. The whole of Hampstead Heath is completely open to you. Visitors are allowed too. We really have very few rules compared to other parks, so I'm led to believe.'

Vince relaxed a little.

'It's a very fair system,' Theresa went on. 'It helps stop over-crowding, too many of one species in one place, management of resources, that sort of thing.'

'Sounds pretty sensible,' Laurie said. Vince wasn't sure if she meant it or if she was just trying to ease his mind.

'You're lucky, actually, we have quite a bit of room in most of the areas right now. And if there's a problem, we are happy to accommodate transfers. So, let's start with you, Vince, my dear. You are a fox, and you are male, correct?'

He nodded.

'Age?'

'Er, nearly five seasons.'

'Right, no health problems? Mange? Fleas? Anything like that?'

'No!' he said defensively.

'Apologies, but we do have to make sure, you understand… And did I hear you say you were from Richmond Park? How lovely! Is that your birthplace?'

'Yes.'

'I'm from there too!' Rita chirped.

'Excellent, well I can tell you this now, Rita, we'll certainly have space for you. Bit of a glut of male magpies at the moment, all looking for mates.' Theresa winked.

'Oh… Good,' Rita said, a hint of disappointment in her voice.

'And Arthur, of course you are unconditionally welcome to any of our areas. You are the first hedgehog we've had in seasons. Rare to see animals from such a long way away, too. But I digress… Vince, your parents were born in Richmond Park too, I assume?'

'Yes. My grandparents were actually from here, though, I think.'

'Really? Well, isn't that lovely! From before the riot, I suppose? Otherwise I'd have to question why they left!' Theresa laughed.

'Yeah, that makes sense,' Vince said. Knowing that Rita and Arthur could settle down here, if they wanted, was a weight off his mind. Rita could do what she liked, of course, but he would have felt terrible if they'd ended up in a place where she wasn't happy.

'Right then, well, luckily for you we've just had a spot come up near Wood Pond. I trust that will suit you?'

'A pond? Are there frogs?'

'Oh, yes! And the clue's in the name, it's by the woods, so lots of cover. Very cosy.'

'Perfect!' Vince grinned at Laurie. 'Can we go there tonight?'

'Well, let's see about Laurie... Fox, female...'

'Five seasons, no mange, no fleas,' she said cheerily.

'Were you born in Richmond Park too, my dear?'

'No, Hammersmith.'

'Hammersmith... park? Sorry, I've not heard of it. Is it new?'

'Er, no. It's just Hammersmith. Not a park. Just... You know... in the city.'

'Right. Your parents, too?'

Laurie nodded.

'I see.' Theresa's smile evaporated.

'What? What is it?' Vince said.

'I do sincerely apologise, but Hampstead Heath operates a strictly park-only members system now. I can't let Laurie stay here, I'm afraid.'

'What? I don't understand...' Vince said.

'It's a shame, I know, but our popularity means we have had to restrict intake. And there are safety concerns too, you understand. You can come and visit, of course. We are very relaxed about that. And if you are mates, then we can arrange a visitation schedule, but—'

'*Visitation schedule?* This is ridiculous. You said there was lots of space. It's not like she'd need an extra den, we'd share...' Vince glanced at Laurie, and she quickly nodded in agreement.

Theresa went on, 'Of course, but there's the additional resources to think of... Food, waste management... Then, of course, if you were to have cubs, that would be an issue… We have to take all this into consideration. I'm sorry.'

'Cubs! We haven't even… Never mind.' Laurie shook her head. 'Is there really nothing you can do? I can't live here at all? Even if it's in another area? Somewhere less nice. I don't care.'

'Less nice?' Theresa laughed. 'We don't have any areas like *that*, my dear.'

Vince clenched his jaw.

'But they're in *love!*' Rita said.

Theresa shrugged. 'There's nothing I can do. I really am terribly sorry.'

Rules. Always rules.

Stupid rules.

Wrong rules.

'Vince, listen…' Laurie began, 'You stay, we'll do the visiting thing, okay? You've come all this way—'

'No!' Vince snapped. 'I want you here.'

'You heard Theresa, I can't. But there's no reason why you can't stay with Arthur and Rita. You nearly died trying to find this place. So did Rita. Don't let it all be for nothing.'

'Nothing? Meeting you wasn't nothing.'

'No, but—'

'Listen,' Theresa said. 'I feel terrible about this, I really do. If you want to stay for tonight, think it over, then you're more than welcome. I'll have to restrict you all to this area, until you decide one way or another, but please let me know first thing in the morning. If you need anything in the meantime, I'll be in those trees, just over there, okay?'

'Thank you,' Rita said.

Vince said nothing.

'I'll be back at sunrise, my dears.' Theresa flapped away, leaving them in solemn silence.

'Don't worry, Vince. We'll sort something out…' Rita said as Theresa disappeared over the trees.

Vince slumped onto the grass. 'How can they have a rule like that? As if one animal is better than another because of where they were born. Or where their parents were born… It's ridiculous. It's unfair. I can't believe after all this…' He dropped his head to the ground and continued through gritted teeth. 'All this time, all this way, and it's no better than stinking Richmond Park or the stinking wetlands.'

Rita's optimism was waning, but she tried her best. 'Come on, Vince, it's not that bad. You heard what she said about the riots. There's no one in charge here. It may not be perfect, but I'm sure you two can work it out. There are other places close by where Laurie could live. She'd only be leaps away…'

'No. I'm not staying without Laurie. End of discussion. And we have to go back home and tell the others about the riot and Edward's lies… If we can get everyone together, we can stand up to Edward and make Richmond Park like it used to be.'

Laurie lowered herself down beside him. 'Why don't you get some rest? It's been a hard few nights. We can talk about it in the morning.'

'Mmm,' Vince closed his eyes. 'Maybe just for a little while. Until Theresa comes back. Then I'll tell her where to shove her egg-sucking pond and her egg-sucking woods. And then we'll head back to Richmond Park and take Edward down a branch. I can't wait to see everyone's faces when they hear about the riot.'

Laurie shot Rita and Arthur a worried look, but stayed silent, before nestling her head into Vince's shoulder. Rita and Arthur shuffled over and joined them. Rita fluffed her feathers and cuddled up against Laurie's warm fur. Keeping his prickles at a safe distance, Arthur curled into a ball.

The animals said their goodnights, but Vince was already dreaming. He and Laurie were catching frogs, laughing as they swiped their paws across the water of the unknown pond. Around them, blankness. An empty green canvas.

13

Laurie was gone when Vince woke up. He scanned the park, but couldn't see her anywhere.

She must have gone to find breakfast.

He stretched, backside in the air, and yawned. A rest had done him good: his wounds had settled to a gentle throb, his muscles not quite as tender. He sniffed the air. The local birds were awake and singing their dawn chorus, diamonds of yellow sunlight flashed through the trees and the grass was damp with dew. Rita and Arthur were still sleeping.

He gave them a quick poke each. 'Wake up, you two, it's morning.'

'Huh?' Rita opened one inky eye.

Arthur unfurled and blinked.

'Theresa will be here soon. Then we'll have to find somewhere else to sleep for the day. There should be somewhere safe on the outskirts,' Vince said.

'Uh huh.' Rita shook her feathers then opened her other eye. 'So, we're definitely not staying, then?'

'No. I told you, I'm not staying without Laurie.'

'Okay, okay! I was just checking. I think it's the right decision.'

'You do?'

'Yes. If they won't let Laurie live here just because she's from the city, then it's not the right place. Even if it is your grandparents' park. Ajadi was right. You shouldn't settle for second best.'

'And to be, um, honest,' Arthur said, 'I didn't like Theresa much anyway. Her feet were far too nice for a pigeon.'

Vince laughed, glad they both understood.

'Where is Laurie, anyway?' Rita said.

'I don't know, I guess she's finding breakfast, but I dread to think what Theresa will say about that...'

'We're about to find out.' Rita pointed at the sky. Theresa was flapping towards them. The dull sound of her wings slapping together grew louder as she descended, before she swooped above the grass and landed, almost managing to make it look elegant.

'Good morning!' she cooed. 'All set and ready for your induction, Vince? I've informed the other foxes in the woods and they're all very excited to meet you.'

'What? No... I'm not staying. I'm just waiting for Laurie to get back and then we're leaving.'

'I'm sorry, perhaps I've misunderstood, then? Laurie said you would be staying. She came to find me just now, before she left. She said you two had... er, how shall I put this? Uncoupled?'

Vince shook his head, mouth open. 'I don't... Understand. She's gone?'

'My apologies, I assumed you knew. So... will you be staying or not? It's just I need—'

'Not. Which way did she go?'

The pigeon pointed to the bridge. Vince turned away and headed towards it, his walk quickly turning to a sprint. Rita and Arthur followed, struggling to keep up.

'Wait! Vince!' Their voices swept over him, but he kept running. Laurie couldn't have got far. Even if she'd run, he could still catch her. But which way did she go? How could he...?

Rita. Of course. He wasn't thinking straight.

He skidded to a stop and doubled back to Rita and Arthur. He panted the words out. 'Rita. Find her. Please.'

She nodded and took to the sky without hesitation.

'We'll walk back the way we came!' he shouted into the air.

'Don't worry,' Arthur said. 'She'll find her. It'll be fine.'

Vince said nothing.

The two of them crossed the bridge, walking at Arthur's pace. The train tracks below barely registered as he stared at the sky. He understood why Laurie had done it. She wanted him to stay and be happy. And maybe Theresa's reaction had made her feel like she wasn't good enough. Or maybe he had got it all wrong as she didn't want to be with him after all. Maybe she'd had second thoughts. But whatever it was, how could she just leave without explaining or saying goodbye? How could she do that? After yesterday; after everything?

He had to find her. Rita *had* to find her.

Vince and Arthur retraced their steps, Arthur trying to reassure Vince that it was 'probably all a silly, um, misunderstanding'. Vince could only nod and mumble in reply, convinced that he would never see Laurie again. The sun was above the trees now, but Vince ignored it. He could sleep later. Arthur would just have to deal with it.

Arthur was tired from yesterday's long walk so the pair only made it to the end of one street, before Rita's silhouette flashed across the sky.

'Rita! Down here!' She spiralled down and perched on a lamp post, but Vince was too preoccupied with her to notice Laurie turn the corner and sit on the pavement opposite.

Rita pointed a wing and Vince's eyes followed it. His stomach somersaulted. 'Laurie!' He ran to her, but stopped short. The fur on her face was wet. She'd been crying.

'Laurie... You left... I don't... How *could* you?' Vince said.

'I had to. I can't be the one who stops you from being happy. I won't,' Laurie replied.

'If this is because of what Theresa said, about you not being from a park...'

'I don't give a scat what that flying rat thinks.' Laurie paused. '*You* don't think that, do you?'

'Of course not!'

'Good. No, it's not about that. It's about you. And Rita. And this whole journey thing. I just don't...' She sighed and shook her head. 'I don't... want to get in the way. You had this big, exciting dream, and you found it. After nearly dying, how many times? You found it. Exactly what you wanted. And now you're saying you don't want it after all? Because of me. Because I turned up in some allotment, called you a poodle, helped almost get you killed… No. It's not fair on you. I'm sorry, but I won't let myself ruin this for you.' She blinked and tears spilled from her eyes.

Vince felt his heart shatter inside him. Laurie was the strongest, fiercest animal he'd ever met, and seeing her cry only made him want to be with her even more. 'No, Laurie, that's not how it is at all…'

'You need to forget about me. You've got everything you wanted now.'

'Yes, I have, because I have *you* now.'

'I was *there*, Vince. At the zoo, remember? You thought about living in Hammersmith with me, then you changed your mind. And that was fine, because I knew you wanted more than that. I wanted you to be happy. I *still do*. So much. That's all I want. That's why I can't let you walk away from Hampstead Heath. I saw your face when we arrived. When you ran across the grass, it was the happiest I've ever seen you. I won't let you abandon that for me.'

Vince shook his head and laughed. 'Laurie, how can you not understand… I was happy because I was with *you*. The heath is… Look, there are other parks. There's only one of you.'

'Are there? How many parks have you been to, now? Four? Five? Hampstead Heath is where your grandparents were born. It's the place you've been looking for this whole time. You won't find anywhere better, Vince. You really won't.'

'Laurie, listen to me, I don't—'

'Don't worry about me, please. I've still got Socks. And I'll pass on the message, about the riot. I'll make sure everyone at Richmond Park finds out, so don't worry about it. Just enjoy your new life, okay? Goodbye, Vince.' She turned and ran.

'No, Laurie, wait!' He chased after her, but she darted left down another street, widening the gap between them. 'Laurie, stop!'

Rita followed overhead, yelling for Arthur to hide and stay put. A female human ran along the pavement puffing from exertion, neon stripes on her clothes glinting in the sunlight. She gasped as the two foxes tore past her, one after the other. Her presence was a sudden reminder that it was no longer night-time, and no longer safe for them out on the streets.

'Laurie, come on! It's daylight! Let's find somewhere to sleep then we can talk in the evening, okay?' he yelled at her backside. Laurie kept running. The road curved around to the left and Vince's ears twisted instinctively towards the hum of a nearby engine.

'Laurie!' On she ran. More humans dotted the path, but she weaved through them with ease. Unused to crowded streets, Vince began to lose ground. The engine noise thrummed louder. Where was it? Behind him? He couldn't stop and look. He couldn't lose sight of Laurie.

The road straightened out again and Laurie was now far in front. More streets branched off on both sides, the paths ending abruptly. Laurie bounded across one and Vince held his breath, until she rejoined the path on the other side. Hot air blasted Vince as the car sailed past him. It was black, an orange light glowing on the front, grey smoke pouring from the pipe at the back.

Laurie looked towards a turning up ahead on the right. It looked narrow, lined with houses. A good place to lose a pursuer. The black car was behind her. She hadn't seen it. 'Laurie! Stop!'

'Laurie! Car!' Rita yelled from the air, but Laurie either couldn't hear or ignored them both. She darted off to the right, jumping from the pavement onto the road. She disappeared behind the car. A screech filled the air.

'Laurie!' Vince skidded to a stop, watching for Laurie to emerge on the other side.

She didn't.

The car's engine revved and it roared away, leaving behind a gritty cloud of fumes and Laurie's body, unmoving in the road.

No!

Rita dived, swooping up to land on the road with a flash of her white-striped wings.

Please be okay. You have to be okay. Please. Please.

Vince checked for more cars before rushing to her. Rita touched Laurie's snout with her beak, looked at Vince, then shook her head.

No.

He circled her body. Her eyes were closed.

No.

He nuzzled her snout. Nothing.

'No...' he whispered.

Rita started to cry. Vince lay down next to Laurie. She was warm. He nestled his head into her, as she had done to him before they'd fallen asleep. He squeezed his eyes shut, but the tears fell anyway.

Rita watched from the pavement as Vince laid beside Laurie's body. Another car arrived, red this time, but he refused to move, lifting only his head to stare blankly at the metal beast until it slowed and swerved around them.

'Vince, I know you don't want to leave her but—'

'I'm not moving.'

'You have to.'

'I don't.'

'Well, maybe we can try to move her...'

'No. Just leave me.' His head dropped again.

Rita didn't know what to do. He had lost everything. Again. And Arthur was still waiting back near the heath. Who knew what might happen to a tiny hedgehog in broad daylight. But could she leave Vince alone? In the road?

She hopped back and forth, trying to think, when a man appeared from one of the side streets. He saw Laurie and Vince, stopped, then headed straight for them.

'Vince, a human's coming.'

'I'm not leaving her.'

The man approached them slowly. The material on his legs was blue and ripped across his knees. His top half was covered with something thick, black, and woolly and the hands poking from it were dark and wrinkled like tree bark. A crooked smile beamed from within a fur-circled mouth, set within an equally dark and aged face. His head-fur was twisted into long rope-like strands and pulled back like a horse's backside, with some of the shorter strands hanging down at the front.

'What do we got 'ere then?' He crouched down next to Vince. 'Ah, 'ello there! Your friend 'ere don't look too good. Let's see...' He reached his hand towards Laurie. Vince growled and thrashed his tail. 'Easy, boy! Just tryin' to 'elp.'

'He's friendly, Vince. Let him help,' Rita said.

Vince backed away, teeth still bared. The man pressed Laurie's side with his fingertips. He pulled the black covering over his head and shook it free from his arms. Underneath his arms were bare, but another, thinner piece of black material covered his chest. He held the material in his hands and scooped Laurie into it, wrapping her tightly.

Vince let out a whine. The man looked straight at him. 'I'll do my best, little fella.' He picked up the bundle containing Laurie and hugged her close to his chest. 'I'll do my best,' he said again, then began to walk back the way he came.

'Follow him, Rita,' Vince cried.

He didn't need to ask her twice.

Edward grunted as he paced back and forth in front of the pond. The squirrels were late with his breakfast. He liked his acorns in a pile on a nearby tree stump, ready and waiting when he woke up. He wasn't particularly hungry, but that was beside the point.

He'd had trouble getting back to sleep after the foxes' intrusion. They'd rankled him more than he'd expected. Word travelled fast in Richmond Park. If the other animals heard that they were standing up to him and getting off lightly, they'd start to follow suit. Destroying their dens and kicking them out wasn't enough, but killing them both, as well as Alice, might cause ripples. He needed something else. A statement.

Ugh. This was all Vince's doing. He should have killed him seasons ago when he had the chance. But he would have to worry about the foxes later. First, he had to speak to Kara before the sun was fully risen and she disappeared for the day.

She was late too, but he didn't want to reprimand her more

than necessary today. She was too useful, and making an enemy of her would be unwise. After some more impatient pacing, he spotted her in the sky. Oblivious of her misdemeanour, she swooped casually overhead and landed in a tree behind him.

'You're late,' Edward said.

'No, I'm not. You woke up early.'

'It's not important. Listen, as grateful as I am for your assistance with the Vince problem, I'm afraid I can't let you hunt any more rabbits.'

'You're joking, right?' Kara flexed her talons, gouging lines in the branch underfoot.

'No. There have been complaints from the rabbits. One of them saw you. I told you to be discreet.'

'There's hundreds of them, it's impossible. And you promised me one rabbit per moon. It won't even make a dent in the population.'

'Maybe not, but I have a duty to respect the needs of every animal in this park.'

'Are you seriously giving me one of your "look how much I care" lines? Who do you think you're talking to? You don't give a scat about the rabbits. And we had a deal. A deal that almost got me killed, by the way.' She turned and waved her patchy tail feathers at him.

'Yes, very nice. But I'm sorry. There's nothing I can do.'

'So, that's it? I fly across London, have a fox killed for you, almost die, and I get nothing...'

'You can hunt the big rats in the golf course, three times a week, as agreed, and you still have your usual privileges.'

'Screw the golf course. I want my rabbits. *As agreed.*'

Edward shook his head, about to speak, when the squirrels appeared, struggling along the ground with armfuls of acorns.

'You're late.'

'It's... It's sunrise... Same as always...' The lead squirrel quivered.

'Don't argue with me. I've been awake for an age. Be on time tomorrow or you and your family can find a new home in the car park.'

'Yes, s-sir.' They carried the nuts to the tree stump and fled into the trees.

Kara watched them scurry away, then turned back to Edward, who was now nibbling at the pile of acorns. 'Can I go?' she said.

Edward swallowed his mouthful. 'Well, I do need someone to check on the foxes. Now that Jake is no longer willing and all this business with Vince... I need to make sure they're staying in line.'

'Unless you're offering rabbits in return, then you can shove it up your fat rump,' Kara said.

Edward frowned. 'Fine. Then that's all.'

He went back to his breakfast pile, the delicate scraping of Kara's talons on the tree the only hint that she had gone. No matter. There were other animals who would be pleased to do the work, other promises he could make. Kara was getting annoying anyway. Too demanding. Too inefficient. How long had it taken her to find Vince? Two nights? Pfft. She was losing her edge. And something had to be done about those squirrels... Simply not good enough. Time to reassess the workforce.

He smiled as a plan formed in his mind. Yes. The park needed a bit of a shake-up, and he knew exactly how to make sure his work got done while also dealing with Sophie. After today, no animal would dare even *think* to call him a twig-head, let alone say it out loud.

'A *fox*, Del? Jesus Christ.' Rita watched through the window as the man she now knew as Del knelt on the floor and placed Laurie in a blanket-lined cardboard box. A woman stood with her arms folded. A long piece of flowery material covered her from neck to knees, splaying out at her waist. Her foot coverings were fluffy and pink, with ears like a rabbit's. 'I thought we agreed, no more animals? After that squirrel shat on my knitting, remember?'

'This is an emergency.' He stroked Laurie's ears.

After shouting to Vince to go and wait with Arthur, Rita had followed the man back to his home on the nearby street, where he'd disappeared through a bright purple door. The building was tall, and she'd rested on each windowsill in turn, waiting for a glimpse of him, until he'd arrived on the top floor. The window was open a crack; enough for her to hear them.

'Shouldn't you take it to a vet? Or call the RSPCA or something?' the woman said.

'A vet won't 'elp a fox. Nah, they'd probably just put her to sleep. She'll be okay with me.'

'Fine, but this is the last one, okay? And if she shits on *anything*…'

'I'm a dead man. Yes I know, darlin'.' He smiled up at the woman, who smiled back.

'Right, I'm off to work. See you tonight.' She unfolded her arms, went over to him and kissed him on the forehead.

'Bye, love.' He watched her leave, then got up and wandered to another room, out of view. The house was messy but vibrant. Flowers filled pots on nearly every surface and the walls were covered with pictures: landscapes, animals and more flowers. Blankets hung over the back of chairs, and a large table was littered with objects she'd never seen before: thin wooden sticks with hair splaying from their ends; pots filled with brightly coloured liquid; large squares of fabric, stretched across wooden frames.

Del returned with a bowl of something, placed it in the box with Laurie and went back to stroking her fur. 'What shall we call you then, pretty lady? How about Scarlett? Like the actress, and because you're red.' He laughed to himself, a deep, friendly chuckle.

The sides of the box were too high for Rita see Laurie clearly, but why would the man talk to her like that if she wasn't alive? She had to trust him, and pray to Mother Nature that he could help her.

She watched for a few more moments then, confident Laurie was in safe hands, fluttered in the direction of where she'd left Arthur, where, hopefully, he would be waiting with Vince.

Vince found Arthur sleeping under a bush in a front garden, almost exactly where they'd left him. Vince curled up next to him, being careful not to wake, or touch, the prickly creature. He couldn't deal with telling him about Laurie. Not yet. Plus, it was daytime, and as good a place to rest as any.

Sleep was not an option, though. His mind raced. Had it been his fault? Could he have shouted louder? Run faster? If he hadn't chased her at all, she wouldn't have tried so hard to get away, and wouldn't have run into the road...

Over and over it played in his mind – the car engine, the shouting, her lifeless body – until Rita's raucous voice roused him from the nightmare.

'Laurie's alive! Wake up, Vince, Arthur! She's alive!'

His heart thumped hard in his chest as he slid out from under the bush. 'Really? Are you sure?'

'Yes! The man made her a bed and gave her some food. He wouldn't do that if she were dead.'

'Maybe, but... Do you think he knows for sure?' Vince said.

'Of course! Humans know these things.'

'I hope so,' Vince said. 'So, now we just wait? What will he do with her?'

'He'll take care of her until she's better, then release her, probably.'

The bush rustled and Arthur emerged, yawning. 'You came back! I thought you were both gone for good. Did you find Laurie?'

Rita explained what had happened and Arthur's face fell. 'She'll be okay, though? Won't she?'

Vince spoke before Rita could reply. 'Don't get your hopes up. Not everything is rainbows and sunshine out here, Arthur.' He crawled back under the bush. All he wanted to do was see Laurie, but since he couldn't do that, sleeping seemed like the next best option. All thoughts of sending a message back to Richmond Park had vanished. Until Laurie was safe and free, nothing else mattered.

Rita sighed. Vince listened from inside the bush as she spoke to Arthur. 'You don't have to stay with us, you know. If you'd rather just go back to Hampstead Heath—'

'No!' he replied. 'I want to be with you and, um, Vince and Laurie. Besides, there are no hedgehogs in Hampstead Heath. I don't want to be alone again.'

'I'm glad you want to stay, and I know Vince is too,' Rita said.

'I'll keep an eye on Laurie, and we'll all decide what to do once it gets dark again, okay? Now, here's an important job for you... Stay with Vince and make sure he doesn't do anything silly.'

Arthur giggled and Vince snorted from the bushes. 'I heard that,' he mumbled.

14

Laurie woke to the sound of running water and a tune, hummed softly by a human. She eased open her eyes and blinked away the grogginess. Something was not right. It felt like evening, but the light above was harsh and orange. Her ribs ached on one side when she breathed, the pain intensifying at any slight movement.

Despite the light, she was comfortable. Wherever she was, it was warm, and the blanket beneath her was almost as soft as fur. A yawn escaped her mouth and a blinding pain cascaded through her bones. She yelped. The water and whoever was humming both stopped, and the sound of footsteps replaced them.

'Ah, Scarlett, you're awake.' The human reached a hand towards her and gently stroked the top of her head. Too stunned and in too much pain to bark, she found herself rather enjoying it. 'Let me get you some chicken.' He disappeared, talking to himself as she heard some kind of packet being ripped open. He returned, a small plate in hand. It certainly smelled like chicken. Cooked, but not like the crunchy, sweet stuff she usually ate back home. The rats would approve. He placed it down in front of her and she gave it another sniff, just to be sure.

Convinced that it wasn't poisoned, she worked her way through the meat, wincing through every laboured swallow, pain erupting across her chest each time. The man watched her until the last morsel was gone and she dropped her head to the blanket, panting through the ache in her ribs. 'It's okay, you're goin' to be fine. Let me wash that up.' He gave her ears a quick scratch and took the empty plate away. The water, and the humming, started up again.

How had she got here? She tried to remember but her brain was foggy. She'd left Vince and the others in Hampstead Heath, hoping to slip away, but Rita had caught her up and convinced her to go back and speak to Vince. She remembered that. Vince was upset. She had run, and he had shouted for her to stop, Rita too, but she hadn't realised why. She'd tried to cross the road to get away from him... But she hadn't made it. A car, probably. She thought they just wanted her to stop. Her mind was elsewhere and her eyes were blurry from tears. Concentrating too hard on trying to get away.

Stupid Laurie. Stupid, stupid, stupid.

At least she was safe now. And not dead. Being dead would not be ideal. Was Vince okay, though? What if he'd followed her into the road and...

The man returned with another plate of chicken. 'I won't tell Charlie if you won't. We'll say it was past its use-by date.' He tapped the side of his nose with a finger. She tucked into the meat, but Vince still plagued her mind. This wasn't how it was supposed to go. But maybe if he thought she was dead, he would go and live in Hampstead Heath, like he should have in the first place.

A door opened and more footsteps filled the room.

'Hello, honey. How was work?' the man said.

A woman's voice spoke. 'Oh, you know, awful. How's the fox?'

'She's awake. I've called her Scarlett.'

'You're obsessed. I've told you, she's out of your league.' The woman laughed. 'And how long will *Scarlett* be staying with us?'

'I don't know. She 'asn't moved, so I don't know if she's broken anythin'. But if there's no broken bones, then I'll let her go in the mornin'. But I was thinkin', I might take 'er somewhere else. Somewhere safer, what d'you reckon? Maybe up by Marion and Pete's? You know, with the big nature reserve?'

'All that way? Why don't you just take her to the heath?'

'That's probably where she came from. All these roads around it, it ain't good for them, Charlie. I seen three dead foxes this week, squashed like pancakes. 'Orrible.'

Laurie shivered. That could have been her. She'd been lucky, but what was this human going to do with her? What if she never saw Vince or Socks again?

'Yes, well, that's London, isn't it? And what about the other fox you saw?' Charlie said.

'If I see him again, maybe I'll try to catch him. Take both of them together.'

'Rescuing an injured fox is one thing, but catching a healthy one just to take it somewhere nicer? You're crazy, Del, but Lord knows I can't stop you when you get one of your ideas in your head. Just promise me she won't be here long, okay? And don't get bitten. Any more tetanus jabs and the hospital will think you're getting high on 'em or something.'

'Yeah, I promise. But look...' Del moved across the room and picked something large and square up from the table. 'What d'you think?' He held up the square. On it, a picture of a fox. Reduced to a few simple lines and shapes, but unmistakably Laurie. Bright orange with green eyes, curled up in a perfect circle, a wreath of leaves like a halo around her.

'Gorgeous, as always.' The woman leaned forward and planted a kiss on the man's lips. 'And it doesn't smell like the real one.' She smiled, tweaking his chin between her thumb and forefinger.

Laurie frowned. *Rude.*

'I gotta' make her eyes greener, though. Look at them...' He came over to Laurie and crouched down next to her. 'Beautiful.'

'They are beautiful, I'll give you that,' Charlie said. 'Rest of her is a bit mangy, though.'

'Don't be rude!' Del said.

'What? She doesn't know what we're saying. Do you?' Charlie bent at the waist and peered into Laurie's box. 'You don't look that hurt. Reckon Del can get rid of you tomorrow, can't he, Scarlett?'

'My name is Laurie,' Laurie said, knowing full well they wouldn't understand her.

Del laughed. 'See! Did you hear that? She said, "Shut up, Charlie, you're the mangy one." Don't listen to her, Scarlett, you're beautiful.'

'I have sharp teeth too,' Laurie said to Charlie. 'Come closer and I'll show you.'

Charlie rested a hand on the man's back and leaned in again.

'Wow, did you hear that? She said, "Shut up Del, you lazy bastard, and go and make your wife a cup of tea."'

'That is one clever fox, right there,' Del said, giving Laurie one last head rub. 'I'd better do what she says.'

The sun was setting and the drop in temperature woke Rita from her slumber. Laurie was still in the box, presumably asleep, when she'd arrived back on the windowsill, so she'd found a tree to perch in while she waited for any improvement.

She hopped along the branch and fluttered to the window, peering through the murky glass. The lights were off inside and neither Del nor the woman were around. Laurie's box was on the floor. Her tail was draped over the edge, swishing lazily from side to side.

She is alive! And she's awake!

'Laurie!' Rita hissed through the tiny gap in the window. 'It's me! Over here!'

Laurie's head turned, and her eyes lit up before her face contorted into a grimace. 'Rita!'

'Oh, don't move! Are you okay? We were so worried.'

'I'm okay. Bruised and sore, but alive. Plus, I've had some of the best chicken of my life and the man made a picture of me and said I was beautiful, so overall, can't complain. Is Vince okay? He didn't get hit too, did he?'

Rita laughed. 'Vince is fine. He's waiting for you. I know what you said about wanting him to stay at Hampstead Heath without you, but he won't. He loves you, Laurie. Come with us. We'll find somewhere else to live, all of us.'

Laurie nodded. Nothing like almost dying to put things into perspective. If he was really that stubborn, then nothing she could do would change his mind. Probably not even her being dead. 'Okay. But tell him he's a poodle for choosing me over that place.'

Rita cocked her head. 'I will, but I don't agree.'

'There are two problems, though,' Laurie said. 'The man said something about taking me somewhere else. Some nature reserve place. Out of London, I think. They said, "up there", so maybe north? But it could be anywhere.'

'I'll have to follow you. Do you know when he's planning on doing it?'

Laurie recounted what the humans had said, and how the woman seemed keen to get rid of her as soon as possible. Then she told Rita the other problem.

'Socks,' Laurie said.

'I'll get a message to him, let him know what's happened. You'll see him again, Laurie. I promise.'

Laurie shook her head. 'No... Not if the human takes me away...'

'We'll figure something out. We will. Vince and Arthur will be waking up now. You sit tight and rest. I'll be back before morning. And don't worry about anything, okay? It'll all be fine.'

'Thanks, Rita. Don't forget to tell Vince—'

'That he's a poodle... I won't.' She hopped off the windowsill and headed back to Vince and Arthur once more.

Rita spent the night under the bush while Vince hunted, bringing back rats for himself and mouthfuls of worms for Arthur, whom, they agreed, they didn't want wandering the gardens on his own. Vince's reaction to Laurie's message had been reserved. He'd smiled, but muttered only, 'I just hope I get to see her again,' before wandering off.

Ever optimistic, Rita slept well, considering her earlier nap in the tree. She was glad to be back to her usual diurnal routine for a while. As the sun rose over London she felt the warmth on her feathers and hopped out onto the pavement to enjoy the daylight. Overnight, fat spiders had strung their webs across the leaves of the bush. She pecked them off, swallowing them whole. She would need a good breakfast if what Laurie had told her was true.

Vince returned to the bush and flopped onto his side with a sigh.

'Are you okay, Vince?' Arthur said. 'Laurie will be alright, don't worry. Rita's going to follow her, then we'll find her and everything will be fine.'

'Maybe. But what if Rita can't follow her? What if the human takes her in a car?' Vince said.

'I can keep up, don't worry,' Rita said, a little hurt that Vince didn't have faith in her.

'It's not that I don't think you can, but what if you get hurt too? I almost got you killed once, now Laurie... I keep putting you all in danger.'

'Vince, I wanted an adventure. Let me have it. I've got nothing to lose, except letting you down.'

'Oh, Rita, don't talk like that. You know—'

'Shush!' Rita said. 'Enough of your whining! Laurie is going to be set free, I'm going to find her and we're all going to live together, do you understand?'

'I just—' Vince started.

'Yes or no?'

'Okay, yes, you win. Just be careful. Please. For me?'

'I'll be careful. For you.'

She flapped away, making what she hoped was her last journey to Del's house. The sooner all this was over and they got back to finding a park to live in, the better. Not for herself, of course, but after all this, Vince and Laurie deserved some peace and quiet.

Rita arrived just in time. Del was eager, already outside locking the purple front door, a large plastic container with a handle on top sitting at his feet. The orange-and-white fur of Laurie's tail poked through a mesh grille at the front.

'Sorry, Scarlett, my dear, it's only for a little while,' he said as he picked up the carry-case and made his way along the road. 'The wife says we don't 'ave room. And she is right about you being smelly, sorry. Don't tell her I said that. Anyway, Del is gonna take you to a much nicer place. Nicer than London. It's a long way, but when we get there... Oooh-wee! You gonna love it!'

Don't get in a car, don't get in a car...

At the end of the street, Del took a left, heading back towards Hampstead Heath, but a short way along the road he cut right, passing through a paved area with tall blocks of flats either side. Rita breathed a sigh of relief. Unless his car was parked nowhere near his house, it didn't look like he'd be driving anywhere.

Rita flew from lamp post to lamp post as Del walked down another narrow road, past an old stone church, then over some railway tracks. She watched the plastic box swing in his hand, and thought about Laurie, curled up inside. It occurred to her that Laurie didn't know she was following, since she'd been expecting to greet her at the window again, so she called her name as loud as she could, hopefully easing her mind.

Eventually, after passing along one final row of houses, Del took a break and paused outside a brown-brick building. An orange sign adorned the brickwork over the entrance but, of course, it was meaningless to her. Rita settled on a brick wall as he set Laurie on the floor and pulled something from his pocket. Rita called Laurie's name again, and this time Laurie replied with a sharp bark. Del crouched down and whispered through the mesh. 'Shhh now, Scarlett. It's okay, my darlin'.' After a quick roll of his shoulders, he picked the box back up and headed into the building.

Del placed whatever it was that he'd taken from his pocket onto a yellow circle, which opened a narrow gate, large enough only to let a single human through. Rita watched him disappear up some stairs. She would have panicked at losing sight of them, but she could already see where the stairs led. A train station. She jumped from the wall and flew upwards, over the building and over the train tracks that ran along the roof and off into the distance in both directions. She was glad Vince wasn't there.

She settled on the corrugated metal roof that hung over the station platform and waited for Del and Laurie to reappear. Del clambered up the final few steps, steadying Laurie's box with his free hand, then made his way to the platform, where he placed Laurie at his feet once more. Although not a car, a train wasn't much better. She could follow the tracks, no problem, but if she couldn't keep up then how would she know where they'd got off?

A distant rumbling vibrated through the tracks and a tinny voice sounded from nowhere. 'The next train on platform three will be the London Overground service to Barking. Please stand behind the yellow line and let any passengers off the train before boarding, thank you.'

The train slid along the rails; a giant metal caterpillar, its long, white body punctuated with orange stripes, with a square face of yellow, blue and black. It slowed, grinding to a lurching halt as it pulled up beside the platform. Seeing it this close, Rita suddenly understood why Vince was so scared of them. The orange doors hissed open and a few humans stepped out and filed away down the stairs as Del lifted Laurie and entered the body of the enormous metal beast.

Could she follow it? It had been travelling slowly into the station, but she knew it would pick up speed once it left. The platform was empty now. She flapped down and peered through the open door. Del and one other human sat, backs to the windows. The train began to beep. It was leaving. Could she...?

The doors hissed again and she leapt towards the opening. The gap narrowed as the doors sliced through the air. She landed inside, her talons slipping on the smooth floor. The doors thumped together behind her, trapping her long tail feathers between them.

'Argh!' she squawked. Del looked over and clicked his teeth with his tongue. He got up, quickly checking Laurie was safe on the seat next to him, and crouched down beside her.

'Oh, little bird! Hold still...' He wrapped his thick fingers around her, cradling her body in his palm while tugging her tail gently from the door with his other hand. Once free, he set her down on the floor and tickled her white chest. 'There you go. Now make sure you get out at the next stop, okay?' He laughed and returned to his seat next to Laurie. The other man on the train looked up at Del, then immediately dropped his head back to the phone in his hand, not even noticing the mini-menagerie in the carriage with him.

Rita shook her feathers and hopped into a corner, from where she could see Del and Laurie, but where she would be less likely to be trampled if the train filled up with passengers. She found it hard to believe that this man was the same species as whoever set the fox trap in the allotments.

They soon arrived at the next station, where more humans got on, staring at Rita and pulling out their phones to snap pictures as they took their seats. Del stayed where he was, but occasionally shouted, 'Watch out for the bird, folks! He's comin' for a ride with me!' to the other humans when their feet got too close for comfort.

'I'm female, actually,' Rita said.

'What a clever bird you are, Mister Magpie,' he responded.

Rita sighed.

The train trundled on, filling and emptying, but Rita noticed that no matter how busy it got, the other humans kept their distance from Del, preferring even to stand and stumble around than sit next to him. It confused her since, despite calling her 'Mister', he was the nicest human she'd ever encountered.

'Humans are weird,' she said to herself.

15

'Park meeting! Park meeting!' A sharp voice filled Sophie's sleeping chamber.

'Huh?' Sophie eased open her eyes and blinked. The den was dark, but she knew it was the morning. She reached a paw out for Jake, suddenly remembering that he wasn't there. After the confrontation with Edward, she couldn't bear to be around him. She told him to leave her alone and, obedient as always, he'd left. She had no idea where he was and she wasn't sure she cared.

How could he do those things? Telling Edward that he didn't want Vince to come back, spying on her and her friends and then lying about it… How could she ever look at him in the same way again?

The voice yelled again. 'Park meeting at the lake, right now! Attendance mandatory for all animals! Get a move on!'

'Okay, okay, I'm coming,' Sophie said through a yawn.

What was Edward up to now? He'd already surprised her by not kicking her out, or trampling her den, after she'd spread the word about what he'd done to Vince and Alice. Jake warned her not to, but she had been too angry to wait. She'd barely slept since, and a horrible feeling grew in the pit of her stomach as she slipped from the den and squinted in the dawn sunlight. The air was cool and wisps of cloud still hung like cobwebs in the pale blue sky.

The owner of the voice – a crow – flapped to the next den and repeated his command. Sophie's friend Marge emerged, groggy and confused, and headed over to join her.

Blake and Bailey had already headed back to Hyde Park, after scraping out a shallow hole under some nearby brambles to rest for a while. Their plans to kill Kara were quickly put aside once Sophie explained the owl's friendly relationship with Edward. After coming face-to-face with the Head Stag, they decided revenge wasn't worth their skulls being crushed under angry hooves.

One by one and two by two, animals emerged from their homes and made their way across the park. Birds soared overhead, smaller mammals crept along behind, but all hunting was on hold until Edward had said whatever he had to say.

Most of the residents were already gathered by Vince's old den – Edward's new sleeping spot – when Sophie arrived. Thousands of animals of countless species. Any human who stumbled upon the gathering would have pinched themselves, but to be extra careful, the deer had formed a wide semi-circle enclosing the creatures and separating them from any stray humans who might walk by.

The atmosphere was nervous and hushed; even some of the deer muttered to one another, speculating about what Edward might have planned. The rabbits arrived altogether – an impressive mass of brown fur, moving as one. Hundreds of tiny songbirds twittered in the centre, alongside the crows, jackdaws and magpies. Kara and the other owls perched on the branches above, under the dark leaf canopy, puffing under their breath about the unsociable time of day. Sophie found a spot on the left-hand side, between the squirrels and the rabbits, a couple of does standing guard behind them. Marge and all the other foxes, with the exception of Jake, joined Sophie. She didn't think he would show up, until she spotted him alone at the very back.

As the rest of the creatures filed in, Edward himself emerged from the trees, six of the largest stags spread out behind him along the straight edge of the semi-circle. Wry smiles crept onto the stags' muzzles as they saw the quiet congregation expanded across the grass, but Edward remained cool, his lips pursed and chin high.

The Head Stag cleared his throat. All whispering ceased and silence fell over the crowd.

His voice boomed over the animals. 'Good morning, everyone. I have called this emergency meeting for three reasons. The first is that I have distressing news. Vince the fox, who left this park of his own accord, has sadly been killed. I asked Kara to send a message, informing him that he was welcome to return, but unfortunately she found him dead in the city. The cause of death is unknown, but a vicious animal or a car accident seems most likely. The city is a dangerous place, and I hope this unfortunate loss serves as a reminder to you all that leaving the safety of our boundary is not something we recommend.'

Sophie rolled her eyes. The crowd murmured, confused. Many had heard Sophie's story, and now clearly didn't know whom to trust.

Edward continued, 'The second reason for this meeting is that I have become aware of a recent decline in standards of behaviour. Some animals have wilfully disregarded rules – rules that are in place to protect you – and, as I'm sure you'll agree, this kind of behaviour is unacceptable.'

Small gasps rose from the animals as they looked around at one another. But Sophie had a pretty good idea who he was talking about.

'One animal in particular believes she is better than the rest of you. She believes the rules don't apply to her.'

The crowd burst into frenzied chatter. Sophie clenched her teeth. She wanted to run, but that would be admitting guilt. That was what Edward wanted.

Jake shot Sophie a worried look. Edward stamped a hoof and a hush fell over the crowd.

'This animal has been reported to be giving our resources to outside animals. Domestic cats, in particular, spreading vicious rumours, and being abusive to other residents.'

The last part's true, at least.

Disapproving murmurs spread across the mass of animals like fire. On cue, the deer behind the foxes sidestepped together, closing the gaps in the barrier and blocking any escape. A trembling Marge looked at Sophie, her eyes wide. 'Don't worry, he's after me,' Sophie whispered.

'But that's not all, I'm afraid,' Edward boomed again, his eyes scanning the sea of residents, settling on Sophie for an almost imperceptible moment. 'Two non-resident foxes from the city were found to be living in the cemetery. They have since been dealt with and no longer pose a risk to you. However, they were invited inside our boundary by the animal in question. Mother knows how long they have been living here, eating your food, murdering your families…'

Sophie flinched as gasps split the air around her. Her mind went to Vince. His dead body out in the city somewhere. If he were here…

'Lies!' Sophie yelled without thinking.

Countless tiny heads painted with anger turned to stare at her. Whispers of her name filled the air, followed by shouts, the noise quickly becoming deafening.

'Sophie!' Jake's shout was only just audible. He started to push his way through the crowd but a deer stepped in front of him and lowered its antlers.

Edward's mouth curled into a smile. 'I wasn't going to name the perpetrator, but it seems she is keen for you all to know who she is.'

'Stop lying!' Sophie shouted. 'The foxes were nothing to do with me. *You* sent Kara to find them and promised them a home in return for killing Vince. Tell them the truth! Tell them you ordered Vince dead!'

The animals around her only grew angrier at her protest, shaking their heads in disgust. The squirrels backed away, shielding their children from the threat of the rogue fox. The other foxes didn't move, but whispered to one another, eyes on Sophie. Marge shot her a desperate look.

'I admit…' Edward ignored Sophie and carried on, everyone quickly turning back to face him, '…I assumed that Vince was the main cause of unease within this park and that his leaving would solve our problems, but it seems he passed his despicable behaviour on to his mate.' He looked directly at Sophie.

The entire park seemed to be on Edward's side. Did they actually believe his lies, or were they just scared of him? She knew the foxes' answers, at least; they'd seen the state of Alice's den. Her instinct to run kicked in. She was faster than most of the animals, but not the deer. It would make her look guilty, but if everyone already thought she was to blame, she had nothing to lose. If she could make it to the boundary, she would be safe.

She went to turn, but one of the deer dealt a swift kick to her side with a front hoof. Sophie cried out and Jake leapt into the crowd, the deer not quick enough to stop him.

'Don't even try it,' the doe said to Sophie. She collapsed onto the grass, dizzy from the pain exploding through her ribs. Jake pushed his way through the protesting animals.

'Leave him,' Edward shouted to the does. 'Let him comfort his mate while he still has the chance.'

Sophie lifted her head. Her blurry vision masked Edward's expression, but she had little doubt there was a smirk plastered across his stupid snout. Jake arrived at her side. 'Mother Nature, are you okay, Soph?'

'Fine,' she breathed. 'But everyone... believes him.' She set her feelings towards Jake aside; she needed all the help she could get.

Edward shushed the animals. 'It goes without saying that she will be dealt with appropriately later, but I will come back to that, after I tell you the third reason I called this meeting. I hope it will reassure you all to know that we, the deer, as the strongest animals here, vow always to bear the great responsibility of protecting the park and all the residents within it. It is truly an honour to serve as your protectors, and to uphold the rules and values of this place we call home.'

Nods spread through the sea of animals. A few cheers even rose up from some small groups.

Sophie dragged herself to her feet, wincing through the pain in her side.

'As you all know,' Edward continued, 'these rules and values form Park Watch, which was put in place many seasons ago to maintain safety and harmony, and to ensure that any animal who is chosen to take on additional duties could be fairly rewarded.'

'*Additional duties* my backside,' Sophie muttered under her breath.

Edward's voice grew louder. 'Building on the continued success of Park Watch, I am pleased to announce an exciting new opportunity for you all.' He paused for effect, and many animals responded predictably with excited whispers. Edward carried on. 'From now on, every resident in Richmond Park – not just those with officially designated duties – will be eligible for rewards.'

More cheers erupted, louder this time. Smiles spread across faces, tails waved back and forth and hind legs stamped on the grass.

Edward opened his mouth to speak again and the noise died down. 'The nature of the rewards themselves will be decided on a case-by-case basis, but they can be earned simply by reporting any rule infraction – large or small – directly to me...'

'This is madness,' Sophie said. 'Can't they see what he's doing?'

'...I hope this new system will encourage everyone to work just a little bit harder for the greater good of the park. Together, we can keep this park safe, peaceful and productive!'

Some animals – those with the least critical thinking skills – cheered again, but many stayed silent. Sophie felt a pang of hope.

A short way from Sophie, a squirrel whispered to another, 'He wants us to tell on each other.'

'Yes, yes!' Sophie hissed at them, 'He wants everyone to be his spies... Tell him you won't do it! All of you!'

The squirrels looked at Sophie with their jet-black eyes. 'But he's in charge. He'll kick us out...'

'He can't kick you all out, can he? Come on, we have to all stand up to him together.'

'Sophie, you're going to get yourself killed,' Jake said.

'Wait, you're the fox that did all those bad things...' the other squirrel said.

Before she could reply, the air disappeared from her lungs as an antler struck her already bruised ribs. A silent yelp escaped her jaws and she fell to the ground, gasping for breath.

'Sophie!' Jake scrabbled towards her and inspected the gash where the tip of the antler had impaled her. He licked the wound to stem the blood flow.

'The fox has something else to say, apparently,' Edward shouted. 'Excellent timing. We shall move on to the business of her punishment. Consider this, everybody, your first infraction report. You all know what she did. You've seen her try to undermine me and disrupt this meeting. What should her punishment be?'

The crowd was silent. Sophie coughed as she tried to get up again. The doe moved to stop her but Jake bared his teeth and thrashed his tail to keep her away.

'No one wants to make a suggestion?' Edward began to pace back and forth along the front row of the crowd. 'There I was, thinking a bit of democratic debate might help improve morale…'

'Kick her out!' a tiny voice yelled out. A rabbit. One of the larger males.

'Ah!' Edward stopped pacing. 'Good, good… Any more? Don't be shy, there are no wrong answers…'

'I say kick her out too!' another rabbit shouted from the crowd. More quickly joined in. 'Yeah, kick her out! We don't want her here!'

Sophie summoned her energy and shouted back. 'Are you serious? Can't you see that he's manipulating you? I haven't even done anything. It's all lies.'

'Listen to her!' Jake joined in. 'Edward is just using you! Sophie did nothing wrong, and Edward's the one who had Vince killed!'

'Residents, who do you trust more?' Edward started pacing again. 'Me, the one who keeps order, who keeps you safe, who is standing up here telling you *facts* in a calm and rational manner? Or the *foxes*? The foxes who spread vicious gossip, who refuse to cooperate, who invite strangers into your home, who try to convince you of their innocence by suggesting that you are *stupid*, somehow, for trusting me.'

'When did I call anyone stupid? You're twisting my words…' She trailed off and locked eyes with Jake. He may have been foolish and naive to trust Edward, but she could see now how his good intentions could have spiralled out of control. She had let herself be manipulated by Edward, as the rabbits were being now.

Edward addressed the crowd again. 'Now, if the vermin are quite finished—'

'VERMIN?' A voice, low and hoarse, called from deep in the trees. Sophie didn't recognise it, and, judging by the rest of the animals' puzzled expressions, neither did they.

Edward's smile dropped from his face as the creature lumbered its way into view.

Kara emerged from the shadow of the tree above. 'You...?' she said.

The creature pointed his long, black-and-white snout towards the branch above him. 'Ah, the moon-faced bird. A pleasure to see you, it is not.'

Rita tried to keep her balance as the train lurched to a halt again. This was stop number four, and it looked like it would be the final one as Del lifted Laurie from between his feet and stood up. He smiled at Rita. 'You comin' with me, bird?' He laughed.

He left the train and Rita followed, flapping up to the roof of the station. 'Well, look at that, Scarlett. I'm Snow White!' He laughed again, this time louder, with his head tipped right back. 'Or maybe Doctor Dolittle, eh? Hey, bird! Can you understand me?'

'Yes!' Rita yelled from the roof. 'But you can't understand me, can you?'

'Nope.' Del shook his head. 'I got nothin'. Just Snow White, then, I guess.' He carried Laurie out of the station and Rita followed, watching from high above.

'It's a bit of a walk, Scarlett, my dear, but I prefer the fresh air, you know? Well, as fresh as it gets around 'ere. Better than bein' squished on the underground trains, especially as I got you with me. Don't think you'd like it down there.' He walked north along a straight road for a short while, before heading east. Rita took to the lamp posts again. Another turn to the left, straight up again, then right, and Del finally arrived at the next place. Another station. This one was busier, with a vast paved area outside where cars and buses hummed in and out. A murder of crows mingled around a rubbish bin, squabbling over the remnants of a bag of chips.

Del stopped for a quick stretch – carrying Laurie seemed to be hard on his arms – then pulled the small object from his pocket again. Rita kept one eye on him, but took the opportunity to ask the crows where exactly she was. After informing her the station was called Tottenham Hale, Rita thanked them and left them to their chips. She scanned the area, but Del was gone. She flew over the station roof and searched the platforms below. He was seated, Laurie between his feet again, on a bench on the west of the train tracks.

Thank Mother.

But where was he going? If she got the next train with him too, who knew how far away she'd end up. Could she follow him all the way back as well? It didn't look like she had much choice...

There was no doubt that Del wouldn't harm her, so she swooped down next to Laurie's carrier. The front mesh door was facing Del, away from the bustle of the platform. 'Hello, Mister Magpie, you been followin' me?' he said.

Rita ignored him. 'Laurie, it's Rita. Are you okay?' She didn't know how much time they had before the train arrived.

Laurie's voice was muffled through the sides of the box. 'Rita! You're here! Oh, Mother, I knew I heard your voice before but when he got on the train I thought I'd lost you... Where are we?'

'Somewhere called Tottenham Hale. It looks like you're getting another train. I'm going to come with you, then follow him all the way back so I can bring Vince and Arthur.'

'No, Rita, it's too far. What if something happens to you? Vince will never make it all the way, anyway. Not on one train, let alone two. Don't risk getting lost.'

'I won't, and I'm not leaving you alone.'

'Rita—'

'You can't stop me, Laurie, so you might as well accept the fact.'

Del laughed and clapped his hands together. 'You 'ear this, everyone? The bird and the fox be talkin' to each other! It's true! Come and listen!'

The people around them looked up from their phones, frowned at Del, then went back to their screens, a wide circle of empty space forming around him. Rita looked up at him. He seemed to understand them better than the other humans, even if he didn't know what they were saying.

Rita hopped on top of Laurie's box and faced Del. 'Where are you taking her?' she said.

'One for sorrow... That's what they say, don't they? But you don't look sad, Mister Magpie,' Del said.

'*Where* are you *taking* her?' Rita turned her head and pointed her beak to the train tracks.

'You comin' on the train with me again? All the way to Broxbourne?'

'Broxbourne? Is that it?' Rita said.

'Oh, you'd love it there. Nice and green. That's why I'm takin' Scarlett. It's a long way, but it's got *biiig* fields and trees and rivers and the air is...' He made a circle with his thumb and finger and clicked his tongue against his teeth again. 'Plus, it's as far as you can get with your travel card. Not a lot of people know that.' He winked at her.

A stilted voice echoed over them. 'The next train calling at platform two will be the six-ten to Cambridge. Calling at Cheshunt, Broxbourne, Roydon...'

That's the one he said. Broxbourne. Two stops.

'Laurie, I know where he's taking you. He says it's a long way,' Rita said.

'Listen, Rita, don't worry about me, okay? Just tell Vince to go back to Hampstead Heath and look after Arthur. There's no way they can make it this far.'

'Laurie, can you do one thing for me?' Rita said, ignoring Laurie's pleas. 'Remember those symbols you left in Hyde Park for Socks to follow? If you can, make some more of those. If I can get Vince and Arthur to this Broxbourne place, make sure we can find you, okay?'

Laurie's voice grew more panicked. 'Oh, *Socks*... Mother Nature... Can you get a message to him? A cat. Find a cat. They all know each other. Tell him thank you for everything, and that I'll always remember him, okay?'

'I will, I promise, but you'll see him again, Laurie. I'll make sure of it. Will you leave us the symbols?'

'Yes, I'll try, but... It's too far... Tell Vince to—'

'Excuse me, Mister Magpie, but Scarlett and I gotta be going now.' Del waved a hand at Rita.

'I think your train is here. I'll see you soon, Laurie. Don't forget the symbols...'

'I won't...'

Rita flapped away and the train pulled into the station. It was different from the last one. Bigger, and all white. Del looked up at her as she settled on the station roof to watch them leave. 'This is where we say goodbye, eh, Mister Magpie?' he called to her.

'Bye!' Rita yelled to him. 'Look after Laurie, please!'

'And a scrack-ack-ack to you too!' The doors opened and he disappeared into the carriage, Laurie in hand.

Rita watched the train roll away, until it was completely out of sight.

'Okay,' she whispered to herself. 'Tottenham Hale. Broxbourne. That's all. Easy. Get them here first. Worry about the train later. Good plan. How hard can it be?'

Sophie and the rest of the residents stared at the badger. He was old, with a torn ear and patchy, grey fur. His nose was streaked with pink welts, probably the result of a recent encounter with some claws. 'Vermin, you say?' he said in his deep growling tone. 'Sid remembers that word.'

'*Sid?* What are you... How...?' Edward said. The crowd was silent, all thoughts of persecution temporarily on hold.

'Remember Sid, do you?' the badger said. 'Sid remembers the twig-headed one, oh yes. I didn't, but came back to me, it all did.'

Sophie looked at Jake, who shrugged. Even the deer behind them were inching away to get a better look at the stranger.

Edward composed himself. 'Actually, after I kicked you out, I never gave you a second thought.'

'Indeed. And a second thought Sid never gave to Richmond Park. Like a dandelion, my brain is. Floated from Sid's memories, it did. Until the red-furred mammal and the pie-bird came by.'

'Red-furred…?' Sophie said under her breath, then shouted to the badger, 'Vince? You met *Vince*?'

'Vince, yes! The red-furred one! Are you his vixen? The one he left behind? Sid has information for you. Well, for Vince. But know how to find him, Sid didn't.'

'What information?' Sophie stepped forward into the throng. The deer behind made no attempt to stop her, since she obviously wasn't trying to escape.

Edward stamped a hoof. 'Enough of this. No more interruptions. Stags, remove this badger! Get that vermin fox back in line!' The deer went to move.

'Wait!' Sid commanded, his voice almost as loud as Edward's. The stags stopped in their tracks.

Sid looked up at Edward and continued, his voice calm. 'The only vermin here, Sid thinks, is you.' Edward opened his mouth, but the badger kept talking. 'I will say what I have to say, then I will leave. No skin off your nose, it is not.' He looked at Sophie. 'The red-furred one is looking for a park, yes? Its location Sid cannot remember, but this one knows…' He pointed a paw at Edward, then looked up at him. '…Correct, am I not?'

'He *knew*…' Sophie whispered to herself, then looked at a confused Jake. 'But he had Vince killed anyway. Why not just tell him and let him go there?'

'Do you think there's something or someone there that Edward didn't want Vince to know about?' Jake asked.

Edward snorted. 'So what if I know where the park is. Vince is dead.'

Sid's face fell. He looked at Sophie, who confirmed it with a nod. 'And the pie-bird, too?' Sid asked.

'Pie-bird?' Sophie frowned.

A voice chirped from the stunned crowd. A starling. 'Excuse me, Mister Badger, do you mean a magpie?'

Sid nodded. 'I suppose that's what most animals call them, yes.'

'Rita! We'd been wondering where she'd gone. It's been quiet without her,' the starling said. The other starlings around her chirped in agreement. A group of crows cawed, 'I hope she's okay.' The ripple spread and birds twittered worriedly to one another, expressing their guilt at not having asked as to her whereabouts until now.

'This is all very touching,' Edward resumed his speech. 'But can I remind everyone what this meeting is—'

'Shut up!' A jackdaw shrieked. 'Rita's missing! She didn't do anything wrong... How can you be so callous?'

Edward rolled his eyes. 'Perhaps you're forgetting that bird's ceaseless noise. Good riddance, I say.'

'Singing's not against the rules,' the starling said. 'Or should we expect the mammals to report us all every single morning from now on?'

'Don't be ridiculous, birds are integral to this park,' Edward said. 'You all know that.'

'Yeah, to do your dirty work,' Sophie said as she scanned the trees, searching for Kara. 'Kara! We know you're up there. What happened to Rita? At least tell us the truth about that.'

Kara emerged from the leaves like a ghost, inching along the branch. 'She's dead. But it was nothing to do with me.'

'But Vince was, wasn't he? You found those foxes and had him killed, didn't you? Tell everyone the truth, Kara.'

Kara looked down at Edward, who frowned back up at her with eyes narrowed almost into slits. She surveyed the crowd before shrugging her wings. 'Yeah. It's all true. Edward said I could hunt a rabbit every moon if I made sure Vince didn't reach that park.'

'You little *runt*!' Edward reared up on his hind legs and brought his front hooves down to the earth with a powerful thud. 'After everything I've done for you...'

'Yeah, like go back on our deal...? Thanks for that, Edward ol' friend, I *really* appreciate it,' Kara shouted. 'I admit I've done some questionable stuff, but at least I always stick to my word.'

'It *was* her! You said it was a hawk! You lied to us too, Edward, didn't you?' a rabbit squeaked from the throng.

Murmurs began to fill the air.

'Lies and deals and dirty work...' Sid spoke to no one in particular. 'Sid thinks he was lucky to leave when he did. Used to be nice here, it did. Sid remembers *that*, indeed.'

The crowd was quiet with confusion. No one knew who this badger was, but he had – purposely or not – chipped away at Edward's authority and revealed the deceit that lay beneath. But the animals needed one final push to wrench away his power, and Sophie had to give it to them.

'We can't trust you to lead us anymore,' Sophie yelled, ignoring her pain and moving further into the throng towards Edward. 'You lied to the rabbits, you lied to Kara, to me and Jake, and you're lying to everyone when you say you want equality here. You only want power for yourself, like you've always done. Park Watch used to be a good thing where everyone could help, but now it's just bribery and favouritism. Now you want everyone to spy on each other, to live in constant fear.'

Edward curled his lip and puffed his broad, russet chest. 'I've let you talk for long enough. Stags, get rid of her. I'll deal with the badger, and the rest of you, go back to your homes. We'll continue this meeting tomorrow.'

'No!' A rabbit ran forward. 'We're not leaving. Admit that you lied about the hawk hunting us. We want to hear it from your own mouth.'

Cries of agreement rose from the crowd.

'This conversation is over,' Edward said, then looked to the does, who were scrambling back to their positions in the circle. 'You! All of you! *Escort* everyone home. *Now!*'

Cries rose from the animals as the does began pushing them with their hooves. One squirrel received a sharp kick, her mate yelling out, 'Hey! Leave her alone!' He lashed out at the deer's foreleg with his teeth. The bite was minor, but the doe flinched and backed away from the throng.

'Stop that, or I'll report you for abuse!' the doe said.

Edward snorted as a growl rumbled from his throat. '*Mother Nature*. Stags, go and help them! Disperse the crowd! Go!'

The stags rushed through the crowd as the squirrel replied,

'Report us? To whom?' He lunged at the doe's leg again and sunk his teeth in. A bead of blood erupted through her fur. More squirrels joined in, flooding around her feet and nipping at her thick flesh.

'Stop! No!' the deer screamed as she stumbled backwards, then found her footing and galloped away to the safety of the trees, a trail of squirrels snapping at the air where she had been. A stag came up behind them, but he was no more of a match for them than the doe. They repeated their attack, growing fiercer with every bite. Some clung on, tearing off tiny chunks of flesh as the stag tried to shake the creatures from his leg. He lowered his antlers and swiped blindly at the gang of squirrels, but it only served for them to jump on board and nip at the thin flesh of his pink ears.

Edward was almost screaming. 'What are you *doing? Crush* the damned things! Cowards! The *lot of you!*' He looked up at Kara and the other owls. 'Help me out, owls. You can have all the rabbits you want. Just get rid of everyone…'

Kara laughed. 'For some reason, I'm not sure they believe you…' She leapt off the branch, then flapped her way back to her hollow. A few of the others followed her, returning to their nests, but some remained to watch in silence from the dark treetops.

Every stag and doe was now whinnying in pain, thrashing their heads and legs furiously. Less ferocious, but greater in number, the rabbits and rats took on a doe each, and drove them both away with grazed, bleeding legs from a barrage of claws and teeth. The song-birds fluttered around the head of a stag, needle-like beaks jabbing at his head and snout. He stumbled about, kicking and shaking the birds away, but they came back, pecking, again and again. The crows, jackdaws and magpies did the same, but quickly found only two or three were needed to see off a single deer. Their jabs were harder and deeper, and drew more blood. The foxes had joined in the fight, snapping their teeth down on any stray legs that came close. Many of the deer had retreated to the trees, but some – Edward's most loyal – stayed to fight, the embarrassment of being chased away by the creatures almost worse than any punishment Edward might dole out later.

Edward snorted and pawed desperately at the ground as his herd were driven away one by one. A leap away to his right, watching everything unfold, was Sid. Sophie and Jake went to join him.

'Sid thinks perhaps power doesn't belong to the biggest and fastest,' Sid said to Sophie and Jake as the last of the deer galloped away.

Edward moved towards them, eyes wide and wild. '*You*. I should have killed all of you as soon as you stepped out of line, like your *friends*.' He reared up on his hind legs, nostrils flaring, sharp hooves dangling over Sophie's head. She could smell his panic.

'SOPHIE!' Jake yelled.

Edward tipped himself forward and his hooves plummeted towards her. Sophie threw herself sideways. His feet slammed down into the grass where her body had been moments before, cutting grooves into the soft earth. Sophie howled as she landed, her bruised ribs screaming inside her. Jake rushed over and helped her to her feet.

'Sid, get out of here! Don't worry about us!' Jake screamed.

Sid shook his head and said, 'Oh dear. Botheration, indeed,' then began to trot away.

'Call off the animals. Make them stop or I'll kill you both. And the badger,' Edward said, one foot off the ground, ready to strike again.

'You'll kill us anyway. And what makes you think *we* can stop them?' Jake said.

Edward clenched his jaw, the muscles in his cheeks twitching. 'Your choice.' He rocked back on his hind legs again, lifting his front feet high in the air. Jake and Sophie scrabbled to get away as Edward sprang forward, leaping clear off the ground. The foxes were quick, but Edward crashed to the ground right behind them, his front hoof landing squarely on Sophie's tail.

She screamed, her paws scrabbling at the dirt as he pinned her to the spot.

'Sophie!' Jake doubled back to face Edward and crouched low, ready to pounce, as Sophie felt the smooth, solid point of an antler press into her spine.

'Come any closer and I'll make sure she dies *very* slowly.' He twisted his hoof, grinding her tail into the ground. She screamed again, claws curling into the dirt.

Jake froze.

'Run, Jake. Please,' she said, staring into his eyes.

'I'm not leaving you,' Jake said.

'This will be kinder, I promise,' Edward said.

She squeezed her eyes shut. Tail still trapped, the antler disappeared from her back and she heard a scrape as he lifted his other front hoof off the ground. She tried to wrestle from his vice but, short of pulling her tail clean off, it was useless.

'Vermin, all of you,' Edward said, then grunted hard as he brought his hoof towards her skull.

'NO!' Jake screamed.

A roar ripped through the air. Sophie's ears filled with the thump of Edward's hoof slamming awkwardly into the dirt, a whisker away from her head. His other hoof disappeared from her tail and she scrabbled away. She twisted her head to find out what had happened, but as Edward stumbled sideways, Jake took his chance. He leapt towards Edward, wrapping his paws around his neck and sunk his teeth into his throat. With a gurgling grunt, Edward thrashed, trying to dislodge Jake. Blood spilled on the grass.

Then Sophie saw.

Jaws clamped around his left hind leg, claws clinging on for dear life, was Sid.

Vince woke with Rita's squawks exploding through his ears and the sun beaming through the leaves above him. He crawled out onto the path, ready to yell at her, when he reminded himself that it was his idea for her to wake him as soon as there was any news about Laurie. He danced a little when she told him that Laurie was fine, and asked how long it would take to reach her.

Rita spoke as quickly as she could, hoping that it would somehow lessen the impact of the words. 'Well, the place is called Tottenham Hale, and Del took Laurie there on the train...'

Vince's face fell.

'*But...*' Rita continued, 'We can walk it. I followed the tracks back here, and we can take the roads this time. If we leave at sunset, and Arthur keeps up a good pace, I think we can be there well before morning, no problem.'

'And that's where Laurie is?'

Rita nodded, a bit too enthusiastically.

'What's it like? You said he was taking her to a big nature reserve,' Vince asked.

'I don't know, I didn't see much of it. But does it matter? You want to find Laurie, don't you?'

'Of course. And we'll try to send the message back to Richmond Park too. Find a bird or a cat?'

'Yep. Don't worry, it'll be fine. Let's all get some sleep. We'll leave as soon as the sun sets, okay?' Rita chirped.

Rita was holding something back. He could tell. She was always pretty cheerful, but she seemed to be over-compensating. Plus, Tottenham Hale didn't sound like a nature reserve. He decided to forget it for now. He trusted her, and maybe being constantly on edge and sick with worry was making him paranoid too.

The two of them retreated into the bush, where Arthur was still curled up, and settled in for the day. It took a while for Vince to drop off to sleep again, with all the anxiety of their upcoming journey swirling around his head and stomach. He'd faced so many dangers already, and he was growing weary. A tiny, selfish part of him wished he could just settle down in Hampstead Heath, see his nights out in peace. But when he closed his eyes to sleep, Ajadi's words still lingered in his mind.

His home was where his heart was, and his heart was with Laurie.

'Jake! Sid!' Sophie shouted as Edward flailed in front of her, the two animals still clinging on. The leg with Sid attached skidded out from under him and he fell sideways, his massive weight dragging him to the dirt. Jake let go of his throat and jumped back, away from his thrashing limbs. Sid opened his mouth too, releasing Edward's leg, and Edward kicked him away. Sid tumbled onto his back, legs waving in the air like an upturned beetle. Jake rushed over to help him to his feet. Still in pain, Sophie stayed where she was, her sore ribs thwarting her attempts to inspect her probably broken tail.

Thanks to Jake's teeth, Edward's neck and chest were covered with dark blood. The deer pulled his forelegs towards him, bending them to rest on his knees, but as he went to straighten his hind legs, his left buckled and he fell, his bulk hitting the floor with a thud once more. He let out a long growl.

The rest of the deer had gone; driven back into the trees by the animals' attacks, or fled in fear before they had the chance. The smaller animals remained, celebrating and comparing battle scars. But when they – one by one – began to notice Edward on the ground, struggling, they inched over, curious to see what they'd missed in all the commotion of the fight.

After another failed attempt to stand, Edward gave up and resigned himself to the ground, forelegs curled under his chest, his wounded leg splayed out awkwardly to the side. Sid's teeth had done more damage than Sophie expected. Edward's rear leg was a mess of torn, exposed muscle and bone, slick with blood.

The animals looked on in shock. The only leader they had ever known, protector of their homes and families, reduced to a helpless wreck on the bloodstained ground.

'Go away, all of you! Get back to your homes or I'll...' He trailed off. 'This isn't over. I'll be fine in a few days.' He winced as his movement pulled at the raw flesh on his throat. 'As long as I'm alive, then I'm in charge, do you understand?'

Sophie, trying to ignore the pain screaming through her tail, spoke as loudly as she could. 'No, Edward. It *is* over, and we won.'

Edward spoke through sharp pants. 'The deer are still... under my command... You just wait... until I'm healed.'

A rabbit piped up. 'We're not scared of you or the deer anymore, Edward.'

'Give it up,' Jake said. 'It's over.'

'No... I...' Edward let his head sink to the ground, a long exhalation rasping through his nostrils. 'How could this happen? I did everything right… Vince never reached the heath… You… You didn't even find out…' He closed his eyes and clenched his jaw.

'Find out what?' Sophie said. 'What is at this heath? Tell us.'

'The deer… They failed. They couldn't control the residents…'

'Sounds familiar,' Jake said dryly.

'No!' Edward grimaced, his wounds reminding him to stay still. 'It was their own fault… Too lenient. They stood idly while the animals organised… They let it happen… Everything was fine here. I knew everything. I had a plan…'

'How did you know? Kara?' Sophie said.

'Surveillance… Another bird… I killed her seasons ago. As soon as she told me everything. No one could know…'

'Twig-headed ones have a habit of underestimating other animals, Sid thinks,' the badger said.

'Never… I knew the power of numbers. I heard what happened there and vowed to never let it happen here. But somehow… without even knowing… without even organising…'

'It's funny, Edward,' Sophie said, 'We should thank you. Because if you'd killed me and Jake straight away you probably would have carried on ruling, for who knows how many seasons. No one was brave enough to stand up to you on their own, but *you* brought the whole park together in one place. *You* organised us. You tried to get them to turn on each other, and on me. And it nearly worked. Everyone believed you, and Sid wasn't enough to persuade them, but you screwed over the *one* animal who would have lied for you. And when she turned on you, everyone was gathered to watch. We couldn't have planned it better ourselves.'

Edward closed his eyes and exhaled again.

'But I refuse to feel sorry for you,' Sophie continued. 'Because all this happened without us even knowing about the other park, which means Vince died for no reason at all.'

Edward was silent.

Sophie looked at the dwindling crowd of animals, then at the blue sky, then finally at Jake. 'I think it's time we got some sleep.'

Jake helped Sophie up, taking some of her weight on the back of his neck.

'Sid, are you staying?' Jake said, once Sophie was stable. 'You're very welcome in the cemetery, but I'm sure Edward won't mind you digging somewhere else if you'd rather,' he laughed.

'Oh, perhaps one sunshine, Sid will stay? Maybe two? A long journey it is, back to Sid's sett. Very kind, you are. Very kind.'

The remaining residents dispersed after giving Sophie their get-well wishes. Edward didn't move, but opened one eye to watch them leave. Jake helped Sophie as they made their way back to their den, with Sid ambling beside them.

After a while, Jake broke the silence. 'Listen, I don't know if this means I'm forgiven... I wouldn't blame you if not. I've made some terrible mistakes. Things Vince would never have done, and—'

'Shush, Jake. It doesn't matter now. Edward manipulated every-one.'

'Not you. You stayed strong the whole time.'

'He got me to hate you for a while,' Sophie said.

'By telling you what *I* did. Vince would never have made a deal with him, gone behind your back, got your friend killed...'

'Stop beating yourself up. Vince was a good fox and, yes, you did some stupid, awful things, and maybe we can't go back to exactly how things were... Alice is dead and I won't ever forget that. But...' She took a deep breath before continuing. 'I won't let Edward destroy us. I know you did it all for me, and I love you. I love you because you're Jake, not Vince.'

Jake sniffed and smiled. 'Okay.'

'And you love me, right? I'm a wonderful, wise vixen, remem-ber?' She smiled back.

'Of course. And beautiful and brilliant. Don't forget that.' Jake laughed, then gave her a gentle nuzzle. She pressed her snout into his warm neck.

Sid frowned at them both. 'On second thinkings, Sid might stay for just the *one* sunshine.'

16

The evening arrived, as it always did, and Rita led Vince and Arthur past the station where she had jumped on the train with Del and Laurie the day before. Arthur's experience of trains was almost zero but, unlike Vince, he showed no signs of fear, asking Rita question after question about them: Where did they come from? Where do they go? What colour are they? How big? How fast? Could he ride one, maybe, one day?

After a while, Arthur grew tired. His short legs were not built to carry him long distances, and Vince was surprised he'd made it so far from Regent's Park without complaining, but he was a tenacious little thing, his only goal to explore London. Not surprising, really, that Rita was happy to chat to him hour after hour, and vice versa.

Despite Vince's urgency to get to Laurie, they all agreed to walk at Arthur's pace, stopping whenever he needed a rest. Arthur was grateful, but clearly felt bad for holding them up. At times, Vince could tell the little hedgehog was panting, desperate for a break, but kept going without a word.

The only animal they spoke to on the way was a ginger cat named Sherbet, and Rita did all the talking, explaining about Laurie and Hampstead Heath.

'Socks, you say? Hammersmith?' Sherbet said between licking his paws. 'Rings a bell, but strictly the Haringey patch, me. Down to the tracks, up to Turnpike Lane, no more, no less.'

'Right, but you know the cat, sorry... Official Feline Administrator... In the next patch over, right?' Rita said.

'Yeah, I know a few. Hawking does Crouch End that way, Princess Whiskers in Wood Green that way...' He pointed his paw.

'Okay, so can you give them all the message and tell them to tell the *next* cats over? Then maybe it will eventually reach Socks,' Rita said.

'That's not a bad plan, you know. Which way is Hammersmith?'

'South-west. Quite far that way.' Vince pointed in the general direction.

'Right you are. Well, I'll tell Hawking, he knows the OFA in Holloway...' Sherbet started to nod, then his smile stretched into a grin. 'Yeah, I think this might work, you know.'

'Thank you so much,' Rita said.

'No worries, always a pleasure to assist anyone in my patch. If you ever find yourself back here, you ask for Sherbet. That's me.'

The group continued on their way, relieved that they had done their best to let Socks know how Laurie was and passed on the story of the Solstice Riot at Hampstead Heath, which they hoped would eventually reach Richmond Park. They only wished, for Laurie's sake, that she'd had a chance to see Socks one last time, but Rita assured them all that she would sort something out. Vince was less optimistic, but went along with it.

They walked in silence for a while as the moon scoured the sky, full and round. It was nearly gone by the time they arrived at Tottenham Hale station.

Vince looked around the desolate, grey space. 'This is it? So, where's Laurie?'

'Well, here's the thing...' Rita began.

'I knew it,' Vince snorted.

'... we have to get on a train.'

'What do you mean, *get on* a train?' Vince pulled a face.

'It means we ride the train along the rails, right, Rita?' Arthur squeaked excitedly.

'No,' Vince said, without thinking. He started to pace back and forth. 'I... I can't. I just can't. Why don't you go and find Laurie, Rita, and... and just bring her back here or something?' It was a ridiculous suggestion, but as far as he was concerned, no more ridiculous than Rita's.

'She's in a nature reserve, Vince. As in, *reserved* for *nature*. Doesn't that sound like somewhere you want to be?' Rita said.

'Yes, but...' Vince closed his eyes for a moment and took a breath. 'Not on a *train*. You saw me walking over that bridge at Hampstead Heath, and we weren't even near the tracks then.'

'You won't be near the tracks. You'll be *on the train*,' Rita said, cocking her head to the side.

'And *where* is the train?' Vince said.

'On the tracks...' Rita mumbled. 'But if you think about it, if you're scared of getting hit by a train, then surely the best place to be is *on* a train?' She waved her wings for emphasis.

'I really don't want to discuss this. Have you even thought about how we'd get on board? With humans around?' Vince sat down. 'You're only one little bird. If a human sees all of us together on a train, they're going to freak out, aren't they? What if one of them picks us up and takes us somewhere, like Del did with Laurie? Then we're in a right mess.'

Rita tilted her head and frowned. She clearly hadn't thought it through.

'Exactly!' Vince sniffed.

'Maybe they are like the roads...?' Arthur piped up. 'Busy in the daytime but empty at night.'

'I think you might be on to something,' Rita said. 'I can watch from the roof and see how busy they are. I doubt there will be any now, but there might be some early in the morning. The first one has got to be quiet, right? Most humans don't wake up with the sun like animals do.'

'Yes, and then we can get on the quietest part and hide some-where. I'm good at hiding,' Arthur said.

'Wait... We're not actually going through with this?' Vince said, mouth open.

'Vince, you know we are. You can do this. What would Laurie be saying if she were here right now?' Rita said, hopping closer to him.

'Well, that's a stupid question, since we're only here because—'

THE FOX OF RICHMOND PARK

'Vince!' Rita said. 'Come on, *hypothetically*, what would she say?'

'That I'm being a poodle,' he mumbled.

'Yes. And *are* you a poodle?' Rita said.

'I don't know what—'

'Ugh! Just shut up and find somewhere safe to wait while I watch for trains, okay? You can do this. We're going to help you. It'll be fine.'

'Yes, Rita,' he mumbled, then under his breath said, 'Laurie's right again, and she's not even here.'

Vince crouched under a bench, Arthur beside him, as Rita paced the metal roof of the station. They had been waiting and napping for hours, but sunrise was not far off now, and Vince was answering more of Arthur's questions to try to take the hedgehog's mind off his empty belly. The nearest bins contained only a few oily scraps of paper and plastic, and insects and worms were nowhere to be found. On the odd occasion that Arthur fell silent for a while, Vince kept himself occupied with thoughts of Laurie, the nature reserve and frogs.

Rita's talons clacked on the roof as she hopped across it, then flapped over to the bench. 'Some humans have arrived,' she said. 'They're unlocking doors and uncovering things. Won't be long, now.'

'Hope so,' Vince said, his own stomach starting to growl.

From the station, a faint voice echoed through the still, early morning air.

'The next train to arrive at platform two will be the four fifty-nine service to Stansted Airport, calling at Cheshunt, Broxbourne, Harlow Town...'

'That's it! That's our train! We need to go!' Rita squawked.

'Go and check for humans,' Vince said.

'Alright, but don't dilly-dally.' She flapped back to the roof. Vince and Arthur crept towards the station entrance. The barriers were closed, but they didn't reach the ground, so they could easily sneak under. But getting into the station wasn't what Vince was worried about. And worried was an understatement. Vince felt sick to his stomach, and his fast-approaching hunger didn't help.

'There's no one here, guys,' Rita shouted.

They crawled under the barriers and, once through, Vince peered down the platform. It was, indeed, completely empty.

'I told you,' Rita said, fluttering down from above. 'Come on. The train's nearly here.'

The rumble vibrated through Vince's bones. Arthur walked towards the edge of the platform with Rita. Vince stayed put. He couldn't see the rails from where he was, and he didn't really want to.

The voice spoke again. 'The train now arriving at platform two is the four fifty-nine…'

'Come on, Vince,' Rita said sternly.

He shook his head. 'I'll… I'll wait until it's here. I don't want to… fall on the tracks or anything.'

'Don't be ridiculous – you won't fall on the tracks. Look, Arthur's not scared, are you?'

Arthur shook his head.

'Arthur's braver than me,' Vince said.

The train screeched into the platform and Vince edged backwards until he was almost back under the barriers. The doors opened with a hiss and a man stepped out. Vince's heart thumped in his ears. Rita flapped through the open door into the carriage, then hopped to the edge and called out. 'It's empty! Quick!'

Arthur followed her, but stopped at the edge. The gap between the train and the platform was too wide for him to cross.

'Vince, Arthur needs help, come on!' Rita yelled.

Vince took a deep breath. The train beeped. He ran towards them, eyes on Arthur.

Don't look at the tracks. Don't look at the tracks.

The doors started to close. He pushed his snout underneath Arthur's backside and lifted. The doors thumped together and Rita disappeared from view. Arthur's front feet were pressed against the slippery train as he balanced on Vince's nose. Rita's voice came through, muffled by the solid metal between them. 'Broxbourne! Get to Broxbourne!'

The train lurched and pulled away with Rita on board. Arthur yelped, his front paws sliding across the white metal. Vince opened his jaws and twisted his neck to catch him, but Arthur panicked and curled up. Spines jabbed into the roof of Vince's mouth and he flinched, dropping Arthur onto the concrete platform. He rolled. Vince lunged with his paw to stop him, but he was too slow. Arthur dropped over the edge and bounced onto the train tracks.

Four stags hovered around Edward in the early morning mist as he tried and failed to stand up for the third time. He'd made it through the night, the stags standing guard around him, but he was in agony. The throbbing in his hind leg had worsened hour by hour, spreading across his entire flank, the pain now excruciating. His breath came out in short pants, drops of spittle hanging from the tip of his lolling tongue. Streaks of foam covered his chestnut fur, whipped up from his frantic staggering and falling. The wound on his throat was still raw, his constant struggling pulling at the damaged flesh.

He didn't want his stags to see him like this, but rather them than the rest of the park. Once he was fit again, he could sort this mess out. Over time, the residents would learn to trust him again. He would apologise for his mistakes, make amends. He was the only animal who could rule Richmond Park. Surely they could see that? A few days and nights of anarchy and they would all come crawling back.

'I think you should rest, Edward. It looks... bad,' one of the stags said.

'I'm *fine*. Where are the rest of you? That skinny stag, and the ugly one? Where are they? You, go and get them. Bring them here.' He collapsed onto his side, blood oozing from the burning wound on his throat.

'Er... They've... Er...' The stag looked down at his hooves.

'Spit it... out,' Edward gasped.

'Quit.'

'*Quit?* What do you... mean... *quit?*'

'Quit... Er... Their service. To you. They're with their families. They said they won't help you anymore. They—'

'*Enough*,' Edward grunted. 'I want all of you to—' Edward's ears pricked along with those of the rest of the stags. The unmistakable sound of a car engine.

The stags backed away from the sound, leaving Edward exposed on the grass. 'Get back here! Protect me!' His chest pounded and saliva dribbled from the corner of his mouth.

A shape came into focus as the engine grew louder. A car. One of the large square ones, driving across the grass. It stopped some way away and the engine cut out. A door opened and a human jumped out. His top half was covered with a dark-green material, his legs with grey.

Edward composed himself, speaking slowly between long breaths. 'Ah, you see... One of the wardens has come... To help me. They must have heard I was hurt. The visitors are probably... Concerned.'

The man approached. He was carrying something.

Edward filled with relief and relaxed. 'See? He's got something for me. Medicine, probably, or something to strap my leg up. Didn't I tell you I'd be fine?'

The stags retreated further. 'Cowards,' Edward shouted. 'The humans are here to help the deer, you *know* that. Listen, human, I appreciate your assistance. It was that damned badger, you know. Came out of nowhere...' The human was nearer now, and Edward could make out more detail. The object under his arm was not medicine. Or something to strap up his leg. Edward's eyes bulged. The stags bolted into the trees.

'No!' Edward panicked and tried to get up, tumbling back to the ground as his wounded leg skidded from under him. He roared in pain. His heart raced at woodpecker speed. 'No, help me, please. It's just my leg, I'll be fine if you just...'

The human frowned and shook his head. 'Poor bastard.' He lifted the shotgun to his shoulder.

'No, human! Stop! *Stop!*' Edward scraped frantically at the dirt with his hooves and pulled his front end up onto his forelegs.

The man braced and the gun made a click.

'Stop! Don't you understand? *I am in charge here!*' Edward shrieked.

The shot boomed over the park. Pain exploded across his chest as the bullet ripped through his lungs. Edward sank to the ground, his last breath rasping from his bloodstained lips.

'No, no, no, no, no... Arthur!' Vince crept to the edge of the platform and peered over. Arthur was still curled up, resting on the gravel between the wall of the platform and the closest rail. The sight of the tracks made him queasy enough, but seeing Arthur down there almost made him vomit. He snapped his head back and reversed.

Arthur let out a squeak. 'Where am... Oh no! Vince! Help me! Vince!'

'Don't worry, Arthur, it's okay. I'll get you out; just stay away from the rails, okay? Don't touch the metal bits, do you understand?'

Arthur's voice wobbled. 'Okay.'

Oh, Mother Nature. What do I do? And Rita's on her own on the train...

He sat back on his haunches and looked around. Where was a human when you needed one? He walked the length of the platform, searching for something he could reach down with. A plank of wood, a rope, anything... He kept close to the building wall, not daring to walk anywhere near the yellow lines that warned him away from the edge.

A noise made his ears twitch. A beep, followed by a whirring. The gates. Someone was coming in. He hid behind a bench and watched as a woman, led by a knee-high dog on a long, red lead, strolled onto the platform and towards him. She wore a thick, brown coat with a brightly-coloured, patterned scarf around her neck and a wide-brimmed hat on her head. On her other arm, she carried a large, black bag in the crook of her elbow. She sat down on the next bench and pulled out her phone.

'Psst. Hey, you!' Vince hissed at the dog. She was white, with tight, curly fur and long, floppy ears. Her bouffant tail wagged frantically.

'Who? Me?' She searched for the voice. 'Who's there?'

'Behind the bench, but stay where you are. I need your help,' Vince whispered. The woman tugged lazily at the lead, but was absorbed in her phone and didn't look up.

The dog looked nervous. 'What kind of help? It's just that, if I'm bad, my human will call me a bad girl and boop me on the nose, and I really don't like it when she does that.'

'Oh, no, nothing bad... No booping, I promise,' Vince said.

'Then, sure!' Her tongue lolled from her mouth. 'What do you need? Tell me, tell me!'

Of all the dogs in all of London...

'My friend has fallen down onto the tracks. I need something to pull him up. Can I use your lead?'

'My lead?' She turned her head. 'Oh! That lead! Erm, that might be difficult, but...' She ran to the woman. Vince leaned around the bench to see what she was doing.

The dog leapt onto the woman's lap, grabbed her scarf in her teeth and pulled. The woman screamed and her phone fell from her hand and smashed on the floor. The scarf came away from her neck in one smooth motion and the dog jumped down and ran back to Vince.

'Coco! What are you doing?' the woman shouted, yanking hard on the lead. 'Bad girl!'

'Will this do?' Coco said, dropping the scarf at Vince's feet as she was dragged backwards. 'Oh no! I think I was bad again...'

'Perfect!' Vince dashed to the scarf and picked it up in his jaws.

He shouted a muffled 'thank you' through the material, before running back to Arthur.

'Bad girl, Coco! What has got into you?' The woman did, indeed, boop her on the nose. 'Oh my *god*, is that a *fox*? It's bad enough I have to be up this early without you destroying my stuff…'

The station's disembodied voice announced the next train, but Vince didn't have time to listen. 'Arthur, you still there?'

'Yes, please hurry, Vince. I think I can feel another, um, train coming.'

'Can you grab this in your teeth?' Vince held the scarf by one end and flicked the other over the edge of the platform.

'I, um, think so.'

Vince felt the rumbling of the train in his paws. Panic seized him, but he'd almost killed Rita and Laurie, and he wasn't about to let a tiny hedgehog get crushed under a train.

'Ready?' Vince said through clenched teeth.

'Yessh!' came the muffled reply.

Vince backed up and felt the weight of Arthur at the end of the scarf. He went slowly, so as not to dislodge him. A flash of the oncoming train caught the corner of his eye. He slammed them shut, creeping backwards and pulling at the scarf until he heard a squeak.

He opened his eyes. The tip of Arthur's nose was poking over the edge of the platform. The train thundered towards them. Vince gave the scarf one last yank. Arthur sailed through the air and bounced onto the concrete, rolling until he hit the building wall. He unfurled and blinked at Vince. 'I'm alive! You did it!'

The woman appeared, Coco dragging her feet behind her. 'Ugh…' She bent down and plucked the scarf from the ground with two dainty fingers. She turned to Coco. 'Gross. Now I have to throw this away.'

Vince collapsed onto the ground. The train came to halt and the doors opened. The woman and Coco stepped on.

'Should we get on?' Arthur said.

'Erm…' Vince pulled himself to his feet. 'COCO?'

Coco's head peered out from the open door.

'This train… Broxbourne?'

'Nope,' Coco replied.

'Thanks!' Vince shouted over the beep, as the woman yanked Coco's head back into the train before the doors slammed on her neck.

'We wait for the next one, I guess,' Vince said. 'Let's find somewhere to wait, *away* from the edge.'

'Um, agreed,' Arthur replied.

Vince and Arthur had been waiting for a while behind the bench when the disembodied voice spoke the name they wanted to hear.

'The next train at platform two will be the five-forty service to Cambridge, calling at Cheshunt, Broxbourne, Roydon…'

'That's us!' Arthur said.

'Yup. Remember what we talked about? No curling up. Hang on to me and don't worry about hurting me, okay? Getting on the train is the most important thing.'

Arthur nodded. A few humans had arrived since the last train left, but they were bleary eyed and concentrating hard on the phones in their hands. Vince was grateful for those phones, and whatever it was that was so fascinating about them.

The rumble of the rails and the roar of the massive engine grew louder, and the train appeared in the distance. After the accident with Arthur, Vince's fear had faded somewhat, and now he was almost excited to see it. The train that would take him to Laurie and Rita. Hopefully.

'Right, let's go.' Vince lowered his belly to the floor and Arthur clambered onto his back, biting down on the scruff of Vince's neck to hold himself still. It was inelegant, but for a few blinks, it would do.

The train pulled up and the people trudged onto it, eyes down. Vince held his breath and rushed to the door, keeping low. He slipped onto the train and the doors slid shut behind him. The humans were all sitting down, spread around the carriage, with most of the seats unoccupied. Vince exhaled and Arthur let go, dropping to the floor of the train with a bump.

'We did it!' Arthur whispered.

'Quick, under there.' Vince dashed under a pair of empty seats, getting as low and as close to the side wall as he could. Arthur wasn't far behind, and tucked himself into the brush of Vince's tail. Vince whispered, 'Now we just have to get off at the right place. Two stops, the voice said.'

'Do you think Rita is, um, okay?' Arthur asked.

'I think Rita's fine. You know why?'

Arthur shook his tiny head.

'Because she's a brave adventurer, like you.'

Arthur giggled.

The train was quiet, the engine the only noise for a while, until it arrived at its first stop. The train voice – different from the station voice – announced the name, but it wasn't theirs. The doors nearest to them opened and a man got on, then sat down in the seat across from them. His clothes were all black, with a thin strip of blue material hanging from his neck, but – unlike the piece of material the woman had worn to keep her neck warm – Vince could see no discernible function for it. He placed a bag on the seat next to him and began to rummage through it.

Vince must have caught his eye, because he suddenly stopped rummaging and moved across the seats to peer at him. The man's eyes widened and he pulled a phone from a pocket on the top of his leg. He held it out in front of him, crouched down, and slowly crept closer to Vince, steadying himself on the seats.

'I think someone's fare dodging,' the man said to nobody in particular, then laughed.

Vince growled, hoping he would go away, but he continued to point the phone at them.

'What's he doing?' Arthur said.

'Socks told me they make memories or something. Don't worry, I won't let him hurt you.'

The man eventually returned to his seat and alternated

between stabbing his fingers at his phone and staring at Vince, a gormless grin plastered across his face. Finally, he pulled a long white string from his bag and spent a while untangling the two round objects hanging from one end before pushing them into his ears. He clicked the other end into the phone, then stuffed it back into his pocket. A grating *tssk* noise emanated from the white bulbs.

Arthur screwed up his face. 'What are those white things? Is he listening to that horrible noise on purpose?'

'I don't know, it looks like it. Humans are weird.'

As the train trundled on, Vince found himself becoming surprisingly relaxed. Maybe it was the warmth, the rhythmic vibrations of the carriage on the rails, or maybe Rita was right; the train really was the safest place for him to be.

He wondered if Laurie had been scared, coming on the train with the human, and wished he could have been there to comfort her. But wishing about the past would get him nowhere. He'd come so far, and nothing would stop him from reaching Laurie now.

After a while, Vince felt the train begin to slow down. 'I think this is us. Get ready.'

The train lurched to a stop, almost sending Arthur rolling across the floor, but he managed to climb up onto Vince's back and grab on with his teeth again before the voice spoke from overheard. 'Broxbourne. This is Broxbourne station.'

'Ready?' Vince said. Arthur grunted a reply. Vince ran, the man turned his head and pulled out his phone again, but Vince was already at the door. It was still closed. 'What?' A few blinks passed and he began to panic but, finally, the now-familiar hiss came and they slid open. A mass of human legs greeted him, followed by gasps and pointed fingers.

'Look at that! A fox! And is that a... *hedgehog*?'

Hands reached into pockets and those already holding their phones thrust them into Vince's face. Some of the humans behind started tutting and pushing, causing the frontmost legs to stumble onto the train. Vince jumped back, startled, but he had to get out.

'Hold on, Arthur!' Vince darted between the first pair of legs, which wobbled atop bizarre shoes with a spike for a heel. The woman let out a shout and fell, crashing into another, and together they sank against the edge of the doors. The rest began to part for him and he weaved his way through until he was out in the open.

Behind him, the group of humans clambered onto the train, snatching glances over their shoulders before the doors closed and blocked their view. The train began to roll away, but Vince stood and watched the open-mouthed and smiling faces through the windows until they were out of sight.

They were strange creatures, humans. More often than not they seemed oblivious to him, until an opportunity to thrust a phone into his face occurred, but he concluded that they were, overall, a good species. Apart from the one who set the trap in the allotments. And the one who invented trains.

Silence settled over the station and Vince lowered Arthur to the ground. In front of them, another set of train tracks ran parallel to the ones they'd arrived on, and a few humans milled around, some staring at them, some not. The animals weren't completely out of danger yet. Vince stood over Arthur and had begun to look for the way out when a familiar voice caught both their ears.

'You made it!' Rita was perched on a fence, on the other side of the tracks. 'What took you so long?'

17

Socks purred as he stretched across his owner's lap, the man's fingers occasionally reaching down to tickle him in his favourite spot behind his ears. His tail hung down, swishing contentedly from side to side.

The man was seated at his kitchen table. His non-stroking hand spooned crunchy flakes into his mouth while the hand that, ideally, should have been focused solely on stroking Socks's ears poked at the phone lying flat on the table. Sound began to play and the man leaned forward, over Socks.

'Wow,' the man said to himself. The noise from the phone sounded like rumbling, and a deep growl. 'Look, Socks, a fox on a train.' He lifted the phone and brought it close to Socks's face. Before Socks realised what was happening, the noise stopped and the moving pictures on the phone changed to a black rectangle with some human writing across it.

Socks frowned. 'I didn't see it! Show me again.' He batted the phone with a paw then looked up at the man's face.

'Hang on, let me restart it.' The man prodded the phone and a fox appeared, growling under some odd-looking chairs. After a few blinks, the picture disappeared again.

'That's Vince! How did you know...?' Socks said.

'You like the fox, Socksy?' the man said. 'Want to watch again?'

'I don't understand...' Socks looked back to the screen. He watched the moving images of Vince again, but was none the wiser about where he was or how his human knew about him. And where was Laurie? He wasn't much of a worrier and he knew she could take care of herself, but she'd been gone a few days now and he couldn't help wondering where she'd got to.

'Right, enough videos for you, Socksy Face. I've got to get to work. Another day, another dollar.' The man sighed as he rose from the chair, tipping Socks off his lap and onto the floor before heading to the sink. Socks moseyed across the kitchen, about to climb into his bed in the corner, when he heard a scratch at the back door.

'Socks? You in there?' It was Monkey, the long-haired tabby from Shepherd's Bush.

'What are you doing over here, Monk?' Socks shouted back.

'Is that your friend? You want to go out?' the man said, reaching over to open the back door. 'Hello, handsome,' he said to Monkey. 'Well, isn't this the coolest cat party around, eh?'

Socks made for the door and meowed a thank you to his human before the door closed behind him. 'Monk, I've just seen the strangest thing... Anyway, everything okay?'

'Yes, yes, everything's fine. I've had a message about your Laurie. Well, from Mister Floof in Notting Hill, actually, but he heard it from... Not important... Anyway, she had a bit of a run in with a car, but don't worry, she's absolutely fine. A human took her in and is taking her somewhere. There's a bird and another fox looking for her. And a hedgehog.'

'Oh, that's Vince and Rita! And a *hedgehog*? Marvellous! So, Vince is okay too?'

'Sounds like it. They're on their way to find her. She's been taken out of London, on a train,' Monkey said.

'That must be where he was when I was watching him...' Socks said, almost to himself.

Monkey frowned. 'Nope, you've lost me there, Socks.'

'Sorry, yes... Don't worry. It's so good to know she's okay and that Vince is on his way to her. Thank you.'

'There's another thing, too,' Monkey said. 'They want a message taken to Richmond Park. Do you know it?'

'I'll find someone who does,' Socks said.

Monkey explained about Hampstead Heath, the riot and Edward's deceit as best he could. The message, having been passed from cat to cat across the width of London, was understandably vague and made little sense to either of them, but Socks hoped Vince's old friends would know what it meant.

When they were done, Monkey said his goodbyes then turned and left Socks alone on the doorstep.

Socks took a moment to wash his paws while he tried to figure out the best course of action. Richmond Park was south. He'd just have to get down to the flyover, tell the next cat over, then they'd take it from there...

He wandered through the back garden, leapt up onto the fence and tiptoed along it until he reached the end of the houses. Dropping down to the pavement, he headed for the road, readying himself to cross it for the first time. If every other Official Feline Administrator could help Laurie and Vince, then he sure as scat could too.

'Rita!' Arthur ran across the platform towards her.

'Arthur, stop!' Vince lunged for him and pulled him back from the edge with a paw. 'We are not going through that again. How do we get out of here?'

'Well, I flew, but there are stairs I think,' Rita said. 'Unless you want to just jump down and cross the tracks? You could easily squeeze through this fence.'

'No thanks.' Vince turned to look for the stairs. 'Ah, over there?' He walked over and looked up. A single human was coming down towards them. 'Arthur, ready for another ride? Might be a bit longer this time. Think you can hang on until we're out?'

Arthur nodded and Vince instructed Rita to meet them outside. The human reached the bottom of the stairs and stopped. He stared at Vince and Arthur, mouth open. 'Woah,' he said.

'Quick, get on.' Vince and Arthur repeated their procedure, Arthur climbing onto the back of his neck in record speed. Vince growled at the human and crept towards him, tail thrashing, hoping it would be enough to move him out of the way.

'Okay, alright mate, there you go...' The man stepped to the side and swept his arms towards the stairs, as if ushering them up.

Vince dashed past him, Arthur clinging on for dear life. He reached the top of the stairs and looked left and right. More humans walked towards him from far down a corridor on the right. To his left seemed like a dead end, but some humans were disappearing off, as if going down more stairs. He looked right again. They looked like they were coming in, so it must be the way out... If he went left down those other stairs, he'd end up back by the train tracks again, wouldn't he?

The longer he waited, the more he risked being trapped, or taken away somewhere by a well-meaning human. And Arthur's teeth wouldn't hold forever. He went right, and carefully ran along the corridor towards the oncoming humans. He didn't look up to see their reactions. Feet stamped around him and shouts floated over his head as he tore through the maze of legs.

More stairs. Down, this time. He took them two by two, turning once, twice, spiralling downwards, until he was at ground level once more. The room opened out and the familiar gates lined the exit. Humans passed through one at a time with shrill beeps and the harsh slamming of plastic and metal. One gate was larger, and the humans seemed to avoid it. Through the gap underneath, Vince had a clear view of the paved area beyond, where white lines marked out spaces for cars. Beyond that, trees.

Rita was hopping on the pavement outside. 'Vince! Arthur! Over here!'

One human stood still on Vince's side of the gates. He seemed to be in charge, pushing buttons on a machine when the gates didn't open properly. The man saw Vince and put his hands up to his face. 'Oh dear!' He turned to the humans waiting behind the gates and shouted over the mechanical din. 'Everyone get back. Let this fella out, please! Get back!' He stood in front of the gates, stopping everyone from passing through.

'Come on, little fella. Off you go.' He beckoned Vince towards him and pointed to the large gate.

Vince made a dash for the gate, ducking low, careful not to knock Arthur off, and ran out of the building. His paws hit pavement and Rita squawked with joy. Arthur dropped to the ground and shook his tiny head. A cheer rose from the humans behind him and he turned to bark his thanks. A wall of phones held at arm's length blocked the humans' faces, but a voice overhead announced a train arriving and the beeping of the gates started up again, the humans quickly falling back into their routine.

Vince turned back to his friends. 'Welcome to Broxbourne,' Rita said with a smile and a glint in her eye.

'Have you found Laurie? Is she okay?' Vince asked.

'Wait and see...' Rita laughed.

'You are the absolute worst,' Vince said, smiling. 'And I haven't forgiven you for lying about having to get on a train.'

'When did I lie? I simply *omitted* a tiny detail. Anyway, you're here now, and since you don't want to cross the tracks, we'll have to go the long way round,' Rita said.

Rita led Vince and Arthur across the car park. The sun was low in the sky, but bright, and the air fresh, absent of London's dust and grit, which caught in his eyes and throat. Vince took a deep breath and savoured the crispness of it in his lungs before slowly exhaling. Vince's relief at arriving was palpable, but he couldn't fully relax until he saw and smelled Laurie with his own eyes and nose.

As they walked further, his eyes rested on a human sign atop a tall grey pole. The striped black-and-white face of a badger stared down at him. It was only a simple picture, but Vince smiled as he remembered Sid, so many days and nights ago now, and wondered what he was up to.

Probably just sleeping.

Rita took them down a slope and over a narrow metal bridge spanning a river. Despite being daylight, it was quiet, and the few humans they encountered stopped and stared, but nothing more. Vince could barely keep his eyes open, but his stomach was wide awake, and empty. His number two priority, after finding Laurie, he decided, was finding something to eat. He looked down at the shallow water flowing under the bridge. Was that a frog he could smell?

They emerged into another car park but skirted the edge, where thick brambles grew up a steep bank that flanked a road. Gradually the bank flattened out and they were level with the traffic.

'Here we are. Just across here,' Rita said, nodding to the field on the other side of the road. A dirt track led into the grass and disappeared through a mass of tall oak and birch trees.

'That's it? Really? We've been walking for barely five blinks,' Vince said.

'I know. Great, isn't it?' Rita said.

'So, Laurie's over there?' Vince said.

'Wait and see!' Rita laughed again.

Cars roared past, rising up on their left as the road ascended.

'It's busy,' Vince said.

'Yeah, but there are some red-yellow-green lights up there that the cars all stop to look at sometimes. We'll just have to time your crossing right.'

They waited on the grass and, sure enough, the cars on their side of the road began to stop, one by one, at the top of the hill. The approaching cars slowed down and joined the queue, until eventually the line of vehicles reached them. Heat from the growling engines filled the air around them. Rita took to the sky.

'You want to climb on to me again?' Vince said to Arthur.

'No. I can do this last one myself,' he replied, brow furrowed in concentration.

Rita called down to them that it was safe to cross.

'Let's go, Arthur.' Vince stepped into the space between the two closest cars, coughing and blinking away the fumes as he peered out the other side. Cars rolled along the far side of the road at speed. Arthur pulled up beside him. Vince started to speak. 'It looks like—'

'No time! Go!' Rita shrieked, before he could finish.

The last car in the moving line roared past and the flow of vehicles stopped, but for how long, they had no idea. Either side of them, engines revved into action. The stationary line of cars was about to move.

'GO!' Rita yelled again.

'Run!' With his nose, Vince pushed Arthur into the middle of the road and held his breath as he scurried across. The tiny hedgehog dived into the long grass on the other side and Vince was suddenly overcome with pride and relief. 'Well done, Arthur! That was amazing!'

'Vince!' Rita shouted.

The car on his left was inching forward, the car on his right about to do the same, and he was dangerously close to its front wheel. He checked the road was clear, then made his final dash. Leaving the machines in his wake, he tumbled into the grass. The cars trundled away up the hill, until a new line began to form and the empty lane now closest to them became a steady stream of roaring engines again.

Arthur peered out from the long grass. 'That was fun! Can we, um, do it again?'

The news of Edward's death spread rapidly and, despite his grievous misdemeanours, after a few nights had passed, the residents of Richmond Park agreed to listen to a statement from the remaining herd members. The deer could no longer instil fear in the animals, even if they wanted to, but it was clear that the herd wanted to start afresh.

Everyone congregated in the deer's old home, by the smaller pond. The atmosphere was jovial, many creatures greeting Sophie and Jake with smiles and waves as they arrived. Once the crowd settled, one of the oldest stags stepped forward and made a moving speech, expressing the regret and shame of the herd, and their intent to live peacefully with the rest of the animals. Sophie listened, Jake at her side, until the deer finished and the animals slowly dispersed.

'Do you think they meant it?' Sophie asked Jake.

'We'll have to wait and see, I guess,' Jake replied.

The pair had agreed to move on from Jake's mistakes, providing he did all the hunting for a few moons. Sophie was injured, after all. It would take a while for her to fully forgive and forget, but dwelling on it wasn't going to help either of them. Richmond Park was evolving, so they had to do the same.

They walked back to their den. Sophie's broken tail hung awkwardly, but the pain was fading night by night. Greeting them when they arrived, washing her ears with a pristine white paw, was a thin tortoiseshell cat.

'The bird over there said this is where the foxes live,' the cat said, blinking her yellow eyes.

'It is,' Jake said. 'Can we help you?'

Sophie instinctively looked over her shoulder, but felt relieved when she remembered that she didn't have to check for deer anymore.

'Other way round, actually. I have a message from Socks, the Official Feline Administrator of Hammersmith.'

'The *what*? We don't know any Socks.' Sophie looked at Jake, who shrugged.

'But you know a fox called Vince, right? Don't tell me I'm in the wrong park…'

'Yes, we knew Vince. Why? What's going on now?' Sophie said.

The cat explained about Vince finding Hampstead Heath, about how the riot had changed things there, and about him getting the train to the countryside with Rita.

Sophie and Jake stared wordlessly at the cat until she finished. 'Wait… Vince *reached* the park?' Sophie said.

'Sounds like it,' the cat replied.

'So, he's not…' Jake looked at Sophie.

'How?' Sophie said.

The cat tilted her head. 'Don't *quite* know what you're asking me there…'

'We thought he was dead,' Sophie said.

'And Rita,' Jake added.

'Dead? No. Well, not before he sent the message. Obviously. He might be now. Who knows?' The cat laughed.

Vince was alive! Kara had got it wrong somehow. Sophie pawed at the ground nervously, not wanting to get her hopes up. It didn't sound like he would ever come back now, but at least he was okay. And although they already knew about the heath and the riot thanks to Edward's confession, the fact that Vince had gone to the trouble of trying to let them know filled her with happiness. He hadn't forgotten about them. And she had to let him know that they hadn't forgotten about him, either.

'We need to speak to Kara,' Sophie said to Jake, then turned back to the cat. 'But can we send a message back with you to this... Socks? Will he somehow be able to pass it on to Vince?'

'We'll do our best,' the cat agreed.

Sophie told the cat everything about Edward and his death, adding that she missed Vince, and hoped he was happy. She also made sure to mention that the birds missed Rita too. The cat repeated it back to them, keen to make sure she didn't forget anything, then turned to leave.

'Wait, we didn't get your name...' Sophie said.

The cat looked over her shoulder. 'Batman,' she said, then with a roll of her eyes added, 'Children,' before going on her way.

The long grass of the field tickled Vince's belly as he walked, once again, northwards. Arthur shuffled along behind, stopping sporadically to dig for worms, while Vince waited patiently for him to catch up. The noise of the road faded blink by blink and, all around them, thick trees shielded them from the ever-rising sun and its springtime warmth. Rita basked in it, spiralling up, wings stretched, as she sang tunelessly and contentedly to herself. Vince whipped insects away with his tail, the smell of soil, pollen and fish filling his nose.

Eventually, Rita landed and told them to wait. Up ahead, a river cut through the earth, its bank dropping straight down to the gently bubbling water. Beyond it, more grass, and trees as far as he could see. Rita flapped ahead and disappeared into one of them.

'The river must be the boundary,' Vince said. 'Maybe she's gone to get the animal in charge.'

'I hope it's not a deer,' Arthur said through a mouthful of worms.

Vince laughed. 'Let's not judge anyone before we've met them, eh?' He squinted in the sun. 'What is she playing at? Is she whispering to someone?' Vince mumbled to himself as Arthur swallowed his meal. 'Maybe she's making sure we're definitely allowed—'

Suddenly an orange-and-white face appeared from behind a tree trunk and a pair of green eyes flashed at him.

'Laurie...' He ran to her.

She emerged from her hiding place and headed towards him, limping heavily on one side. 'Vince!' she called.

'You're hurt...' Vince whispered. Their noses touched and he buried his face in her soft neck. 'I'm so glad to see you. I thought you were...'

'Just a bit bruised,' Laurie whispered. 'Top tip, don't run into roads without looking.'

Vince inspected her side, rubbing it with his cheek. She winced at his touch. 'Okay, maybe a *lot* bruised. Did you come on the train? Rita found me, she said you missed it...'

'Can I tell you later? I'm *so* hungry. Are we allowed inside yet or do we have to wait for whoever's in charge here?' Vince said, looking around.

A grin spread across Laurie's snout. Rita joined them and chuckled.

'What's so funny?' Arthur squeaked at Vince's feet.

'We *are* inside. There's no one in charge, Vince,' Laurie laughed.

Vince couldn't speak. He blinked and looked around. The trees, the grass, the river...

'Are you sure?' It was too good to be true. There had to be something else. Something they were too scared to mention, for fear of disappointing him.

'Well, I've been here for a whole day and night and no one's tried to kill me, so yes, pretty sure,' Laurie said. 'Oh, and Arthur? There's some animals I need to introduce to you after sunset...' She winked.

'Hedgehogs? *Really?*' Arthur bobbed up and down in the grass.

'Yep! A whole family. I told them all about you.'

Arthur giggled.

'Laurie... This is... I can't believe it. If my parents could see this... And my grandparents...'

'Come on... Let me show you something.' Laurie gave him a nudge and turned with a flick of her tail and walked towards the river. He followed and sat on the bank beside her. A shoal of plump fish swayed in the water, swimming against the lazy current. Further down, packed together in a thick carpet of algae, was a knot of frogs, their green skin glistening in the sun.

Kara was munching on a mouse when Sophie and Jake arrived at the base of her tree. 'What do you want? I'm about to go to sleep.'

'We'll be quick. We've just had a message,' Jake said.

'From Vince,' Sophie finished.

Kara frowned. 'He made it, then?'

'You said he was killed!' Sophie shouted.

'Calm down. We're all mates now, aren't we?' Kara smirked. 'He looked dead when I left. Those other foxes tried to kill me so I wasn't about to stick around and check for a heartbeat or anything. He must have pulled through. Mother knows I wasn't about to tell Edward that I wasn't sure.'

Sophie smiled at Jake. Vince *was* alive. Not only that, but it meant Edward's talk of the city being too dangerous really was rat scat. They'd suspected as much, but it was good to have proof.

Now that Edward's rules had been abolished, anyone could leave and explore if they wanted to. Outsiders could even come inside to live now, too, and as the news of Edward's death spread, not a night went by without at least one city animal arriving. They were usually greeted by their own kind, and given introductions and a tour of the park before settling in as permanent residents.

Sophie pointed her snout up at Kara again. 'We never got a chance to thank you for telling the truth about Edward.'

Kara laughed. 'Save your thanks. I didn't do it for you, or the park. He screwed me over and I wanted to get back at him.'

'Well, thank you anyway. It meant a lot to everyone,' Sophie said, then with a smirk added, 'We'll see you around, I guess, *mate*.'

Kara smiled. 'Sure. I'm thinking of leaving, though. Maybe even find that heath myself.'

Jake widened his eyes. 'Oh? I never had you down as the travelling type.'

'I saw a few places when I was looking for Vince. Now Edward's

gone, might be nice to spread my wings a bit. Finally catch some rabbits. Now, if you don't mind, my dinner is getting cold.'

They said their goodbyes and left, heading back to the cemetery.
As they walked, Sophie asked Jake how he felt about going outside
the boundary. He pulled a face. 'Not for ever,' Sophie added. 'Just take
a little walk one night. See what's out there?'

'I can tell you're not going to stop asking me until we do it, and
there's no way you're going on your own, so I guess I have no choice,'
he said, laughing.

'Correct,' she said, nudging him with her nose.

Sophie and Jake had almost reached their den when Marge came
running towards them. 'Come quickly!' she shouted. 'We found
something.'

'Found what?' Jake said as they upped their speed to follow her.
She was heading in the direction of her own den.

'A human thing. Made of metal,' Marge replied, her eyes wide.
'It's hidden in the bushes.'

Most of the skulk were crowded around the mysterious object,
the vegetation trampled and torn away so they could get a better look
at it. Some of the recent arrivals hung back, watching from behind the
tall gravestones or the still-loose mounds of earth next to their newly
dug dens.

Sophie went for a closer look. A box made of thick wire, almost
like the fences, with an opening at one end. Scraps of meat littered the
bottom.

'Don't touch it!' a voice called from behind her, but it wasn't
Jake. She turned to see Gregory – one of the former city foxes – staring at her. He'd shown up the day after Edward's death, but mostly
kept himself to himself. 'It's a trap. If you go in, it'll lock you inside.
Watch…' He searched the ground and picked up a large stone in his
jaws. The other foxes backed away as he approached the trap. Lowering himself to face the open side, he tossed the stone into the wire box
with a flick of his head. The weight of it released a catch and, with an
ear-shattering clang, a previously unnoticed solid metal door sprang

down from the roof and closed off the opening. The stone, alongside the meat, lay still and imprisoned inside.

Marge's mouth fell open. 'I... I almost went inside it... I smelled the meat... Oh, Mother, can you imagine if I had?'

'You've really never seen one?' Gregory let out a short laugh. Marge recoiled, embarrassed.

'No, we haven't,' Sophie said sharply. 'They must be a city thing. Why would they want to trap us?'

'To get rid of us. Or Marge, it looks like, in this case.'

Tears filled Marge's eyes. Sophie frowned. 'Can you try to be a bit more sensitive, please? This is serious. Why Marge, though?'

Gregory shrugged. 'We're all the same to them. And I doubt this is the only one.'

'But why, *now*?' Jake said.

'There's too many of us.' Marge sniffed. 'There are dens everywhere now. Since you city foxes started arriving.' She glared at Gregory through wet eyes.

'*You* welcomed us here,' Gregory said, fur bristling.

'That's right, we did. And there's plenty of room and food for us all. We shouldn't blame anyone,' Sophie said to Marge.

'Easy for you to say. You don't have one of these *things* right outside your den,' Marge wailed.

'I know you're scared, but now that we know what they are, we can avoid them, right?' Sophie looked at Gregory for reassurance, but received none. She looked around at the rest of the foxes. 'If you smell meat, be very careful, okay? And if you find more of these traps, let everyone know straight away. Now, let's just try to carry on as normal. I'm sure once the humans realise they can't catch us then they'll take them away and that'll be the end of it.' Everyone nodded except Gregory, who simply smirked before turning and walking away.

The rest of the foxes followed suit, dispersing quickly to their dens, but Sophie couldn't help but hear snatches of whispers as they all padded away.

'... do you really believe...'

'... city foxes...'

'… one outside my den then I'll…'

'…put her in charge, anyway?'

Jake sidled up to Sophie and she relaxed slightly, unaware she had been so tense. Together, they returned to their sleeping chamber.

Sophie curled up in the bed of leaves, but made no effort to sleep. Jake joined her and sensed her unease. 'Maybe the deer can get rid of the traps for us? Or move them? We can ask them tomorrow. Try not to worry too much.'

'Mmm,' Sophie replied. 'It's not just the traps, though. If the humans think there are too many of us, then they'll just try something else, won't they? And what happens if one of us does get trapped, or worse? Marge already blames the new foxes. How long before everyone else starts to? We can't start preventing animals from coming to live here… Not after everything that's happened… Can we? And you heard them talking about me, as if I put myself in charge… I don't even want to be in charge, Jake! I don't want *anyone* to be in charge! That was the whole point… Ugh!' She pulled her tail over her face.

Jake snuggled closer. 'I know, but going over and over all the possible scenarios isn't going to help. And we can always leave, Soph. Find a new home, like Vince did. You were talking about it earlier. Start afresh.'

Sophie pulled her head out from under her brush and looked into Jake's eyes. 'I just wanted to explore, maybe for a night or two… We helped make this place decent again, we can't just up and leave when things start to get hard. This is my home. *Our* home. This is where I want to be. Me and you and, eventually, our cubs.'

'Cubs?' Jake swallowed.

'Yes,' Sophie said.

Jake smiled. 'We'll make it work, whatever happens to the park. Me, you and our cubs.'

Sophie beamed and nuzzled into Jake's warm neck. 'Just one thing,' she whispered into his fur. 'If we have a boy, I want to call him Vince.'

Jake pulled away. 'Um… Okay… I mean, I…'

Sophie threw back her head and laughed.

'You!' Jake swiped at her nose with a paw. Sophie dodged it and gave him a nip on the ear in retaliation. They gave each other a quick nuzzle before a yawn escaped from Sophie jaws.

As they settled back down to sleep, Jake whispered, 'Try not to worry, Soph. It's not up to you to sort all the problems out.'

'I know.' Sophie closed her eyes, then added, under her breath, 'It's not up to anyone anymore, is it?'

Beneath the glowing moon, Vince took a step back from the pile of earth he'd just dragged from the hole in the ground. 'There. All done.'

Laurie sniffed at the hole. 'Very nice. Almost as nice as my empty shop on the high street.'

Vince pulled a face.

'I'm joking. It's perfect!' She laughed.

'You haven't even looked inside yet!'

'Vince, *I* dug half of it. You *watched* me do it earlier, remember?' Laurie prodded him with her nose.

'I know, but... Just go inside.' He pushed her towards the entrance and followed her into their new sleeping chamber.

She gasped as she saw what he'd done. A blanket of downy grey feathers covered a layer of leaves. Scattered across the feathers, hundreds of vivid flower petals gently rested; yellows, pinks, reds and purples.

'You like it?' he said.

'Oh, Vince, I *love* it. It's beautiful. You did this while I was hunting?'

'Yes.' He looked at his paws.

'*You*...' She nuzzled his neck and sighed. 'I wish Socks were here.'

'I know, but I'm sure he got the message. And Rita's been talking about going back at some point. A holiday, she keeps saying.'

'Yeah. I just wish I could see him. I was going to say he would like it here, but there's a distinct lack of human laps and ear scratches, so I'm not sure that's true.' Laurie smiled. 'Oh, by the way, Arthur finally dragged himself away from his new family to tell me how you rescued him from the train tracks.'

Vince looked at his paws again.

'Don't get embarrassed! I know how scared you were of the trains. It must have been really hard,' Laurie said.

'Yeah. Although if Coco hadn't turned up, I don't know what I would have done.'

'Who's Coco?'

'Didn't Arthur tell you? There was this white dog, with curly fur and a stupid tail. She grabbed her human's scarf for me.'

'White with curly fur?' Laurie cocked her head. 'How big?'

'Bit bigger than me, why?'

Suddenly, an air-splitting sound burst into the chamber. 'Huooh! Huooh! Kee-kee-kee!'

'*Mother Nature*... ROSIE! Can you please be quiet for *two* blinks?' Laurie yelled up through the passage.

'Sooor-*ry*,' the voice replied. 'But Rita wants you. We both do.'

'Alright, we're coming... You know, when I first met Rita,' Vince said to Laurie as they made their way outside, 'I thought, *that's it*. That's the most annoying birdsong I can *ever* hear. No other bird can *ever* be as loud, as tuneless, or as sleep-destroying as Rita. It was comforting, really. I'd heard the worst, so anything else was an improvement.'

'And then you met Rosie,' Laurie said.

'And then I met Rosie.'

'At least Rita's happy,' Laurie said. 'They get on so well.'

'Oh, I'm not doubting their happiness. I just wish they could be happy *quietly*.' Vince laughed. He was joking, really. Rita had taken to Broxbourne like a duck to water, building an enormous domed nest in the biggest oak tree she could find, singing from sunrise to sunset. Rosie introduced herself not long after, and they'd been inseparable ever since. It had only been a couple of nights, but it was like they'd known each other for years.

They emerged into the cold night air. Rosie stood next to Rita, their snow-white chests puffed out beside each other, but that was where the similarity ended. Rosie towered over Rita, and her yellow beak, grey wings and webbed, pink feet were not those of a magpie, but a gull. A very large, very noisy gull.

'We wanted to give you a moving-in present,' Rita said.

'Oh, how sweet,' Laurie said.

'We made up a song for you!' Rosie grinned.

'Oh… Great…' Laurie shot Vince a wide-eyed look.

'What's this about, um, a song? Can I hear?' Arthur came scurrying out from under a nearby bush, which, he claimed almost daily 'had the best worms'.

'Of course, the more the merrier,' Laurie said, beckoning him over. Vince lay on the grass and curled his tail around himself. Laurie settled in next to him, Arthur in front.

'So, about that dog…' Laurie whispered.

'A poodle?' Vince replied. Laurie nodded and they both laughed, her tail shaking, just as it had the day they met, and the way it always did when she was genuinely happy.

Rosie cleared her throat. 'Okay, sooo, just so you know, the song is *quite* long…'

'Do you mind?' Rita said, blinking her black eyes at Vince.

Vince looked at Laurie and smiled. 'Not at all. I can't wait to hear it,' he said. And he meant every word.

Acknowledgements

I would like to thank everyone at Unbound who thought my idea for a modern-day animal story was worth pursuing. Even more thanks go to the many pledgers whose support and hard-earned money gave me the motivation to write until I reached 'The End'.

Patrons

Dania Al-Lamy
Jade Bartolf
Mark Bowsher
Ann Carrier
Nicola Cumberlidge
Heather Delaney
Kate Dreyer
Caroline Gale
Eleanor Goodman
Heather Hayden
Maia Honan
Julia James
SarahLouise McDonald
Catharine Mee
Jennifer Rushworth
Will Smith
Warren Smith
Jamie Speakman
Ewertton Tadeu
Sophie Williams
Amanda Willmore